A LITTLE BIT OF HOLIDAY MAGIC

BY
MELISSA McCLONE

MILLS
BOON

First published in Great Britain 2013
by Mills & Boon, an imprint of Harlequin (UK) Limited,
Eton House, 18-24 Paradise Road, Richmond, Surrey TW9 1SR

© Melissa Martinez McClone 2013

ISBN: 978 0 263 90156 6

23-1113

Harlequin (UK) policy is to use papers that are natural, renewable and recyclable products and made from wood grown in sustainable forests. The logging and manufacturing processes conform to the legal environmental regulations of the country of origin.

Printed and bound in Spain
by Blackprint CPI, Barcelona

With a degree in mechanical engineering from Stanford University, the last thing **Melissa McClone** ever thought she would be doing was writing romance novels. But analysing engines for a major US airline just couldn't compete with her 'happily-ever-afters'. When she isn't writing, caring for her three young children or doing laundry, Melissa loves to curl up on the couch with a cup of tea, her cats, and a good book. She enjoys watching home decorating shows to get ideas for her house—a 1939 cottage that is *slowly* being renovated. Melissa lives in Lake Oswego, Oregon, with her own real-life hero husband, two daughters, a son, two lovable but oh-so-spoiled indoor cats, and a no-longer-stray outdoor kitty that has decided to call the garage home.

Melissa loves to hear from her readers. You can write to her at PO Box 63, Lake Oswego, OR 97034, USA, or contact her via her website: www.melissamcclone.com.

In Memory of Elizabeth Brooks.
Thank you for the wonderful memories and always
believing I could be a writer.
Special thanks to: Karyn Barr, Roger Carstens,
Alice Burton, Lori Freeland, Lisa Hayden, Terri Reed,
Jennifer Shirk, Margie Lawson and her
Nov. '12 Fab 30 class.

CHAPTER ONE

PLEASE, TRUCK. DON'T die on me.

Grace Bad-luck-is-my-middle-name Wilcox gripped the pick-up's steering wheel tighter, as if willpower alone would keep the sputtering engine running in the middle of a blizzard on Mount Hood. A CD of cheery Christmas carols played, but frazzled nerves kept her from singing along.

The tire chains crunched on the snow. The wipers' frenetic back-and-forth struggled to keep the windshield clear of falling snow. The engine coughed, a croupy-seal-bark sound.

She raised her foot off the accelerator.

A gut-clenching grinding noise shook the cab, confirming her fear.

Forget reaching the Oregon coast tonight. The truck wasn't going to survive the drive over Mount Hood.

Stranded in a snowstorm with her three-year-old son.

Shivers racked her body, a mix of panic, fear and bone-chilling cold. The heater had stopped working an hour ago. Her fleece jacket and knit gloves weren't enough to keep her warm.

Grace pressed on the gas pedal, praying for a miracle. She glanced in the rearview mirror to the backseat of the truck's extended cab.

Liam slept in his car seat with his head on a blue stuffed elephant named Peanut, and his body covered with sleeping bags and blankets.

A ball of warmth settled at the center of Grace's chest. Liam—the one bright light in her otherwise dark life. The reason she kept going. "I hope you're having sweet dreams, baby."

Because reality sucked.

Except when you were a little kid and trusted your mom to keep you safe.

And she would keep him safe. That was her job. Though she was failing at being a good mommy tonight.

Liam must be exhausted. It was nearly eleven o'clock, hours past his bedtime, and they'd spent another long day on the road, their progress hampered by harsh winter weather.

"Looks like Astoria will have to wait one more day."

Her voice trembled from the cold, disappointment, fear.

If only we were there now.

The small northern Oregon coastal town, about a three-hour drive from Mount Hood, would be their home. She could make a new life for herself, and most especially, Liam.

With only one working headlight, Grace struggled to see the road due to the wind-driven snow.

The engine clanked and rattled and thunked.

She needed to find a place to stay the night before the truck gave out. She glimpsed something, a pole. No, a sign.

Grace made out the words *Hood Hamlet*. An arrow pointed right.

She had no idea what Hood Hamlet was—she assumed not a Shakespeare character in a hoodie—but anything had to be better than being stuck on the side of the road in this freezing weather all night. She flipped on the blinker, even though no one else was crazy enough to be driving in these conditions, and turned right.

Deep snow. A foot more than was on the highway. No tracks.

The truck plowed ahead, slowed by the road conditions and her nerves. The snow muffled the sounds of the tire chains, but the disturbing engine noises increased in frequency and volume.

Not good.

White-knuckled, she clutched the steering wheel as if it were a lifeline.

Hood Hamlet, please don't let me down.

The snow and darkness, pitch-black except for the one head-light, made seeing more than a foot or two ahead impossible.

She leaned forward, squinting, trying to see.

The windshield fogged on the inside. Frost built up on the outside.

A T in the road lay ahead. But no sign to direct her, nothing to let her know she was close to Hood Hamlet.

Right or left?

Grace chose right. That turn seemed easier to negotiate with the road conditions. She eased the steering wheel toward the passenger's side.

The truck skidded, sliding sideward.

Air rushed from her lungs. Her fingers dug into the steering wheel. "No. No. No."

Turn into the slide.

Hadn't Damon told her that when she was learning to drive? Wait. That was for front-wheel drive cars, not his truck.

She turned the steering wheel the other way.

The truck straightened.

Grace glanced back at Liam, who was still sleeping. "Maybe our luck's changing."

The truck slid again.

She tried to correct, but the vehicle spun in the opposite direction. Round and round, like a merry-go-round with afterburners.

Her pulse accelerated into the stratosphere.

The world passed by in slow motion, appearing through the windshield wipers like blurry photographs.

Trees. Snow. More snow.

Round and round.

Grace couldn't tell what was real, what was her imagination. The roar of her heartbeat drowned out the music.

It'll be okay, babe.

Damon. Tears stung her eyes at the memory of his voice. Nothing had been okay since he'd died.

A wall of snow appeared in front of her.

Every muscle in her body tensed. Panic ricocheted through her. Grace closed her eyes. She screamed, clutched the steering wheel with all her strength. If only she could hold on to Liam…

"Damon, help us."

A prayer. A plea.

The truck jolted with an awful metallic, crumpling sound. Something exploded, hitting her in the face. A horrible smell filled her nostrils. "Oh."

The engine died.

Liam wailed.

Adrenaline surged. Her face stung. She coughed. "Liam."

He screamed louder. The soul-piercing sound stole her breath and her hope.

Hands shaking, she struggled with her seat belt. The air bag had deflated and lay on her lap. She had to get to her son. "Be right there, baby."

He sobbed, alternating between hiccups and cries, each stabbing her aching heart. "P-nut. Where P-nut?"

"I'll find him." Grace unfastened the belt, turned, reached back. Her face burned. It hurt to breathe. She couldn't see anything, but felt around. "Fleece blanket, cookies, jacket. Peanut has to be here."

She hit the switch on the cab lamp above her.

Light flooded the truck. The engine might not work, but thankfully, the battery still did.

Crocodile tears streamed down Liam's cheeks. "P-nut."

Grace glimpsed blue fuzz stuck between the front and back seats. She pulled out the stuffed animal. Pushed the elephant into Liam's mitten-covered hands. "Here's Peanut."

The tears stopped flowing. He cuddled his favorite toy. "Mine."

"Do you hurt anywhere?"

"No." He kissed the elephant. "I fine. Peanut fine, too."

A lump clogged her throat. The relief was short-lived. If she didn't do something fast, they were going to freeze.

She tucked blankets and sleeping bags around him again in between coughs.

"Mommy needs to check the truck." And get help. She grabbed her cell phone. Dead. Of course it was. She hadn't been able to find her charger since driving through Utah. "Stay here and keep Peanut warm. I'll be right back."

Grace pulled on her handle. The door wouldn't budge. "Come on."

She tried again. Nothing.

She crawled to the passenger seat and tried that handle. On her third attempt the door opened, pushing away a drift.

Thank goodness. She stumbled out of the truck. Her canvas sneakers sank into the soft snow. Her toes curled from the icy cold.

Wind whipped. Freezing air stung her lungs. Fear doubled with every passing second.

Crossing her arms over her chest and tucking her gloved but trembling hands beneath her armpits, she closed the door with her hip. She needed to keep Liam protected from the cold.

The truck was stuck in a seven-feet-tall snowbank. The shell over the back of the pickup looked fine. She couldn't see the damage to the driver's side, but based on the impact sounds she expected it to be crunched.

"Help," Grace yelled, though she doubted anyone was around. She couldn't see anything in the darkness with snow falling. "Can anyone hear me?"

The wind swallowed her voice. A weight pressed down on her.

She couldn't give up.

Her son needed her to be strong.

If Grace hadn't had Liam, she would have given up the night the army rang her doorbell to tell her Damon, her Ranger husband, a man she'd loved since she was fifteen, had been killed in Afghanistan. Damon had saved three soldiers before dying, but the word *hero* could never fill the gaping hole his death left in her and their son's life. A hole still present two and a half years later.

Damon had always said, *"It'll be okay, babe."*

She repeated his words. *"It'll be okay. It'll be okay."*

All she had to do was find shelter. Get Liam out of the cold. Everything else could wait until daylight.

Grace looked around.

Snow and trees.

That was all she could see.

Stupid snow and stupid trees.

Driving across country from Georgia to Oregon two weeks before Christmas had been stupid. Sure, she'd finally graduated college, but she should have stuck it out another few months until the weather improved.

What was I thinking?

Making new Christmas memories, not dwelling on old ones. Ringing in the New Year in a different place, not wondering what might have been. Meeting new people instead of saying good-bye to old friends transferring out of the Rangers or heading downrange on another deployment, not knowing who wouldn't be coming home this time.

Snow coated her jacket and jeans. Her hair, too. Her gloved hands tingled. She shoved them in her pockets.

"I'm sorry." Her teeth chattered. She blinked away tears. "Should have stayed in Georgia."

It'll be okay, babe.

Grace wished she could believe things would be okay. She glanced back at the truck. At the light illuminating cab. At Liam.

No giving up.

The snow helped the burning sensation on her skin. She wasn't coughing. It no longer hurt to breathe. All good things. And this road had to lead somewhere, to people, right?

She forced her tired legs forward to find help, her feet completely covered in snow. Wetness seeped into her shoes, sending icy chills up her legs.

Grace glanced back at the truck, not wanting to lose sight of her son. Looking forward again, she shielded her eyes from the snowflakes coming at her sideways like miniature daggers. She scanned right to left.

Snow, trees and…

Santa Claus?

She blinked. Refocused.

A lit-up Santa beckoned in the distance. Beyond the figure was a house strung with multicolored Christmas lights.

It'll be okay, babe.

It was going to be okay. At least for tonight. Grace looked up into the swirling snow. "Thank you, Damon."

* * *

"No worries. I have power, Mom." Bill Paulson walked out of the kitchen holding a bottle of beer in one hand and the phone against his ear in the other. "This is your third call tonight. It's late. Go to bed. I'll be by in the morning to plow your driveway. I have to check the rental properties, too."

"Unless the snow keeps falling."

Her hopeful words were not unexpected. His mom preferred him stuck inside and safe, rather than on another outdoor adventure. She seemed to forget he was thirty-three, not thirteen. Though, admittedly, sometimes he acted more like a kid than an adult.

"It better stop snowing." He sat in his favorite chair, a big, comfortable leather recliner. Sports highlights played on the TV, with the volume muted. Flames danced and wood crackled in the fireplace. "I don't want to lose another day on the mountain."

A drawn-out, oh-so-familiar sigh came across the line, annoying him like a tickle in the throat before a full-blown cold erupted. He loved his mom, but he knew what was coming next.

"There's more to life than climbing and skiing," she said.

"You don't climb or ski."

"No, but you do."

"My life rocks," Bill said. "There's nothing like helping people in trouble get down the mountain, or carving the first tracks in two feet of fresh powder, then crawling into a comfy, warm bed after a day on the hill."

Especially if he wasn't alone. Which, unfortunately, he was tonight.

"You're headstrong like your father. Always off doing your own thing."

Bill knew that disapproving-mother tone all too well. He'd grown up hearing how much he was like his dad, a man who was never around to support and love her. But this was different. His mom didn't understand the pull of the mountain. The allure of the adrenaline rush. The satisfaction of a successful mission. She was too worried Bill would end up hurt or dead. That could happen one of these days, but still…

Time to change the subject before she laid on another guilt trip. He didn't want to end up letting her down again. "This morning I put up the Santa you brought over. Got the lights strung on the eaves, too."

"Wonderful. How's the tree coming along?"

Two ornaments—a snowboard and a snowshoe—hung from the branches of a seven-foot noble fir. Bill had a box full of more ornaments, but he'd gotten bored trimming the tree. Decorating with a sexy snow bunny for a helper would have been more fun. "The tree's coming along. I've even got a present under there."

He wasn't about to tell his mom the gift was a wedding present for Leanne Thomas and Christian Welton, two firefighters getting married on Saturday. Soon Bill would be the only member of their crew still single.

He didn't mind.

Marriage was fine for other people. Somehow his parents had remained together in spite of spending so much time apart. Maybe when Bill hit forty he would reconsider matrimony as an option. Then again, maybe not. He didn't need another woman dependent on him, like his mom. A woman who would think he wasn't a good enough man, husband, father, and kept waiting for him to screw up.

"I'm happy to finish decorating your tree," Mom said.

He had no doubt she would happily show up to decorate his whole house, wearing an embroidered Christmas sweater and jingle bells dangling from her earlobes. With her husband away most of the time, she focused her attention and energy on Bill. Always had. After she'd miscarried during a difficult pregnancy, she'd turned into a hovering, don't-let-the-kid-out-of-your sight, over-protective mom. His turning eighteen, twenty-one, thirty hadn't lessened the mother hen tendencies. "Give me another week."

"We'll talk tomorrow." She made a smacking sound, her version of a good-night kiss over the phone. "Sleep well, dear."

"Will do." Too bad he'd be sleeping alone. Stormy nights were perfect for going to bed with a hot woman. But the December dating deadline—the second Monday in December, when men stopped seeing women, in order to avoid spending the holidays with them—had passed. Even friends with benefits expected more than he was willing to give this time of year. "'Night, Mom."

He placed the phone on the end table, sat in the recliner and took a long pull of beer. This year's seasonal brew from the Wy'East Brewing Company went down smoothly.

He glanced at a photograph hanging on the wall—of Jake Porter, Leanne, Nick Bishop, Tim Moreno and himself at Smith Rock during a sunny day of rock climbing in central Oregon. He raised his bottle in memory of Nick, who'd died during a climb on Mount Hood's Reid Headwall at Christmastime nine years ago.

Wind rattled the windows.

Storm, storm, go away. Billy Paulson wants to play.

He downed the rest of the beer.

Game highlights gave way to a sports talk show.

He flipped through the channels, not bothering to turn up the sound. News. Chick flick. Syndicated comedy. The same boring shows.

Bill heard what sounded like a knock.

No one would be out tonight. Must be a branch against the house.

Another knock.

He stood.

The knocking continued. Rapid. Loud.

Not a branch. More like someone in trouble.

Bill ran, opened the door.

Cold wind slammed into his body. Bits of ice pelted his face. Swirling snow blinded his eyes.

He blinked. Focused.

A woman stood on the porch. A woman holding a bunch of blankets. A woman covered with snow.

Bill ushered her inside, then closed the door.

Dark, wet hair obscured her face. Her teeth chattered. Her jeans and jacket were soaked. She wore wet gloves.

He brushed snow off her jacket, icy wetness chilled his palms. "What's going on?"

"S-slid into a s-snowbank."

"Were you buckled up?"

"Yes."

"Did you hit your head?"

"No. Air b-bag."

"Back or neck pain?"

"No."

"Does anything hurt?"

"F-f-face was b-burning. H-hard to breathe. B-but that's better now." She shivered. "Just c-c-old."

Bill pushed the wet hair off her face to get a better look at her.

Wide amber eyes. Flushed cheeks. Runny nose.

Full, generous lips.

The kind of lips a man, at least this man, dreamed about tasting and kissing and...

Her lips trembled.

Focus, Paulson. "Let's get you out of that wet jacket."

She held out the pile of blankets. "M-m-my s-son."

Adrenaline shot through Bill. He grabbed the child and laid him on the rug in front of the living room fireplace. "Is he injured?"

"I d-don't think so."

Bill peeled away the wet top covering. "How old is he?"

She struggled out of her gloves and pink fleece jacket, nothing more than a waterlogged sponge now. "Three."

Another blanket came off, this one dryer than the last. "What's his name?"

The woman slipped off canvas sneakers. She wasn't wearing socks. Not exactly dressed for the weather. What in the world was she doing driving around in a snowstorm?

"Liam." She stepped away from the puddle of water pooling by her shoes. "I'm G-Grace. Grace Wilcox."

"Bill Paulson."

"Mommy," a small, scared voice said from beneath a blue fleece blanket.

Grace kneeled next to the boy. She wore a short-sleeved T-shirt. Goose bumps covered her arms. "R-right here, honey."

Bill raised the blue blanket. "Liam?"

A small boy with dark hair and pale skin looked up with

quarter-size blue eyes. He wore red mittens and forest-green footie pajamas.

Bill gave the kid his best fireman smile. "Hello, little dude."

Liam's lips quivered. "Mommy."

Grace pulled his mitten-covered hand onto her lap. "It's okay."

Okay? Only if she was talking about them being out of the storm. Maybe she had hit her head or maybe she was drunk.

Bill didn't smell alcohol. She didn't show any obvious signs of impairment, except for driving late at night in a blizzard. "Was Liam in a car seat?"

Her do-I-look-like-a-bad-mother glare hit Bill like an ice pick in the forehead. "Of course my son was in a car seat. He was in the backseat."

"Just a question." Bill didn't see any cuts or bruises. "No offense intended."

He touched the boy's shoulder.

She grabbed the top of Bill's hand, her fingers, as cold as Popsicles, dug into his skin. "What are you doing?"

"Checking your son." Bill didn't need to look over to know an anxious mother was watching his every move. "I'm a firefighter with Hood Hamlet Fire and Rescue. I have EMT training and am a wilderness first responder with OMSAR."

"OMSAR?"

Definitely not from around here if she didn't know what that was. He shot her a sideways glance. Anxious, but attractive with wide-set eyes, high cheekbones, straight nose and full lips. Mid-twenties, if that. "Oregon Mountain Search and Rescue."

Her gaze went from distrustful to relieved. "Looks like I picked the right house."

"Da-arn straight." Bill didn't want to curse in front of the kid. "No visible signs of trauma. Does anything hurt, buddy?"

The little guy scrunched up his nose. "P-Nut."

Bill looked at Grace. "Huh?"

"Peanut is right here." She handed the child a stuffed animal. "Tell Mr. Paulson if anything hurts, okay?"

The kid's eyes glistened. Tears would fall in 3...2...1.

"Tummy." Liam's voice cracked.

Internal injury? Bill's throat tightened. "I need to check Liam's abdomen."

Color drained from the woman's face. She rubbed her hands over her mouth. "Maybe we should call 9-1-1."

"I am 9-1-1, minus the truck, flashing lights and uniform." Bill grabbed the pajama zipper and pulled. "Relax. I know what I'm doing. If he needs help, we'll get it."

"Hungry," Liam said.

Bill's hand stalled. "You want something to eat?"

The little boy nodded.

"Wanting food is a good sign." Bill examined Liam. No redness or marks from where the car seat straps may have hit his body. No signs of distress or shock or concussion. The kid seemed fine. "How does a cookie sound?"

A grin brighter than the lights on the Christmas tree erupted on the kid's face. "Cookie! I want cookie, puh-lease."

Bill's throat relaxed, allowing him to breathe easier. The kid was going to be okay. But the mom was another story. Not quite panicked, but cold and suspicious.

The dark circles under her eyes told only half the story. Exhausted, check. Stressed, check. Nervous, two checks. Her eyes darted back and forth, unable to focus on one thing too long. But with each pass, her gaze lingered on him a second longer than the last. Her wariness pissed him off. She seemed to forget *she'd* knocked on *his* door tonight.

"Do you want a cookie?" he asked. "Chocolate chip. My mom made them."

Grace gnawed on her lip. "No, thanks."

Bill rose. He grabbed two chocolate chip cookies from the snowman-shaped cookie jar on the kitchen counter, then returned to the living room. He handed one to Liam, who'd removed his mittens, and the other to Grace, who looked as if he'd given her a grenade with the pin pulled.

Her confused gaze bounced from the cookie to Bill. "I didn't want one."

"You look like you need one." He watched Liam munch his cookie. "Nothing wrong with his appetite."

"Unless I'm trying to feed him veggies."

Grace's lighthearted tone surprised Bill, but it was good to see her sense of humor come out. "Who wants to eat icky green and orange things?" he asked.

The kid and Peanut nodded.

"Green and orange *things*—" Grace emphasized the last word "—help a person grow to be tall and strong. I'm sure Mr. Paulson didn't become a firefighter by eating junk food and drinking soda."

Grace sounded like a mom. Duh. She was one. He wasn't helping her out here. "Your mom's correct, Liam. Eat lots of vegetables, fruit and protein if you want to grow up to be tall and strong like me."

She stared down her nose at Bill. "Modest."

Her tone and look screamed *not interested.* That only piqued his. "Humility is a virtue."

Grace opened her mouth, but didn't say a word. She looked away, then took a bite of her cookie.

Bill knelt next to her. Wet hair dampened Grace's shirt. She wasn't busty, but had curves in the places that mattered. She smelled good in spite of being wet, a mix of vanilla and cinnamon and something he couldn't place. "Let's see how you're doing."

Holding the cookie, she crossed her arms tight over her chest. "I'm okay. The snow washed away the powder from the air bag."

"Looking you over won't take long."

She scooted back. "I'm good."

He cut the distance between them. "Let me make sure."

Grace stood. Every motion seemed to take effort. A battle of fatigue and stress and shock, one she was losing. "You've done enough."

His gaze ran the length of her, checking for obvious injuries. He didn't see any. "Show me where the seat belt straps hit you."

"It's not necessary. I told you, the air bag—"

"If you stiffened prior to impact, you're going to be sore."

"I'm—"

"I'm trying to do my job here. That's all. Please let me examine you." He was losing patience. "I have to determine if you need to go to the hospital tonight."

She nibbled on her lip.

"Would it make a difference if I put on my uniform?" he asked.

"None whatsoever." Her firm voice left no doubt she was serious. "I appreciate you letting us get warm, but I need to find a place to stay tonight."

"You're not going anywhere unless it's the hospital."

She glanced out the window. "But—"

"The weather's wicked. You're staying here tonight. I'll keep an eye on you."

Forget deer in headlights. Grace's expression made her look as if she'd been flattened by a semi. "That's—"

"Your only option."

Her mouth twisted.

He wasn't deterred. "I have two spare bedrooms. Use one or both." Bill pointed to her coat. "You may feel warmer without your wet jacket and shoes, but you need to change clothes."

Grace rubbed the back of her neck.

"Sore?" he asked.

"Fine." She moistened her lips. "All my clothes are in the truck."

"I have something you can wear. Be right back." Bill sprinted to his bedroom and grabbed a pair of flannel pajamas, a Christmas gift last year from his parents. Well, from his mom. His dad usually arrived home on Christmas Eve and was out the door on the twenty-sixth, leaving Bill to become his mom's entire world again. Maybe if he'd had a sibling, a little brother or sister, things would be different. Better. But Bill hadn't called for help soon enough. His mother had lost her baby and couldn't have another.

Back in the living room, he handed the pajamas to Grace. "They'll be big on you."

She stared at them as if he'd handed her a French maid outfit to wear, complete with fishnet stockings and a feather duster.

Her jaw tightened. "You want me to wear your pajamas?"

He pressed his lips together to keep from smiling. "They're

practically new. I've only worn the bottoms a couple times. Flannel is warm. You might be hypothermic."

Her suspicious gaze targeted him once more. It was a good thing she wasn't armed, or he would be a goner.

"You're really a firefighter and mountain rescuer?"

"Check the pictures on the mantel." He pointed to framed articles and photographs. "And the walls."

Looking around, Grace held the pajamas in front of her like a shield.

Okay, he got it. Got her.

No wedding ring, and a kid had made her cautious. That was smart. She didn't know him. Didn't know her having a child meant he considered her off-limits, a look-don't-touch, modern-day leper.

"My job is to help people in trouble. I do that when I'm on the mountain, too," he said. "That's all I'm trying to do here."

"It's just…" Grace glanced at Liam, who was playing with Peanut. She touched the boy's head. "I've never been stranded—with a stranger."

"No worries. I understand. But you're safe here. If it makes you feel any better, the bedroom doors lock."

Her eyes darkened. "From the inside or outside?"

That would be funny if she didn't sound so serious. "I have an idea. I'll call the sheriff's office. Let them know about your truck, so they can get it towed. Then you can talk to the sheriff or a deputy. They'll appease your concerns about staying here tonight."

"The sheriff and his deputies will vouch for you?" Only a deaf person would miss her please-someone-tell-me-he's-not-psychotic plea.

"I've lived in Hood Hamlet my whole life. I know everybody."

Grace's gaze took in the articles and photographs hanging on the wall again. The tension in her face, especially around her mouth, lessened. "Okay. Let's call the sheriff. I doubt there's more than one black pickup stuck in a snowbank around here, but in case there is, mine has Georgia plates."

"Long way from home."

She shrugged.

Must be a story there. Not his business.

Even if he was curious…

CHAPTER TWO

FIVE MINUTES LATER, Bill took the phone from Grace, who held on to his pajamas with her other hand. The lines creasing her forehead had disappeared, but the wariness in her eyes remained. He hoped that look wasn't due to something the sheriff had said. "All good now?"

"The sheriff said Liam and I would be safe with you." Her voice sounded stronger, but her words had a nervous edge. She rubbed her fingertips against the pajamas. "He's going to take care of my truck."

"Truck," Liam repeated. "I like trucks. Big ones."

"Me, too." The kid was cute. So was the mom. If she would quit acting as if Bill was a murderer. She shifted her weight from foot to foot. At least her toes weren't frostbitten. "Something's still bothering you."

Her hands stopped fidgeting with the pajamas. "You're perceptive."

"Sometimes." Bill wasn't about to play games with Grace after what she'd been through. "Tell me what's going on."

She looked at Liam, looked at his EMT and wilderness first aid books on the shelf, a snowboard, an old fire helmet, looked at everything in the living room except Bill.

He took a step closer. "Something's got you wigged out."

Grace rubbed her lips together. "The sheriff thinks you should, um, check me. See if we…I…need to go to the hospital."

That would do it. "Good idea."

"No. I don't. Need to go, that is." Her gaze still avoided his. "I'm a little sore. Nothing else."

Liam played with Peanut, seemingly oblivious to everything else.

"Most people are sore after an accident." Bill didn't know if she was afraid of going to the hospital or of him. He'd guess the latter, but wished she'd look at him so he could try to see if something else was going on with her. "The rush of adrenaline can mask injuries. You should be examined."

Grace nodded, but looked as if she'd rather face a dentist and gynecologist at the same time than be checked by him. She ran her teeth over her lower lip.

"I promise I don't bite," he teased.

She blushed. Her bright red cheeks made her look like a teenager.

He motioned to a chair. "Do you want to sit?"

"I'd rather stand."

Figures. When Bill was on a call or out in the field on a rescue mission, he tried to keep the patient at ease. Joking around with Grace wasn't working. He'd try talking to her. "Where do you live in Georgia?"

"Columbus."

"You don't sound Southern."

"I grew up in the Midwest. Iowa."

"Cornfields and the Iowa Hawkeyes."

Her amber eyes twinkled. "And country fairs."

"Let me guess. You were the Corn Queen."

Her grin brightened her face. Not only pretty, unexpectedly beautiful.

Air stuck in his throat. He struggled to breathe.

She struck a royal pose, lifting her chin and shifting her shoulders back. "Corn Princess."

Bill had no idea why he'd reacted to her. Must be tired. "Sash and tiara?"

"Corn-on-the-cob scepter, too."

"Real Iowan corn?"

"Only the finest." She gave Liam a royal wave. "I was the envy of the corn court until an unfortunate incident with one of the 4-H goats."

"Poor goat."

"Poor corn." She made an exaggerated sad face. "After the goat encounter, I was a princess without a scepter."

Okay, this was more like it. Smiling and joking and raising Bill's temperature ten degrees. "So what brings her highness out of the land of sweet tea and juicy peaches across the Mississippi River and over the Rockies to the verdant Pacific Northwest?"

She stared at Liam. Her eyes softened. "Astoria."

"Ah. Nice little coastal town, if you don't mind being at sea level." Bill preferred living in the mountains. "Do you have family there?"

"No, but I thought why not try something different."

Her voice sounded shaky. Nerves?

Or something more? "That's a big move."

She shrugged, but tight lines formed around her mouth. "I've moved a lot."

"I've moved twice, not counting my stint at the fire academy. Once from my parents' house to an apartment, then into this house." Bill stood next to Grace. The top of her head came to the tip of his nose. "Show me where you're sore."

She pointed to her left shoulder, where the seat belt would have hit.

He touched the spot. "Does this hurt?"

"Slightly tender." She glanced at his hand on her, then looked away. "I can't remember all the moves we've made. My husband was in the army."

Was. Past tense. She hadn't said ex-husband, but she wasn't wearing a wedding band. Bill knew some folks didn't wear rings. Others lost them. Or pawned them. "Is your husband waiting for you in Astoria?"

She bent down and stroked Liam's hair. "He's…dead."

Her words cut Bill at the knees. He opened his mouth to apologize, to say something, anything, but nothing came out. She was so young with a kid.

Just like Hannah, Nick's wife.

A million memories rushed back, memories Bill had hoped to forget. The smell of death when his rescue team had found the bodies of Nick and Iain, still roped together. The sound of grief when he'd spent days at Nick's house, trying to comfort the Bishop family. The taste of regret when Bill had realized nothing he did or said would make things better for Hannah and her two young kids.

He had felt so useless back then. He forced himself to breathe now. At least he could do something for Grace. "I'm sorry."

"Thank you." The words came automatically, as if programmed in and spoken without thinking.

Her gaze, full of affection, remained on Liam, who kept himself entertained with the toy elephant.

Bill thought he could reach out and touch the love she was sending her son. A small knot formed in his chest. Ached behind his ribs. He didn't know what was going on, but he didn't like how he wanted to hold Grace until she looked at him the same way.

Not that she would. He had a habit of failing the women in his life. Just like his dad.

"Columbus, Georgia." Bill forced the words from his dry throat. "Is that where your husband was stationed?"

"Yes. Fort Benning. Damon was a Ranger. He was killed in action in Afghanistan two and a half years ago."

Damn. That sucked. "A real hero."

"Yes. Highly decorated. He loved what he did."

Grace's affection for her late husband filled her voice. Love never played into Bill's relationships. He much preferred the other *L* word. *Lust.* Love was too messy, too complicated. It was capable of causing pain and grief, like Grace must have endured with her husband's death. "Our service members have paid a high price in the Middle East, but your husband leaves behind a legacy of memories, and Liam."

Her gaze went from her son to Bill. "Is there, um, anything else you need to check?"

He looked at his hand on her shoulder. Damn. Still touching her. He lowered his arm. "Any headache or sore neck now?"

"No."

If her headrest wasn't set properly she could have whiplash. He rubbed his hands together so they wouldn't be cold against her skin, and stepped behind her. "I'm going to move your hair to check your neck."

"That's fine." Her tight tone made him think otherwise.

Bill pushed her long wet hair over to one side. His fingertips brushed her neck.

She inhaled sharply. Tensed.

"Sorry." He liked the feel of her soft skin. If only she wasn't so cold. But he knew ways to warm her up. Lots of ways.

Stop. Right there.

Bill might have the reputation of being a player, but he didn't play with patients. He touched her neck again. "Does this area hurt?"

Her back stiffened. "Not really."

He wasn't buying it. "You feel something."

"Nothing major." She sounded nonchalant, as if she had a splinter in her finger, nothing more. "A dull ache."

He moved his hand lower. "What about here?"

"Very dull. Almost nothing."

He moved in front of her. "Show me where the seat belt hit you."

Grace pointed to her left shoulder, then diagonally across her chest and over her hips.

"Does your abdomen or lower back hurt?"

"No."

"Hips?"

"All good."

"We can hold off a trip to the hospital tonight. Depending on how you feel tomorrow, you might want to see a doctor."

"Okay."

"Time for you to get out of those wet clothes. You can change in the bathroom. First door on the right." Bill motioned to Liam. "The little dude and I will make cocoa."

Liam clapped the elephant's paws together. "Cocoa. Cocoa."

Bill offered her the phone. "Take this with you. You can call whoever you need to, and let them know what's happened."

Sadness filled her gaze. "Thanks, but there's no one to call."

With that, Grace walked down the hall. Denim clung to her hips, showing off her curves and the sway of her hips.

Nice butt.

Hot.

Whoa.

Not going to happen. Not with a mom. Definitely not with a widow.

He liked rescuing damsels in distress, but only long enough to see them back on their feet and be rewarded for his efforts. He might help moms, but he didn't date them. Ever.

Mothers with children equaled commitment.

He'd rather hang in base camp, drinking and playing cards, than attempt that summit. Married friends might be happy, but they had provided enough *beta* on the climb. Marriage took commitment and hard work. An instant family wasn't on Bill's list of peaks to bag.

Hot or not, Grace and her son were his houseguests, period.

The bathroom door closed.

Liam sidled up next to Bill, pressing against his leg.

He glanced down. "Guess it's you and me, kid."

Liam held up his elephant.

"And Peanut." The expectant look in the little boy's eyes reminded Bill of the schoolkids who toured the station on field trips. Sitting behind the steering wheel wasn't enough. Sirens needed to blare and lights flash. And helmets. The kids all had to wear the helmet. "I bet you want another cookie."

"Please. Cocoa, too."

Kids were the same whether they came from Hood Hamlet, Oregon, or Columbus, Georgia. "Marshmallows or whipped cream?"

"Both."

A small hand clasped Bill's larger one. Squeezed.

Warmth shot up his arm. Boy, that felt good. And not because Liam's tiny fingers weren't so cold any longer.

Inquisitive eyes full of adoration gazed up at Bill, making him feel like a superhero.

Something tugged inside his chest. Something he'd never experienced before. Something he didn't understand. He shook off the unfamiliar and unwelcome feeling.

Must be all the excitement around here.

This wasn't the evening he'd expected to spend. A cute kid wanting to make hot chocolate with him in the kitchen. A pretty mom changing into his pajamas in the bathroom. But Bill was not unhappy the way tonight was turning out.

Company and cookies and cocoa beat decorating the Christmas tree any day.

Even at midnight.

It's going to be okay.

In the bathroom, Grace repeated Damon's words. She stripped out of her clothes and dried herself off with a blue towel hanging on the rack.

Why wouldn't it be okay?

She was naked, standing in a strange man's house, about to put on a strange man's pajamas, wondering if the strange man was too good to be true.

According to the sheriff, Bill Paulson was a kind, caring, generous man. She shouldn't be surprised, since she believed Damon had helped her find this refuge from the storm.

But she doubted her late husband would appreciate the hum racing through her body. A hum that had nothing to do with the drive or the crash or the strangeness of the night, and everything to do with her handsome rescuer. The only way to describe the feeling was first-date jitters. Except this was no date. And Bill...

He reminded her of Damon. The two men had similar coloring and take-charge personalities. Bill exuded the same strength, confidence and heat as her husband.

Too bad the similarities ended there.

Damon had always been attractive, but his looks became rugged over the years due to scars from shrapnel and a nose broken twice. Not exactly world-weary, but not happy-go-lucky like Bill Paulson, whose gorgeous features belonged on the pages of an outdoor magazine layout. Bill wasn't quite a pretty boy, especially with the sexy razor stubble, but close.

No doubt she was in shock.

That would explain her noticing every little thing about him. Reacting, too.

Touching Bill's hand had felt good, his skin warm and rough against hers. His touching her had felt even better, his hand on her shoulder, calming and sure, as if it belonged there.

But when he'd touched her neck…intimate, almost sexual, albeit unintentional…

She missed…that. A man's touch.

Don't think about him.

At least not *that* way.

Annoyed with herself, she shrugged on the pajama shirt. The soft flannel brushed her like a caress. The friction of fabric over dry skin warmed her, even though the pajamas were too big.

The sleeves hung over her hands. She rolled them to her wrists, then fastened the front buttons with trembling fingers. Her hands didn't shake from the cold, but from the situation.

Nerves.

She stepped into the pants. The hems pooled at her feet. She cuffed them.

The waistband slid down her hips. She rolled the top, determined to make this work.

Nerves weren't her only issue. A touch of guilt, too.

Something's got you wigged out.

Yeah, him.

Of all the houses on Mount Hood, she would pick the one belonging to a firefighter and mountain rescuer. The hottest guy she'd been alone with since, well, Damon had deployed.

Grace grimaced at her starstruck reflection. Had she looked this goofy while talking to Bill? She hoped not. Either way, she was being silly, acting like a teenager with a crush, not an adult, not a mom.

So what if Bill Paulson was a nice piece of eye candy? So what if he had a killer smile? So what if the concern in his bright, baby-blue eyes for her and Liam had sent an unexpected burst of heat rushing through her veins?

Tomorrow he would be one more person who had passed through her life. Nothing more.

All she had to do was survive tonight.

How hard could that be?

Grace shuffled from the bathroom and down the hallway, the carpet runner soft beneath her feet.

In the living room, a sense of warmth and homey goodness surrounded her. She'd been so frantic earlier she hadn't noticed the house. Now she took in the hardwood floors, beamed ceiling, river rock fireplace, wood mantel covered with photographs, and beautifully lit Christmas tree.

She wiggled her toes.

More cabin than house.

Inviting and comfortable.

The kind of place she'd dreamed of living someday. The kind of place where a kid could grow up happy. The kind of place a family could call home.

The scent of the Christmas tree hung in the air along with a touch of smoke from the burning fire. The beer bottle on the wooden end table and the gigantic leather recliner seemed typical for a bachelor pad, but the couch with color-contrasting pillows and coordinating throw blanket seemed out of place for a guy living alone. A far cry from her cheap apartment in Columbus.

Was there a girlfriend or wife in the picture? Maybe an ex who had lived here and decorated?

Male laughter, rich and deep and smooth, washed over her like water from a hot shower, heating her from the outside in. Forget feeling warm; she was downright feverish.

She'd forgotten the appeal of a man's laugh, the happiness and humor contagious. A higher pitched squeal joined in. That laugh, one she knew better than her own, brought a smile to her lips.

Liam.

Her chest tightened.

He could be such a serious boy. She was pleased he was having so much fun.

Grace entered the charming kitchen, with its dining area separated by a breakfast bar.

Bill sat at the table with her son, who was wrapped in a blanket, his little hands around a mug. Peanut sat on the table with his own mug in front of him.

What kind of guy would fix a cup of hot chocolate for a stuffed animal?

The sheriff had told her Bill Paulson was a cross between an Eagle Scout and an X Games champ. Yeah, that seemed to sum him up.

Grace moved behind Liam. She placed her hands on his narrow shoulders. "It looks like you boys did fine on your own."

Bill stood, his manners excellent. "Your cocoa is on the counter."

She noticed the steaming mug. "Liam doesn't drink his very hot."

"I've been around kids. I put ice cubes in his and Peanut's cups in case they decided to share."

She appreciated his treating Peanut like a living, breathing elephant, not a stuffed one. "Liam could spill on your blanket."

"It's washable. Isn't that right, little dude?"

Liam looked up at Bill. Her son had a case of hero worship. "That's right, big dude."

"Okay, then." Grace took her cup from the counter and sipped. "This is delicious."

Bill raised his cup. "My mom makes her own cocoa mix."

Liam took another sip. "It's yum."

Interesting. Her son seemed perfectly content to be away from her. Usually he didn't want to be out of eyesight.

A twinge of regret pinched Grace's heart. She'd done everything she could to be a good parent, but that didn't seem to be enough. Liam liked having Bill—a man—around. Well, her son better enjoy the company because tomorrow they would be on their own again.

"You have a very nice home." She wouldn't expect a single guy's house to be so clean, with homemade cocoa and cookies at the ready. "Thanks for everything."

Bill gave her the once-over.

Grace knew better than to be flattered, especially since she couldn't tell what he thought of her. Probably not much, given she was wearing his baggy pajamas, had no makeup on and her hair was a scraggly mess.

Her appearance wasn't due only to traveling. She hadn't cared how she looked since Damon died. She couldn't remember the last time she'd had her hair cut. She hadn't thought about her hair, her nails, her looks.

Until now.

She combed her fingers through damp strands, all too aware of how she'd let herself go these past two and a half years. Not that she wanted a man in their life. She could have stayed in Columbus and married Kyle if she'd wanted a husband.

Liam needs a father. You need a husband. You'll grow to love me.

As if saying "I do" was all it took to make a marriage work. Grace shook the memory of Staff Sergeant Kyle Gabriel's proposal from her mind. She dropped her hand to her side. "I don't know how I'll repay you for tonight."

"No need." Bill motioned to the empty chair next to Liam. "Send me a postcard once you're settled in Astoria, and we'll call it good."

Relief washed over Grace, grateful that he hadn't asked for more, for something she might not want to give. A postcard would be easy. She would have to remember to get his address. She sat. "I can manage that."

"You mentioned trying something different by moving to Astoria. Why there and not a bigger city?"

"The Goonies."

"Excuse me?"

"There's a movie called *The Goonies,*" she explained. "When I was dating my husband, Damon was saving money to buy his truck, so we didn't go out on dates that cost a lot of money. One time he came over to my house to watch movies. We saw *The Goonies.* Damon said when we got married we should go to Astoria for our honeymoon."

"Astoria, Oregon?"

She shrugged, waiting for hot tears to prick her eyes. Surprisingly, they didn't come. Sadness and grief ebbed like the tides. "It sounded cool to a couple of kids from Iowa. We didn't have the money for a honeymoon after we eloped. We got married at city hall. Two excited kids—me in my Sunday best and Damon in his army dress uniform—with a bouquet of carnations and two plain gold wedding bands. Going to Astoria ended up on our to-do list."

"You and your son are doing it now."

Grace nodded. She thought Damon would approve.

Liam yawned.

She took the mug from his hand. A preemptive move. "Tired, baby?"

He shook his head. "P-nut tired. He ready for nighty-night."

"It's been a long day for Peanut. You, too." Bill pulled out Liam's chair. "I'll show you the guest rooms."

"One room is fine." She stared at the dirty cups and spoons on the table. "Less of a mess to clean up tomorrow."

"Help yourself to the spare toothbrushes and toothpaste in the bathroom drawer."

"Have a lot of unexpected guests?" she asked.

"Not a lot, but I like to be prepared." He winked. "You never know who might knock on the door."

His tone teased, but Grace doubted his houseguests were stranded like her and Liam. Most likely they were attractive young females eager to spend the night.

The realization unsettled her.

Maybe she was wrong.

For all she knew, he had a girlfriend or a fiancée. The thought didn't make her feel better.

"Thanks. I appreciate your hospitality. I hope having us here won't cause you any problems with your…girlfriend."

"No worries," he said. "I don't have a girlfriend."

Yay. Single. Grace stiffened. Being happy he was available was a crazy reaction, but oh well. She was only human.

And out of his league.

She needed a haircut, a good night's sleep, a job and the ability to converse with a hot guy without losing her cool.

Not only out of his league, in a different grade. Grace was a kindergartner when dealing with the opposite sex. Bill was working on his master's thesis.

"Come on, Liam." She reached for her son. "Let's get you to bed."

Liam held his arms out to Bill.

Hurt flashed through Grace. Her chest tightened. She struggled to breathe.

"What can I say?" Bill's smile lit up his face and took her breath away. "Kids love me."

"Women, too?" The words came out before Grace could stop them. She wanted to cringe, hide, run away. But where was she going to go? She swallowed a sigh.

Bill's lopsided grin defined the word *charming*. "Most women. Except those who think I'm a psychotic killer."

He meant her. His lighthearted tone told Grace he wasn't upset. If anything, he made her suspicions sound…endearing. But she was still embarrassed.

"I'll carry him to the guest room." He lifted Liam up. "Don't forget Peanut."

Liam hugged the elephant and settled comfortably in Bill's arms, against Bill's chest. "Peanut like to be carried."

"Good," Bill said. "Because I like to carry."

Watching the two was bittersweet for Grace. The last time Damon had carried their son, Liam had been a year old, barely walking. Babbling, not talking.

Don't look back.

Grace was moving west to start over. She couldn't change the past. Damon was never coming back. She needed to look forward for both her and Liam's sake.

She followed Bill down the hallway to a room with a queen-size cherry sleigh bed and matching dresser and nightstand. A patchwork quilt covered the bed, with coordinating shams on the pillows. Framed pictures hung on the wall. The room sure beat a cheap motel with paper-thin walls, or an expensive hotel she couldn't afford.

"This is lovely." But odd considering the house belonged to a single guy. "Did you decorate the room yourself?"

"My mom helped me with the entire house. She thought my apartment was too much a man cave. I give her full credit for making sure everything coordinated."

"Your mother did a good job."

Holding Liam with one arm, Bill pulled down the covers. He gently set the little boy on the bed. "There you go, bud."

Liam thrust out his lower lip. "Not tired. More cocoa and cookies."

"I'll take you to the bathroom," Grace said. "Then I bet you and Peanut will be ready for bed."

At least she hoped so, because she didn't think her heavy eyelids would remain open much longer. Her feet ached for rest. Her brain wanted to shut down for the night.

"Want Bill." Liam's tiny fingers wiggled, reaching for the firefighter. "P-nut want Bill, too."

Grace opened her mouth to speak, but couldn't. This was the first time Liam had asked for someone else. She tried to ignore the prick of hurt, telling herself this was no big deal.

Bill knelt next to the bed, giving her son the height advantage. "Listen. I'm going to be in the room next to the bathroom. That's across the hall. When you wake up, we can have breakfast. Chocolate chip pancakes sound good?"

Liam nodded about a hundred times.

"We'll make a snowman if the storm lets up." Bill stood. "But you and Peanut need to be well rested, okay?"

Another nod from Liam. This time Peanut joined in.

Grace mouthed a thank-you.

Bill stepped away from the bed. "Give me your keys. I'll get your suitcases out of the truck."

She thought for a moment, touched her hand to her face. "Oh, no. I left the keys in the ignition. I wasn't thinking straight."

"You've been through a lot."

He had no idea. "Our suitcase is on the floor in front of the passenger seat. Everything else we own is in the back."

Compassion filled his eyes, not the usual pity people lavished on a widow.

She appreciated that.

Bill glanced toward the window. "Under a tarp or do you have a shell?"

"Shell."

"I hope there aren't any cracks from the accident."

"If there are, I don't want to know." She looked at Liam, who was bouncing Peanut on the bed as if the mattress was a trampoline. "Not until morning."

Bill drew his hand across his mouth as if he were zipping his lips.

The gesture was kidlike and sweet at the same time. "Thanks."

His gaze rested on Liam. "It's not easy being a single parent."

The sincerity of Bill's voice made Grace wonder if he knew someone who'd lost a spouse. She thought about asking, but didn't want to pry. "You do what you have to do. I'm not the first wife to have lost her husband. Or Liam his father."

"It still sucks."

Bill's words cut through the pleasantries—aka crap—people said to her, trying to make the bad stuff bearable. "Yes, it does. But you're right about having memories and Liam. That's made all the difference. And now we have our own Ranger angel looking out for us. Damon definitely had our six tonight."

A thoughtful expression formed on Bill's face. "You're lucky you walked away from that snowbank without any injuries."

"True, but that's not what I meant." Grace smiled up at him, a smile straight from her heart, something usually reserved for Liam alone. "I was talking about us finding you."

CHAPTER THREE

THE SMELL OF freshly brewed coffee enticed Grace to open her heavy eyelids. The scent made her mouth water and her tummy grumble. A cup of java and one of Damon's banana walnut muffins sounded so—

Wait a minute.

Her husband was dead. She was in bed.

Who made the coffee?

She blinked, disoriented and confused.

Light filtered through the window blinds. Not her apartment. Not anyplace she recognized.

Grace bolted upright.

Tall dresser, closet door, closed bedroom door.

Memories of the night before exploded in her mind. Driving in the blizzard. Crashing into the snowbank. Stumbling to Bill Paulson's front door. She hadn't been dreaming. Last night had been real.

Grace stretched her sleep-drenched arms and arched her back, like a drowsy cat waking from a much-needed nap.

She'd slept through the night. No bad dreams to wake her.

Amazing, considering she hadn't had a full night's sleep since Damon's death, and odd, since she was sleeping in a strange house in a stranger's guest room. Maybe this move to Astoria hadn't been the worst idea since skinny jeans.

Wind shook the window. The storm hadn't let up.

"We sure aren't in Columbus anymore, baby."

Grace moved her hand to the right to touch her son. Her fingers hit the mattress. "Liam?"

The spot next to her was empty.

No Liam.

No Peanut.

Her stomach clenched. Her heartbeat roared in her ears. "Liam."

No answer.

A million and one thoughts raced through her head, none of them good.

She scrambled out of bed, threw open the door and raced down the hallway. Every muscle bunched.

The sheriff had vouched for Bill Paulson. She'd been taken with the handsome firefighter herself. But Bill wasn't used to having kids in the house. What if he'd left cleaning solution where Liam could reach it? What if he'd left a door unlocked and Liam had wandered out of the house? What if? What if? What if?

Every nerve ending twitched. Her stomach roiled. She thought she might be physically ill.

It'll be okay, babe.

If only she could believe that.

"You'd better not do that again, Liam." Bill's voice, loud and boisterous, sounded from the kitchen. "I'm warning you."

Liam wasn't outside, but the knowledge didn't loosen the tension in her shoulders. Something was going on.

Grace accelerated her pace, lengthening her stride. She rounded the corner. Skidded to a stop.

On the floor between the dining area and breakfast bar, Bill sat crisscross applesauce with Liam and at least thirty dominoes set up in a row.

"I mean it this time." Bill tried to sound serious, but his mouth curved upward, a big grin tugging at his lips. "Don't touch the dominoes!"

Defiance gleamed in Liam's gaze. Mischief, too. He raised his arm, made a small fist and pushed over the first domino. The rest cascaded one on top of the other.

"You did it again!" Bill placed his hand over his heart and tumbled to the floor as if he'd been knocked over, too. "What are we going to do, Peanut? Liam won't listen."

Her son giggled.

The sheer delight in his voice warmed Grace's insides. Her pulse slowed. Her heart rate returned to normal. A bolt of guilt flashed through her at being so quick to think the worst of Bill Paulson when she'd woken up without Liam next to her.

Liam clapped. "Again. Again."

"Okay, kid. But only for you." Bill reset the dominoes, a job that took patience and a steady hand. "One more time."

Liam spread his fingers. "Ten more."

Grace wondered how many times they'd played this game. Knowing Liam, at least ten, but Bill didn't seem to mind.

"Two more," Bill countered. "I'm getting hungry."

"Four more. I help cook."

"You strike a hard bargain, little dude." He stuck out his arm. "But it's a deal."

Liam shook Bill's hand. "Deal."

The guys from Damon's squad, Liam's honorary uncles, visited when they could, but over the past two years they'd dropped by less and less. Some attended professional development schools. Some went to Special Forces training. Some joined other military units. Some left the army. Their group of friends had gotten smaller, but Liam had never been this animated with them, people he'd known his entire life. He rarely acted this way with her. Only Peanut. Liam's one and only friend.

Though Bill Paulson could probably qualify as her son's friend now. The guy had the right touch with Liam.

Jealousy stabbed Grace, an unexpected emotion. One she didn't like.

So what if her son had a new friend? Bill was nothing more than a nice guy who'd offered them shelter for the night. Something she would expect from a man who rescued people for a living, but she hadn't imagined a bachelor being so in tune with a three-year-old.

Watching Bill and her son play together made her feel older than twenty-six. Sure, she got on the floor, and didn't mind a big mess with art projects or mud. But she was always so tired, as if she carried a hundred-pound pack all day, struggling to keep herself balanced and not fall over like one of those dominoes.

Unlike Bill. No tired eyes. No sagging shoulders. Only smiles and an innate strength she felt from the doorway.

She tucked her hair behind her ears. "Good morning."

Liam jumped to his feet and ran toward her. "Mommy."

The excitement in his voice warmed Grace's heart. This was more like it. She scooped him up, eager to have him in her arms. "I woke up, and you weren't in bed."

Liam gave her a wet kiss. "I wake up. Peanut, too. You asleep so I get Bill."

"You mean Mr. Paulson."

"That's my dad's name." Bill stood. "Liam can call me by my first name."

"Okay." She relented only because they would be leaving today. She cuddled her son close. Sniffed. "You smell like cookies."

Liam pointed to his new best friend. "Big dude."

Bill's cheeks reddened. "Liam wanted to wait until you were up to have breakfast, but we were a little hungry."

"Hungry men eat cookies." Liam spoke the words with a growly voice, as if mimicking someone.

Bill's entire face turned red. He cleared his throat. "Cookies have flour, eggs and milk in them. Not that different from pancakes."

"Cookies are healthy." Liam bent his arm to show off his biceps. "Make me strong. Like Bill."

Grace covered her mouth with her hand and bit back laughter. "I can let cookies before breakfast slide this one time."

Bill's grin made him look more like one of Liam's peers than hers. "I appreciate that."

"It's the least I can do after being able to sleep in. That never happens." Or hadn't since Damon's final deployment. Grace was reminded of what she and Liam had lost in the mountains of Afghanistan, of what other people took for granted, without giving their good fortune a second thought. "I hope Liam didn't wake you up too early."

"I was awake when he knocked on my door. No reason for both of us to be up at the crack of dawn." Bill studied her with his watchful gaze. "I hope you weren't worried when he wasn't in bed."

She hugged Liam tight, remembering her fear waking up without him. He was all she had. "I had a moment of panic until I heard you in the kitchen."

Liam pushed away from her. "I winning."

Grace placed him on the floor. "You always win."

"And here I thought I had the age advantage," Bill joked. "Liam's quite the domino shark. He's kicking my bu—er, behind."

She appreciated the way Bill watched his language.

"I shark. Let's play," Liam shouted.

"Duty calls." Bill set up more dominoes. "Breakfast will have to wait a few more minutes."

"You boys play." Grace knew having a guy to play with was a big deal for her son. She'd let him have his fun. "I'll fix breakfast."

Bill's gaze met hers. "I don't mind cooking."

"Neither do I."

"You're a guest."

"And you're sweet." She meant each word. "Consider my cooking breakfast a bonus on top of the postcard I'll be sending."

He glanced at a waiting Liam, then back at her.

"Okay." He returned to setting up dominoes. "It's better this way. The guys at the station aren't that keen on my cooking."

"I find that hard to believe." He seemed like the kind of man who could do anything, including setting up dominoes while carrying on a conversation. "It's hard to ruin pancakes."

"Unless you burn them, turning breakfast into a three-alarm call."

"You're a firefighter," she said. "I'm sure you can take care of any flames."

"Oh, I know how to put out fires." He looked up with a mischievous grin. "I also know how to start them."

His words, flirtatious and suggestive, hung in the air. His gaze remained on her.

Grace's pulse skittered. Attraction buzzed all the way to her toes. Something passed between them. Something palpable. Something unsettling.

She looked away. Gulped.

"I have everything you need." He returned to the dominoes. "On the counter."

She opened her mouth to speak, but nothing came from her Mojave-dry throat. "Thanks," she finally said.

She shuffled to the kitchen in her bare feet, eager to put distance between them.

A few words from a gorgeous guy? A look? And she was incapacitated?

So not good.

Pancake mix sat on the counter, along with measuring cups, a wooden spoon, eggs and a stainless-steel bowl.

What was happening to her? She wasn't in shock. She didn't need more sleep. Maybe loneliness had finally sent her over the edge.

Grace measured the flour mixture. Her hand trembled and her vision blurred. She managed to fill the cup and dump the contents into the mixing bowl without making too much of a mess. She added water and eggs. Stirring the batter, she slowly regained her composure.

Dominoes clattered against the hardwood floor.

Liam laughed. "Oops."

Bill released a drawn-out sigh. "We'll have to try that again."

Her son clapped. "Again. Again."

"I've figured out your M.O.," their host said. "You don't do anything once."

Bill impressed Grace. "You pick up quick. Are you sure you aren't married with kids?" she asked him.

"Nope. Most of my friends are married, but my life is good, and I'm happy. Marriage and kids can wait until those things change. And if they don't change, then I'll be happily single."

"Wait until you meet the right woman."

"Why settle for one when there are so many out there?"

"So cavalier."

He shrugged. "Some of my friends have great marriages. Others not so good. My parents have struggled with a long-distance marriage."

Grace's life had started the day she fell in love with Damon. He'd wanted to spend the rest of his life with her, but being a Ranger kept him away from home and cut his life short. "Being married takes work whether you're together or not. Damon and I were apart a lot. Loving someone isn't easy. But we managed. Had a child. Were a family."

"My parents and I have never been much of a family. My dad is always away because of his job. His traveling is hard on my mom. Makes me wonder if the family thing is for me."

"If you don't know, it's good you're waiting to settle down."

"Thanks for saying that. Everyone else has been telling me to grow up because I'm missing out."

"I never said you weren't missing out," Grace teased.

She felt sorry for Bill. He could play all he wanted and be as sweet as could be, but she would never change places with him. At least she had Liam. One day, Bill was going to find himself lonelier than her.

"Cartoons. Cartoons," Liam chanted. "Peanut wants to watch cartoons."

Bill looked at her. "Is Liam allowed to watch TV?"

"Yes, but I limit how much."

"That's good," Bill said. "Kids should be outside playing and making snow angels, not sitting on the couch inside."

"You sure don't act like a confirmed bachelor who doesn't want kids."

"I may not want children of my own, but that doesn't mean I don't like other people's."

"Fair enough," she said. "You're the perfect playmate and babysitter rolled into one. If you ever get tired of being a firefighter, you'd make great manny."

His brow furrowed. "A what?"

"A male nanny."

He rose to his feet with the grace of an athlete. "I've been known to babysit a time or two. Though I'm the call of last resort."

That surprised her.

"Come on, little dude." He picked up Liam and grabbed Peanut. "You get the best seat in the house. My favorite chair."

Bill carried them into the living room. Thirty seconds later, the sound of cartoons filled the air. Liam squealed.

Her son seemed to like whatever Bill did. Of course, being a playmate or friend was easy. Being a parent and disciplinarian not so much.

Bill joined her in the kitchen. "How are the pancakes coming along?"

"Stirring the batter now."

"You've got a great kid."

"Thanks. But he has his moments."

"Don't we all."

Grace tried to focus on cooking, but curiosity about the handsome firefighter filled her mind with questions. "You said you don't plan on settling down anytime soon, but you must, um, date."

The second the words left her mouth she regretted them. Talk about awkward. But wanting to know more about him had gotten the best of her.

"Yeah, I do," he answered, as if she were asking if he put butter on his toast. "But I won't be dating again until December."

She added chocolate chips to the batter. "You don't look like the Grinch."

"I'm not. I love Christmas."

"Most people like having someone to date for the holidays."

"I'm not most people."

She would agree with that. "So why won't you date until after Christmas?"

"Too many family obligations."

"Do you have lots of brothers and sisters?"

"Just my mom and dad. I meant a date's family."

"You lost me."

"Nothing worse than being dragged to countless family gatherings, with everyone asking when's the wedding, even if you only started dating."

All she'd wanted to do while dating Damon was think and talk about their future. But she knew guys weren't like that. "That would get old."

"Didn't your family do that?"

"No, my family didn't want me getting serious with Damon. His family felt the same way."

"Why?"

"They thought we were too young. I was fifteen when we started dating. Nineteen when we wed. My parents couldn't forgive me for eloping and marrying a man who'd joined the military instead of going to college. They haven't spoken to me since. Damon's folks were furious when he enlisted. They'd asked me to talk him out of it. Our getting married only made things worse."

"You'd think both sets of parents would be proud of what Damon was doing. The sacrifice he and you were making."

Bill had no idea how horrible both sets of parents had acted. "We made our choices. They made theirs."

He glanced around the doorway into the living room, then back at Grace. "Have you started dating again?"

Answering should be simple, but the unexpectedly personal question startled her. "A few months ago I went out with another Ranger."

"It didn't work out."

"He proposed. On the third date."

"Whoa."

"That's exactly what I thought." She poured batter onto the skillet. "Kyle is a sweet guy from Damon's platoon, but I wasn't sure if he was serious about marriage or trying to do the right thing by a fallen mate."

"Sounds like a good man, either way."

"He is, but…"

"But?"

She remembered Kyle, all earnest and sincere, proposing while Liam napped on the couch. She was all for being practical, but Kyle was a friend, nothing more. "I wasn't in love with him. We went on a few more dates, then it was time for him to deploy and…"

"Hard to go through that again."

"I wasn't going through it again." She hadn't been ready to marry another hero. She didn't want to love a man and give her all, but not be his priority.

God. Country. Army. Family.

That was how Damon's priorities fell. The army and serving a greater good had always come before her and Liam. She'd known where she'd fallen on the list going into the marriage, had accepted her place, respected it, because she was young, and her love for Damon was that strong.

But she was not about to accept being second, third or fourth again. Not for any man.

Grace and Liam deserved to be the number one priority. She would never settle for anything less.

"Breakfast was delicious." Sitting at the table, Bill leaned back in the chair, his stomach full and a satisfied smile on his face. He liked having a woman cook breakfast for him, especially one with sleep-rumpled hair, wearing his pajamas. The circles under Grace's eyes had faded. She must have slept well last night. That pleased him. "Thanks."

"You're welcome." Glancing out the window, she dragged her upper teeth over her bottom lip. "The snow is coming down hard."

"This morning's weather forecast predicts it will fall all day and into the night. A real bummer."

Her features tensed. "I'm sorry if we're in your way."

"You're not in the way." Bill annunciated each word. He needed to be careful what he said. Grace took things too personally. "I'm bummed the weather will keep me from skiing today. I have to be at the station early tomorrow morning, so I'll miss making first tracks in the freshies."

Grace gave him a blank stare.

"Powder," he clarified. "You don't ski."

"There are ski resorts in Iowa, but skiing wasn't something Damon and I ever tried."

Bill couldn't tell from her tone whether she was interested in the sport or not. "It's never too late to learn."

"I doubt there's a ski resort near Astoria."

Not interested. Too bad. Bet she would like skiing if she gave it a try. "No, but the mountain will always be here."

"Maybe when Liam is older."

"He's old enough now."

She stared at her son, who was picking chocolate chips out of his pancakes. "He's three."

Liam raised four fingers. "Almost four."

"That's the age I learned to ski."

"But you lived on the mountain." Grace's words rushed out. "I bet everyone in Hood Hamlet skis when they're in preschool."

Bill didn't know if she was trying to convince him or herself. "Many do, but lots of kids who don't live here learn to ski at a young age. The earlier, the better. That way there's no fear."

She shook her head. "Fear seems healthy, considering you're speeding down a mountain."

"Kids have a lower center of gravity and don't have as far to fall. Helmets protect them." Liam had chocolate and maple syrup smeared on his chin. Bill could count the number of family breakfasts he'd had, growing up, with both his mom and dad at the table. That was too bad because this was…nice. "Want me to teach you how to ski, little dude?"

Liam raised his hands in the air. "Ski…!"

Grace shook her head. "He doesn't know what skiing is."

"I'll show him."

"Maybe if we were staying—"

"Look out the window. You're not going anywhere."

"You can't go to the mountain today. Tomorrow you work."

Okay, she had a point. Bill shouldn't have offered to teach Liam to ski. He shouldn't have flirted with Grace before breakfast, either. He might find her attractive, but he didn't want her to think he was romantically interested in her.

"Just an idea." A bad one, except… Bill's dad might be alive, but he'd never been around long enough to show him how to do anything. Liam's father was dead. The kid was going to need someone to teach him about the outdoors and other guy stuff. "But who knows how long it'll take them to fix your truck."

Grace's lips parted, a combination of shock and panic. "I thought I could leave today."

Maybe Bill should have included denial in the mix. "Not in *this* weather."

"Once the storm passes…"

Damn. She had no idea about how long bodywork could take. Neither did he, but the vehicle wouldn't be ready today. "A claims adjustor from your insurance company needs to assess the damage before your truck can be repaired. Sometimes they don't have to do it in person, but other times they will."

Her head dropped slightly. She touched her forehead with both hands, rubbing her temples as if trying to put out a fire.

He wished she would relax. "Thad Humphreys owns the body shop. He's a good guy. A great mechanic. Talk to him before you start worrying."

Her hands froze. "Who says I'm worrying?"

She was the epitome of worry. Bill didn't like that. "No one."

Grace lowered her arms to her side. "I have a lot on my mind."

"I'm sure you do." He wanted to help her, but some things he couldn't do. "I hate to add to your list of things to do, but you should contact your insurance company and file a claim."

"I called them after Liam fell asleep last night. I didn't think you'd mind me using your phone."

Not a complete damsel in distress. "I don't."

"I wonder if they've towed the truck."

"Not yet."

Her shoulders slumped.

He didn't like seeing her so dejected. "I bet as soon as there's a break in the weather, they'll be right out."

Her mouth twisted.

"This isn't what you wanted to happen, but try to enjoy yourself." He wished she didn't seem so concerned all the time. "Relax."

"I need to clean up the kitchen."

"The dishes can wait."

Someone needed to show Grace how to lighten up and have fun. Bill knew how to make that happen.

Not in his usual way.

He needed to get her on the mountain and fill her lungs with fresh air and put a smile on her face that would last longer than a blink. Too bad the weather wasn't cooperating.

"Snowman, snowman," Liam chanted.

"It's snowing too hard." Bill hated to disappoint the kid, but safety first. "We're going to have to stay inside for now."

Liam pouted.

"I'm sure we can find something else to do," Grace said.

Bill reviewed the options for kid fun inside his house. Not much beyond TV, Xbox and a few board games. And then he remembered. "I could use some help decorating my Christmas tree."

Liam bounced Peanut on the table. "Tree. Tree."

"He's in." Bill flashed Grace a charming grin. Not the one that encouraged beautiful, sexy women to type their numbers into his cell phone. The I'm-a-good-guy-you-can-trust-me grin he used on everybody else. "What about you?"

The look on her face made him think she was doing calculus in her head. "Uh, sure, but would it be okay if I took a shower first?"

Sexy images of bare skin, hot water and steam filled his head. He would like nothing better than to join her.

Bill swallowed. "Go ahead. I'll take care of the kitchen."

Grace rose. "My suitcase?"

"In the living room by the front door." He started clearing the table, leaving Liam to finish gorging himself on chocolate chips dipped in maple syrup. Two of Bill's favorite foods. "I didn't see any cracks in the shell last night. I went ahead and grabbed a couple of plastic bins from the back. One had a few toys in it."

"Thanks," she said. "The conditions must have been horrendous."

"I've been out in worse."

"With OMSAR?"

"In June, during a mission, my team had to spend the night in a snow cave."

"You must have been freezing."

"It was fun."

She studied him. "You like to have fun."

"Fun is the name of the game."

Having them here was fun. A different kind of fun than Bill was used to having, but he had no complaints. Even if nudity wasn't involved. Which it wouldn't be. Not with Grace. Only wholesome, kid-friendly fun. Still, he had a feeling he wouldn't have to worry about being bored.

That was good.

Bill carried more dishes to the counter.

His dad claimed boredom was the enemy. Bill hated being bored. He liked a variety of activities. One thing—an activity or a woman—never held his attention for long. Another reason why settling down held zero appeal.

His parents had celebrated their thirty-fifth wedding anniversary this year, but Bill wondered why his dad had gone the wife-and-kid-route in the first place. The man worked all over the globe, wherever his job in the oil industry took him. He never wanted to be home, had never wanted them to visit him on site. His dad never wanted them around, period.

Bill hated hearing his mom say he was like his father. He didn't want to be like his dad. Didn't want to break his wife's heart each time he left, and wasn't there when she needed him. He didn't want to break promises to his kid, who loved him more than anything. He didn't want his family to ever question whether he loved them back or not.

But he *was* like his father. Bill had failed his mother during her pregnancy. He'd failed helping Hannah after Nick died. He'd failed his best friend, Leanne, by not realizing she'd been spending her holidays alone.

Bill wouldn't get involved in a serious relationship.

He didn't want to fail and hurt another woman.

Not after seeing what his mom had gone through over the years, and was still going through when his dad was away.

Bill couldn't do that to a child.

Not after wondering if he'd done something to make his dad not want to be around.

No way. That wouldn't be fun or fair.

CHAPTER FOUR

"WINTER WONDERLAND" PLAYED on Bill's living room speakers. Light snow fell outside the wood-framed windows. Grace might as well be standing inside a snow globe. She knew exactly how the enclosed glass bubble world would feel. Cozy and comfortable and safe.

How she felt right now.

Unbelievable. Under the circumstances.

Bill dug through a big box. "There's an ornament in here you'll like, little dude."

"I'll help." Liam set Peanut on the floor.

At the breakfast table, the handsome firefighter had wanted her to relax. She'd figured that wasn't possible. Two hours later, she realized she'd been wrong. Grace half laughed.

Bill glanced her way. "You look more relaxed."

Someone could flip her make-believe world upside down to shake the snow, and still she knew today would be okay. An odd feeling, given the uncertainty over her truck. "Surprisingly, I am."

"Look at that, bud, your mom is chillin' in Hood Hamlet."

Liam grinned. "Chillin' Mommy."

"I can't remember the last time I *chilled,* but the Christmas spirit around here is contagious." Bill's faded jeans and blue henley shirt could easily be a red velvet Santa suit that matched the hat he wore. "I'm waiting for you to start ho-ho-hoing."

He put his hands on his flat stomach and leaned back. "Ho-ho-ho."

Liam burst out laughing.

Grace appreciated Bill's sense of humor. "How do you make everything so much fun?"

He shrugged. "It's a gift."

"A wonderful gift." Bill helped Grace focus on the present. Something she hadn't done in far too long. Humming along to the song, she hung a silver bell on the tree.

The branch bounced.

The bell rang. The chime lingered on the fir-scented air.

Arms outstretched, Liam ran to the front door, where a two-inch-wide red leather strap with four gold bells hung from the doorknob. He pulled on the strap, ringing them.

Bill sang the chorus from "Jingle Bells."

Grace joined in.

The singing invigorated Liam. With each shake, his impish grin widened. He bounced from foot to foot, excited and offbeat.

The song ended, but Liam didn't stop ringing the bells. If he had pointy ears and shoes, he would make the perfect elf to Bill's Santa. The thought blanketed her heart with warmth.

She adjusted a silver ball on the tree. "The jingling makes me think of a horse-drawn sleigh."

Bill gave Liam a thumbs-up. "Ever been on one?" he asked her.

"No, but I saw one in a Hallmark Christmas movie on TV."

Liam's ringing went on and on and on.

Grinning, Bill shook his head. "The little dude likes the bells."

"Liam loves all types of bells." She motioned her son back to the tree. "I'll hang the strap somewhere out of reach."

"Don't. The front door is perfect." Bill's gaze traveled from the miniature village on the end table, past a clock on the wall that played carols on the hour, over a stuffed Christmas moose on the entertainment unit to a nativity scene set on the mantel. "Thanks for putting out the decorations. The house is ready for Santa."

Memories of a revolving iridescent tree that changed colors rushed back. Her mom had loved anything unique when it came to Christmas. The more bizarre the decoration, the better. But Grace had been uninvited from all holidays, her cards and presents returned unopened the year she'd married Damon.

Grace preferred rustic and homespun decor, like the kind she'd found in the additional boxes of Christmas decorations Bill had brought out. She'd had a blast finding spots for each item. She couldn't wait for him to see his snowman-themed guest bath or his candy-cane kitchen. "You're welcome, but decorating was my pleasure."

She'd made halfhearted attempts to make Christmas special for Liam, but he'd been too young to know what was happening, and she'd felt so alone after Damon died. But today was different.

After years of apartment living, she'd dreamed about spending Christmas in a house, decking the halls and trimming a real tree. Only today was no dream. Everything was real, from sitting around the table eating breakfast like a family, to spending the day with Bill, who was proving to be…well, maybe a little too perfect.

The perfect host, anyway.

No man was perfect.

A guy like Bill, a first responder and hero, someone who risked his life and put the needs of others ahead of his own family, was far from Grace's idea of Mr. Right. If she were interested in finding Mr. Right.

She wasn't.

Maybe after she made a life for herself in Astoria, and Liam was older. But she had no reason to be thinking about that now.

Time to embrace the feeling of family and enjoy the glad tidings tied up in a shiny ribbon. Maybe this would be the start of a new tradition for her and Liam.

She'd never seen him happier.

"Look at this." Bill showed Liam an ornament. "My dad gave me this fire engine when I told him I wanted to be a firefighter. It's one of my favorites. Put it on the tree for me."

Liam's mouth formed an O.

Bill handed over the ornament.

Her son held the miniature fire truck as he would a priceless treasure.

"Find an empty branch," Bill encouraged.

Liam scanned the tall tree. He raised his arm toward a bare branch, but came four inches short. The ornament dangled from his little fingers.

Grace's heart lurched. If he let go…

Liam rose on his tiptoes.

She held her breath.

Bill's smile didn't waver. "Almost there, buddy."

He didn't sound concerned at all.

She nibbled a fingernail.

The tip of Liam's tongue stuck out between his lips. He stretched again, but fell short. Dropping onto his heels, he puckered his lips.

Bill rubbed his whisker-covered chin. Liam hadn't given the guy time to shower this morning, let alone shave.

The stubble gave Bill a dangerous edge. She wondered if the whiskers would scratch her face if he kissed her. Not that she wanted to be kissed by him. Or anybody else.

"That's a good branch you picked out, but why stop there?" Bill asked. "Help me put the fire truck toward the top."

Liam nodded, his eyes twinkling with excitement.

Bill lifted him into the air.

"Higher," Liam commanded, then giggled.

With a whoop and a holler, Bill obliged.

Liam beamed like the brightest star in the sky on Christmas Eve.

Grace placed her hand over her thrumming heart. She loved seeing her son so happy. They both needed to laugh more. That would be one of her New Year's resolutions.

Liam pointed at her. "Mommy's turn. Lift her up."

Heat rushed up her neck. "I'm too heavy."

Setting Liam on the ground, Bill grinned wryly. "You're not even close to being too heavy."

Liam grabbed a Nutcracker ballerina from the box and handed the ornament to her. "Go on, Mommy. Lots of empty branches up top."

The thought of Bill's large, warm hands around her waist made Grace want to fan herself. He could make her skin dance and her blood boil with a simple touch. But she shouldn't. She couldn't. "Thanks, but I wouldn't want you to hurt your back."

"Remember, all those green fruits and veggies made me

strong." Bill's voice lowered to a deep and oh-so-sexy tone. "I can handle you."

Her heart tripped. "I'm not sure I can handle *you*."

He raised a brow. "You never know unless you try."

Temptation flared. Grace loved a challenge. That was how she'd ended up dating Damon back in high school. But she was no longer a teenager caught up in that first blush of love.

This morning, the line between daydreams and reality was blurring. Grace couldn't be reckless with her heart. She couldn't be reckless with Liam. She had to be careful. Not douse the spark waiting to ignite inside her with a full container of lighter fluid.

She raised her chin, meeting Bill's gaze straight on. "I could try, but it's not worth the risk. What if you're wrong and throw your back out? You won't be able to finish decorating the tree, or make a snowman if the weather improves, or go to work in the morning."

She and her son had never experienced this kind of family time preparing for the holidays. Having Bill a part of it was special. No sense letting fear ruin the day for Liam.

Bill studied her. "You're practical."

Grace expected to hear teasing in his voice, not…respect. "Being practical goes with being a mom."

Bill swept Liam into the air again. "You're a lucky guy to have such a great mom."

Her heart went pitter-pat like the Little Drummer Boy's stick against his drum. Her life revolved around being Liam's mom. There was no better compliment. "Thanks."

Holding on to a glittery green ball, Liam nodded. "Best mommy ever."

Grace's chest tightened. All she'd ever wanted to be was a great mom. A great wife, too. Maybe someday she'd get another chance at the latter. "You're the best son ever."

Liam nodded. "And Bill best daddy."

The word *daddy* floated on the air, a comic strip dialogue bubble looming over Bill's head.

Her joy evaporated. Her stomach churned. Her heart hurt. He was going to burst Liam's bubble and…

Bill casually ruffled her son's hair. "That's the nicest thing anyone's ever said to me, little dude. Where do you want to hang the ball?"

Grace released the breath she'd been holding.

Liam pointed to one of the upper branches. "There."

"You've got this." Bill lifted him higher.

Her son hooked the ornament on the tree and was lowered to the floor. He dived into the box of ornaments. "More. More."

"Let's put them all on," Bill said.

Maybe she'd overreacted, hearing Liam call another man Daddy. Maybe she'd been the only one feeling uncomfortable. Maybe Bill could smooth over an awkward moment like buttercream icing on a wedding cake.

A *wedding* cake?

Her insides trembled.

Maybe she'd better forget this holiday fun and run as far away from Bill as she could during the next break in the storm. Not that she had a way to leave besides her two feet. Darn it.

Grace could count on one hand the times Liam had said the word *daddy*. He didn't remember his father. He'd been too young. But she told him stories about Damon and showed him pictures. Liam had seen other kids and their daddies at preschool and at the college day care where he'd stayed while she attended classes.

Guess he thought Bill looked like a daddy.

A superhot daddy.

Don't go there.

Getting her son a daddy wasn't on her to-do list. Or her Christmas list.

Bill Paulson was not the answer to their prayers. He was not going to wrap himself up in a big bow. He was a one-day savior, not a long-term one.

Not that Grace needed saving.

She needed to get a grip on her fantasies and kick him out of the starring role.

He touched her shoulder. "You okay?"

Grace startled. No, she wasn't okay, but she nodded, not wanting to admit the truth. She needed to protect her son's heart. How was she going to do that? And protect herself, too.

She glanced out the window. Still snowing. That meant she was stuck here with Liam's idea of a daddy. And Bill happily acting the part.

His eyes didn't let go. "You look miles away."

She wished she was miles away. Away from him and the sugarplum temptation of his make-believe world, where all was safe and perfect.

Grace, of all people, knew better.

She gave her head a hard shake. "Just thinking."

"About me?" he teased.

Her cheeks flamed. If he only knew…

He made her feel things she'd buried deep inside her when she'd laid her husband to rest at Arlington. She would rather face a roomful of black widow spiders than tell him the truth.

"About today." Which was true. "I've never decorated a live Christmas tree before. They sell them, but we used an artificial one."

"Then we're even. I've never decorated a fake tree."

"I can't imagine buying a fake tree when your backyard is a forest."

"True, but most of the trees outside are too big for in here. I applied for a permit to cut this one down. I do that every year."

"Of course you did." She didn't hesitate a moment. "You follow the rules."

He glanced at Liam, who lay on the floor flying an angel ornament in the air, then back at her. Bill's mouth curved into an inviting you-know-you-want-me smile. "Depends on the rule."

Enough charm and sensuality infused his words to ignite a ball of heat in her belly.

Not good, Grace. Not good at all.

Her mouth went dry. Her mind raced, imagining what rules he'd broken, where and how. And with whom.

She tried hard to be good, to do what was right. Would she ever have the chance to do something…naughty, or was she stuck being nice?

Liam handed her an angel ornament. "Here, Mommy."

"Thanks, sweetie." Grace focused her attention on the angel with feather wings and a gold pipe-cleaner halo, over the picture of a little girl's face. "Who is this?"

"Kendall Bishop-Willingham." The tender smile on Bill's face suggested Kendall was someone special. "She's the daughter of my friends Hannah and Garrett."

"Beautiful."

Bill nodded. "Each year Kendall and her two younger brothers give me ornaments. Without them I'd have nothing but round balls and bells."

Liam ran to the door and jingled the bells. The sound got louder and louder until she couldn't hear the Christmas carols playing.

Bill shook his head with a laugh. "I said the magic word."

"Bells," she and Bill shouted at the same time.

Liam danced. He rang the bells again.

Her gaze met Bill's. Something passed between them, the same connection she'd experienced last night.

She wanted to look away, but couldn't.

He seemed in no hurry, either.

A bell-size lump formed in her throat.

"More. More." Liam's chant broke the spell. "Need to decorate."

For the best. Common sense told Grace that, yet a part of her wished the connection could have continued. She inhaled deeply and looked to her son.

Liam pulled a red ball from the ornament box. "Up. I want to put on this one."

"Sure thing, buddy." Bill raised her son into the air again. "By the time we're finished with the tree, I won't need a workout."

Bill sounded so content. Nothing seemed to bother him, except not being able to ski. This must be what an always-up-for-a-good-time kind of guy was like.

What would he think if she told him she hadn't been to a gym in nearly three years? Or hadn't eaten a meal with another adult in two months, until last night? Their worlds were so different. She kept forgetting that when she was with him.

Grace hung the angel on the tree.

She couldn't imagine having Bill's carefree life. She worked hard, paid her bills, cared for her son, cooked and cleaned. After that? No time. No energy. No sleep. Nothing left for her.

"Look, Mommy." Liam hung the red ball on the tree. "Shiny and pretty like you."

Her affection for him overflowed.

Liam meant everything to her.

Unlike Bill's, her life wasn't perfect. Her heart was missing a huge chunk. Her faith was battered. Her nights were lonely. But she had her son. He was all she needed. Anything—anyone— else would be a bonus, an indulgence, like whipped cream on ice cream, and a cherry on top.

Moving away from the tree, Bill brushed her shoulder with his arm. "Sorry."

Her pulse skittered. Heat emanated from the point of contact. Grace took a calming breath. It didn't help.

Forget bonuses. Whipped cream was full of calories and fat. No need for indulgences. maraschino cherries were sticky, full of chemicals and food coloring.

She glanced at the handsome firefighter.

Totally unnecessary. Bad for her.

And to be avoided at all costs.

After lunch, Bill stood next to the six-foot snowman in his front yard. He had summited Denali, scaled peaks in Patagonia, skied in Chamonix. He enjoyed vacations that pushed him to the physical limits, whether on another continent or here on Mount Hood. Building a snowman with Grace and Liam was the last thing he'd expected to be doing on his day off. Surprisingly, it didn't suck.

Snowflakes fell from the sky, much lighter than the blanket of white that had poured down earlier. The sharp scent of pine tickled his nose. His breath hung in the air. Familiar sights and smells, until he looked at his house and saw a blue elephant sitting on the living room windowsill.

Not so typical.

His childhood memories of snow days revolved around playing with his friends. Today was Bill's first experience of family time in the snow, the kind of day he'd always wanted to spend with his parents when he was a kid. But his dad had always been away, or too busy when he was home. His mom had been game for about thirty minutes, until she thought the temperature was too cold.

Bill enjoyed this afternoon's interlude from reality more than he thought he would. He'd liked being called Daddy, and liked having the kid look up to him. For a few hours, Bill could be the kind of father he wished his dad had been. And no one would be hurt when he went back to being a fun-loving, womanizing bachelor. A win-win for all involved.

Liam stuck out his tongue, trying to catch a snowflake.

Grace held up a camera. She wore one of his soft shell jackets over her zip-up fleece. Strands of brown hair stuck out from under the colorful stripped wool beanie, also his. A pair of black gloves kept her hands warm. She looked wintery cute, like a photo from a Hood Hamlet Visitors Center brochure.

"Got it." She focused the lens on Bill. "Your turn."

He struck a serious pose, if pretending to be an artist sculpting snow could be deemed serious.

Liam jumped into the picture. Not easy with knee-high snow and so many articles of clothing he looked like the Michelin Man. The poor kid had to be sweating beneath all the layers Grace had made him wear.

The condensation from her sigh floated away on the air.

Bill had to laugh. "Photo bomb."

"I don't think he knows what that is." She lowered her camera. The cold had turned her cheeks rosy. Her eyes were clear and bright. "At least I hope not."

"Then the kid's a natural." Bill patted Liam's fleece cap. "Because he's got the method down."

"It's nice to see him clown around."

Grace's lighthearted tone thrilled Bill. Emptying her pickup and watching the truck be towed away had seemed to release the remaining grip she held on herself after decorating the tree.

Bad stuff happened.

Life went on.

Now she was smiling. Singing Christmas carols. Playing.

He couldn't be happier.

Liam tugged on Bill's arm. "Frosty needs nose."

"Yes, he does." Bill looked around. "I brought out a carrot."

"Abra-dabra." The kid pulled one arm from behind his back. He clutched the carrot in his mitten-covered hand. "One nose."

"Nice trick, little dude." Bill gave a thumbs-up. "You'll have to teach me that later."

Grace positioned herself to take a picture. "Be careful."

Bill rolled his eyes. Mothers could caution, but kids needed to be kids. Get into scraps, jams and fights. Knock over a snowman or two.

"Liam's so padded he looks like he's wearing bubble wrap," Bill said. "He'll be fine if he falls."

The kid might even bounce.

"Liam's not used to snow." Her mouth tightened. "You've worked hard on the snowman. He could fall on top of it."

She didn't seem used to the white stuff, either.

"Snow is soft. More forgiving than grass. And snowmen have short life expectancies." Bill held out his arms. "Come on, bud. Frosty needs his nose."

Liam flew into them. With so many layers, Bill couldn't feel the little body underneath. It was like holding on to a stuffed animal.

Grace snapped more pictures. The kid stuck in the carrot.

"That's much better."

The click of the camera continued.

"Good job." Bill released Liam. "Does Frosty need anything else?"

The kid studied the snowman like an art dealer appraising a van Gogh. "Frosty good."

She took another picture. "Awesome."

The darkening sky told Bill more snow was on the way. Best

to make the most of the reprieve from the storm. "Time to make snow angels."

"Snow angels?" Liam's scarf muffled the words.

Grace stepped forward. "Georgia Christmases are more green than white. We've never done that before."

"Then it's a good thing you came to Hood Hamlet, because we always have white Christmases." Bill held Liam's hand. Bill's dad never taught him to do anything outdoors. It had been his mom, then Nick and Jake. "I grew up making angels. I'll show you how."

Bill walked to a canvas of fresh snow in front of a semicircle of tall pines. He released Liam's hand. "Do you know how to do a jumping jack?"

Liam did five.

"That's all you have to do, except you're not standing up." Bill lay on the snow with his arms extended. The cold seeped into him, a familiar feeling. "Get down like this, then do a jumping jack."

He flapped his arms up and down, scissored his legs in and out, flattening the snow on either side of his body. He carefully rose, then motioned to his creation. "Look what I made."

"Angel. Angel." Liam's eyes widened. "I want to make one."

"You can make as many as you want." Bill looked at Grace. "Trigger finger ready?"

She positioned her camera. "The first one is going on video."

"Start here, bud." Bill pointed to a patch of snow. "Lie down."

Liam did.

Bill talked him through the steps.

The padding of winter clothing hampered the boy's movements, but he didn't give up. The grin on his face grew with each sweep of snow. Giggles filled the air.

Bill clapped, his gloves muting the sound. Playing with Liam and making Grace smile was like a siren's call, but no matter how seductive, he wasn't ready for a family long-term. He would end up blowing it just as his dad kept doing. Bill needed to hold on to reality. His reality. "You're an expert angel-making boy."

"Again. Again."

"Let me help you up so you can make another." He held out his arm and pulled Liam to his feet, then glanced at Grace. "I'm going to have a yardful of angel Liams."

"He doesn't—"

"It's fine." Bill aimed a disarming smile in her direction. One he hoped told her she could relax. All was well. And would remain that way today.

Liam fell on his butt. Instead of standing, he made an angel right there.

Grace snapped a picture.

Bill motioned to a fresh patch of snow. "Give me the camera. I want to see you make a snow angel."

She just clutched it tighter. "I'm taking pictures so I can make a scrapbook page."

"Capturing memories is good, but making them is better."

Her nose scrunched. "I like both kinds."

"You make the angel. I'll take the pictures."

She gripped the camera. "I don't—"

"Mommy angel." Liam was covered in snow and smiling. "Mommy needs to make an angel."

Her mouth quirked.

Way to go, little dude.

Grace was trapped.

About time.

Bill couldn't get her up in the tree this morning, but he'd damn well get her down in the snow now.

Come on, Gracie. Let go. Show me what you're made of.

CHAPTER FIVE

MORE SNOW FELL from the sky, bigger flakes than before. Bill extended his arm toward Grace. "I'll make sure I get this on video, too."

She gave up her camera, then stuck out her tongue.

He focused the lens on her. "Do that again."

She feigned innocence, raising her hands in the air, palms up. "Do what?"

Grace Wilcox had a devilish side. That intrigued him. A good thing she wasn't going to be here long or he might do something he would regret. "Make your snow angel."

"I'm going to get all wet."

Oh, boy. He could have fun with that line. But he wouldn't. He couldn't with Liam within earshot. Bill would watch out for the kid the way he wished his dad would have cared for him. That was the least he could do until the two Wilcoxes left Hood Hamlet. "It's only water. You'll dry."

See? He could be good. Even though he would rather be bad.

"Last night you were worried about hypothermia," she said.

"Today I'm not." He hit the record button on the video mode. "Show your mom what to do."

Liam instructed her with enthusiasm. The two made a set of mother-and-son figures, then another and another. Snow covered them until they looked like yetis from the Himalayas. Happy ones. Smiling ones.

That pleased Bill.

He filmed them and took pictures. She would have memories for her book or wall. A few to tuck away in her heart. He would have some, too. Memories were all he could afford from this time with them. No matter how much he was enjoying himself. A day or two of being a family guy was his limit. At least that was how long his dad could last at home.

"Enough angel making for me." Grace stood, brushing the snow off front and backside.

Bill enjoyed the show, then handed her the camera. "I only cut your head off in a few shots."

She made a face.

He raised his hands. "Kidding."

Liam made his way toward them.

"Are you ever serious?" she asked.

Oh, Bill could be very serious, especially in the horizontal position. "Sometimes when I'm on a call or a mission."

"Only sometimes?"

"Life's short. It's meant to be enjoyed. Let's just say I'm glad you knocked on my door."

"Us, too." Grace walked to the three-feet-tall Santa decoration with a lightbulb inside the molded plastic figure. She brushed off the light cover of snow. "The least I can do is clean up this jolly fellow, who showed us the way to your house."

Liam threw snowballs at Frosty.

Bill joined her on that side of the yard. "What do you mean?"

"It was so dark and snowy I couldn't see anything, until I glimpsed Santa glowing like a lighthouse."

"I put him out in the yard yesterday."

"Lucky timing."

Of course someone not from around here would chalk up good fortune to luck, but he knew better. "Not luck. Christmas magic."

"Right. Flying reindeers and dancing elves."

He recognized the doubt in her eyes. "You mock, but Christmas magic exists in Hood Hamlet. I've seen it myself. Things happen on the mountain this time of year—accidents, lost climbers—that should end in tragedy but end happily instead. Even my skeptical best friend, Leanne, now believes."

Grace's forehead creased. "Your best friend is a woman?"

He nodded. "Since we were nine."

"What changed your friend's mind?"

"Love."

Grace straightened.

That had gotten her attention. But not surprising. Women wanted to find love.

"Leanne is getting married on Saturday. Her gift is under the tree," Bill stated.

"Falling in love? Getting engaged? Those things changed her mind?"

He nodded. "Christmas magic is a big deal around here. The town's second annual Christmas Magic Festival was held on Saturday."

"Guess the magic kept the snow away until Sunday so the celebration could go on."

"It sure did," he said. "Maybe Christmas magic brought you to Hood Hamlet last night."

"Maybe." She spoke with a wistful expression on her face. "Or maybe it was an angel."

"Christmas is a time for miracles, but I haven't had much experience with angels except the snow kind," Bill said. "I'll stick with magic."

"You do that." She glanced at Liam. "I'm going to stick with my angel the next time I need a Christmas miracle."

Bill wouldn't mind sticking with *her*.

Whoa. Where had that come from?

He wasn't up for sticking with anyone. Not for more than a night. Maybe two if they had fun together.

Maybe the temperature had dropped more than he realized. Time to head inside and warm up. He was thinking nonsense right now. "The snow's picking up. Let's warm up inside and make ourselves some hot cocoa. We can check if there's an update on your truck."

Her soft smile kicked his gut with the force of an ornery mountain goat. He made himself breathe.

Something was at work here. Not magic. Physical chemistry.

That would explain the way he felt. But he couldn't fool around with Grace no matter how appealing the thought might be.

"You're a good guy, Bill Paulson."

"Thanks."

He'd been good all day, but his bad boy side wanted to come out and play with Grace.

Standing in Bill's kitchen, Grace adjusted the phone receiver to better hear Thad Humphreys, the owner of the Hood Hamlet Garage and Body Shop. She was having trouble concentrating on what he was saying. Her fingers stung from the ice that had slipped into her gloves while outside playing. Her mind whirled from the fun she'd had with Bill.

She needed a break, some distance from him.

The guy was charming and handsome and oh so sweet to her son. She'd found herself wishing Christmas magic could be true, and maybe she'd get something special—maybe someone special—from Santa this year. Silly. A few hours of fun didn't change anything.

"Your truck has over one hundred eighty thousand miles on it," Thad said. "The damage from the collision is pretty significant, plus the engine is shot. The claims adjustor will likely total the vehicle."

Air rushed from her lungs. Hands trembling, she clutched the phone receiver. "Total it?"

"Yeah, I'm sorry. But there's a way you can still keep the truck if you don't want to buy a new one."

Buy a new one. The words added a hundred pounds of weight to each of her shoulders. Shoulders that hadn't felt burdened thirty minutes ago.

"I just wanted to give you a heads-up," Thad said.

Grace wanted to hang up, go back to playing outside and trying not to notice how blue Bill's eyes were when the light hit them right. But she knew that wasn't possible. There was no going back.

She swallowed around the snowball-size lump in her throat. "Thanks."

"I'm sure this isn't what you expected to hear."

"No."

"I'm happy to discuss your options. But think about whether

you want to fix the truck or buy a new one." Sympathy filled Thad's voice. Who better than a mechanic to understand the sentimental attachment to a vehicle? "The claims adjustor isn't available until Wednesday. You have a couple of days to decide."

Wednesday. Two days from now.

She tightened her grasp on the phone. "Okay. Thanks. Goodbye."

Grace disconnected from the call, placed the phone in its charger, slumped against the refrigerator.

Where would she stay? What would she do about the truck that had meant the world to Damon?

She blinked, not wanting to cry.

Laughter floated into the kitchen from the living room. She'd learned good times didn't last. Another lesson she'd forgotten in this house until Thad's phone call. At least Liam sounded happy. That made one of them.

She leaned against the kitchen counter, her usual source for support.

Two days to make a decision.

She'd spent a year debating whether to leave Columbus or not. Months deciding where to go. Weeks selling furniture and books and clothes and baby gear so she could fit all she had into Damon's truck.

A truck not worth repairing.

It's going to be okay, babe.

No, it wasn't.

Goose bumps covered her arms, ones that had nothing to do with the cold.

The truck had been Damon's most treasured possession. Selling his other things had been bearable because the truck was the only thing that mattered to him. He'd purchased the vehicle his senior year of high school from a local farmer, after doing maintenance on it for years. He loved working on the truck, keeping the vehicle in running order. She'd never had to worry about having mechanical problems. But the old truck's performance had suffered without Damon's TLC.

Along with everything else.

Grace had no idea what another truck might cost, or if she needed a pickup at all. Except how would she get their stuff to Astoria in a car?

Damon had trusted her to make decisions, whether he was home or away. But he'd always been an email or Skype conversation away when she needed input. Now every decision she'd made since burying her husband filled her with doubts.

Her stomach churned.

Was she doing the right thing?

Should she get rid of the truck?

Could she let it go?

She had no one to turn to for advice. Except Bill, whose greatest concern was what woman he would kiss at midnight on New Year's Eve. Okay, that wasn't fair.

Grace blew out a puff of air. She would figure this out on her own. The way she always did.

She straightened, tucked her hair behind her ears, then walked into the living room.

Bill was crawling on his hands and knees. Liam sat on his back, giggling and full of excitement.

Not even the truck crisis could keep a smile away. "What is going on?"

"I cowboy. This is my horse." Liam held on to Bill's shirt collar. "Giddy-up, horsey."

Bill trotted across the floor like an obedient pony. Back and forth he moved, adjusting his speed based on his rider's commands.

Grace watched in wonder. Bill was going above and beyond, even for a nice guy. And her son was enjoying it greatly. Liam didn't remember being in his daddy's arms or in a baby pack against Damon's chest. "How did you get roped into being a horse?"

Looking at her, Bill neighed.

The guy was too much. "I didn't get that."

Liam made a face at her. "A horsey can't talk, Mommy!"

"Oh, I forgot." She wrung her hands, full of nervous energy. "Well, have fun. Looks like we're going to be in Hood Hamlet a few more days. I'm going to find us a place to stay so we can get out of your horse's hair."

Bill stopped crawling. "The truck."

Grace rubbed the back of her tight neck. She tilted her head toward Liam. "Maybe we can talk later. Things are sort of a mess."

Bill's gaze met hers, a sympathetic glance that told her he understood. "You're welcome to stay here as long as you're in Hood Hamlet."

A lump formed in her throat. "I—"

"Here. Here," her son chanted. "I want to stay with big dude."

Bill raised an eyebrow. "Liam thinks staying here is a good idea."

She swallowed. "Liam also thinks filling the toilet with a squad of toy soldiers is fun."

Bill glanced over his shoulder. "Don't do that here, bud, okay?"

"Okay," Liam said.

Bill looked back at her. "We're good."

Grace wasn't so sure. Liam hadn't left Bill's side all day. Dominoes. Breakfast. Tree trimming. Lunch. Playing in the snow. Horsey. The kid treated him like a wind-up plaything, and Bill was more than happy to oblige. Spending more time here might hurt Liam when they left for Astoria.

Her son had been too young to remember Damon leaving and not coming home, but he might be old enough to remember Bill. "Thanks, but you don't need us hanging around. You must have stuff to do."

"Not in this weather. The only thing on my agenda is work tomorrow."

"What if it keeps snowing?" she asked.

"Nothing keeps a firefighter away from the job. I have a four-wheel drive truck with a plow on the front. I work a twenty-four hour shift. This place will be all yours."

Her mouth fell open. "You trust us here alone?"

Bill's appreciative gaze raked over her, sending chills down her spine, the good kind, ones she hadn't felt in a very long time.

"You don't look like the type to take advantage of anyone."

Of course not. She looked like a frazzled mom trying to care for a curious three-year-old, with nowhere to go and no vehicle to take them there. But something about Bill's easygoing tone challenged her. She raised her chin. "Looks can be deceiving."

His brows slanted. "Got some crimes to confess?"

She tapped her finger against her chin. "Do you think I'd tell you if I did?"

The connection between them flared, stronger than ever. Hot, inviting, oh so tempting.

Crush. A foolish crush.

Self-preservation called for her retreat. But Grace couldn't stop staring. She didn't blink. She didn't move.

She stood mesmerized.

Bill looked away first, but Grace didn't feel as if she'd won. He was only keeping her guessing.

His casual shrug belied his darkening eyes. "Doesn't matter to me if you have some deep dark secrets. All I have here is stuff."

She glanced around, trying to calm her rapid pulse. A glass of ice water might cool her off. Or she could step outside. "Nice stuff."

"Replaceable." A faraway look filled his eyes. "People don't understand. When there's a fire they lose their minds over how this is gone or that is ruined. Sometimes we have to hold people back or pull them out of burning buildings over stuff. I get that it's hard to lose pictures and mementos, but nothing's worth saving except loved ones."

"You've seen some bad things."

He glanced over his shoulder at Liam once more. "Occupational hazard."

"I can't imagine."

"Don't." He spoke sharply, then his features relaxed into a smile. "Life is too precious to dwell on the negative stuff."

"You seem to have no problem focusing on the positive."

"Only way to go." He crawled across the floor with Liam on his back. "I bet the little dude makes it easy for you to do the same."

"Yes." Though not always.

Maybe she should follow Bill's advice. Expecting something to go wrong wasn't a good way to live. It wasn't how she and Damon had lived before that final deployment.

"So you'll stay?"

A "no" sat poised at the tip of her tongue. Thinking positively was one thing. Buying trouble was another. Something told her Bill Paulson could be big trouble. Her lips parted—

"Before you say no, hear me out." He moved closer. "Giving you a place to stay is the least I can do. It's my way of saying thank you for the sacrifices your family has made for our country."

Liam raised his arms and cheered. "Stay. Stay with Bill."

Holding on to the boy, Bill reared like a stallion, graceful and wild. Smiling like a fiend.

Grace tapped her fingers against her lips. "It could be a couple of days or longer. Thad thinks, um, things shouldn't be fixed."

Liam slid off Bill's back. Both stood.

"All the more reason to stay." Bill spoke as if this was nothing more than a weekend sleepover where they'd watch DVDs and eat popcorn and candy. "Don't waste money on a hotel when you have a free place here. Liam needs a Christmas tree and room to play. I have both."

Not to mention an adult-size playmate.

Liam nodded, as if he understood what Bill was saying.

"I won't be around much," he continued. "After my shift, I'm off for forty-eight hours. I spend most of that time on the mountain. Trust me, I won't be a good host."

"That's hard to believe. You've been amazing."

"You're easy to please, Grace." He looked down at his legs being hugged by Liam. "You, too, cowboy."

Bill's schedule alleviated her fears about Liam getting too attached. She had money, thanks to insurance and military benefits, but she wanted to be frugal. Still, she hesitated. "But Christmas is coming…."

"Let's take it a day at a time."

Both Liam and Bill were looking at her, waiting for her to

decide. She couldn't think of any reason not to stay, but found herself balking. Bill rattled her nerves.

Liam tilted his head. "Puh-lease, Mommy."

"Listen to the kid," Bill said.

"If we stay, I don't want to be treated as a guest. I'll buy groceries. Cook. Clean."

"Not necessary."

She was outnumbered, but not about to give in. "Not negotiable."

"Then it's a deal." Bill held his hand up to her son. "Looks like you're staying, little dude."

Liam high-fived his new playmate. "Yay!"

"Nothing like Hood Hamlet in December." Bill shot her a sideways glance, making her pulse jump. "You won't regret this."

Grace hoped not. She'd lived with enough regrets. She didn't want to have to live with any more.

The next morning Bill entered the station stifling a yawn. The smell of freshly brewed coffee filled the air. He needed caffeine pronto. The little dude hadn't slept well last night. No one else in the house had, either.

That was what he got for telling Grace to stay. He didn't regret the invitation, though he'd given her little choice.

Why *had* he worked so hard to convince her? Why did it matter where she went?

He'd never thought the whole family thing was attractive, but something about spending more time with Grace and Liam had sucked him in. His common sense had fled or maybe gone into hibernation.

He crossed the apparatus bay, his steps echoing against the concrete floor, not another soul in sight. Everyone must be waiting for morning briefing from the chief. Bill hoped someone had brought breakfast. This morning he'd wanted to leave his house as quietly as possible, so hadn't grabbed any food.

A bad move according to his grumbling stomach.

Grace would agree and tell him breakfast was the most important meal of the day. Too bad they couldn't have eaten together.

Weird how he couldn't stop thinking about her.

Bill had tried to help last night, but his presence had been only a hindrance in getting Liam back to sleep. The little dude had wailed like a banshee with him around. So much for being good with kids.

He'd retreated to his room, trying not to think of having an after midnight play session with Grace. Hot, heavy fun. He was good at that. But…

Grace + Liam = off-limits.

Bill couldn't forget that, even if math had never been his best subject.

He headed toward the living quarters, basic but comfortable with a television area, large dining room and kitchen. The bunk-rooms were upstairs, along with the bathrooms.

Bill hoped Grace and Liam were still asleep. She had to be tired. He didn't know how she handled being a single parent. Not that she had a choice. At least his dad flew home a couple times a year, around major holidays. That had to count for something, right? Grace had no one. Not even parents she could call.

Maybe she could nap today. A vision of her in bed made him grin.

Bill pushed through the door. An argument about the upcoming Seattle Seahawks game on Sunday raised the decibels by a factor of two. A heated debate over the best local ski area—Timberline, Mount Hood Meadows or Ski Bowl—for fresh powder ensued. Two men bragged about the hot babes they'd bagged the other night. No doubt one of the guys was Riley Hansen.

In the dining room, both B and C shifts sat around the table. Every person had a coffee cup in hand. Three pink boxes of doughnuts and a stack of napkins rested in the center of the table. A typical morning at shift change.

"Good morning, fellows. And Thomas." Bill nodded toward his best friend, Leanne Thomas, who worked with him on C shift.

She sat next to her fiancé, Christian Welton, who had been moved by the chief to B shift after the engagement was made public. Leanne held an old-fashioned glazed doughnut. "Traffic was heavy this morning. Lots of folks heading up the mountain," she commented.

"I don't blame them." Brady O'Ryan, the other paramedic on the crew, refilled his cup. "Everyone wants to make first tracks in the fresh powder."

Bill grabbed a chocolate-frosted doughnut covered with candy sprinkles. "Me, too."

Hansen snickered. "Sucks to be a C shifter."

"I don't see any of you B boys hightailing it out of here to make your mark," Thomas said, with the attitude that had earned her respect at the station.

"Hey, babe." Welton put his arm around the back of her chair. "I'm one of those B boys now."

Her expression softened. "Maybe after we're married, Chief will move you back to Hood Hamlet's elite C squad."

The B boys groaned.

Bill laughed. "Better watch it, guys, or Thomas will dream up yet another physical training torture."

She winked. "Damn straight. And this one will be tougher than the last."

Thomas's last program had nearly killed them all, Bill included. His muscles ached from the memory of the world-class athlete cardio and strength training regimen.

"I've got my skis with me," she told him. "Christian and I are heading up the hill as soon as I'm off. Want to come with us?"

"You're on." But Bill wanted to check on Grace and Liam first. He decided against mentioning them in front of the whole crew. "I'll need to swing by home to grab mine."

"Hey," Welton said. "I heard there was some excitement on your street two nights ago."

"A pickup in a snowbank," Bill said.

Leanne wiped her mouth with a napkin. "Drunk?"

"No, someone trying to make it over the mountain." He didn't want to talk about this now.

"In a blizzard?" Christian shook his head. "Must not be from around here."

Bill stared into his coffee cup. Grace hadn't been stupid. She'd just never driven through the Cascades in winter before. "They're not."

"Injuries?" O'Ryan asked.

Bill eyed what remained in the pink boxes, debating if he wanted another doughnut. "Just sore. They were buckled in. Had air bags."

Thomas raised her cup. "Lucky."

"Very." Though Grace might not agree. Her truck was in bad shape according to Thad. Bill sipped his coffee. "The pickup might be totaled."

"Wonder how they ended up on your street from the highway?" Welton asked. "It's not exactly Main Street."

"No idea." Bill hadn't thought about that. Now he was curious. "I'll have to ask Grace."

Silence fell over the table.

Thomas leaned forward. "Grace?"

Damn. Everyone was looking at him.

"The driver of the pickup." He tried to backtrack slowly, like a truck stuck in a rut. "She showed up at my house needing help."

"Unbelievable." Hansen rolled his eyes, the gesture matching the disdain in his voice. "Even when Paulson can't date a woman, they show up in the middle of the night knocking on his door."

Bill straightened. "It's not like that."

"So she's not hot," O'Ryan said.

He looked up. "I never said that. But she's a mom."

Thomas elbowed him. "Moms can be cute."

"Moms can be hot," O'Ryan said.

Hansen sneered. "Ever hear the term MILF?"

Thomas glared, shutting them all up. "Were Grace's kids in the truck?"

"One kid," Bill answered, knowing how hard car accidents involving kids were for Leanne. Her parents and two brothers had been killed in a crash on Highway 26. She'd been the lone survivor. "He's fine, but had a rough time last night. Kept waking up."

Thomas's forehead wrinkled. "How do you know that?"

Now everyone knew everything. Bill never had been good at keeping secrets. Especially here. He'd had no siblings growing up, but these people were his brothers and sister. Irritating at times, but still family. Though not quite the same as what he'd felt with Grace and Liam.

Bill shrugged. "They're staying at my house."

Looks flew across the room faster than freestylers off the jumps at Timberline's aerial park. Bill sucked it up and waited.

"This woman…" O'Ryan sounded surprisingly earnest. Sometimes he could be a jerk. "She's there now? While you're here?"

Bill nodded. "They were asleep when I left."

Hansen hung his head. "Bad move."

"Why is that?" Bill asked.

Leanne touched his arm. "You don't know them."

"I do now. What would you do? It's a woman and a kid with a wrecked vehicle." He glanced at each of the firefighters. "Which one of you would have done it differently?"

No one. Bill knew that in his heart.

Hansen shook his head. "How can you be such a player and so stupid about women at the same time?"

"She could be trying to get her hooks into you," O'Ryan said. "A mom looking for a sugar daddy for herself and kid."

"I bet a U-Haul truck is at your house now and some sketchy looking dude is loading everything you own to sell on Craigslist," Hansen said.

Bill's jaw tightened. "Grace is not like that."

"You're not at all suspicious?" Thomas asked.

"It's the other way around." He remembered the wariness in Grace's eyes the night she arrived. He was so glad she smiled now. "She called the sheriff on Sunday night. She wasn't sure if it was safe to stay at my house."

Thomas smiled. "Sounds like a smart woman."

"Grace is," Bill said. "She's a widow. Her husband was a Ranger killed in Afghanistan. She's on her way from Columbus, Georgia, to Astoria to make a new start. Or was until she hit the snowbank. Helping her out is the least I can do."

No one said anything for a minute.

Hansen snickered. "At least that's the story she told you."

A series of tones sounded. "Rescue 1 and Engine 3 respond-

ing to car accident. Automobile versus pedestrian on the corner of Main Street and Second Avenue," the female dispatcher announced.

Everyone from C shift rose from the table.

Bill headed toward his bunker gear.

O'Ryan followed him. "Way to go, finding a way around no dating in December."

"Huh?"

"Having wild monkey sex with your new roomie, Grace."

Only in Bill's dreams. Though sex would be the easy part. The rest was what he couldn't handle. He removed his shoes and stepped into his bunker pants and boots. "I'm not doing this to get laid. Plus she's got a kid."

"So what?" O'Ryan shrugged on his jacket. "The chick's only passing through town. Sex is sex."

Bill balled his hands, ready to punch the guy. But the clock was ticking. He grabbed his helmet. "How would you know about sex? I thought you were saving yourself for your wedding night."

He climbed into the rig.

Damn O'Ryan. Bill didn't want to be thinking about Grace and sex.

The engine pulled out of the bay, lights flashing and sirens roaring.

This wasn't the time to fantasize. Grace wasn't a woman to lust after, not with appealing and playful images running through his mind and sending his temperature spiraling. He shouldn't be thinking about her romantically at all. He couldn't give her what she needed, what she deserved.

Bill hoped she heard good news about her truck. The sooner she was on her way to Astoria, the better off they all would be.

CHAPTER SIX

THE SOUND OF the garbage disposal woke Grace. Sunlight streamed through the edges of the window blinds.

Morning already?

She didn't want to believe it. Neither did her heavy, let's-go-back-to-sleep eyelids.

The digital clock on the nightstand read 8:26 a.m.

Not early, even if it felt that way.

Grace rolled onto to her side toward Liam. He slept like a hibernating bear. Since he'd been up and down all night, she wasn't surprised.

Too bad she couldn't blame Liam for her exhaustion. Images of the truck and Bill had etched themselves into her mind. A swirling mix of dreams and thoughts had made for a sleepless night. She hoped her and Liam's restlessness hadn't kept Bill awake. He needed his sleep if he was going to be working a twenty-four hour shift.

Another noise sounded—cabinets creaking open and shut.

Bill must be going in late this morning. She could apologize for Liam's behavior.

Grace slid out of bed, careful not to wake Liam. He would be cranky enough, with Bill at work. She didn't need her son tired, too.

In the hallway, she rolled up the waistband on Bill's pajama pants. Liam had wanted her to wear them again last night. She liked the softness of flannel even if the jammies didn't fit.

She shuffled down the hallway.

A faucet ran.

Weird.

She'd cleaned the kitchen before going to bed last night. Maybe Bill had made himself breakfast. But she didn't smell food. No coffee. And he'd said nothing would keep him from work.

She slowed her pace and lightened her step. If Bill was at work, who was in the kitchen?

She peeked around the corner.

A fiftysomething woman stood at the sink looking down at the running water, a blue sponge in her hand. Her short brown hair was stylishly cut, her makeup perfectly applied. Candy cane earrings dangled from her earlobes. Snowmen covered her red sweater. Not exactly what a cleaning woman would wear. Or a prowler.

Grace waited, watched, grew impatient. She couldn't stand here spying all day. "Hello."

The woman looked up. She gasped.

Grace held up her hands. "I'm sorry if I startled you."

"Who are you?"

"Grace Wilcox." She waited for the woman to offer her name. She didn't. "Bill's, um, guest."

"I'm Mrs. Paulson." Her gaze ran the length of Grace, taking in her messy hair and too big pajamas. "Bill's mother."

The unfriendly tone bristled. Grace overcame the urge to snap back. She needed to be polite. This was Bill's mom. "Nice to meet you. I love your chocolate chip cookies and cocoa mix."

Mrs. Paulson pursed her lips. "You're not the usual type my son brings home."

To sleep with.

The words were unspoken, but implied.

Grace didn't know what to say. Knowing someone for what—thirty-six hours?—didn't make them friends, but after spending yesterday together they weren't strangers. "I'm not…"

"His lover?"

Heat rose up Grace's neck. Her cheeks flamed. "Gosh, no. I'm staying here, but in another bedroom."

Mrs. Paulson's brows arched. "Well, you're creative. I haven't heard that one before."

The accusation in her voice twisted Grace's insides a dozen

directions. She shouldn't care what Bill's mother thought of her. Yet standing straight was difficult when all Grace wanted to do was squirm. "It's the truth."

"He doesn't usually have his women stay when he's at work."

His women. His here-for-a-good-time women. Grace wasn't one of them. She raised her chin. "I'm from out of town. I hit a patch of ice and my truck slid into a snowbank, so I ended up on Bill's doorstep."

The words rushed from her mouth like water from a fire hydrant. Needing to shut up, she clamped her lips together.

"This happened last night?" Mrs. Paulson asked.

Grace rubbed her face. "The night before."

"You're not injured?"

Funny, the woman sounded as if she might care. "No."

Mrs. Paulson's lip curled. "So you spent yesterday here, too."

Grace angled her body toward the doorway, wishing Liam would wake up screaming for her. Anything to escape Mrs. Paulson's demeaning glare and resist the growing itch to tell her off. "Yes."

"Leave his pajamas in the bathroom." The woman's dismissal was clear. "I'll wash them after you go."

Mrs. Paulson was a mama bear; no blaming her for that. She seemed to have no patience for Bill's womanizing. Grace agreed with her there, but needed to take a stand. "I'm not going anywhere."

"But—"

"Big dude…!" Arms outstretched, Liam skidded around the corner in his footie pajamas. One look at Mrs. Paulson had him darting behind Grace quicker than a camera flash.

"It's okay." She reached behind to reassure him. "This is Bill's mom, Mrs. Paulson."

Liam peeked around Grace's hip, then hid again.

A puzzled expression crossed Mrs. Paulson's face. "Who is this?"

"My son. Liam."

An unexpected smile replaced Mrs. Paulson's scowl. The change was dramatic. She looked ten years younger and ten times nicer. She must like kids better than women wearing her son's jammies. "Hello, Liam."

His little fingers dug into Grace's legs.

She patted his hand, trying to release his death grip on her. "It's okay."

"How old are you, Liam?" Mrs. Paulson asked.

He stuck three fingers out to the side, then added a fourth.

"Three and a half," Grace said.

Liam poked his head out. "Almost four."

"Almost four," Mrs. Paulson repeated. "You're a big boy."

Liam jumped to the left like a jack-in-the-box on its side. "Big and strong like Bill."

"Yes, you are." She studied him, then looked at Grace. "You said you were from out of town."

"Georgia."

"What brings you to Hood Hamlet?"

"Just passing through."

Liam looked around. "Bill? Where's he?"

"At work," Grace said.

Liam's lower lip stuck out. Quivered. "Want Bill. Time to play."

She touched her son's shoulder. "We talked about this last night. Bill's working at the fire station."

Liam stared at the floor as if his world had come to an end.

Grace had to admit she, too, would rather be speaking with Bill than Mrs. Paulson. Damon's mom hadn't liked her much, either. Maybe it was a mother-with-sons thing. Grace vowed not to be like that when Liam brought a girlfriend home someday. "Your son is my son's new best friend."

"I'm not surprised. Bill's a kid at heart. That boy will never grow up. Though I wish he'd find a good woman and settle down." Mrs. Paulson removed a cookie from the cookie jar and gave it to Liam. "This will make you feel better."

Grace sighed. "This is the second day in a row he's had a cookie for breakfast. He'll be spoiled rotten by the time we leave."

"Nothing wrong with a little spoiling," Mrs. Paulson said. "I do that with Bill. I was wondering why the house looked cleaner than usual this morning. You must have dusted and vacuumed. Decorated the tree and the house, too."

The woman didn't sound pleased, but Grace wasn't going to let Bill's mother get to her. She had allowed that to happen with Damon's mom. "The least I could do. I'm so grateful for Bill's hospitality. I plan on doing as much as I can for him in return."

"Thoughtful, but unnecessary. I come over the mornings he works at the station, to help out. He claims I do too much for him, but he gets distracted with his rescue work, climbing and skiing. Someone needs to take care of him."

Grace didn't know what to say. From the time she was twelve she'd done laundry, cleaned the house, washed dishes and cooked meals. Her parents' high expectations had led Grace to work hard around the house and at school to make good grades. As long as she met their demands, everything was fine. If she didn't, they'd made her feel like a stray cat they regretted bringing into the house. "Bill's lucky to have a mother who wants to do so much for him."

Mrs. Paulson focused on Liam, who ate the cookie. "You'll understand when your son gets older. They grow up so fast."

Grow up were the key words here. Grace hoped by the time Liam was thirty he would want to take care of himself, and she would let him.

Mrs. Paulson walked back to the kitchen. "What would you like for breakfast, Liam?"

"Eggs and toast, please," he answered.

The woman beamed brightly. "Such manners."

The surprise in her voice made Grace grit her teeth. "I can make you breakfast, Liam. I'm sure Mrs. Paulson has a lot to do this morning."

"Not as much as I had planned, thanks to you." The words didn't sound like a compliment. "I'm happy to scramble eggs and make toast."

"With jelly." Liam followed the woman into the kitchen, as if being related to Bill automatically made her another friend. "I help."

"I'd love your help. Bill used to help me cook when he was

your age." The smile on Mrs. Paulson's face turned genuine. She looked at Grace with appreciation. The woman must be lonely. "Go ahead, take a shower and get dressed. I'll watch Liam."

No way. Bill's mom might be lonely, but Grace wasn't about to leave her son with her. "Thanks, but Liam isn't used to being around people he doesn't know."

Mrs. Paulson tsked. "Don't you worry. Liam will be fine with me. Won't you?"

"I fine." He opened the refrigerator for her. "Eggs inside here."

With her head in the fridge, Mrs. Paulson waved in Grace's direction. "Go on, now."

Liam mimicked the gesture. "Go, Mommy."

Something about the Paulson family made Liam feel comfortable, in a way he'd never been with anyone but her. Grace, on the other hand, felt nothing but tension, a different kind with Bill than with his mother.

Grace didn't like to be dismissed, especially by her son. Mrs. Paulson approved of Liam, not her. Bill's mother likely thought she was another one of Bill's women du jour. But tense run-ins with Damon's mom had taught Grace not to get huffy. She'd have to earn Mrs. Paulson's respect with charm, no matter how much it irked.

And she shouldn't be complaining.

A shower alone would be great. Her second one in as many days. A record.

"Thank you, Mrs. Paulson," Grace said with a slow Southern smile and sweet drawl she'd learned in Georgia. "I sure do appreciate the help."

The older woman looked startled. "Why, you're welcome, Grace. I promise, Liam will be fine. If he needs you, we'll come get you."

She nodded, then walked down the hall, thinking. She didn't know why she'd tried so hard to end their tense meeting with a draw. She and Liam would likely be gone the next time Bill's mom showed up.

Grace might not understand her behavior, but she knew one

thing—no woman would meet Mrs. Paulson's standards for her son.

Thank goodness Bill didn't plan on settling down anytime soon. He would need years to find a wife his mom considered to be a "good woman."

Bill's shift flew by, with not a lot of downtime between calls except for a five-hour stretch of sleep. Now it was Wednesday morning. Time to head out.

He wondered how Grace and Liam had fared alone.

Bill hoped they were doing well, stuck in his house for the past twenty-four hours. He hadn't thought to leave them transportation or his cell number or a key. Most of his houseguests spent the night and were gone the next morning. No one ever stayed longer.

"Paulson." Thomas had changed into ski clothing—insulated pants and soft shell jacket. Two long braids hung from her pink-and-purple fleece cap. She might be "one of the guys," but according to Christian she liked girlie things, too. "See you on the hill."

Bill would swing by home, check on his houseguests, grab his gear and be on his way. "Won't take me long."

Fifteen minutes later, he opened his front door.

Christmas carols played. The scents of cinnamon and vanilla filled the air.

He took another sniff. His mouth watered. Whatever was cooking smelled delicious.

He closed the door behind him.

Liam ran from the kitchen-dining area, his arms outstretched and mouth open. He barreled into Bill, hugging him tight. "Big dude is home."

Warmth pressed down on the center of his chest. No one had ever welcomed him home like this. He lifted Liam into his arms. "How's it going, bud?"

Liam cuddled and rested his head against Bill's shoulder. "Going great now."

A figure-eight-shaped knot formed in Bill's throat. He tightened his grip on the boy, who squeezed back, his little fingers holding on as if Bill was as important to him as his beloved Peanut.

Unexpected warmth flowed through Bill. This was a different feeling than holding a soft, sweet-smelling woman. Different, but good. He didn't want to let go of the kid.

Whoa. What was he thinking? Maybe five hours of sleep last night hadn't been enough. "Where's your elephant?"

Liam squirmed.

Bill placed him on the ground.

The kid ran to the kitchen, darting past Grace, who stood in the doorway. She wore a pair of boot-cut jeans and a baggy forest-green, long-sleeved T-shirt that hid her waistline and chest. The kind of shirt women wore when they didn't want a man to notice their assets.

But Bill already knew.

Grace was luscious. His good manners, not her camouflage shirt, kept her safe from prying eyes and fingers. Though the thought of slipping his hands up her shirt made his mind go blank and his temperature rise.

Stop. He'd gone over this. Seducing Grace would be wrong. She needed someone reliable, someone long-term, someone not destined to repeat the mistakes of his father.

Bill wasn't about to hurt a woman and child with false promises and vows.

"Good morning." She wiped her hands on a dish towel. "Your welcoming committee has been waiting for you. Liam has been up since six."

Bill wished she wanted to be part of the committee, too. He liked being welcomed home. Especially with her wearing those jeans. Unlike her blouse, the denim hugged the curve of her hips nicely, leaving nothing to his imagination. "No sleeping in for you."

"I'm used to it. How was your shift?"

"The same as usual. Whatever you're making smells delicious."

Grace and the aroma of her cooking dragged him in like a tractor beam.

"Baked French toast." She glanced back in the direction Liam had gone. "It's almost ready if you want some."

Bill looked at his watch. He was supposed to be meeting Thomas and Welton to ski, but he didn't want to be rude. He would text Leanne to let her know he was running late. "Sounds great."

"I'll add another place setting to the table."

His table never had place settings. Not until Grace arrived. He liked coming home to food cooking, and sitting at the table together for a meal, something he had only at his parents' house during holidays.

He followed her into the kitchen.

Liam sat on the floor next to the plastic bin full of toys Bill had brought in from the truck. Laughing, the kid held Peanut with one hand and an airplane with the other.

"Settling in," Bill said.

"I hope that's okay."

She sounded nervous. He wanted to reassure her. "It's fine." And it was. Surprisingly.

He liked coming home not to an empty house, but one full of warmth and laughter and home cooking. This was what Hughes, Porter and Moreno must mean when they talked about their families and wanting to be home. Well, except the cooking for Hughes. His wife, Zoe, could burn water. "I didn't leave you with transportation if you needed groceries or something."

"You're pretty stocked with groceries for a guy who lives alone." Grace motioned to the bag of powdered sugar, the can of whipped cream and what looked like defrosted berries. "We had everything we needed and then some, thanks to your mom."

His stomach plummeted to his feet and kept right on going. "My mom was here?"

"Tuesday morning."

He smacked his forehead with his palm. "I forgot to tell her not to come."

"We were both a little…startled. Your mom thought I was one of your women."

"She didn't."

"She called me your lover."

"I'm sorry." And he was. "My mom has definite views about the women I date. She doesn't approve of any of them. Thinks I can do better."

"At least she loves you."

He still couldn't believe how badly her parents had treated her and Liam. "I'm sorry about your folks. Maybe time has softened their hearts."

"I've tried. I finally gave up. They want nothing to do with us." Grace's voice held no regret, only resignation. "Your mom's a little over the top, but it's nice to see a parent care so much for her child."

"I'm all my mom has."

"Only kid?" Grace asked.

"Yeah. When I was seven, she got pregnant again, but she miscarried and couldn't have any more children."

"That had to have been rough."

He blamed himself. "My dad wasn't here when it happened. Just me. I had no idea my mom was in such bad shape."

"You were only seven. How would you know?"

Bill shrugged.

"Where was your dad?"

"Away. He works in the petroleum industry. When he's not on an oil platform in the Gulf, he's in the Middle East. It's been that way for as long as I remember," Bill said. "If my dad spent more time here in Hood Hamlet, my mom could focus on him, not me."

"Is your dad old enough to retire?"

"Nope. I'm going to have to suck it up until then."

"You're a good son."

He had no choice. At times he appreciated everything his mom did for him. Other times he hated it. But what could he do? She was his mother. "I'm her only son. Any word from the claims adjustor?"

Grace checked the oven and added two minutes to the timer. "I should hear something today. Thad says the body damage is fixable. But the engine isn't."

"The snowbank took out the engine?"

"The motor started sounding funny as soon as we crossed the Georgia state line. But I thought we'd make it."

"What are you going to do?"

"Hear what the adjustor says first. The truck belonged to my husband, so I'd rather not get rid of it."

"Thad's a great mechanic. He'll take care of you and your pickup. I'm happy to do whatever I can."

Gratitude shone in her eyes. "Thanks so much. For everything."

"You're welcome." Bill wasn't quite sure why he said the words. He hadn't done anything. Not really. Giving her a place to stay wasn't costing him anything. Playing with her kid was fun. Spending time with her was no hardship at all.

He wished he could do…more.

He wanted to wipe away the worry from her forehead. He wanted to erase the dark circles below her eyes. He wanted to kiss away the tightness around her mouth. He focused on her full lips. No colored lipstick, shiny gloss or plumper needed.

He wanted to kiss her.

Badly.

His heart rate increased, accelerating like a snare drum roll. His temperature rose twenty degrees as he thought about his lips against hers. His gaze lingered on his target, waiting for a sign, an invitation.

Look away, a voice cautioned.

Bill didn't. He couldn't.

Not when everything inside of him was screaming, *Kiss her!*

Buzz-z-z.

The oven timer blared.

What the hell was he doing? Thinking?

He looked away, stepped back, took a deep breath.

This wasn't only about kissing her. Something about Grace affected him at a much deeper level, in a way no other woman had. She had him thinking about meals together, kids. He didn't like that.

Liam ran to the table. "Breakfast!"

Grace walked to the oven. "Yes, it's time for breakfast."

For them, yes. Not Bill.

She bent over to remove the pan from the oven, giving him a great view of her butt.

Curvy. Sexy.

Damn. Bill rubbed his hand over his chin. He needed to get out of here before he did something he would regret. Something he couldn't take back. "Can you make mine to go?"

Confusion clouded her eyes. "Sure."

Bill didn't blame Grace for the uncertainty in her voice. He'd said yes to breakfast. He hadn't stopped her from setting the table. But he couldn't forget he wasn't part of the Wilcox family. They weren't part of his. "I'm supposed to go skiing with a friend from the station. I thought I'd have enough time…."

"Not a problem."

Grace used an oven mitt and a hot pad to remove the casserole dish. She placed the baked French toast on the stove.

Oh, man, that looked and smelled like heaven on earth. His stomach rumbled. Nothing like home cooking.

She opened a cabinet. "I saw a plastic container in here some-where."

He felt like a jerk for bolting on breakfast. "The cabinet on the left."

"Sit, Big Dude." Liam sounded like a little prince with his command. "Eat."

Bill wanted to join the kid at the table. He wanted to spend the day with Liam and Grace, but couldn't give in to temptation.

He'd never experienced this soothing warmth flowing through his veins, this desire to cancel a day skiing and kick around at home. This wasn't about getting naked and doing the horizontal mamba. That he understood. This was…different.

Whatever was going on, sweet as it felt, had to end. Right now.

Bill had everything he needed to be happy—friends, the mountain, powder and a cell phone contact list full of hot wom-en's numbers. No reason to let some kid, his mom and her home cooking change anything.

Bill was going to stick to the way he did things.

He was not going to mess up her life. Or his.

"No can do, bud." Bill went to ruffle the kid's hair, but thought better of it. He pulled his hand back, plastered his arm against his side. "But I'll be home later."

Much later.

After he skied hard, the only thing he'd want to do was fall into bed.

Alone.

CHAPTER SEVEN

EARLY EVENING, BILL entered the Hood Hamlet Brewpub with Thomas and Welton. Their stomachs and throats demanded payment for a long day skiing. The booths and tables were full, so they snagged three stools at the bar. A perfect way to spend an evening—with beer, burgers and good friends.

Multicolored lights from the garland hanging above them made the glossy wood surface look polka-dotted. Christmas carols played from overhead speakers. OMSAR friends—Sean and Zoe Hughes and Tim and Rita Moreno—were crammed into a booth near the fireplace.

The bartender set three pints on the bar.

Bill raised his beer, stared at the dark ale and creamy foam on top. "Nothing like one of Porter's microbrews after a bluebird day on the mountain."

"You deserve a pint or two after hitting the slopes so hard today." Welton lifted his pint. "Looked like you were trying to outrun an avalanche."

Thomas swiveled toward Bill, staring over the rim of her glass with a pointed look. "Or a woman."

"Don't know what you're talking about." He shifted on the leather-covered bar stool. His muscles ached from making tracks and carving turns. A good feeling, like when he'd been home this morning.

He shook the thought from his head, the way he'd been doing all day whenever Grace and her son crossed his mind. He shouldn't be thinking about her. She deserved a lot more than a guy like him could give. "Just enjoying the powder."

Thomas faced forward. "Mom alert."

Grace was here? Anticipation surged. Bill straightened, glanced over his shoulder.

His mother was marching toward him with a fiery look in her eyes. The smiling snowman on her sweater emphasized how badly her lips were puckered. He doubted she'd been sucking lemons.

That meant one thing.

Dad had let her down. Again.

Bill tightened his grasp on his glass.

Only his father had that kind of effect on her. Dad must have called to say he wasn't coming home for Christmas. So much for enjoying a little après-ski with his friends. But if his mom put out a distress call, he was the first responder. He couldn't always fix her problems or meet her needs, but he could at least be there for her. Unlike his dad.

Bill gulped the rest of his beer, set the empty glass on the bar, then turned around with his you're-the-best-mom-ever smile. "Hey, Mom. What are you doing here?"

She stood, arms crossed, as if she'd clocked him going ninety with a radar gun. A corner of her mouth twitched. "Is he yours?"

"Huh?"

"Liam." She took a step closer and lowered her voice. "Is he your son?"

The air whooshed from Bill's lungs. "What in the hell are you talking about?"

"Don't swear."

"Don't provoke me."

Her gaze narrowed. "Liam looks like a younger you. Same coloring. Mannerisms."

"The kid is three. He looks like a lot of people."

Bill is the best daddy.

He'd thought Liam's words were sweet the other day. Now Bill forced himself to breathe, to loosen the tension knotting his insides. And tried not to admit how much he liked hearing those words. He'd be a crappy dad. He didn't have a father to use as a role model. He wouldn't know how to be a good dad.

"He's not mine." Bill kept his voice even, his tone calm. Losing his cool with his mother would only make this worse. "Met the kid and his mom for the first time on Sunday night."

"But—"

"No buts." Rumors spread faster than the norovirus in Hood Hamlet. Though he trusted Thomas and Welton, who were facing the bartender and pretending not to be eavesdropping, but no doubt listening. "Liam's father was an Army Ranger killed in Afghanistan. A true American hero, named Damon Wilcox."

His mother started to speak, then stopped herself. "Grace is a widow?"

Bill nodded.

His mother wrung her hands.

Dread shot down his spine like a snowboard without a leash on a steep, black diamond run. "Please tell me you didn't mention this to Grace."

"I didn't, but… Why didn't you tell me about Grace and Liam?"

Bill rubbed his chin. "Nothing to tell."

"She and her son are staying at your house."

"Temporarily."

"They've been there since Sunday."

"It's only Wednesday."

"So they're leaving soon."

"That's the plan."

"Grace is attractive. Strong. Stands up for herself."

Funny, those were the most positive compliments his mother had ever said about a woman he'd gone out with. Not that he and Grace were dating. He weighed how to best respond. "Yes, but she's not my type."

The truth, but that hadn't stopped him thinking about the way she hummed Christmas carols, and how cute she looked in his pajamas, and the sexy way she filled out her jeans. No worries. He appreciated women. That didn't mean he wanted to go out with all of them.

"I thought your type was female and over the age of eighteen," his mother said.

"Drop it." Bill's words came out sharper than he intended.

"Grace and Liam staying with me is no big deal. Her truck's wrecked. She's trying to figure things out. I'm doing what anyone else in town would do for the family of a fallen hero. End of story."

Her mother arched a finely plucked brow. "If you say so."

"I do." His jaw tensed. He didn't want to talk about this any longer. "Anything else?"

"No, except…"

Here we go. He needed a refill. Maybe two. "What?"

"Be careful."

"Don't go all Mama Bear on me." Frustration laced each word. "There's no need for you to worry about me where Grace is concerned."

"I'm not worried about you. Everyone in Hood Hamlet knows you're a big flirt and charmer, with no intention of settling down with one woman." The lines around his mother's mouth deepened. "But Grace doesn't know you or your reputation. Be careful you don't break her heart."

Surprise hit first, followed by a stab of guilt. "You're way off base here."

"Am I?"

"Completely. I don't hit on women with kids."

Never had. Never would.

Even if she was pretty, with a sweet smile, made amazing baked French toast, and showed backbone, struggling to build a life for her and her son. Okay, Bill had flirted a little and convinced her to stay with him, but he refused to follow his standard operating position and take things further. "I admire Grace. She's got…"

"Gumption."

"Yes," he agreed. "I'm not going to put any moves on her."

"Then I guess I have nothing else to say." His mother patted his shoulder. "If you drink too much, call. I'll drive you home."

A noise sounded next to him. Thomas. Laughing under her breath.

Bill fought the urge to roll his eyes. "Thanks for the offer, Mom, but I know my limits."

"I hope so." With that, she left the brewpub.

"Dude." Welton gave Bill a sympathetic look. "The next round's on me."

"This has to go into the annals of Mama Bear Paulson lore." Thomas's laughter spilled out. She wiped the corner of her eye. "I thought she was going to pull out a swab and DNA you right here."

"I can't believe your mom's worried about Grace," Welton said. "Never thought I'd see the day Mrs. Paulson thought angel Bill could do wrong, but all Hood Hamlet, including your mother, knows you're a heartbreaker."

"Shut up." Tonight was looking like a good night to get drunk. But Bill would walk home before calling his mom.

Hansen walked up. "Get enough freshies today?"

O'Ryan stood next to him, looking off into the dining area.

The bartender placed three more pints on the bar.

Nothing beat a Wy'East Brewing Company beer. Except for a free one. Bill reached for his glass. "I can never get enough."

O'Ryan nudged Hansen. "Who's the hot babe with Thad Humphreys?"

Thomas sighed. "Guys…"

"If you know her, Thomas, you gotta tell me her name," O'Ryan urged. "I think I'm in love."

Hansen snickered. "Lust, dude. Love is for fools."

"You're the fool if you feel that way." Leanne glanced back. "She's pretty, but I've never seen her before."

O'Riley sighed. "Someone has to know who she is."

Hansen looked over. "Her rack could be bigger, but I'd forget about the no dating in December decree for a piece of that action."

Leanne sneered. "Hard to believe you don't have a girlfriend with such sweet talk, Hansen."

Always willing to admire a pretty woman, Bill swung his stool around. He scanned the tables in the back room until his gaze zeroed in on Thad at a table with…Grace and Liam.

Bill's heart slammed against his ribs. He slid from his seat, pushing back the stool until it crashed into the bar. His hands clenched, balling into fists, wanting to punch something, someone. He swore, releasing a tirade about one of the nicest guys in town, even knowing Thad was working on Grace's truck.

"Just a hunch, but I'd say the woman's name is Grace." Leanne dug her fingers into Bill's shoulder, holding him back. "Your eyes are green when they should be blue. Don't fly off like a kamikaze. Sit and cool off for a minute."

Bill didn't get jealous; he simply moved on. The way he felt now was illogical, yet he couldn't help himself.

Hansen's eyes widened. "Isn't Grace the name of the mom who's staying with you?"

He nodded, his stomach churning.

The smiling threesome looked cozy and comfortable, like a family out to dinner and a movie. Thad was single and liked pretty ladies as much as the rest of them. The mechanic's interest in Grace might not be one hundred percent professional. Of course it wasn't. The guy had taken Grace and her son out to eat. This was as close to a date as they came.

"Dibs," O'Ryan called.

"Looks like Thad got dibs in first," Leanne teased.

O'Ryan shrugged. "I'll settle for seconds. She looks sweet. Perfect to kiss under the mistletoe or unwrap on Christmas Eve."

Bill's jaw clenched. Every single muscle bunched. He leveled a death-ray glare at the paramedic. "Don't even think about it."

At the Hood Hamlet Brewpub, Grace squirted ketchup onto Liam's plate. She smiled at Thad, the handsome owner of the body shop. "Thanks for the ride to and from your garage. Stopping for dinner was a great idea. Looks like we were lucky to get a table."

Thad wiped his mouth with a napkin. "The brewpub is a big hangout for tourists and locals, even on weeknights."

Grace wondered if that included Bill. She glanced around, but didn't see him. "Well, I'm not surprised. The food's great. I love the pretzels and dipping sauce."

"House specialty." Thad leaned closer, a serious gleam in his eyes. "Do you have any more questions about your truck?"

"No, you've been very thorough."

"It won't take long for us to do some research tonight. The claims adjustor will up her lowball offer."

"I appreciate your help."

"Least I can do." Thad smiled at her and Liam, who dipped French fries in the ketchup. "You two didn't have the best introduction to Hood Hamlet."

"People are making up for our troubles." The atmosphere in the pub was friendly, warm and welcoming. "Does everyone in Hood Hamlet go out of their way to help strangers?"

"Not only strangers, but each other."

"It must be nice to live here. I—"

Liam dropped his fry. He reached sideways, toward the empty seat at the table. "Bill. Bill."

Grace looked up.

Bill was striding toward them full of purpose as if he owned not only the brewpub but the town. His jaw was set. His lips narrowed. His gaze was focused on one thing—her.

Grace's heart jumped, followed by a cartwheel and a somersault.

His carelessly styled, ski-tousled hair shifted with each step. His long-sleeved T-shirt stretched across muscular arms and shoulders. His black ski pants emphasized long, strong legs.

Her pulse sped up. Heat rushed through her veins. She reached for her glass of water and drank. Okay, gulped.

Thad cleared his throat, then stood, his posture stiff. He shook Bill's hand. "Care to join us?"

Bill sat in the chair opposite her. He ruffled Liam's hair. "Enjoying dinner, little dude?"

"Yummy." Liam handed him a French fry. "Eat."

Bill did, his watchful gaze on Grace.

She scooted back in her chair, not liking his predatory stare, as if he wanted a taste of her rather than the French fry.

She tucked her hair behind her ears and looked down, critiquing her clothes. Not that she had much beside jeans, track pants and T-shirts to wear. At least what she wore was clean.

Because the way Bill's gaze had locked in on her made her feel desirable. For the first time in years she felt like a whole woman, not the broken widow of a heroic Ranger. The attention gave her a needed boost of confidence in the female department.

"Get a lot of skiing in?" Thad asked.

"One of the best days up there in a while." Bill looked from Grace to Thad. "Showing Grace and Liam the hot spots in town tonight?"

Thad's smile hardened. "It was either that or have them eat dinner alone at your house."

Veins twitched. Lips thinned. Eyes narrowed.

Weird. She thought they were friends. "Thad drove us to his garage so I could speak with the claims adjustor."

"What's the verdict on the truck?" Bill broke from his stare-down to be civil.

The decisions Grace would have to make soon hit with sudden force, like the long, fast-moving freight trains they'd seen driving across the plain states.

Liam handed him another French fry. "The truck is broken, isn't it, Mommy?"

"Yes, it's very broken." She glanced at her plate, and her half-eaten order of halibut and chips. Her appetite had disappeared. "Thad's been explaining my options."

Bill smirked at the mechanic. "Nice of you to go to so much trouble."

"Just trying to help Grace and Liam." Thad's square jaw jutted forward. "Like you giving them a place to stay."

"That's what we do in Hood Hamlet."

"Exactly."

The undercurrent at the table bothered Grace. Both men were great. Thad was sweet, and Bill made her tummy tingle. Without the other, each guy had been pleasant and kind. Together, not so much. She didn't know their history, but recognized the territorial posturing. She'd seen it in Columbus.

Men.

As if one man's hospitality to two strangers was an affront to the other. She didn't get it. Them.

Liam seemed oblivious to what was going on. He sucked on

the straw in his chocolate milk, his small hand touching Bill's larger one.

"So how's Muffy?" A French fry dangled from Bill's fingers. A mischievous smile lit up his face. "I heard the two of you have been dating."

Grace rolled her eyes and took a long sip of her pale ale.

Thad cleared his throat. "We've gone out a few times. Nothing serious. You went out with her, too."

"Once or twice. I'm not dating anyone now."

"Oh, yeah. It's December." Thad emphasized the month. "Some guys would rather let women fend for themselves at the holidays than cough up money to buy them a present. You've always been a fan of leaving women waiting."

Oh, brother. This could take all night. Grace shoved aside her plate, propped an elbow on the table and leaned her head against her hand, forgotten.

The two men stared at each other, as if sizing up a rival or trying to make him back down.

Forget cutting the tension with a knife. They would need an ax or a chainsaw.

The din of the customers around them rose. Their silence increased the pressure at the table.

Time to intervene. She didn't think logic would help, but needed to say something. "A car might be more practical for me than a truck."

Both men startled, then nodded.

Good. She had their attention. "Though I'm attached to the old pickup and I need a way to get our things to Astoria."

"I have a truck," Thad said.

"So do I." Bill put more ketchup on Liam's plate. "I'm happy to drive your things to the coast."

"Same here," Thad said. "I have an aunt in Long Beach. That's across the Columbia River and a little north. I can stay with her."

Bill grimaced. "You can make the drive there and back in a day."

"Unless Grace needs help unpacking."

"Grace has moved a lot. She knows how to unpack."

Thad shrugged, undaunted. "She still might want help."

Bill scooted forward. "I'm happy to help, too."

She made a T with her hands. "Time out, guys. I was just making conversation. I don't know what I'm going to do yet."

The two men kept glancing at each other, as if checking the other's position.

Liam climbed out of his seat and onto Bill's lap.

Thad's nostrils flared.

Grace shot forward with a thrill.

Okay, she was twenty-six, not sixteen, but she'd never had two guys act this way over her. It was…nice. Immature and silly, but flattering.

"Hey." A pretty woman with braided brown hair and warm brown eyes stood next to their table, with a tall, handsome man behind her. "Enjoying yourselves?"

Thad pressed his lips together.

Bill took a French fry off Liam's plate.

Someone needed to be polite. Grace smiled. "The food is delicious. The beer, too."

"I'm Leanne Thomas. This is Christian Welton." The woman extended her arm. "You must be Grace. Paulson—I mean Bill—mentioned you."

She shook the woman's hand. Bill had called Leanne his best friend. "I'm Grace Wilcox. This is my son, Liam."

Liam burrowed his head between Bill's neck and shoulder.

"Sorry to interrupt your dinner, but I wanted to tell Bill our table's ready. Looks like I was just in time—" Leanne motioned to Bill and Thad "—otherwise these two might have had a territorial pissing match right here in the dining room. Jake wouldn't have liked that."

Bill and Thad united to glare at Leanne.

Grace swallowed her laugh and eyed the woman with respect.

"Jake Porter owns the brewpub," Christian said to Grace.

Liam reached across Bill and grabbed a French fry.

"We wouldn't want to upset the owner," Grace said. "Thanks for diffusing the, um, situation."

Christian winked. "We're firefighters. That's what we do."

The iceberg-size diamond engagement ring on Leanne's finger sparkled. Grace remembered what Bill had said. "I hear congratulations are in order."

"Thank you." Eyes twinkling and face beaming, Leanne held her fiancée's hand. "We're getting married on Saturday."

She looked at Christian with such pure love that Grace's heart ached. She missed having that mutual adoration with someone. The squabbling between Bill and Thad might amuse her, but was no substitute. Not even close. "Best wishes for a happy life together."

The server brought the check.

Bill reached out his hand. "I'll take it."

"No, I will." Thad tried to snatch the bill. "You didn't eat."

Bill kept his arm extended. "My treat for you helping Grace."

"I got it, dude. I invited her to dinner," Thad countered.

They fought like boys seeing who got to shoot the new Nerf gun first. A town the size of Hood Hamlet probably didn't have many single women to choose from. Grace must be the new toy the guys wanted to play with. She sighed, then looked at Leanne. "Are they normally like this?"

"No. Not these two." A puzzled expression crossed Leanne's face. She stared at Bill with Liam on his lap. "This behavior is highly unusual."

Grace was ready to go back to Bill's place. She took the black portfolio from the server. "Dinner is my treat."

Both men protested.

"Sorry, boys." Grace scanned the bill for the total and calculated the tip. She'd always been good with numbers. Now she had a degree in accounting. "You snooze, you lose."

Leanne laughed. "You're going to fit in well around here."

"Thanks, but I won't be here long." Grace removed two twenties and a ten from her wallet, then slid the money inside the folder. "Liam and I will be on our way to Astoria soon."

"Too bad." Leanne sounded genuinely disappointed. "But Astoria isn't that far away."

"Less than three hours," Bill said.

"One hundred and fifty miles at the most," Thad said at the same time.

"As I said, not far." Leanne grinned like a bride on a shopping spree in Tiffany's. "Come on, Bill. Time for dinner."

Leanne and Christian walked to an empty table on the far side of the dining area. Bill remained seated.

"Go on," Grace urged him. "We're finished."

Bill didn't move. "You need a ride home."

"I'm driving them back to the house," Thad said.

"I will."

"Liam's car seat is in my truck."

"I know how to install a car seat," Bill said. "The station holds clinics."

Grace put a hand on his shoulder. "Relax, okay? Liam's tired. You haven't eaten. We're going home with Thad."

"No, you're not," Bill said.

"Yes, I am."

Thad shook his head. "I have to drive Grace home so we can put together a counteroffer for the claims adjustor."

"Counteroffer?" Bill asked.

"The claims adjustor wants to total the truck, but gave Grace a lowball offer," Thad explained. "I'm going to help her research what the truck is worth."

"Then get going. I take it you know what will sway the adjustor."

Thad nodded.

Bill stood, then put Liam back in his seat. "Tomorrow, I'll take Grace to look at a replacement."

Thad rose. "I'll put together a list of reliable, safe vehicles. But don't buy anything without me."

"I'm right here, guys," Grace said to no one in particular.

"Paulson," Leanne shouted. "Get your sorry ass over here. I'm hungry."

His gaze locked on Grace. "I'm starving."

Her pulse skittered.

"Dinner won't take long." Bill's gaze raked over her as if she would be dessert. "I'll be home soon."

Liam clapped.

Grace gulped.

Bill's words sounded like a warning.

Yet anticipation zipped from the top of her head to the bottom of her toes. Awareness of the man thrummed through her veins.

If Grace knew what was good for her, she would call it a night before he arrived home.

Or maybe she would put Liam to bed and take her chances.

Dessert might be exactly what she needed.

CHAPTER EIGHT

Turning his truck onto the driveway, Bill hit the garage door opener. No sign of Thad or his pickup.

Good. Bill didn't want to get into a fight.

The garage door lifted.

His headlights lit up the boxes and plastic bins from Grace's pickup. He tightened his grip on the leather-covered steering wheel.

He wasn't proud of his behavior at the brewpub, but seeing Grace with Thad had turned him into a caveman. He had wanted to stomp on any guy who eyed her as O'Ryan did, or took her to dinner, like Thad. Bill had never felt that way about anyone.

Not even Cocoa Marsh, the only woman he'd ever thought about dating more than a few times.

Bill drove into the garage.

He'd been bummed about Cocoa hooking up with her ex-flame, gold medal snowboarder Rex Billings. Until Bill had met a cute snow bunny a week later. What was that girl's name? She'd been blonde and hot enough to make him forget why he'd been attracted to Cocoa in the first place.

He turned off the ignition and removed the keys.

Over dinner, Leanne had called him on his behavior, rather his "childish, territorial chest-puffing." She could be such a hard-nose, but he loved her like a sister. Still, he wasn't about to open up to her.

Not after the abuse he'd received at the station over Cocoa, Leanne's former roommate. Discussing Grace was off-limits with everyone.

He'd backtracked during dinner. Shot from the hip, hoping

something he said about boys being boys appeased her. Lied his butt off.

What else could he do?

Admit he thought Grace was hot? That he liked spending time with her and her kid? That he wanted them to stay in Hood Hamlet as long as possible?

Nope. Bill couldn't admit any of those things.

Because they weren't true. Not really.

He exited the truck.

Bill was just a little lonely due to no dating in December. He didn't want a girlfriend. He didn't want a relationship. He sure as hell didn't want a ready-made family.

Monogamy and commitment were not in his DNA. He wasn't going to fail like his dad by saying "I do," when the only words out of his mouth should be "I can't."

He opened the door to the laundry room.

Grace was attractive. But she didn't seem like a fling kind of woman. More like an on-bended-knee-proposal kind. A forever kind.

That was why his mom worried he'd break Grace's heart. Leanne had warned him off over dinner. Even Christian had pointed out Grace had to be stressed, and needed friends with no agenda.

No problem.

Bill would keep his distance. Be her friend, her bud, her pal. He would treat her like Thomas. Okay, maybe he'd be nicer than that.

Inside the house, he shrugged off his jacket and tossed it on the dryer.

He accepted he wasn't the right guy for Grace, but knew Thad Humphreys wasn't, either.

Sure, Thad was an upright, responsible, respectable citizen. No one in Hood Hamlet would disagree.

Bill walked through the dining area to the living room.

The mechanic spent every New Year's Eve giving free rides to drunk drivers and towing their cars home. He'd dropped out of college at age nineteen to take over his family's garage and support his mother and sisters, after his father had a massive coronary and died at the age of forty-two. Thad had made sure Hannah Bishop's cars ran perfectly, maintaining them for free after Nick died and before she'd married Garrett Willingham.

A good man.

But not the one for Grace, and by default, Liam, since the two were a package deal.

Bill's gut told him Thad was wrong for her. Instincts had kept Bill alive and out of trouble all his life. He trusted his instinct to be right now.

He needed to make sure Grace left town with a reliable vehicle and her heart in one piece. Totally possible. Totally his plan.

Giggles sounded from down the hall.

Liam.

Water ran.

The bathtub.

The door to the hall bathroom was closed, but he heard voices, and water splashed.

Taking a shower sounded good. He needed to wash away the smells of the mountain and sweat. A steady stream of icy water would clear his head and put him in the right frame of mind to see Grace.

Ten minutes later, Bill dried off, feeling clean and smelling better. He'd calmed down about Thad, too. Grace was moving to Astoria to make a fresh start. Getting involved with Thad or anyone in Hood Hamlet would be a complication, something she didn't seem to like. Bill didn't like them, either.

He slid into a pair of flannel sleep pants, then reached for a shirt.

The phone rang.

The receiver wasn't in the charger on the nightstand. He tossed the shirt on the bed, jogged out to the living room and answered the phone. "Hello."

"I hope you're not upset with me."

His mother sounded contrite. She should be.

"Not upset." He cradled the phone against his shoulder as he tied the drawstrings at his waistband. "But you shouldn't go off half-cocked about things and people you know nothing about."

"Perhaps it was wishful thinking on my part."

Yeah, right. She'd been upset, not hopeful. But the last thing he needed was her grandma clock to start ticking. "Just so you know... Not. Going. To. Happen."

"Going skiing tomorrow?"

He was grateful she'd changed the subject. "After I take Grace to look at cars."

"Liam will hate car shopping," his mother said.

"We'll bring toys."

Silence filled the line.

"I'll come over and watch him," his mother offered. "That way Grace can concentrate on looking at cars and not worry about Liam."

"I'll ask her."

"I'll be ready in case she says yes and you want to get an early start."

His mother sounded so enthusiastic about babysitting. That wasn't like her. She volunteered in the nursery at church on Sundays, giving her something to do besides hovering over him. "It's my day off. No early starts unless we're talking Alpine climbing," he answered.

"Let me know what time." His mother made her familiar smacking-kiss noise. "Sweet dreams."

He said good-night and disconnected from the call.

A door shut.

Bill turned and saw Grace standing with an odd expression on her face. "Where's Liam?"

"Asleep. Baths do that to him sometimes." She motioned to the phone in his hand. "Need to make a call?"

"I was talking with my mom. She offered to watch Liam tomorrow while we look at cars."

"You don't have to take me out."

"We're going." His wanting to take her had nothing to do with Thad Humphreys. Bill wanted to help Grace. Getting her a safe, reliable vehicle was the first step to her leaving town. He returned the phone to the charger. "We can take Liam with us if you don't want to leave him with my mom."

Grace walked toward him. "I'm sure Liam would rather stay home and play with your mom than have to look at cars for a few hours."

The baggy T-shirt Grace wore didn't hide the bounce of her breasts. Her hips swayed seductively.

His temperature spiked.

The tip of Grace's tongue darted out and dragged across her lower lip.

Damn, she was sexy.

Look, don't touch.

Except looking might get him in trouble tonight. *Pretend she's Leanne or Zoe or Carly or Hannah.* But all he could see was Grace. "I'll, um, let my mom know. Did Thad help you get what you needed?"

"Yes, he did. He was so helpful. A very nice guy."

Helpful. Nice. Bill wanted to choke. But he was going to be good guy, too, and not say a word. For Grace's sake. "Glad it worked out."

Her eyes shone, sparkled, as if full of tiny diamonds. "Tonight at the brewpub, you and Thad were going at each other."

"Men being men. Nothing else."

"That's what Thad said, too."

Bill rocked back on his heels. "Did he say anything else?"

She closed the distance between them. "Just that he was happy to help me however he could."

"I'm happy to do the same."

"I appreciate that." Something flickered in Grace's eyes. She touched his shoulder.

Her fingertips seared his skin. He sucked in a breath. "What…?"

"You have tattoos."

Heat emanated from the point of contact. His pulse kicked up a notch. Okay, three. "A couple."

"Who's Nick?"

Bill tried to think. Not easy to do with her so close, touching him. He took a deep breath. Focused.

Oh, yeah. The memorial tattoo.

"Nick was a good friend killed climbing Mount Hood." Warmth flooded Bill. He tried not to think about Grace's fingertips outlining the scrolled name. "We grew up together. Hung out. He taught me to climb, fish, hunt. Pretty much everything having to do with the outdoors. He was a couple of years older. The closest thing to a big brother Leanne and I had. Nick was a total jokester, too. He wore the stupidest Santa hat. The ball lit up and turned different colors. We used to give him so much crap over that hat."

"Sounds like a good guy."

"The best. I think about him every day."

Grace trailed her finger down Bill's arm, making his nerve endings dance and spark. "This tattoo looks job related."

"A helmet with our squad name." He ground out the words. If she didn't stop touching him, he was going to want to touch her. He needed another cold shower or a whopping dose of reality. "Did your, um, husband have any tattoos?"

Her lips parted. She pressed her arm against her side. Her hands balled, then she released them.

A mix of regret and relief washed over Bill. He missed her touch, but knew this was for the best—the best for Grace.

She raised her hand and brushed his right biceps, her fingers soft and warm.

Damn, he hadn't expected her to touch him again, but he liked it. More than he should.

"Damon had several." She drew an arc across Bill's skin, sending pleasurable sensations bursting from his nerve endings. "A Ranger Scroll from the 3/75 here."

"Three seventy-five?"

"Third battalion." She traced a line to the back of Bill's shoulders, starting sparks shooting down his arm. "He had the Ranger DUI here."

Bill had no idea what was going on. He didn't care, even if he should. He'd given her the chance to stop. She was the one who started it. Both times. Talk about a turn-on. "I have a feeling that doesn't mean driving under the influence."

"Distinctive Unit Insignia." She drew something on his shoulder blade, making his temperature shoot up another ten degrees. "It's the insignia on a Ranger's tan beret, a shield with four quadrants. One with a sun, another a star and two with a lightning bolt."

Her hand remained on Bill.

His heart pounded, so loud he was aware of each beat. Blood rushed where he didn't want it to go.

Common sense told him to back away. Too bad he was never one to do what he was told when a beautiful woman was touching him.

Might as well go all in. "Did your husband have any others?"

She ran her fingertip up across Bill's right shoulder to the left side of his chest.

Something fluttered, a tightness, a pang.

"One was right here." She drew a heart. "For me."

His groin tightened. His temperature spiraled until he was downright feverish. All he could think about was kissing her hard on the lips until neither of them could breathe or see straight.

But he couldn't, could he?

Bill tried to focus. He attempted to shut off the X-rated fantasies playing in his mind. All the words of caution from his mom, Thomas and Welton, along with his own, echoed in his brain. He couldn't offer what Grace wanted or needed. Yet here they were....

His gaze locked on hers. "What are you doing?"

She lifted her chin, giving him a great view of her neck, a neck that should be showered with kisses. His kisses.

Her face flushed. "I...I don't know."

That made two of them. "If you don't stop, I'm going to kiss you."

The corners of her mouth curved into a slow smile. "Not if I kiss you first."

Oh, my. Oh, my. Oh, my.

Grace couldn't believe she'd said the words aloud. Oh, she'd been thinking them. Insane.

She forced herself to breathe. Not an easy task when each breath was coming quicker and quicker.

A come-here-sexy-lady grin crinkled the corners of Bill's eyes. "I'm waiting."

Oh, boy. She had never been flirty or forward. Not ever. But seeing Bill shirtless had ignited a fire deep inside her belly. Her fingers had tingled, aching to touch him. She'd wanted two servings of dessert.

Temporary insanity?

More likely loneliness and raging hormones.

But she couldn't help herself.

Memories had stirred. Feelings. Desire.

She'd needed to touch him. So she had.

And now...

Grace stared at his wide shoulders and muscular arms. Her gaze lowered to his solid chest and rock-hard abs. The waistband of his pajama pants rode low on his hips.

She looked up at his face. His mouth. Lips.

One kiss. That was all she wanted. A little kiss.

Something to remember him by. Something secret. Something hers alone.

Grace rose up on her tiptoes. She brushed her lips against his.

Sparks erupted. Heat flared.

Wowza. Forget fireworks. They could have their own Fourth of July celebration right here in December.

She pressed harder against his mouth, soaking up his heat and taste. Her nerve endings shivered. She wanted more.

"Grace..." It sounded like a half groan, half plea. "We shouldn't."

His words proved Bill was a good guy. But she didn't want to stop. "Please. A little more."

There. She wasn't being greedy.

Bill answered her with more kisses. His lips parted, moved skillfully over hers. Tasting, teasing, pleasing.

Grace's legs wobbled, her knees weak from the sensations shooting straight to her toes. Light-headed from the kisses, she leaned against his firm chest.

So strong.

His arms wrapped around her, embracing her with strength

and warmth and a sense of belonging she'd never thought she'd feel again.

Stop, a little voice cautioned.

She knew she should.

Everything she was feeling and thinking was telling her to stop.

But she didn't want to stop.

Grace didn't know if she'd ever be kissed this way again. She wanted to make the most of it while she could.

Tongues tangled and danced.

She ran her hands over the muscular ridges of his back and through his damp hair. She couldn't get enough of Bill's kisses, of him.

She was…home.

Panic ripped through her.

Not home. A temporary place. In temporary arms.

He cupped her bottom, pulling her even closer.

She went eagerly, pressing against him. She arched—

"Mommy?"

Grace jumped back as if she'd been shocked by ten thousand volts.

She turned to see Liam, his hair sticking up. He stood in the hallway, holding Peanut against his heart.

Oh, no. She covered her bruised and throbbing lips with her hands. Tried to calm her breathing, cool the heat in her cheeks, pull down the bottom of her shirt.

Bill, his breathing as ragged as hers, walked over to her son and knelt. "What's up, little dude?"

Liam stared at the ground. "Peanut woke up. Mommy wasn't there."

Bill touched the stuffed animal. "As you can see, Peanut, your mommy's right here."

Liam nodded.

Grace pulled herself together and joined them. Kneeling in turn, she touched his shoulder. "Did you wonder where I was?"

Another nod.

She hugged him. "I'm sorry I wasn't there beside you, but it wasn't my bedtime yet."

Liam wrapped his arms around her neck. "Sleep. Sleep."

The last thing she wanted to do was sleep. That meant she should go to bed. "We can sleep now."

She was a mom—Liam's mom. Her son needed her and she needed him. Even if her lips wanted more kisses.

More kisses weren't a smart idea.

The hunger in Bill's eyes matched the way she felt inside. Thank goodness Liam had woken up, or things might have gone further than she intended. "I need to get him to bed."

"I know." Bill brushed his hand over Liam's hair. "Sleep tight, bud."

The little boy's thumb was in his mouth. His eyelids drooped.

Bill cupped Grace's face. "We'll talk about this later."

She'd tried hard to set a good example for Liam, but tonight…

Heat spread up her neck. She couldn't believe her son had caught her making out with the big dude.

Grace stood, then carried Liam to the guest bedroom. She glanced back at Bill. "Let's forget it ever happened."

"I won't be forgetting anytime soon."

Neither would she. But she would have to try.

The bedroom door was open. She stepped inside the room. "Good night."

Bill stood in the doorway. "Sweet dreams."

His gaze, full of desire, made her shiver with want.

Darn the man. She'd likely be having hot dreams because of his toe-curling kisses. "See you in the morning."

"I'll be seeing you sooner." He winked. "In my dreams."

Her mouth dropped open. She stood with her son in her arms, her heart roaring in her ears.

Wicked laughter lit his eyes. Bill twisted the lock on her side of the knob. "Good night, Liam. Gracie."

He closed the door. The latched clicked.

Gracie? No one called her Gracie. Oh, they'd tried. Damon had given up and called her babe. She'd been named Grace and that was what she wanted to hear.

But the name didn't sound so bad coming from Bill's lips.

She laid Liam and Peanut on the bed and covered them with the sheet and comforter. Her son was sound asleep in a minute.

Grace changed into an Iowa Hawkeyes nightshirt.

Bill Paulson spelled ten types of trouble. He might be a good guy, but his kisses had Bad Boy scribbled all over them. Fun for a moment, dangerous for any longer.

She was clever enough to know better than to mess around with a man like him.

But clever or not, she wanted to kiss the bad boy again. And again. And again.

What was she going to do?

It'll be okay, babe.

"Quiet."

Usually, she welcomed Damon's words and the assurance they promised, but not tonight.

Not when her lips throbbed, not when her heart ached, not when she wanted to fall asleep in another man's arms.

Not any man's. Bill's.

Grace covered Liam with another blanket. He didn't stir.

She would brush her teeth, floss, wash her face, then crawl under the covers to hide. She might not be able to forget the kisses she'd shared with Bill, but maybe she could pretend those kisses had never happened, that she imagined or dreamed them.

That would allow her to sleep.

And she needed sleep. Almost as much as she'd needed kisses.

Bill leaned against the wall next to the guest bedroom door. He didn't know how long he'd been standing in the hallway. He didn't care.

He couldn't remember how many women he'd dated, how many women he'd kissed. But not one had made him want all of her—mind, body and soul—like Grace Wilcox.

He'd felt like a randy teen kissing her, almost losing control, falling over the edge and embarrassing both of them. Well, him.

That had never happened before.

Not even the first time making out with Maggie Freeman in the storeroom of her father's general store on Main Street.

Thanks to Grace, Bill ached with need. He wanted to touch her again, hold her again, taste her again. He shouldn't feel that way about any woman, especially one with a kid. He was too much like his dad to be a forever type family guy. But when she'd touched him, he'd gone mad with desire. When she'd kissed him, he'd struggled to remain in control. When she'd kept kissing him, he hadn't wanted to stop.

The guest bedroom door opened.

Crap. Bill straightened.

Grace stepped into the hallway. Her long brown hair was messy and tangled, as if she'd changed quickly. A baggy nightshirt hid delicious curves, but the knee-length hem gave him a great view of her calves.

Toned muscle. Smooth, pale skin.

Sexy.

What the hell was wrong with him? He was getting turned on looking at her lower legs.

They were great calves, though.

She left the door ajar.

"Forget something?" He tried sounding casual, as if he hadn't been skulking outside her door, fantasizing.

Grace drew back. Her brow furrowed. "What are you doing here?"

"Thinking about you."

She started to speak, then pressed her lips together. Her gaze bounced from Bill to the guest bedroom door. "I don't have time for this. I need to get back to Liam."

She hurried past Bill, like a gust of wind roaring through the Columbia Gorge. Only this squall swirled around him with a sweet aroma of jasmine and vanilla.

The bathroom door closed. Locked.

Bill fought disappointment and rising frustration. He should have said something different, something more. But retreating wasn't an option. He needed to figure out what was going on.

Maybe he'd misjudged the impact of her kisses. Blown them

out of proportion. He hadn't kissed a woman in over a week. He could be imaging things to be better than they were. That would explain his over-the-top reaction.

Bill needed to get her and her kisses out of his system. He knew exactly how to do that.

Kiss her again.

One more kiss would disprove this nonsense. Another kiss would be nice. Special, even. But not enough to change his world—his perfect world.

Kissing her again was a good plan. If Grace agreed…

Minutes ticked by.

Bill waited. He wasn't the kind of guy to swan dive into a foot of water over some woman, let alone a kiss.

All Hood Hamlet, including your mom, knows you're a heart-breaker.

Welton's words echoed in Bill's head. He'd worn the title of heartbreaker like a badge of honor, stepping into the role after Jake Porter and Sean Hughes married. Being called a player brought a rush of pride. Everyone knew, everyone expected that kind of behavior from him.

Everyone but Grace.

Bill didn't want her to find out about his reputation. She didn't seem the type to be impressed by his womanizing, even though he got involved only with women who understood the rules and how he felt about relationships. But Grace might not absolve him of responsibility for any resulting broken hearts.

Not that she had anything to worry about. He would be careful and keep her safe.

But he needed to know if her kisses really made him feel so incredible, so invincible. Or if the December dating hiatus made him kiss-hungry for any pretty woman.

Testing his hypothesis, as his friend volcanologist Sarah Purcell would say, made sense. Another kiss—a test one—wouldn't take long.

The door to the bathroom opened.

His pulse jolted like a Thoroughbred out of the starting gate. But he was feeling like the long shot in the race.

Standing in the doorway, Grace sucked in a breath. "You're still here."

"I want to talk." Not exactly true, but saying "I want to kiss" might freak her out.

"Liam might wake up." She glanced at the bedroom door. "I should get in there."

She should, but Bill didn't want her to go. Not yet. "It won't take long."

The bridge of Grace's nose crinkled, matching the creases on her forehead. She crossed her arms over her chest. "What?"

Truth time. "I want to finish what we started."

She wet her lips. Her eyes darkened, but he couldn't tell if that was due to annoyance or desire. "Here?"

Bill nodded, itching to reach for her.

She looked down at the hardwood floor. "I don't think that's a good idea."

"It's a great idea." Her pulse point, visible at the V of her neckline, beat rapidly. So she wasn't so immune to the charged air between them. Anticipation made him smile. "Think of it as a test. Kissing again will allow us to see it's no big deal."

"You thought it was a big deal?"

"I'm not sure what to think right now."

"That makes two of us. But you shouldn't kiss me again."

"No more kissing?" Bill leaned closer, near enough that she could feel his warm breath against her. "In case you forgot, Gracie, you kissed me."

She flushed. "True, but you kissed me back."

"A gentleman always kisses back."

"That's why you did it? You were being polite?"

His words had hit a nerve with her.

"I'm joking." He raised her chin with his fingertips. "I had to kiss you because were standing under mistletoe."

Grace glanced back at the living room. "There's no… You think this is funny."

"It is funny. You're funny." He let go of her face. "After we kiss, we'll know. We can have a good laugh about all this and move on."

"I have a feeling I'm being led into a trap."

"Never."

Indecision and doubt filled her eyes. "One kiss."

Excitement built in Bill's chest. "One is all I'm asking for."

He lowered his mouth to hers.

Their lips met, soft as a whisper at dawn.

A spark jolted through him. Forget a faint sound, this kiss was an in-your-face, ear-shattering shout.

Exactly like before.

Tingles erupted. Blood boiled. Sensations pulsed through him. Even more than their first kiss.

She tasted like peppermint, her toothpaste. And warm, like her caring, giving heart.

He was the one caught in a trap, snared by Grace's kiss. He wanted to keep kissing her, but he would keep his word. He'd said one. That was all he would take.

At least tonight.

Bill slowly, regretfully drew it to an end. Not a fluke. He hasn't been imagining things. He hadn't blown anything out of proportion.

Grace's kisses were different. Better. Sexier. Hotter. And the reason he'd been struggling to think straight. "Thanks."

"Satisfied?"

"Very," he admitted. "I figured out what I needed to know."

"Me, too." Without meeting his eyes, she slipped into the bedroom and closed the door behind her.

"Good night, Gracie."

He touched his lips.

One more kiss was not going to be enough.

Bill knew that without an ounce of uncertainty.

Kisses like this didn't happen every day. They would be fools to waste her time stuck in Hood Hamlet.

All he had to do was convince Grace they could be together without him breaking her heart. He would be careful not to hurt her. He *couldn't* hurt her. But the longing in her eyes, on her lips, told him she needed kisses as much as he did.

Maybe even more.

CHAPTER NINE

THE NEXT AFTERNOON, Grace walked along Hood Hamlet's wooden sidewalk with Bill. Christmas lights twinkled in store windows. Snippets of carols drifted out of shops with the opening and closing of doors. Snow fell from the darkening skies, matching the storm brewing inside her.

She stole a sideways glance at Bill, taking in his wool beanie, red plaid parka, gray cargo pants and boots. So handsome, all rugged and outdoorsy and male. She wished she wouldn't notice how he dressed. She wished she could stop thinking about kissing him.

Bill was obviously over their kisses. He hadn't mentioned a word about last night as they'd driven down the mountain this morning and checked out vehicles in the towns of Gresham and Sandy. He hadn't brought up the kisses while sharing a pepperoni-and-mushroom pizza at a small Italian café on their way back up the mountain.

The kisses must have scored "no big deal" on his test.

She would have given them an A+. She'd been up half the night reliving every moment and wanting more.

Grace adjusted the scarf around her neck for the third time in ten minutes. Time to move on. She needed to stop tying herself in knots about what happened last night. She should be happy Bill was taking time on his day off to look at cars and show her Hood Hamlet. Not many people would do that. At least not for her.

Two teenage boys strutted toward them, a swagger to their steps and snowboards resting on their shoulders. The words

Hood Hamlet Snowboarding Academy were embroidered on their jackets.

"Those dudes aren't going to get out of our way." Bill slipped his arm around Grace's waist, then pulled her toward a coffee shop. "Wouldn't want you to get knocked down."

Too late. Kissing him had knocked her flat on her face. His touch threatened to do the same thing.

Grace wore a camisole and sweater under her, well, Bill's jacket. In spite of three layers of clothing, tingles and warmth made her all too aware of his hand on her. Of course, having his muscular body against her and his hot breath on her neck weren't helping.

The way he protected her, putting himself between her and the teenagers, sent her pulse sprinting. She'd been taking care of herself for so long, she'd forgotten how nice it was not to have to do everything. Bill made her feel special, treasured.

The snowboarders passed, dropping four letter words like confetti.

"Dudes," Bill called to the boys. "Remember your manners. Doubt you want Johnny to know you're prowling Main Street like a couple of gangstas."

The teens nodded sheepishly. Apologized. Ran.

Grace watched them disappear around the corner, trying to compose herself. "Whoever Johnny is must instill great fear in those kids."

Bill edged away from her. "A little fear, but Johnny Gearhart aims for respect. He's a former snowboarding champion and runs the school."

She fell into step with Bill, ignoring the urge to take his hand. That was what she would have done walking next to Damon. Funny and disconcerting that she wanted to do the same thing now.

"So what do you think of Hood Hamlet?"

"Charming." The Alpine village defined the word, especially with the buildings and streets decked out for the holidays. Garlands and lights draped the storefronts. Wreaths hung on windows and doors. The old-fashioned streetlamps were wrapped in red and white strips like candy canes. "The town looks like a Christmas card."

"It does, but Hood Hamlet's beautiful no matter what time of year." He glanced around with a satisfied look on his face. "I wouldn't want to live anywhere else."

"I can see why." She watched a man dart across the road to pick up a dropped package for a woman juggling shopping bags. "The people seem nice, too."

"We have a few grumpy old-timers who yell at kids. A Scrooge or two who like to hear themselves say 'Bah-humbug' every December, and some teens who make trouble, but the majority are hardworking, good-natured folks."

Two men in a snowboard shop waved to a woman on the sidewalk outside.

Grace had been to Main Street twice. Each time this quaint town called to her—to her heart—like no other place she'd lived. "I wonder if Astoria's like this."

"Astoria is bigger, but you'll find friendly people. You might have to look harder."

She stopped in front of a window display with a "hill" made of white cottony fabric and an old-fashioned toboggan. "Probably won't find much snow there."

No snowmen or snowball fights or snow angels. She sighed, already missing Hood Hamlet.

Bill shot her a sideways glance. "Thinking you might want to stick around town awhile?"

Heat flamed in her cheeks. She wasn't one to long for what she couldn't have. She continued along the sidewalk. "Just making conversation."

"That's what you were doing last night."

He meant at the brewpub, but she couldn't stop thinking about the feel of his skin, the touch of his hands, the taste of his lips.

Do. Not. Go. There.

She cleared her dry throat. "Liam's never had a white Christmas."

"He needs to have one. Spend Christmas in Hood Hamlet."

Her gaze jerked to him. "I wasn't fishing for an invitation."

"I know, but I'm inviting you. Experience Hood Hamlet at its finest. You might see Christmas magic in action."

She let his words sink in. Appealing, yes. Practical, no. "But the twenty-fifth…"

"Is only a week away."

Snow was the reason she was stuck in Hood Hamlet, though the truck's engine might have given out, anyway. The thought of a white Christmas was enticing. This town might not be magical, but it was darn close to a TV Christmas movie setting. The memories made here would last forever. But that would mean more time being tempted by Bill and his kisses. Talk about dangerous. "I…"

"Do you have a place to stay in Astoria?"

Her stomach tensed. "No, but there are temporary rentals available."

"What about a job?"

"No. But thanks to Damon's life insurance and monthly survivor benefit checks, I don't need one right away. I have a degree in accounting and plan on looking for a part-time position once we're settled. Maybe find something during the tax season."

Too long an explanation when a no would have sufficed, but being around Bill made her nervous. She rattled on like a forgotten kettle.

He waved to someone driving by in a blue pickup. "Know anybody in Astoria?"

This one was simple to answer. "No."

"Then why do you need to be there for Christmas?"

Grace didn't. Bill skillfully had her cornered. If she and her son stayed here, Liam could play in the snow after opening his presents. They would be celebrating the holiday in a house with a fireplace to hang stockings on Christmas Eve. She could explain to Liam how Santa came down the chimney. All positives, except… "I don't want to overstay our welcome."

"It's not like you'll be here forever."

No, but forever didn't sound so bad.

She shook some sense into herself.

Forever was as much a fantasy as Christmas magic.

"Stay until the twenty-sixth," he suggested.

"The twenty-sixth?"

"That would give you twelve days in Hood Hamlet. Perfect amount of time, given the holiday season."

She wouldn't go that far. Having an end date made her feel better, but something remained unspoken. The elephant in the room, but its name wasn't Peanut. "What about, um, last night?"

"You mean us kissing?"

She glanced around. "Shhh. Someone might hear you."

"Kissing isn't against the law."

"I felt like I was breaking a few laws."

He eyed her with interest. "Oh, really."

Darn. She hadn't meant to say the words aloud. "Isn't that a pretty wreath hanging on the candy shop?"

"Don't change the subject." He pulled her into an alcove next to the hardware store. "I want you to stay in Hood Hamlet for two reasons. The first is your son. He needs a white Christmas. The second is I want to spend more time with you. There's something between us."

Her heart bumped. Then reality set in. "When we kiss?"

"You felt it, too."

"I did."

"Let's explore the chemistry and enjoy each other while you're in town."

He made being strictly physical sound so easy. But the thought of getting closer terrified her. "What happens when it's over?"

"You go to Astoria like you planned. Until then we'll have fun."

Fun. She had a feeling they had different definitions of the word.

"I don't—" she lowered her voice "—sleep around. I've only been with…"

"Your husband."

She nodded.

"I respect that. I respect you." Bill gazed into her eyes, placed his arms on either side of her with his palms against the wall. "Most people underestimate me, but I'm a man of my word. I won't ask you to do something you're not ready for or don't want. But I'm not going to lie. Kissing you was one of the highlights of my year. And it's been a very good year. I'd like to indulge in a few more kisses, if you're game."

She was. But she'd never approached kissing so casually before. Not with Damon. Not with Kyle. "What if I want to stay for Christmas, but I'm not sure about…us?"

The word *us* sounded funny coming from her lips.

"I want you and Liam to stay no matter what you decide about you and me. Don't answer right now. Think about it."

Grace had a feeling all she would be doing was thinking about it. Imagining it. Craving it. "I will. Thanks."

"Come on. I want to show you something." Bill grabbed her hand and pulled her forward. "Welton Wines & Chocolates is up ahead."

The change of topic brought welcome relief. "The name sounds delicious."

"Christian makes the wines. His cousin Owen is a chocolatier."

"Sounds like two people you want to have as friends."

"Want to go in?" Bill asked.

That sounded better than debating his offer. "I'd rather not miss out on two of my favorite things. But first we should see if your mother minds staying with Liam a little longer."

"No worries. She sent me a text saying not to come home. They're decorating sugar cookies."

Grace's throat clogged with emotion. Her parents had returned his birth notice, unread. Damon's parents had chosen not to be a part of Liam's life. Anger, then grief, had severed the ties completely. Her son had never decorated Christmas cookies with a doting grandmother, had no idea what that would be like. Not until today. The Paulson family's kindness overwhelmed Grace. "I don't want to take advantage of your mom."

"My mom's loving this," Bill said. "She gets lonely, especially when I'm not around. I call and text when I'm working, or if I'm not planning to see her."

"Thoughtful of you."

"I'd like to think so, but she's not happy with me. Chewed me out the other night in the brewpub."

"Why?"

"My mom has strong opinions about my behavior. Especially with women."

"I'm sure that can be a pain, but there are worse things. My parents only cared about me when I did what they wanted."

Bill gave the boardwalk a scuffing kick. "I still can't believe they won't see you."

Resignation fought with loss. She shrugged.

He huffed out a grunt that sounded like "their loss." Then he smiled, making her feel warmer inside. "After hearing about your parents, I shouldn't complain about my dad. He's great at what he does, which is why he's in such high demand far away from us. It's like having a part-time dad. There but kind of not."

Grace nodded. "Sometimes you just have to look at what you have, not what you lost. If you're like your dad in any way, he must be an okay guy. And your mom…she wants to do whatever she can for you. You're lucky to have so many people who love you."

Bill was quiet, his head bobbing slightly, before he looked at her thoughtfully. "You're a kind woman, Grace. My dad will like you. I hope he makes it home for Christmas this year so you can meet him. And I appreciate what my mom does. I am lucky, but I wish she had others to mother hen."

"Your mom likes being with Liam. Maybe you could find other kids for her to spend time with and help."

"Great idea." Bill opened the door. A bell jingled. A smile spread across his face. "Liam would like this place."

"He'd like the bell." The aromas of chocolate and wine filled the air. "And the chocolate."

Bill's eyes twinkled, like Santa here to make her Christmas wishes come true. "What do you like?"

You. Strike that. "Dark and red."

"Bill, Grace." Leanne waved from a back table where she sat with two women. "Come join us."

Grace followed Bill past the display of handmade chocolates on one side and a wine bar on the other to an area of café tables.

Leanne rose. "Grace Wilcox, I want you to meet Zoe Hughes and Carly Porter. Two of my closest friends."

"Nice to meet you." Zoe Hughes was a beautiful woman with long, shiny brown hair, designer clothes and a large baby bump. "I'd stand, but my back has been killing me all day. I think this kid will be our first and last. Hard to believe I still have more than three months to go before this little one arrives."

Grace smiled. "I remember that feeling. Enjoy the peace and quiet while you can."

Carly nodded, her blond ponytail bouncing. A stylish and very pretty woman, she wore a purple sweater with a colorful scarf artfully tied. "Maybe when they go to college it'll happen again."

"Let's not go there." Zoe touched her round belly. "I can't even imagine the terrible twos."

"Don't," Grace and Carly said at the same time.

Leanne shivered. "I'll stick to babysitting."

Grace noticed they were gift wrapping rectangular boxes in red foil paper, white satin ribbon and a sprig of holly. "Getting ready for the holidays?"

"My wedding," Leanne said. "My friend Sarah came up with the idea for these favor boxes. I thought I had everything finished, until she asked me to send her a pic of them wrapped."

"So we're wrapping," Carly said.

Zoe held up a roll of ribbon. "And decorating."

Leanne looked at Bill. "We could use help."

He shook his head. "I'm all thumbs when it comes to gift wrapping."

Grace recalled the present under his Christmas tree, a total mess of crinkled paper and too much tape. "This I can confirm."

Everyone looked at her.

She bit her lip. "I, um, have seen his efforts."

"She's right," Bill agreed. "I suck at wrapping."

"We'll give you a pass this time." Leanne studied him. "I thought you'd be skiing, even though it's probably a whiteout up there by now."

He shrugged. "Had a few things to do."

She raised a brow. "Your mom does everything for you."

The woman's tone made Bill sound like a mama's boy. Grace felt a strong urge to come to his defense. "Bill took me to look at cars and trucks. Mine's in the garage."

The three women exchanged curious glances.

Uh-oh. Grace had the feeling she'd shared too much.

Leanne waved her hand. "Make yourself useful, Paulson. Help Owen load the cases of wine for the reception."

"Aye, aye, Captain." He gave a mock salute. "I trust you'll entertain Grace."

"Hell, no," Leanne said. "I'm going to put her to work."

Honored to be included, she sat. "I'm happy to help."

"Be back soon." Bill walked toward the back of the shop.

Picking up a pair of scissors and a roll of wrapping paper, Grace felt his attention on her. She looked up.

He was glancing back over his shoulder. "Send someone to get me if you need anything."

She nodded.

"So you're staying with Bill?" Carly asked.

"Yes." Grace cut wrapping paper to fit the favor box. "He's been so kind. The answer to our prayers."

A strange tension settled over the table, different from last night.

Zoe looked at Leanne, then back at Carly. "Bill's a great guy."

"He'd do anything to help anybody," Carly agreed.

"True, but let's cut to the chase. You're new in town so we thought you should know." Leanne gave Grace a sympathetic look. "Bill's a player."

Grace cut wrapping paper off one end of the box. She clutched the scissors too hard and the foil ripped. "I know."

The other women looked at her with confused expressions.

"How do you know?" Leanne asked.

Grace didn't understand why Bill's friends were warning her about him, as if she was blind. Part of her was offended.

But another part appreciated their concern. She'd left behind a network of support at Fort Benning, aka the Wives Club. She taped the wrapping paper. "Bill told me he's happy being single and doesn't plan on settling down anytime soon. His mom said something about the number of women he brings home. I've always been good at math. It wasn't difficult to add things together."

"That's good you figured it out." Leanne rubbed her face. "Bill's great with women. Just look at how well he treats his mom."

Carly leaned toward Grace. "He's a total catch. That's part of the problem. Women want him."

Zoe nodded. "But he backs off before any real commitment can happen."

"He backs off before they're dressed," Leanne said.

Grace tied a white ribbon around the wrapped present, then she pulled the ends so tight the holly's stem bent.

She reminded herself she shouldn't be angry. These women were trying to help her, protect her heart, even if their methods were too blunt. "Just so you know, Bill has been a complete gentleman. When he had to examine me for injuries, he made me feel safe by making sure I knew exactly what he was doing. He treats my son like a little prince."

Carly creased the ends of the wrapping paper. "Bill's always been a sweetheart."

"Except for the incident with Thad at the brewpub, I couldn't ask for a more gracious host." Grace tore off a piece of tape and handed it to Carly. "He invited me to spend Christmas in Hood Hamlet."

"Nothing beats this town for the holidays," Zoe said. "My family is flying in to celebrate with us."

Leanne's gaze didn't soften as expected. Her milk-chocolate eyes darkened to the color of 86% cacao. "Have you agreed to spend Christmas here, Grace?"

"Yes, I have."

Leanne tugged on one of her braids, her lips pressed tightly together.

That was when Grace knew. This was as much about protecting Bill's heart as hers. "Are you trying to warn me about Bill, or make sure I don't end up hurting him?"

A sheepish expression crossed Leanne's face. "I'm sorry. It's just that the Bill you've described isn't typical. He's my best friend, but the way he acts around you is…different."

Zoe placed a finished package into a box. "My husband predicts that when Bill falls, he'll fall hard."

"And that would be the end of Paulson as we know him, according to *my* husband," Carly added.

Grace's insides twisted. She scooted back in her chair, disconcerted. "There's not going to be any falling for anybody, trust me. Bill is great, but if you had to guess the type of woman he'd fall for I'm sure it would be a snow bunny." Looking around the table, she saw the three women hiding their smiles. "As for me, I'm done with heroes. So we're good. No worries about anyone getting crushed. He's a friend, someone I'm happy I met. End of story."

In the alley behind the shop, Bill handed a case of wine bottles to Christian's cousin, Owen Slayter, who stood inside the delivery truck. Bill glanced at the back door of Welton Wines & Chocolates, wondering how Grace was doing.

He had no doubt his friends would make her feel welcome, but the women would be peppering her with questions. He didn't want anyone saying something that hurt Grace, even unintentionally.

Maybe he shouldn't have left her alone. But he didn't want to leave Owen to deal with loading the wine on his own.

Bill picked up another box. "This is going to be some reception."

"If you think there's going to be a lot of wine, you're right. But wait until you see the chocolates. My best creations yet."

"Leanne loves chocolate."

"Anything for my new cousin-in-law." Owen took the box from Bill and stacked it with the others. "I hear you have a houseguest."

"Two."

"A kid doesn't count."

Bill pictured Liam's hair standing straight up when he got out of bed. His impish grin when something intrigued him. His impromptu hugs, full of warmth when least expected. "This one does."

"I didn't know you liked kids."

"I love kids." Especially Liam.

"Riley Hansen said the mom is pretty."

"She is, if you like fresh-faced, natural types."

"My only type is someone new in Hood Hamlet. Other than the tourists and snow bunnies, it's slim pickings."

"There are a few available women you can date."

"The key word is *few*." Owen stared off into the distance. "Christian got lucky with Leanne."

Christian might be younger, but he was strong enough to keep up with Leanne, on the mountain or off it. That was the kind of man she needed. "I'd agree with you there."

"You're the last of your crew who's unattached. When are you going to find yourself a wife?" Owen asked with an almost straight face.

An image of Grace flashed in Bill's mind. Not her smiling face, but a kiss-him-until-he-needs-a-cold-shower one.

"Who needs a wife when you can have an unlimited number of girlfriends?" He'd spoken those words before. This time they tasted sour. He didn't want to analyze why. "Are you and Christian still looking for someone to do your books?"

"We are. Part-time. In the New Year."

Bill thought about Grace. "I know someone with an accounting degree. Might be interested."

"Have them call or stop by after Christmas."

If she had a job here, she wouldn't need to go to Astoria except to sightsee. "Have your best man speech ready?"

"It's gonna go viral." Owen placed another case in the truck. "We're talking the sentimentality of a Hallmark card, humor of a stand-up comic and anecdotes of a bestselling memoir."

"You haven't started."

"No. I have two more days. Plenty of time to come up with something."

Bill's cell phone buzzed. He pulled it out, then read the text. Adrenaline pulsed through him. "Mission call out."

Swearing, Owen looked down at the leg he'd broken a little over a year ago. His injury had forced him and Christian to hunker down in a snow cave until OMSAR could reach them.

Bill tucked his phone in his pocket. "Sorry to leave you with all these boxes, but I have to go."

"No worries. I've got this." Owen's gaze met his. "Stay safe."

"Always."

Inside the shop, Bill approached Grace and the others. The women were wrapping and smiling and chatting. More than three quarters of the boxes had been done. "You've been productive."

"Grace wrapped over half of these," Leanne said. "She's amazing."

"Yes, she is." A warm sensation flowed through him. "We need to go. I have an hour to get my gear together and head to a briefing. Two climbers are lost."

Grace stood, grabbing her purse. "I'm ready."

"I didn't hear a text come in." Leanne fished her cell phone from her purse. "Yep. There's a call out."

Carly's face paled, whiter than snow. She gripped the edge of the table. "You can't go, Leanne."

"Of course I'm going." Leanne stood. "We need to put this stuff away."

Carly's lips trembled. Fear filled her eyes. "Bill…"

He knew exactly what Carly was thinking. Rather, who she was thinking about—her brother, Nick, and her fiancé, Iain. They'd died climbing two days before she was supposed to get married on Christmas Eve.

Bill touched Leanne's shoulder. "Sit. Finish the favors."

"Cut the crap, Paulson." Flames flickered in her eyes. "I have to go."

His gaze locked on hers. She wasn't going to like this, but he didn't care. "You may be the bride, but it's not a hundred percent about you. Stay here with Carly and Zoe."

A range of emotion flickered across Leanne's face. She scowled.

No way in hell was she going up the mountain two days before her wedding. "What would Nick say?" Bill asked her.

Leanne's eyes narrowed to slits. "Not fair."

His gaze didn't waver. He hated playing the Nick card, but she'd left him no choice. "I'm right."

Leanne pursed her lips. "Who knows what the mission is?"

Bill wasn't going to be swayed. "Doesn't matter."

"Christmas magic—"

"Didn't save my brother or fiancé," Carly interrupted with a firm voice. "I'm not superstitious, Leanne. But the timing is too similar. You do more than your share. Sit this one out."

Zoe touched Carly's hand. The two women had spent long hours, sometimes days, waiting for their husbands to return home from rescue missions. That bond was something Leanne wouldn't understand, since she was always out with the unit.

But Grace got it. Understanding and compassion shone in the depths of her eyes. She placed her arm around Carly's shoulder, proving what a special woman Grace Wilcox was, to comfort someone she'd just met.

Leanne didn't say a word.

She didn't have to.

Bill had been her best friend since they were nine. He knew that look as well as he knew his own reflection. She was not going to sit this mission out. The more they pushed her, the harder she would fight back.

Fine. Bill knew the one person who could talk sense into Leanne. Her fiancé wasn't a member of OMSAR, but Christian was a climber, and protective of his future wife.

Bill ripped out his cell phone. "Let's see what Christian has to say about this."

Panic flashed in Leanne's eyes. "You wouldn't."

Grace pressed her lips together, as if trying not to smile.

Bill tapped his phone. "Already calling."

Leanne dived for the cell. She missed his hand by an inch.

"Too fast for you, Thomas."

Her eyes grew steely. "Hang up. This isn't a discussion I want to have with Christian. He indulges me enough with my OMSAR responsibilities. I...won't go."

Bill tapped his screen. "I'll make sure you know what's happening up there."

Leanne cursed, sat and grabbed a favor box that needed to be wrapped.

"Looks like my work is done." He motioned to Grace. "Let's go."

Carly squeezed Grace's hand. "Thanks."

Grace's smile brightened her face, taking Bill's breath away. "You're welcome."

"It was great getting to know you." Zoe rubbed her lower back. "I hope we see you again before you leave town."

Grace looked at each woman. "I'll be heading out on the twenty-sixth."

Unless she got a job here. And he would have a vacancy in one of his rental properties in January. This might work out.

She stepped toward him. "Ready?"

The mission briefing. Bill had forgotten. That had never happened before.

He followed her out the door, ignoring the jingling bell and the way her hair swayed.

Grace messed with his head. And even though he wanted her to stay in town, he'd better make sure she didn't mess with his heart.

CHAPTER TEN

BACK AT BILL'S house, Grace watched him check his pack in the living room. Her admiration for him had tripled as she'd watched him handle Leanne. His compassion for Carly, unspoken but visible, showed the caring, protective man he was.

Bill Paulson had a big heart where his friends were concerned. Too bad he wanted to have fun, not find someone to be with for the rest of his life. He preferred multiple women. Not that Grace wanted to be one—or his one and only, if he changed his mind about settling down.

She glanced out the living room window with a sense of foreboding.

Snow fell from the sky, lighter than on Sunday night and Monday morning, but she couldn't imagine anyone going out in this kind of weather, let alone up a mountain.

No one but a hero.

Like Damon.

And Bill.

Her heart cracked, a mix of grief and anxiety spilling out. She pasted on a smile, something she'd perfected during video chats with her husband. "Almost ready?"

"Yes."

He pulled a strap through a buckle. The sound of nylon against plastic ratcheted her concern.

"It didn't take long." Nerves threatened to get the best of her. She rubbed her thumb against her fingertips. She would have preferred to pace, but that might disturb Bill. "You've got this down to a science."

"I've been doing mountain rescue since I was eighteen. It's

second nature. But I recheck my gear to make sure I've got everything."

That was the most he'd said since leaving Leanne and her friends. Bill had been silent on the drive home, appearing preoccupied. When they'd arrived he'd said goodbye to his mom, put an exhausted Liam down for a nap, and then disappeared into the third bedroom, aka the gear room.

A deer outside the window snagged Grace's attention. Big, fluffy snowflakes surrounded the animal. The scene was pretty, but the snow was heavier, falling faster than sixty seconds ago.

She shivered and moved closer to the fireplace. Heat from the flames didn't take away the chill. She knew little about mountain rescue, but given the location and conditions, it sounded dangerous. "How long will the rescue take?"

"No idea, but I'm supposed to work tomorrow morning." Bill unclipped a carabiner from one loop and hooked it on another. "Depending on how the mission goes, I might not be home until Saturday. If you need anything—"

"Your mother gave me her phone number." Grace remembered the look of worry they'd exchanged before she'd left. On the way out the door, she'd told Grace to call her Susannah. "Your mom is going to stop by tomorrow. I'll—we'll—be fine."

Grace was fine now. Except for the churning in her gut, the goose bumps on her skin, the fear in her heart. She crossed her arms over her chest and squeezed tight, but didn't feel any better. She wouldn't feel better until she knew Bill was safe.

He glanced her way. "Don't let my mom get to you."

"What?"

He stood. "You seem worried."

"I am, but not about your mom." *Oh, no.* Grace cringed. She hadn't meant to let him know how she was feeling. Now wasn't the time to ask where the snow shovel was or get his opinion on her truck. She would figure those things out herself. Bill had more important things on his mind. "I mean…"

"I know what you mean, Gracie." He walked toward her, his tunnel vision focus gone. "Rescuer safety is the number one priority on any mission. No reason to worry."

"You must think I'm being silly."

He placed his hand on her shoulder. His gentle touch provided comfort and warmth, exactly what she needed. She fought the urge to lean closer to him.

Bill smiled. "Not silly. Sweet."

Don't go.

The words reverberated through her, so loudly she thought she'd spoken them.

But Bill remained smiling. Not his charming come-hither grin, or the you-know-you-want-me smile. This one was warm and sincere and affectionate. He'd looked this way at Liam, but never her. Not until now.

Grace liked that very much. She wanted to throw herself against his chest, have him wrap his strong arms around her and tell her everything would be okay.

What was going on?

Having a husband who'd deployed and trained for months at a time had taught her to be independent. Not always easy, especially as a newlywed and then a new mother, but she'd managed on her own. She'd had no choice after Damon died.

But to be feeling this way with Bill...

Her snow globe world tilted. Everything was shaken up. Turned upside down. Flooded by emotion and unshed tears.

Uh-oh. Maybe Grace had fallen for Bill a little. That would explain her worry, right?

He tapped his finger on her forehead. "Tell me what's going on inside here."

Heat rose to her cheeks. "Nothing."

"Come on."

"It's just... Watching you get ready..." Grace chewed the inside of her lip. "I didn't know when Damon was going into danger. I never knew how he prepared for a patrol or what he was thinking when he headed out. He never talked about the details, what he saw or what he did. And I couldn't ask."

"You can ask me anything. Anytime."

She looked down. "I don't want to distract you. I'm sorry if I have."

"Hey, don't be sorry. I asked about you because I wanted to know."

"Damon rarely asked. If he did, he didn't press when I wouldn't answer." She rubbed her neck, thinking about their long-distance conversations. She'd been thankful for each minute. "I never wanted him to be distracted. I wanted to make sure he came back. But he…didn't."

Bill cupped her face with his callused palm. He stroked her cheek with his thumb. "I'm coming back, Gracie."

Her worry didn't disappear, but his confidence eased some concerns. "You better."

His hand was on her face, a half smile on his. "Trust me."

Grace had trusted him more than she'd trusted anyone else in the past two and a half years. She swallowed. "I do."

His gaze lingered on her, as intimate as a caress. He lowered his mouth and kissed her softly, a kiss full of affection and promise. He lowered his hand and stepped back. "I know you haven't given me your decision, but I couldn't help myself."

She mustered every ounce of strength not to touch her lips. "Take care and stay safe."

"Always." His smile deepened. He kissed her forehead, then slung his pack onto his back. "See you soon, Gracie."

He walked out. A few moments later, he backed his pickup out of the garage.

Touching her lips, Grace watched him drive away. The truck's taillights grew smaller until they disappeared into the snow-filled air. An icky, helpless feeling threatened to swamp her. She rubbed her arms, trying to chase away another chill.

It'll be okay, babe.

Grace sure hoped so, because everything felt wrong.

"Watch out for him, Damon. Please, watch out for him."

Inside Wy'East Day Lodge, the air buzzed with anticipation. Bill sat with Rescue Team 2 leader Sean Hughes and unit members Jake Porter and Tim Moreno at one of the long, cafeteria-style tables. Following the briefing with Sheriff Deputy Will Townsend, the four had been assigned on a team together. Like old times. Like when they went looking for…

Nick and Iain.

Bill downed the rest of his coffee. The liquid tasted like lukewarm sludge. He'd rather have a cup of the French roast Grace had brewed this morning.

Grace.

The thought of her brought a smile to his face. He hoped she wasn't still worrying about him.

I'm coming back, Gracie.

Damn straight he was. He had to make sure Liam got his white Christmas. Bill wanted to make sure Grace was…okay. And a few more kisses wouldn't suck.

Sean Hughes held a printout with the weather report. "Any questions on what we're doing?"

"Ride the snowcat, climb up, locate the two yahoos—I mean subjects—who failed to mark way points on their GPS going up to the summit, so now can't find their way down in a whiteout, then bring them back," Moreno said. "Pretty clear-cut to me."

Bill gave Moreno a nod of approval. "You should be the one giving the briefings."

Porter picked up his cup. "Seems like building some sort of shelter to block the wind would be prudent. Are we certain the two *subjects* haven't moved?"

Sean glanced up from the weather report. "According to tweets, the subjects have not moved."

"Tweets?" Bill stared, dumbfounded. "The dudes are on Twitter, talking about being lost in a whiteout and wasting their cell phone batteries?"

"Yes, but remember they're stuck, not lost," Sean corrected. "We have the GPS coordinates of their location."

Moreno swore. "Too bad we can't let the Twitterverse talk them down."

"Not an option." Hughes pressed his lips together, not even a hint of a smile peeking through. The snowboard mogul had his game face on during rescues, but he was a casual kind of guy, who liked nothing better than to kick back with Zoe. "All we need is for them to fall."

Bill inhaled deeply. "Then it's up to us."

Porter nodded. "Let's get them down so we can go home to our lovely ladies."

An image of Grace, her hesitant smile and her concerned eyes, popped into Bill's head. He couldn't wait to get back home to her, show her everything was okay.

Moreno snickered. "Bill gets to go home to his mom."

Bill grimaced. "You're such a comic, Moreno."

"With you around, it's easy."

Sean glanced at the clock on the wall. He grabbed his pack and helmet. "Time to catch our ride."

Gathering his gear, Bill remembered how Grace had watched him get ready. Usually he had no problem pushing everything from his mind except the mission.

Not today.

He had always assumed his dad forgot about his family completely when he was away working. But maybe he'd thought about Bill and his mom back home.

Bill couldn't stop thinking about Grace. Her sweet smile, her nurturing heart, her hot kisses. She'd been worried about him, not wanting to distract him, yet curious about what he was doing. An adorable contrast.

He followed the others out of the cafeteria. "Do you tell your wives about our missions?"

Sean glanced back. "Zoe's an associate member, so she knows what we do. But she found some photos I'd taken of a body recovery...."

Porter made a face. "Not good."

"I told her morning sickness made her throw up, not the pictures." Hughes stopped by the door. The snowcat wasn't there yet. "She didn't buy it."

"Smart woman," Bill said.

Moreno toyed with his gloves. "I'd love to tell Rita what we do, but she doesn't want to know anything except when I'll be calling it quits."

Bill shook his head. "Harsh."

"Yeah," Tim admitted. "But I love her. One of these days she'll drop the hammer and force the issue. I'll have to quit going out in the field, and plant myself at base operations."

Bill's mouth gaped. "Dude."

"Hey, she's my wife. Not much else I can do if she draws the line."

Grace would be different. She'd been married to an Army Ranger, a job way more dangerous than anything Bill did with OMSAR or the fire department. She probably wouldn't mind his mountain rescue work.

What the hell?

He did not need to be thinking about marriage.

It must be Leanne's upcoming wedding on his mind.

"Carly knows what goes on," Porter said. "She climbs, and grew up with OMSAR. If she wants to know specifics, I tell her. But usually she doesn't ask."

Bill double-checked the straps on his helmet. "Thanks."

"Why do you want to know?" Sean asked.

Bill shrugged. "Something Grace said before I left."

Jake's forehead furrowed. "The woman who's staying at your house?"

He nodded.

Sean let loose several four-letter words that would make a sailor blush. "If you're taking advantage of a woman, a widow, stuck in a difficult situation—"

"Chill." Bill raised his gloved hands. "We're just…friends."

Friends who'd shared some hot kisses, but no one here needed to know that detail.

Moreno made a noise that sounded like a half laugh, half snort. "I know what you do with your so-called friends."

Sean's jaw hardened. "Keep your pants zipped with this one."

Bill laughed. "Interesting advice coming from a guy who left a trail of broken hearts until Zoe."

Porter grabbed Sean's pack and held him back. "Don't even think about it."

Hughes put his hands up. "You're right. I was that kind of guy before."

"Me, too," Jake admitted. "But once you meet that special woman, you change."

Hughes nodded. "You always say you don't want to settle down, so why do you care?"

"I don't care." Bill shouldn't have opened his big mouth. "Just making conversation."

"Good. Your reputation is worse than ours was," Moreno said. "Finding a woman to look past that won't be easy."

The snowcat lumbered toward the lodge.

Hughes opened the door. "Time to hit it, boys."

The frigid conditions smacked Bill in the face. The weather would make for a long day. If they didn't find the climbers, a longer night. But whether the two subjects were yahoos or just unlucky, they would be rescued the same as anyone else. OMSAR folks might joke or tease or argue, but that kept the mood lighter on crappy days like today.

The four of them crunched through the snow to where the snowcat rumbled, idling.

Bill loaded his gear, then climbed inside, followed by the others.

Sean Hughes squeezed in next to him. "Just giving you crap, Paulson. No hard feelings. But be careful. Women can be more beautiful and dangerous than a snow cornice."

Bill accepted the apology with a nod, but couldn't stop thinking about what his friends had said about his reputation. Regret was heavy and unexpected as the snowcat plodded up the mountain.

This was whacked. Bill shouldn't care what Grace thought of him going through women so quickly. He needed to get his head on straight. He loved everything about mountain rescue and going out in the field.

So why wasn't he focused on the mission? Why was he thinking about Grace, as if she was more important?

* * *

Hours passed. Daylight faded. Grace played with Liam, anticipating the sound of the garage door being raised. She fixed dinner, listening to the radio for updates. She put Liam to bed, wondering if she should call Bill's mom to see if she'd heard anything. He wouldn't be stepping on IEDs, or caught in a firefight, but the mountain held its own dangers with the cold temperatures, shifting snow and darkness.

Grace hate-hate-hated this icky feeling gnawing at her gut, turning her stomach into stone. Eating was difficult with no appetite. Sleeping, forget about it. Though Liam was fast asleep.

She had to do something besides sit and worry.

Grace paced the hallway, but that didn't help lessen her anxiety. She checked the news again. The two climbers had been found and brought down, but she heard nothing about the status of the rescuers. Maybe cleaning would settle her nerves. She worked on the hall bathroom, then moved to the kitchen.

She scrubbed the counter, glancing at the clock on the microwave oven. Five minutes had passed since the last time she'd looked. She'd believed time couldn't go more slowly than it had during Damon's deployments. She'd been wrong.

When he'd been downrange, she'd never known what he was doing. A blessing, she realized. She had gone about her day with Liam, thinking, praying and worrying about Damon, sure. But that was different than waiting for Bill now.

Something clicked, a noise from the far side of the dining area. She froze.

The sound came from the laundry room. The door to the garage.

Bill.

Grace released the breath she'd been holding.

Please be okay. Please be okay.

He stepped out of the laundry room. His hair was a tangled mess, in need of a wash and a comb. His face was dirty, with a streak of dried blood from a scratch on his cheek.

He'd never looked more gorgeous.

Her heart sighed. "You're home."

His tired eyes brightened. "I told you I'd be back, Gracie."

She nodded.

Bill opened his arms. "Come here."

She ran to him, threw her arms around his wide shoulders, hugged him tight and kissed him. Hard.

He tasted like salt and coffee. He smelled like a guy who'd spent the past ten hours climbing a mountain.

Grace couldn't get enough of him.

But this was more than she could take. These long hours had reminded her of how much she could bear. In her heart, she knew this was as much a goodbye kiss as it was hello. She pulled away from him.

Heroes were to be supported, honored, respected, whether on the front lines or first responders. But she couldn't love one. Not again.

He grinned. "That's what I call a homecoming. Let me shower and then we can pick up where we left off."

"Eat, shower and go to bed." She'd loved a hero once. She'd allowed his obligations for country, army and mission to come before her and their family. She'd put herself last and never said a word to him about how his priorities made her feel as a wife and mother. "You have to be exhausted."

"I'm good." Bill traced her lips with his fingertip. "Your kiss gave me new energy."

He lowered his mouth to hers.

She turned her head. "Let me heat you up dinner."

Grace headed to the kitchen. She liked Bill, appreciated his sense of humor, his kindness, his playfulness, but she had learned one thing watching him go off on his rescue mission. Her heart wasn't up for loving this particular hero.

No matter how wonderful he might be.

Bill followed her. "I'd rather taste you."

He wasn't making this easy. She removed the plate she'd made him from the fridge. "I'm happy you're home. Safe."

"I'm happy you're here. Safe."

Grace needed to make sure she remained safe. She placed the

plate in the microwave, set the timer and hit Start. "I made a decision. About you and me."

He flashed her a charming, lop-sided grin. "Wasn't the kiss your answer?"

If only it could be… She took a steadying breath. "No."

"No to the kiss being the answer."

"No is my answer."

His face fell. "I don't understand. I thought…"

His obvious disappointment splintered her heart. "I was married to one hero. I can't get involved with another."

With a tender look that threatened to do her in, he tucked a strand of hair behind her ear. "Forget about being involved. Let's stick to kissing."

His lighthearted tone made it only worse. "We… I can't."

He leaned against the counter. "I need a better explanation than 'I can't.'"

She faced him. "Damon put his service first. Family was never his priority. I knew that going in, was okay with that, but I can't get involved with another hero, even…casually."

"I'm not like Damon. Not at all." Bill brushed his hand through his hair. "I'm not proud of this, but I use the word *hero* so I can pick up girls."

As if a guy as gorgeous needed any lines. His killer smile could bring a woman to her knees. "You're still a hero. A firefighter and a mountain rescuer. You go when people need help."

"I'm doing my job. What I was trained to do."

"A hero is a hero. It's in your DNA. You put yourself at risk for others. Like Damon."

"There are a few risks, but we take precautions. It's not the same as being in combat. Damon was a patriot, one of the damn few out there willing to put his life on the line to preserve our way of life back home."

"What about when we needed him at home with us?"

"I can't tell you the number of times I thought the same thing about my dad. You made me remember something my mom told me. She said my father was working for us. That his job enabled us to stay in Hood Hamlet and live a good life." Bill held Grace's hand, his thumb stroking her skin. "You might not have felt like a priority, but did you ever think Damon was putting you first by fighting to protect you?"

"No, I never thought that. He was about honor and serving a greater good. Duty over love." Her throat tightened. She pulled her hand away. "I knew what he did was important, but I still felt neglected, like I didn't matter. Then he reenlisted. Said his Rangers needed him. When Liam and I needed him."

The words spilled from her lips. Words bottled up for years. Words she avoided because they were selfish, but not untrue. "Why can I say these things to you when I couldn't admit them to my husband?"

"Maybe you would if he was here."

"That's just it. I wouldn't. We served in the army together. We played our roles. I won't do that again."

"Then don't," Bill said matter-of-factly. "Enjoy Christmas and seven days of hot kisses with me."

The microwave timer buzzed. Grace removed the plate, grabbed a fork from the drawer and a napkin from the counter. She placed the items on the breakfast bar. "We'll stay for Christmas, but I can't…"

"Can't or won't?"

"Same difference."

"Not the same at all." He stood in front of her, his gaze intense and pointed. "I knew you were lots of things, Grace, but I never thought you'd be afraid."

She flinched. "What do you think I'm afraid of?"

"I have no idea, but I know fear when I see it."

"You don't know what you're talking about." She motioned to the plate of steaming food. "Eat."

"Thanks, but I've lost my appetite." He rubbed the back of his neck. "I'm going to bed. I'm working tomorrow, so I won't see you until Saturday."

Bill walked out of the kitchen without a glance back.

The house creaked. The wind howled. Grace shivered.

What did she have to be afraid of? She'd lost her husband.

Her truck had been totaled. Except for Liam she didn't have anything else left to lose.

Well, except maybe her heart.

Not that Bill wanted her heart, only her…kisses.

CHAPTER ELEVEN

At 8:06 Saturday morning, Bill exited the station. The cold temperature stung his lungs. His boots crunched on the parking lot's snow. His gaze shot to Hood's summit.

Heading straight for Timberline sounded like his smartest move. Physical exertion on the climb up and the rush of adrenaline skiing down would help him forget.

Forget about Grace. Forget she didn't want him. Forget the feeling of helplessness of knowing nothing he did or said would change the way she felt.

I can't.

The two words stabbed at Bill. She would never be his. Disappointment weighed heavily. So did regret. He'd said similar words to women wanting to tame and domesticate him.

I can't date exclusively. I can't make a commitment. I can't be a family man.

His own words hammered his head and his heart. His dad couldn't seem to be a family man, but did that mean Bill should accept the same fate without at least trying? Maybe he could do more if he took baby steps.

Not that Grace would care if he tried.

A hero is a hero. It's in your DNA.

Bitterness coated Bill's mouth. Most women wanted to go out with firefighters because of their jobs. But Grace made wanting to help others sound like a vice, not a virtue.

He jumped into his truck.

Bill needed to wipe her from his memory bank. There were plenty of other women who wanted to date him. Why worry about the one who didn't? One who would be leaving him behind.

He turned on his left blinker, then remembered the envelope in his pocket.

Damn, Thomas.

Leanne had stopped by the station and asked him to make a "special" delivery. He thought the gesture was, well, misguided. But she was the bride, and he would do this for her.

A few minutes later he stood on his porch, eager to dart into the house, make his delivery, then escape. He opened the door.

Grace sat on the floor in front of the fireplace. She jumped, toppling a tower of blocks in the process. Colorful pieces flew across the room.

Liam leaped to his feet and ran, dragging Peanut. "Bill…!"

He closed the door, then swooped the boy into the air. "Good morning, little dude."

Grace remained on the floor, surrounded by blocks and other toys. She wore a pair of black track pants and a U.S. Army sweatshirt. Her hair was pulled back in a ponytail, and she had no makeup on her face. But she looked…beautiful. Too bad her lips were pressed together and her forehead wrinkled.

Bill's chest muscles tightened into a thousand tiny knots. He hated the anxious expression on her face.

Liam hugged him tightly. "Peanut missed you."

"I missed Peanut, too." Bill kissed the elephant, then looked back at Grace. Like it or not, he'd missed her, too. "Good morning."

The lines around her mouth deepened. "Hey."

He handed her the envelope. "This is for you."

She opened the flap and removed an ivory card with a vellum covering. "A wedding invitation?"

"Short notice, since Leanne and Christian are saying I do this afternoon, but they want you to attend." He set Liam on his feet and motioned to the blocks on the floor. Liam picked them up. "She would have delivered the invitation herself, but she's a little busy."

Grace reread the invitation. She didn't sound upset, more… amused. "Well, she is getting married."

"You'll go?"

Her gaze met his, her expression an unsettling mixture of worry and hope. "Liam."

"They've hired babysitters, so you're covered."

"I…"

Her hesitation hooked his heart, reeling him in. Forget skiing. He didn't need to be slogging up a glacier or speeding down one. The only place he wanted to be was with Grace and Liam. "The reception is being held at the community center, which has a preschool. The kids will hang out and eat popcorn and pizza."

Liam grinned. "Pizza. Pizza."

Her son's enthusiasm didn't seem to sway Grace. Bill would try to convince her. He didn't want to leave them, but staying home wasn't an option.

"Pizza's always good." He wanted to wipe the turmoil from Grace's eyes and put a big smile on her face. "The little dude's been stuck with adults since you got to Hood Hamlet. He needs playtime with other kids."

"Kids. Kids." Liam danced in a circle, waving his arms, wiggling his hips and kicking his feet. "I want to play with kids."

"Go, have fun, let loose. Thad will be there. Carly and Zoe, too." Grace couldn't say yes to more kisses, but maybe Bill could get her to say yes to the wedding. "Leanne appreciated your help the other day. She said there's no reason for you to be sitting home on a Saturday night when they have plenty of room, food and wine. Not to mention chocolates."

Grace reread the invitation. "I don't want to intrude."

"Leanne told me if you said no I'm supposed to kidnap you and bring you, anyway."

Grace's startled gaze flew to his. "She did not."

"She did. I'll do it, so you might as well say yes."

Liam crawled under the coffee table to reach the remaining blocks.

"Leanne and Christian want me there?" The uncertainty in Grace's voice matched the doubt in her eyes.

Oh, hell. Bill wanted to hold her. Hug her. Make her know she had friends in Hood Hamlet, a community, a home.

"They do." He might not get any more kisses. In less than a

week she would be gone. But they had tonight to laugh, eat, drink and dance. One night for the two of them. And a hundred other wedding guests. "I want you to go, too. With me."

"Go, Mommy, go." Liam climbed out from under the table. "We'll have fun."

"O-kay." She didn't sound as excited as her son, but she hadn't said no. "I'm going to have to find something to wear. My dresses aren't suitable for this weather."

"Let's go shopping." The words exploded from Bill's mouth like steam blasts from a volcano. He couldn't wait to see her in a clingy, sexy dress and heels. "There's a mall down the mountain."

Grace eyed him warily. "You want to go to the mall on the Saturday before Christmas to look at dresses? Do you want them to take away your man card?"

"My man card is safe. I'm always up for an adventure."

"The mall will be crazy."

"Crazy fun," Bill countered. "Santa's Workshop is there. What's Christmas without talking to the old guy in red?"

Liam jumped across the room like a kangaroo and pointed out the window to the figure in the yard. "Santa."

Bill grinned. "The decision has been made. Grab your coats and let's go."

A high school choir belted out Christmas carols near the mall's forty-foot, decked out tree. The chorus from "All I Want for Christmas" stuck in Bill's head. All he wanted was to grab Grace and Liam by the hand, turn around and head back up the mountain.

If only Santa and his workshop could be found in an authentic ski chalet.

He hated how artificial everything looked. Overinflated, sparkly ornaments hung from the ceiling. Holiday sale notices plastered in every window and over every doorway begged for attention and customers. Automated holiday characters greeted shoppers, telling them to pick up their reward card at the mall info kiosk. Not that anyone rushing from store to store, juggling shopping bags, listened or noticed.

What had he been thinking, wanting to come here today?

He hadn't been thinking.

That was his problem.

Being around Grace short-circuited his brain.

She held Liam's hand.

Bill ran interference in front of them. If that made him "heroic," so be it. No one was going to bowl Grace and Liam over on his watch.

"Ready to bolt?" she asked.

"Nope." Bill wouldn't give her the satisfaction of being right. He touched his back pocket, where he kept his wallet. "Still there. That's a relief."

Grace's forehead creased. "What?"

"My man card." Joking might lighten his mood. He didn't go shopping at Christmastime, not unless you counted Freeman's General Store on Main Street and the gift shop at Timberline. "I thought someone might have taken it."

She beamed brighter than the shimmering snowman behind her left shoulder. "Remember, this was your idea."

"I take full responsibility for us being here. So where do you want to start?"

Liam pointed at Santa's Workshop, complete with fake snow, penguins, polar bears and North Pole sign. Inside the structure—built with unobstructed views on three sides to entice more children—the jolly old fellow sat on a huge leather chair, with a crying baby on his lap. "There's Santa."

Grace sighed. "Look at the line."

The queue of fidgeting families zigzagged between roped candy cane poles.

Coming today hadn't been Bill's best idea, but Liam was pulling Grace's arm out of its socket, trying to get closer to Kris Kringle. The least Bill could do was get them out of this crazy place quicker. "Why don't Liam and I wait in line to see Santa while you shop for a dress?"

Liam nodded like a bobble-head doll.

"You boys will do anything to get out of shopping," Grace teased.

Bill would much rather watch Grace try on dresses, preferably midthigh and strapless, with high-heeled, strappy shoes that showed off her toned legs. "I'm doing this for the little dude."

Liam pointed to himself. "That's me."

"I rarely get a chance to shop on my own." She glanced at the line, then back at her son. "Will you be good for Bill?"

Liam nodded. "Always good for big dude."

"That's true," Grace admitted. "He listens to you better than he listens to me."

Bill stood taller. "I have the magic touch when it comes to kids."

"You do with Liam," she agreed.

As if on cue, tiny fingers laced with Bill's larger ones.

A protective instinct welled up inside him. He would do anything for the kid. No questions asked.

Bill squeezed the small hand entwined with his. "Come on, Liam. Your mommy has serious shopping to do. You can figure out what you want for Christmas while we stand in line."

"I know what I want." Liam's voice sounded certain for an almost-four-year-old.

Grace combed her fingers through his hair. "What, baby?"

Liam shook his head. "I only tell Santa."

Bill would get it out of the kid. "When you finish shopping, meet us here."

She looked at the people snaking their way around Santa's Workshop. "You'll probably still be in line."

He nodded. "I'll make it fun." Somehow.

"Santa." The kid pulled on Bill's hand. "Let's go see Santa."

After a few steps, he glanced back. Grace wasn't there. "So are you going to tell me what you want for Christmas, little dude?"

"Nope."

"I thought we were buds."

"We are. But it's a secret."

Bill could honor that. To a point. He would eavesdrop when the time came. He wanted to make this the perfect white Christmas for Liam and Grace. That meant finding them each the perfect present, even if he had to make a trip here tomorrow.

The kids in front of them must not have been too greedy, because the line moved quickly. Many of the children were well behaved—careful not to mess up their party dresses or buttoned-down shirts with ties—but Bill wouldn't trade any of them for Liam. His kid was as perfect as kids came.

Not his, he corrected with a surprising regret.

"Santa's taking a break to feed the reindeer," a squat elf with a Jersey accent announced.

The kids cheered at the word *reindeer*. The adults groaned.

With Santa out of sight, kids became impatient. Parents, too. Time dragged, like when waiting for high winds to die down so the ski lifts would reopen.

Liam didn't complain. He didn't make a sound, but stood quietly with his hands at his sides and his gaze focused on Santa's empty chair.

Bill whipped out his cell phone, unlocked the screen and pulled up a game. "Play with this."

Fifteen minutes later, Santa returned, walking with a cane. The line moved again. Not quite quick as a wink, they reached the front of the line.

Liam bounced from toe to toe, bursting with a sudden excitement. "Santa."

The kid's wonder made Bill grin like a fool. If dealing with the glittery facade of Christmas at the mall was what it took to see such awe in Liam's eyes, Bill was in. "We're next."

The elf from Jersey, wearing a pointy hat, ears and shoes, greeted them. He handed Bill a sheet of paper full of portrait options and prices. "Welcome to Santa's Workshop. What photo package do you want?"

Bill glanced at the sheet, expecting to see a handful of choices, not twenty-three.

The elf hovered, the scent of onions strong on his breath.

Liam grabbed hold of Bill's hand, inching closer with each passing second.

"A7." Not the most expensive one—no key chains—but the package had the most photographs and included two poses. Bill thought Grace would like more memories to hang on her walls.

Walls in Astoria.

He rubbed his temples to chase the impending headache away. Having a key chain to keep wouldn't have been bad.

"A7," the elf yelled to another elf behind the camera. "Go up and tell Santa what you want for Christmas."

Liam released Bill's hand, marched up the two steps and climbed on Santa's lap with no hesitation.

Brave for a three-year-old who had been frightened by the elf's loud presence, but not surprising, given the strong woman raising the kid.

"Ho, ho, ho." Santa's real beard was white and neatly trimmed. His blue eyes twinkled behind a pair of wire-rimmed glasses low on the bridge of his nose. His top-of-the-line red suit had a wide black belt with a shiny gold buckle. His black boots shone, as if polished that morning. Impressive for a mall rent-a-Santa. "Tell me what you want for Christmas, young man."

Liam cupped his hands around his mouth, leaned closer and whispered into Santa's ear.

Bill stepped forward, but he still couldn't hear.

Damn. He hadn't expected the kid to be so stealthy about his Christmas list.

Santa tapped his finger against his pink cheek. "That's a big request, Liam. Are you sure that's all you want for Christmas?"

Liam nodded. "Pos-i-tive."

"I'll see what I can do." Santa handed him a candy cane, then motioned to Bill. "Join us for a picture."

Another nod from Liam.

No way would he disappoint his little dude. The package did come with two poses. "Sure thing."

Bill positioned himself next to the chair. He placed a hand on Liam's shoulder.

"Smile at the birdie," the camera elf said.

Bill did.

Flash.

The light blinded him, filling his vision with dancing spots. He blinked. Once. Twice. Okay, that was better.

"What would you like for Christmas?"

He glanced around, then looked at Santa. "Are you talking to me?"

Santa smiled, the balls of his cheeks looking rosier. "Tell me what *you* want for Christmas."

Bill looked at Liam, who was examining a robotic polar bear. "I don't want anything. I have everything I need."

Santa adjusted his glasses. "Are you sure about that?"

"I bought new skis last month. I have more climbing gear than I could use in a lifetime. If there's anything else I need, I don't know what it could be."

"Search your heart." Santa sounded like a self-help radio personality. "That's how you'll figure out not only what you want, but what you need."

"O-kay." Bill tried to humor the old guy. Maybe Santa had been a psychologist and was now retired. "Later, Santa."

He walked toward Liam, who waited patiently for him by the exit.

"Bill," Santa called.

How did the guy know his name? That was odd. Bill hadn't told him. He glanced over his shoulder.

"Don't take too long to figure it out," Santa said. "Twelve days will be over before you know it."

The Twelve Days of Christmas didn't start until the twenty-fifth. Santa must have drunk too much reindeer juice during his break.

Bill picked up Liam, who waved at Santa. "Let's pay for your pictures, then see if your mommy found a dress."

At the photo counter, Bill glanced back at the workshop. Sure enough, Santa was watching them. The guy was taking his job too seriously if he thought Bill needed Santa's one-size-fits-all advice. Time to get out of there.

Liam held on to Bill. "Santa bring me what I want."

"What is that?"

"Not telling."

Grace stood ten feet away. She held a shopping bag in one hand and waved with the other.

Bill's heart thudded. Her smile drew him toward her like a

bear to honey. She was just as sweet. Too bad he couldn't have another taste.

"How did it go?" she asked.

He handed her the white envelope containing the photographs and a CD with digital copies. "Great, except for Dr. Santa wanting to give life advice."

Grace made a face. "What?"

"Nothing." The old guy's words played over and over in Bill's head. Time to turn down the volume. "Let me guess. You found a dress."

"And shoes." Grace's face glowed. "Shopping was a real treat thanks to you."

Her words sent a burst of confidence through him. Maybe he could convince her to give him a chance.

"Treat. Treat," Liam chanted.

Grace laughed.

The bubbly sound seeped into Bill, making him feel toasty warm and a little buzzed, as if he'd downed a hot chocolate laced with a shot of peppermint schnapps. He liked the feeling. He liked how they felt like a family. "Let's hit the food court. I'm buying."

Grace touched his shoulder for a nanosecond. "You paid for the Santa pictures. I'm buying."

"S-sure." He normally would have fought a little harder, except he wanted to know why the imprint of her palm burned his shoulder.

Maybe that whacked-out Santa was onto something.

Because there might be something Bill wanted for Christmas, after all—Grace.

"You look beau-ti-ful, Mommy." Liam sat on the edge of the bed. "You're green like a Christmas tree."

She hugged her son, getting a whiff of sugar and dirt even though snow covered the ground. Must be a boy thing, or he'd been playing in Bill's gear room. "Thank you. The color of the dress reminded me of Christmas."

"I like green. But blue is my favorite color." Liam hugged his stuffed elephant. "Peanut's, too."

"Do you want to take Peanut with you tonight?"

Liam nodded. "Bill said I could."

Bill. Grace smoothed the dress, hoping he liked it. Not that his opinion mattered. Well, maybe a little.

Which was ridiculous.

This wasn't a date.

They were friends. Nothing more.

"Are you going to wear your tags?" Liam asked.

Damon's dog tags. She kept them with her wedding band and Gold Star pin. "No, I don't think they'd go with my dress."

Grace had been wearing them less and less over the past few months. She hadn't put them on once since arriving in Hood Hamlet. But she had a feeling Damon didn't mind.

As long as she was happy and safe.

She'd felt that way here until Bill's rescue mission. Now she was counting the hours, waiting for the day after Christmas to arrive so she could leave. The longer she stayed, the less safe she felt.

A knock sounded. "Ready?"

Liam jumped off the bed and opened the door. "Look at my pretty mommy."

Bill's appreciative gaze ran the length of her. "Very pretty."

Heat rushed to her cheeks. "Thanks. You look…incredible."

Smokin' hot was a better term.

She'd never been swayed by a guy all dressed up and looking fancy. But in the black tuxedo and bow tie, Bill Paulson was the most handsome man she'd ever seen.

He tugged on his collar. "I don't know why anyone would choose to wear a monkey suit."

"To look suave and debonair," she said. "If the British need another MI-6 agent, you'd be the perfect man for the job."

Bill rolled his shoulders. "I feel like a penguin."

Liam giggled. "I like penguins."

Bill waddled around the room with his arms pressed against his sides.

Grace shook her head. "When someone gives you a compliment, you're supposed to say thank you."

He stopped moving. "Thank you."

"You're welcome." Bill not only looked like the next super-spy, but he could be a groom. He was only missing his...bride.

She swallowed. Hard. "Are you a member of the wedding party?"

He adjusted his bow tie. "Groomsman and usher."

The way he fidgeted was cute. She would never have expected him to be so flustered getting dressed up. "Big wedding party?"

"Not too big. Christian's cousin Owen is the best man. His brother-in-law, Jeff, is a groomsman, along with me. Cocoa Marsh Billings is the matron of honor. She used to be Leanne's roommate. Christian's sister, Brianna, and Hannah Willingham are the bridesmaids. Hannah's three kids—Kendall, Austin and Tyler—are the flower girl and ring bearers. The fire chief is sitting in as father of the bride. He's always had a soft spot for Leanne, though he'd deny it to his grave."

The hearth-and-home aspect of Hood Hamlet was hard to ignore. "She told me she lost her family in a car accident, but found a family of friends in Hood Hamlet," Grace murmured.

"A few of us have." Bill's gaze lingered on her. "Your hair looks elegant."

"Thanks." She'd found a few accessories and bobby pins while searching through her boxes, enough to do her hair in a French twist. "I wasn't sure how to wear it when I couldn't find my flat iron. I'm sure it's in one of the boxes in the garage."

"The up-do looks good."

"I'm impressed you know what an up-do is."

"My best friend is getting married tonight. We are the only single ones left. That means I've been hearing about wedding and bride stuff for fifty-one weeks. That includes watching wedding shows."

"I'm surprised you haven't freaked out."

"Thomas provided lots of beer and food."

"That made all the difference."

"It wasn't my wedding, so I was good."

Of course he was. Bill was a confirmed bachelor. A player.

His words should make Grace feel better about not wanting to get involved temporarily. Instead she felt worse.

She looked at her shoes, a pair of sparkly, strappy heels. A total splurge. Impractical for the weather. A Christmas present to herself. She doubted women in Hood Hamlet would be wearing snow boots to the wedding, no matter the conditions.

"Nice shoes," Bill said.

She glanced up.

Mischief gleamed in his eyes. "I'm going to have to hold on to you tight so you don't slip on the sidewalk."

Liam nodded with a wise-beyond-his-years expression. "Bill never let me fall. You be fine, Mommy."

"That's right." Bill touched her son's narrow shoulder. "I'll take very good care of your mommy."

Uh-oh. Grace's tummy tingled with anticipation. The opposite reaction she should be having. Maybe she should have said no to the shoes and worn a pair of safe, bulky snow boots instead.

Leaving the vestibule and entering the church, Bill sneaked another peek at Grace. She looked stunning in the green, long-sleeved lace dress, which clung to her curves and fell almost to her knees.

Classy, elegant, sexy.

The hint of creamy skin through the lacy arms was hotter than any low neckline he'd ever seen. The slit up the back gave tantalizing glimpses of toned thighs. Much better than short hemlines that left almost nothing to the imagination.

With her hair up and light makeup on her face, he couldn't stop looking at her. Then again, his gaze strayed her way when she was wearing sweats and no makeup, too. She'd burrowed her way under his skin.

And he might not be the only one who felt that way.

He noticed men seated in the rough-hewn log pews glancing back, taking second and third looks at Grace. Thad craned his neck so badly he was going to hurt himself.

Protective instincts flared.

Bill placed his hand at the small of her back, possessively, as close to claiming Grace as his date as he dared. No one needed to know they'd come as friends.

Friends.

The word tasted sour, as if he'd gargled with vinegar to ward off a sore throat. But what could he do? Having Grace at the wedding, as his friend, was better than her sitting alone at home. Even if he might wind up playing bodyguard once the reception began.

Grace took a wedding program from a white basket. She glanced around, a look of awe on her face. "I love this church. Rustic yet lovely."

Trees with Christmas lights, poinsettias, roses and candles decorated the altar area. At the end of each pew hung boughs of pine and sprigs of holly tied together by red ribbons. Christian's grandfather was generously paying for the wedding reception. He'd suggested Timberline Lodge, but the community center held special meaning for Leanne and Christian and was their first choice of venues.

Bill and Grace reached the aisle. He extended his arm. "Bride or groom?"

"Bride."

He imagined Grace as the bride, wearing a flowing white wedding gown and a veil on her head, and holding flowers in her hands. She would walk down the carpeted aisle, like now, except he wouldn't be at her side escorting her. He would be standing at the front of the church by the altar, waiting for her to come to him.

What the…

Okay, he liked spending time with Grace and Liam. Hanging with the two of them was the closest thing to family time Bill had. But he sure as hell wasn't ready to have his own family.

No way.

Baby steps.

That meant dating.

The same woman.

More than once or twice.

Not flying off a cliff hoping the landing would be cushioned by powder.

He might not want to be like his dad, but he wasn't going to do anything stupid, either.

Especially not with Grace.

Not with Liam's white Christmas on the line.

Bill was not going to screw this up.

CHAPTER TWELVE

GRACE DIDN'T KNOW if Hood Hamlet's legendary Christmas magic existed, but something—maybe a smattering of holiday pixie dust—had turned the community center into an enchanted, romantic winter wedding land.

Votive candles surrounded the elegant red rose and pine centerpieces on white linen covered round tables. She sat at a table, the last person remaining after dinner and cake, caught up in the emotions of the surprising day.

Bill approached the table carrying two glasses of champagne. He gave her one.

Hood Hamlet's finest first responders from the sheriff's office, fire and rescue and OMSAR were in attendance. But not even the handsome bridegroom could hold a candle to Bill. Looking at him made her tummy tingle.

He sat next to her. "Enjoying yourself?"

"Immensely." She glanced around the room. Bright lights twinkled through white tulle gathered with holly and red ribbon. Star-shaped bulbs illuminated Christmas trees decorated with red hearts and white doves. The favors she'd wrapped were piled under the branches of two trees. Wedding presents surrounded the other trees. "The ceremony was touching. The reception is beautiful. Leanne and Christian are so in love."

"You like weddings."

"I haven't been to that many, but it must be wonderful to have so many family members and friends here to share their day."

The DJ invited the bride and groom to the wooden dance floor. A romantic ballad played. A spotlight shone on the happy couple.

Christian and Leanne danced, her white gown swishing with

every movement. The groom twirled his bride under a sprig of mistletoe, lowered her into a dip and kissed her.

Applause erupted.

Grace sighed.

Bill raised his glass to the beautiful couple. "A special day indeed."

"I've never had second thoughts about eloping." Grace stared at the newlyweds twirling around the dance floor. "But experiencing the community and love surrounding Leanne and Christian today is pretty awesome."

The DJ spun another tune. Couples poured onto the dance floor.

Carly and Jake Porter. Zoe and Sean Hughes. Rita and Tim Moreno. Cocoa and Rex Billings. Sarah and Cullen Gray. Hannah and Garrett Willingham. Others joined in. She couldn't keep the names straight, but the smiling couples looked so in love.

Maybe something was in the water or the fresh mountain air.

Grace sipped champagne, trying to keep her gaze from straying to Bill.

The song ended.

"I want all the single ladies out on the dance floor," the DJ, wearing a red sparkly vest and matching bow tie, announced into the microphone.

Bill placed his arm on the back of her chair. "Aren't you going up there?"

She shrugged. "I'd rather let someone who wants the bouquet to catch it."

"I don't think that's how it works."

Leanne made her way through the crowd to Grace. "You need to get out there."

"The bride has spoken," Bill murmured under his breath.

"I've only begun, Paulson." Leanne's gaze challenged his. "You'd better be out there to catch the garter or you'll pay."

The two were like brother and sister. Even bickering, their love shone through.

Leanne pulled Grace onto the dance floor. "We have one more single lady."

"No holdouts allowed," the DJ said. "It's tradition."

Kendall, a young girl around thirteen or so, and a junior bridesmaid, rubbed her hands together. Her eyes twinkled. "I love traditions. Everyone in Hood Hamlet does."

Grace didn't know what to say.

Leanne stood on the DJ's platform with Christian at her side. She turned her back to the crowd.

No big deal. All Grace had to do was stand here and smile, and pretend this wasn't the last place she wanted to be.

The DJ raised his microphone. "On the count of three. One."

Women around her raised their hands in preparation.

Grace pressed hers to her sides.

"Two." The guests joined in the countdown. "Three."

Leanne swung her arm over her head, whipping the bouquet into flight.

The flowers flew through the air.

A woman in a silky purple dress jumped. Her fingertips missed the handle by inches.

Kendall rushed forward. She overshot the distance. The bouquet soared past her.

Right toward Grace. Her heart sank. She raised her hands to protect her face.

The bouquet hit them, dead center.

Darn. Grace gripped the handle.

Leanne beamed like a blushing bride should on her wedding day. She motioned for Grace to join her on the platform.

Grace forced herself to move, her steps dragging. Her feet felt heavy, as if she were wearing weighted moon boots that kept astronauts from floating off into space. That didn't sound like such a bad fate.

Guests watched her. Bill had to be watching, too.

The DJ gave her the once-over, then a nod of approval as if she'd passed his is-she-attractive-enough test.

Heat rose up her chest toward her neck. She couldn't remember the last time she'd been the center of attention in a crowd this big. Not since high school when, as the second in her senior class, she'd given the salutatorian speech at graduation.

The last time her parents had been proud of her.

The sweet scent of the roses tickled Grace's nose, bringing her back to the present. She clutched the bouquet like a life preserver, as if a plastic handle and a few flowers could save her from this fate. Nerves threatened to overwhelm her.

"Now let's get all the single guys up here, so we can see what lucky gentleman catches the garter."

Men replaced the single women on the dance floor, including Thad and Owen. Grace caught a glimpse of familiar brown hair.

Bill.

His gaze met hers. He smiled, an understanding I-know-you-hate-this-but-hang-in-there-it'll-be-over-soon smile.

Her heart stuttered. Her knees went weak.

Holding these lovely flowers, knowing what a wedding in Hood Hamlet could be like, she imagined him standing at the altar waiting for her to walk down the aisle, slipping a ring onto her finger, kissing her after being pronounced man and wife.

Heaven help her. She was falling for him. Falling hard.

She swallowed around the diamond-engagement-ring-size lump in her throat.

She may have already fallen.

Striptease music pulsed while Christian playfully removed a lacy blue garter from Leanne's thigh. The groom turned his back to the guests.

The semicircle of single men stood waiting.

"Remember, it's only slightly contagious, guys," Dr. Cullen Gray said, his arm draped around his wife, Sarah, a volcanologist on Mount Baker.

Sean Hughes held Zoe in front of him, his hands on her bulging stomach. He laughed. "But once you're infected, there is no cure."

"You won't mind." Rex Billings toyed with his gorgeous wife's long blond hair. "You might wish you'd come across the germs sooner."

Other guests heckled the bachelors.

"Are you ready, gents?" the DJ asked. "On the count of three. One. Two. Three."

Christian turned his back to them. He shot the garter behind him. The high trajectory took the lace-trimmed fabric toward some mistletoe hanging overhead. The garter hit the leaves, dropped straight down and landed on the floor.

No one moved for a second. Maybe two.

Thad and Owen reached for the garter at the same time.

But then Bill snatched it off the ground.

People cheered. Hollered. Booed.

Bill placed the garter over his biceps and took the ribbing from friends like a good sport. His words from the night they'd met rushed back to Grace.

Most of my friends are married, but my life is good, and I'm happy. Marriage and kids can wait until those things change.

She couldn't believe he'd grabbed the garter, if that was how he felt. Granted, catching it or the bouquet didn't mean you *would* be getting married next. She sure wouldn't.

The two other men wanted the garter. Why had Bill picked it up?

For Leanne.

That would explain his actions.

"Time for another dance." The DJ started another romantic ballad. "The bride and groom will dance, and the two who caught the bouquet and garter."

Grace and Bill.

Maybe he'd picked up the garter so he could dance with her. Except…he'd danced with her already. She'd danced with Thad and Owen, too, so jealousy wouldn't have been a motive.

Bill held out his arm toward her. The smile on his face showed no regrets. "May I have this dance?"

Grace clasped his hand, liking the feel and warmth of his skin. "I believe the dance is tradition."

"You're catching on to how things work around here." The crinkles at the corner of his eyes deepened with his grin. He led her to the dance floor. "Tradition means a lot."

"Is that why you picked up the garter? Tradition?"

He glanced at the blue satin displayed proudly on his arm. "I wanted the garter because of you."

"Me?"

"You've danced with enough other guys. The rest of the night you're mine."

Mine.

"I'm staking my claim," he continued.

Grace wanted to be his. "With a garter?"

"Damn straight."

Her heart swelled with love for the man.

Love?

Oh, no. She'd fallen in love with Bill.

A man who didn't want to get married.

A man who wasn't ready to have kids.

A man who was a hero.

But this wasn't the same love she'd felt for Damon. That had been a sweet, mad rush of young love, the two of them taking on more than they'd bargained for at a young age, and making the best of things while they grew up fast. She felt a thrill and excitement with Bill, tingles and chills and heat, but something was different. They hadn't known each other long, but they felt like partners, able to talk, and support each other, rather than Grace trying to be the sole support of everything and figure things out on her own. Maybe age had matured her. Or motherhood.

Bill took her into his arms and wowed her with his fancy footwork.

They'd danced a fast song before, but she much preferred the slower tempo. "You're a great dancer."

"My mom made me take lessons." He twirled her. "If you'd rather, we can hang all over each other like teenagers and rock back and forth while I try to grind on you."

Grace laughed. "I'd rather dance like this."

"Figured as much."

The lyrics spoke about one true love and forever. Two things she'd lost in the mountains of Afghanistan. Two things she wouldn't mind rediscovering on Mount Hood. She sighed.

"What?" Bill asked.

She didn't, couldn't answer.

The sound of silverware tapping on glass—the signal for the bride and groom to kiss—grew louder and louder.

She looked at Leanne, who pointed overhead.

Grace and Bill were dancing under the mistletoe.

She bit her lip. "What do we do?"

"Kiss."

Panic spurted through her. "We're here as friends."

Grace needed to be practical about things, about life. This wasn't a perfect snow globe world. Forget fairy tales. She wouldn't live happily ever after here in Hood Hamlet, even if the fantasy called to her in her dreams. "Friends don't kiss."

Not the way she feared she would end up kissing him—hard, passionately, in front of all these people.

He shrugged. "Blame it on tradition."

"Traditions. Christmas magic." She tilted her chin. "Is there anything else I need to know about Hood Hamlet?"

"Just kiss me, Gracie."

Her heart slammed against her rib cage.

The clinking of flatware against glass continued. The growing sound matched the roar of blood through her veins.

She wanted to kiss him, more than anything.

But should she?

Kiss me, Gracie.

Bill stood with Grace in his arms, a spotlight shining on them. His heart pounded in his chest. Adrenaline flowed, as if this were the crux of a climb, sketchy with a ton of exposure, not a slow dance at a wedding surrounded by friends.

Grace's soulful, brave eyes stared into his.

A vise tightened around his heart.

She'd been through so much. He'd wanted to let her decide about the kiss, not push her into one. But making her kiss him wasn't fair. Bill made his living helping people, rescuing them when needed. That was why he'd helped Grace in the first place. He had to help her now.

He parted his lips.

Grace rose up and brushed her mouth across his.

Heaven.

The touch of her lips against his rocked his world.

Heaven on earth.

That was the only way to describe her kiss, so sweet and warm and full of Grace.

He would never be able to get enough of her kisses.

Bill tightened his hold, not wanting her to get away.

She pulled back, ending the kiss as quickly as she'd started it.

A flame burned deep in his belly. His pulse raced. His lips ached for more kisses. For more Grace.

She smiled shyly, but her darker-than-usual eyes told him she'd felt the same pleasure and desire as him.

Wedding guests clapped. Someone whistled.

Bill heard the noise, but nothing could pull his attention from Grace. She was beautiful and courageous and in his arms.

Her eyelids fluttered. "We should keep dancing."

He would rather keep kissing, but danced instead.

Pride in Grace rocketed through Bill, filling every crack and crevice inside him, ones he hadn't known existed. "Thanks for playing along with another tradition."

Her nose crinkled. "Couldn't disappoint Leanne and Christian."

Bill didn't want to disappoint Grace.

"Didn't you see Leanne giving you the evil eye?" she asked.

Bill saw only the woman in his arms. "No."

His chest tightened. Ached.

He spun Grace to a corner of the dance floor. Her head dropped back her and her laughter filled the air.

Grace didn't want to be his. Okay, he got that. But he couldn't let her walk out of his life without taking wonderful memories of her time in Hood Hamlet.

When she looked back on her days here, Bill wanted her to smile and think fondly of this town, of him. He knew exactly where to start.

Grace and Liam deserved a memorable Christmas.

With a little help, he might be able to pull off something... magical tonight.

* * *

Leaving the Community Center, Grace didn't know whether to laugh or cry. Emotions flickered through her, like a light being turned on and off by Liam.

Bill carried her tired son in one arm and held on to Grace with the other. "That was fun."

"Amazing." Someone had shoveled the sidewalk leading to the parking lot, but she was careful with her steps. "I met so many great people. I didn't have to worry about Liam all evening. We danced so much my feet hurt."

So did her heart, but she didn't want to think about that.

"Your mom is a fantastic dancer, little dude."

"Yep." Liam didn't raise his head. He stuck his thumb in his mouth.

"He knows." Grace pulled up his hood so he wouldn't catch a chill. "We've danced around the house on occasion."

Bill slanted her a glance. "I haven't seen you dancing."

"You haven't been there the entire time."

"I'll be gone more this coming week."

"The holidays?"

He nodded. "I'm switching shifts due to the holiday. I'm off my regular shift on Monday, but working Tuesday, the twenty-fourth."

His words pierced her like an icicle falling from the eaves. A direct hit to her aching heart.

Alone. She and Liam would be alone on Christmas Eve. Again.

A heavy feeling soaked through her limbs, weighing her down. She nearly stumbled, and forced herself to pick up her feet.

It shouldn't matter if they were alone. She and Liam were used to spending Christmas alone. No big deal, right? She hated that every fiber of her being was shouting that it did matter. A lot.

Because she'd imagined Christmas in Hood Hamlet to be special, dare she say…magical?

Grace cleared her dry throat. "Do people usually switch shifts during the holidays?"

"It depends." He stopped on the corner. "I should be off, but Leanne usually takes the Christmas Eve shift so guys with families can celebrate at home. I offered to do it, since she'll be on her honeymoon."

"But you have a family." The words burst out of Grace's mouth before she could stop herself. "I mean, that's a thoughtful gesture, but you have your mom and dad."

"They'll survive until I arrive. I'm off at 8:00 a.m. My dad will be jet-lagged, so the festivities never start early. Besides, this won't be a typical Christmas Day."

"Because you have houseguests. Us."

"You and Liam are going to be the best part of my Christmas." The sincerity in his voice told her he was telling the truth. "But the annual Christmas afternoon snowshoeing trip I go on has been canceled. I'm bummed about that."

She could tell from the disappointment on his face. "What happened?"

"Too many people are going to be away." He looked down Main Street, with its myriad Christmas lights. "Leanne and Christian will be in Thailand. Hannah and Garrett in Seattle. Rita and Tim at her parents' in Portland. Zoe isn't feeling up to snowshoeing, and there's no way in hell Sean will leave her on Christmas Day even though her entire family is flying in from the East Coast for the holiday. That leaves me, Carly and Jake. So they…we…decided to cancel."

Nothing seemed to bother Bill except his parents, but this had. She squeezed his arm. "Snowshoeing on Christmas means a lot to you."

"What makes you say that?"

"You haven't talked that much about one thing since I've been here."

"Guilty." He half laughed. "We stopped going after Nick and Iain died. When Carly came back to Hood Hamlet six years later, we started again. I don't want us to end up with another mega-years hiatus. Sorry."

"No need to apologize." She wanted to make him feel better. "Find other people to go on your adventure. Then hang out with your parents. We'll be waiting when you get home."

"I meant to tell you. My mother wants you and Liam to join us for dinner on Christmas Day. If you have other plans…"

Liam pulled his thumb out of his mouth. "Nana." Somehow Liam had turned Susannah into Nana. Bill's mom didn't seem to mind, and had started calling herself that when Liam was around. "I want to spend Christmas with Nana."

Frustration pricked at the back of Grace's neck. Being alone with her son on Christmas Day wasn't her first choice, but she didn't appreciate Bill bringing this up in front of Liam, getting his hopes up. She felt ambushed…trapped…forced to say yes. "No other plans."

Bill rubbed her son's head. "You'll get to go over to Nana's on Christmas."

"Yay." Liam stuck his thumb back in and closed his eyes.

"I kinda put you on the spot," Bill said to her.

Grace hadn't had to contend with someone else's input on plans in years. She crossed her arms over her chest. "Kinda?"

"I'm not good at this sort of thing."

"What thing?"

"The man and woman thing."

That must be his way of saying a relationship. She would be happy to put his mind at ease. "I'm not good at it, either. But there's nothing going on, so no worries."

In a few days she would say goodbye to the man she'd fallen in love with and this special town. Would her son remember the firefighter-mountain rescuer who came to their aid? Did she want him to remember?

The white lights on the giant tree in the center of town reminded her of stars. Wishing upon a star wouldn't help them. Even if Christmas magic existed, a relationship would never work.

Bill wasn't ready to commit to having a family.

Grace wasn't ready to commit to a man like him.

Shivering, she realized they'd walked in the opposite direction from the parking lot. "Can we go to the truck?"

"Nope," Bill said. "I have a surprise for you."

"It's cold."

"Not that cold."

"It's late."

"Nine o'clock is still early."

She rubbed her arms. "Not when you're three."

"Almost four," Bill and Liam said at the same time.

The two of them were so…

Don't go there.

Every muscle in Grace tensed. She was supposed to stay in Hood Hamlet until the twenty-sixth, but didn't know if she could last that long. Not when each moment with Bill felt so bittersweet. She couldn't leave now, could she?

Bill touched her son's nose.

Liam giggled.

No, she couldn't leave.

Not with Liam expecting to go to Nana's for Christmas dinner.

Bill nudged her. "Relax, Gracie. Trust me."

She'd relaxed. She'd trusted. She'd fallen in love.

Oh, boy. Listening to him again was the last thing Grace should do. She blew out a breath.

The condensation floated on the cold, night air.

Liam stiffened in Bill's arms. "Bells. I hear bells."

She listened and heard them, too. "Christmas magic?"

Bill pointed down Main Street. "A sleigh ride."

A sleigh with lanterns hanging off the side, drawn by a large chestnut horse, trotted in their direction.

She stared in disbelief and delight. No wonder they'd walked this way.

The sleigh pulled to a stop in front of them. The driver, wearing a black stovepipe hat and Dickens-style clothing, climbed down. He placed a step at the back of the sleigh.

Liam squirmed.

Bill set him on the ground. "Don't get too close to the horse."

The little boy stared in awe. "Wow."

Wow was right. Grace looked at Bill with a sense of wonder. She had no idea what he was doing, but a part of her was thrilled.

Bill took her hand. "Climb aboard."

She did. Liam followed, then Bill.

The bench seat was padded on the back and bottom. Comfy.

With her son between them, Bill covered them with wool blankets. "This should keep us warm on the way home."

"What about your truck?" she asked.

"Jake drove it to my house. Carly followed him."

Grace wanted to hug Bill, kiss him and tell him how she felt about him. But she didn't dare. "Thank you for going to so much trouble."

"No trouble at all."

The sleigh took them down Main Street and various side streets to see the holiday lights and decorations. They oohed and awed at the sights. Jingle bells provided the backdrop music.

Grace looked at Bill, overcome by her love for this man who would do something so special for her and Liam. She sniffled, holding back tears of joy and a few of regret. "This is so wonderful."

"Cold?" Bill asked.

"A little."

He added another blanket on top of them, placed his arm on the back of the seat and drew them toward him. "Better?"

She relished the feel of his arm around her. "Perfect."

And it was.

Tiny snowflakes fell from the sky, the final touch to an enchanted evening.

She looked back and caught a flake on her tongue.

Bill laughed. "Christmas magic."

Her gaze met his. "Who needs Christmas magic when we have you?"

Too bad tonight couldn't last...forever.

Too bad this couldn't last.

Bill kept the days leading up to Christmas full of holiday fun. Breakfast with Santa. The light display at the Portland International Raceway. Sledding at the sno-park. Making gingerbread houses with Carly, Jake and Nicole.

Skiing hadn't entered Bill's mind, even though he'd ended up with Monday off, too, due to switching shifts.

All he wanted was to spend as much time with Grace and Liam as he could. That satisfied him as much as being on the mountain, but in a different way. Bill loved Leanne like a sister and never thought he'd be closer to any other woman besides his mom. But with Grace, he'd found something more, someone who not only understood and accepted him, but also made him want to be a better man.

Each day brought the twenty-sixth closer. His collar kept tightening, but what could he do?

CHAPTER THIRTEEN

THE EARLY HOURS of Christmas Day arrived with a fresh snow-fall and a two-alarm house fire. Bill preferred busy shifts, but not like this. Fortunately, the fire was contained quickly, with no injuries or casualties.

No doubt Christmas magic at work.

Back at the station, he showered, then lay in his bunk, trying to sleep. But he couldn't stop thinking about Grace and Liam. Last night, his mother had texted him that she and his dad had taken Grace and Liam to Christmas Eve services at church and then out for dinner.

A nice gesture by his parents.

He hoped nothing had gone wrong.

Someone snored in the room next door—O'Ryan.

Bill's father had arrived yesterday, on Christmas Eve. No doubt he'd driven straight to the mall to do his Christmas shopping. But then again, several of the firefighting crew had stopped by the general store after lunch. Even Bill had picked up a couple things. Maybe he should cut his dad some slack.

Bill looked at the clock: 4:02 a.m. All he could think about was Grace.

Grace. Grace. Grace.

She was on his mind constantly.

He wanted to give her everything, not because she'd lost her husband or been through rough times, but because he wanted to see her laugh and smile and enjoy life. He didn't want her to look as if she was waiting for the next bad thing to happen. The way she'd looked when he'd answered the door eleven days ago.

But Bill didn't know how to start. Because he had no doubt he would fail.

His stomach churned. Maybe he shouldn't have eaten so many brownies for dessert.

A medical call at six o'clock woke the station.

At eight o'clock, Bill looked at the next shift like a Get Out of Jail Free card. He didn't hang around the station. He didn't want to hear who got what for Christmas. No one minded when he cut out a few minutes into the briefing. He wanted to get home and see Grace and Liam.

The kid had been so excited about Santa coming. Porter and Hughes had offered to climb on the roof last night and leave footprints and reindeer droppings. Liam must be bouncing like a ball this morning, thinking Santa had been there.

Filled with anticipation and excitement, Bill pulled into the driveway.

A crossover SUV was parked on the street in front of his house. Must be Grace's new car. Used, but with low mileage according to Thad, who had called Bill yesterday and said that Grace had reluctantly signed over the truck and taken the settlement from the insurance company. Together, Thad and Bill had come up with a way to help her.

His parents' car was parked on the street behind the SUV.

Bill quickened his pace, his boots sinking into the snow. He opened the front door.

The aromas of coffee, bacon and something baking hit him first. A Christmas carol played. Peals of laughter filled the air.

Liam.

Grace.

Sweet music to his ears.

Bill closed the door. He expected to see Liam running toward him, and a mess of torn wrapping paper, discarded bows and empty boxes.

The little dude was a no-show. All the presents were still under the tree, gifts wrapped in brightly colored paper and tied with pretty ribbons. Stockings stuffed with goodies hung from the fireplace.

He stared, dumbfounded. It was Christmas morning. He glanced at the clock: 8:07. But nothing had been opened.

Realization pummeled Bill in the gut.

They were waiting for him to get home.

He could understand Grace doing that, but Liam? Talk about sheer torture for the poor kid.

Bill stood at the doorway to the kitchen and dining area.

His mother and Grace were in the kitchen, cooking breakfast—eggs, bacon and something delicious-smelling in the oven. Both women wore aprons and chatted, but as always, Grace drew his eyes and touched his heart.

The swing of her hair and the smile on her face sucked the breath out of him. Caring and genuine and strong... She didn't need him or any man to rescue her. She was doing fine on her own.

His father sat with Liam at the dining room table, smiling, talking and building a wall with big LEGOs. His dad's hair had grayed since the last time he'd been home, in the spring. His face was tan, but his wrinkles were deeper. His eyes looked tired, but full of warmth gazing at Liam.

Bill couldn't believe his dad was playing with the little dude. His father had never spent time like that with him, but he couldn't be happier for Liam. The kid deserved all the attention and love he could get.

Affection for the little dude threatened to swamp Bill. He never knew he could care so much for a little kid and a woman.

Not just any woman.

Grace.

These four people were his family.

Bill clutched the door frame, overcome with emotion.

He remembered what the mall Santa had said.

Search your heart. That's how you'll figure out not only what you want, but what you need.

Bill had searched his heart. The answer kept coming up the same. He wanted Grace and Liam more than anything else in the world. They deserved better than him, but he needed them.

He loved Grace. He loved Liam.

Bill loved them with everything inside him. He had to make this work.

He'd learned from his dad what not to do. Don't leave your family alone. Bill had learned from years of dating what he didn't want. A night or two with blend-together women.

No one had forced him to be like his dad, and he wasn't. Not really. Bill might like adventure, but he was dependable, devoted to his mom and rooted in Hood Hamlet.

No one had forced him to date all those women. He'd stopped. He hadn't spared one glance or thought about another woman since Grace had entered his life.

But was it enough?

Santa had said something else.

Don't take too long to figure it out. Twelve days will be here before you know it.

Not the Twelve Days of Christmas.

The twelve days Grace was planning to stay in Hood Hamlet. Today was day eleven.

Hope poured through Bill. He still had time.

He had no idea how to convince a woman like Grace to take a chance on a guy like him. But he had to do something. Make promises. Kiss her. Hold her boxes in his garage hostage until she agreed to stay. He would try anything.

What was the worst thing that could happen?

She could say no. She likely would say no. Break his heart. Leave for Astoria. And he'd be miserable.

But the same thing would happen if he didn't try. If he let her go without asking her to stay, he would regret it for the rest of his life.

Come on, Christmas magic, don't let me down.

He took a deep breath, gathered his strength and mustered his courage. "Merry Christmas."

His mother greeted him with a smile. Grace, too.

Liam scampered out of his chair and flung himself against Bill's leg.

His father stood. "Good to see you, son."

Bill touched Liam's shoulder. "Welcome home, Dad."

"Give Bill a chance to say hello to his father." Grace opened the lid of the cookie jar. "You can have one of Nana's cookies."

Liam ran into the kitchen.

Bill's dad hugged him. "A lot's happened since I was here last. You're not the same kid."

Bill glanced toward the kitchen, at Grace and Liam. "Everyone has to grow up sometime."

"That's what your mother said last night." His dad smiled softly. "I always knew you'd be a much better father than I ever was to you. Maybe I'll do better being a grandpa."

Regret and insecurity filled his voice. If Bill had ever doubted his father's love, he didn't now. A lump burned in his throat. "You'll do fine. I know you did the best you could."

"It was easy to let your mom do everything. She's such a strong woman and never seemed to need me around. You're just like her." Pride gleamed in his father's eyes. "I never had to worry because I knew you were there for her when I couldn't be."

"I'll always be here. For both of you." An unfamiliar contentment settled over Bill. He looked at Liam. "Who wants to see what Santa brought?"

Best. Christmas. Ever.

Grace sat on Bill's couch, watching him and Liam play with her son's new train set. The house was a mess, but she didn't care. No one did. They could clean tomorrow.

Bill's dad handed her a mug of spiced cider. Neil Paulson looked like an older version of his son, handsome and athletic. "Enjoy, Grace."

From today on, the scent of cloves and allspice would remind her of Christmas morning and Bill. "Thanks."

His father smiled. "Children make Christmas so special."

"Yes, they do." This was the first Christmas since Damon's death that she'd enjoyed herself. The past years she'd gone through the motions for Liam's sake. She'd been waiting for the normal grief to come, but so far it hadn't.

Progress. Maybe.

Or maybe her happiness had to do with being in Hood Hamlet with Bill. Grace wished Christmas magic could make things work between them. She would allow herself the luxury of wishing and daydreaming today. Tomorrow, when she packed her bags and left for Astoria, she would have to be practical.

The train chugged around the tracks, whistle blowing.

Liam placed his stuffed animal in one of the cars. "Peanut wants to go for ride."

Grace snapped a picture.

Bill's gaze met hers, sending her pulse racing. No matter how many times she told herself not to react to him, she still did.

"You haven't opened your present from me," he said.

"I can open it now."

"It's not under the tree." Standing, he looked at his parents. "Will you watch Liam?"

"Happily." Susannah beamed, waving her hand. "Take your time. We're fine here with him."

Bill led Grace to the garage. "Close your eyes."

She did.

A door opened.

She wiggled her toes in anticipation.

He led her down a step. "You can look now."

Damon's truck minus much of the front end was tied with the biggest red ribbon she'd ever seen.

She gasped, covered her mouth with her hands. "The truck was totaled. I used the settlement for a down payment on the car."

"Thad bought the salvage rights, then sold them to me." Bill placed his hand at the small of her back and led her closer. "It still needs a lot of work, but we'll get the truck running again. Not that you need two vehicles, but I thought you might…"

His voice trailed off.

"It's the perfect gift." Tears stung her eyes at his thoughtfulness. "You have no idea."

"Anything for you, Grace."

"Thank you." She hugged him, soaking up the strength and smell of him. She didn't want to let go, but self-preservation sent her backing out of his arms. "Thank you so very much."

"I'm happy to keep the truck here," Bill offered. "So Thad can work on it."

"That would be great." And would give them a reason to keep in touch. Okay, now she was being silly.

"I was thinking you might want to forget about Astoria and stay here."

His words filled her with hope. "You want us to stay?"

"It makes the most sense," he said. "Astoria is a nice place, but you don't know anyone there. You have friends in Hood Hamlet. People who care about you and Liam."

"People."

"Me, Grace. I care. I want you and Liam to stay."

She opened her mouth to speak, but no words came out.

"Hood Hamlet is a great community. I have rental properties. You and Liam could move into one. A house with a yard. Get a dog or a cat. Or both. You won't have a view of the Pacific Ocean, but you'll have Mount Hood."

Everything he said was valid. But where did Bill and his caring for them fit in? "I love it here, but—"

"I want you to stay because I need you to stay."

Her heart pounded so loudly she was sure everyone in Hood Hamlet could hear it. "I'm touched."

"We'll make this work. I'll do whatever it takes."

He was so sweet. This was breaking her heart. "I…"

She didn't know what to say.

"You will always be first with me." His breath hitched. "I love you. I love Liam, too."

The unexpected words shot through Grace, filling her with a mix of conflicting emotions—happiness, fear, joy, regret. Knees weak, she leaned against the truck.

"I thought my life was perfect. Then you and Liam showed up on my doorstep that night, frozen and wet and hurting." The sincerity in Bill's voice bruised her heart more. "I thought I was helping you, but you and Liam were the ones helping me. I never thought I wanted a family, but thanks to you I realized what *perfect* is all about. You. Me. Liam. A family. We belong together."

She closed her eyes, afraid that if she opened them, all this—

his words, Bill himself—would vanish. "I want to believe this could work."

"Believe, Gracie."

"I wish I could." But something was holding her back. "I'm scared. You were right about me. I'm afraid."

"That makes two of us, because you scare the hell out of me, Gracie."

The door to the kitchen swung open suddenly. "Get in here," Neil all but shouted.

Bill's gaze met hers.

"Liam," they said at the same time.

Bill grabbed her hand, and they ran to the living room.

Liam sat by the tree with two stacks of ripped pieces of wrapping paper.

Seeing her son brought a wave of relief. She'd thought something had happened to him. "What's going on, baby?"

He raised his chin. "Time for more presents."

"We'll continue our talk later," Bill said to her, then joined him on the floor. "What are these?"

Liam picked up the first pile of wrapping scraps. "This one is for Mommy."

"How sweet." She'd never gotten a present from him. This was the first Christmas in years she'd had packages with her name on the tag that she hadn't purchased. "I wonder what it could be?"

"Open it, Mommy."

Grace unwrapped the gift, pulling off scrap after scrap of paper until she came across the back of an envelope. She turned it over. The word *Free* was scribbled in the corner where a stamp would go. Her name and address in Columbus and an APO AE address were written, too. She knew the handwriting as well as her own.

Damon's.

Her heart lurched. Her hand trembled.

Bill grabbed hold of her. "Grace."

"You're so pale, dear," Susannah said.

Neil held out the throw from the couch. "Would you like a blanket?"

She looked at her son. "Liam…"

He smiled. "Read it, Mommy."

Her fingers shook as she unsealed the envelope. She removed a familiar looking sheet of paper. She'd sent Damon the stationery in her last care package. She unfolded the letter and read the date aloud.

Her world exploded. Or maybe it was her heart. All she knew was this, whatever this was, had been written right before Damon had been killed.

Her vision blurred. She lowered the letter. "I—I can't."

"I will." Holding her with one arm, Bill took the paper and read:

"Dear Grace,

"Thanks for the care package. Once again you prove to be the best army wife ever. You always know what to send me. The other night you sounded sad. I know it's hard to be apart. You tell me to stay safe, and I'm trying. I want to come back to you and our son more than anything in the world.

"But what I'm doing over here, it's for you, babe. I know you think I love my job. I do, but not as much as I love you. Every day I spend away from you and Liam is a day I've spent protecting you. Keeping you safe. Making sure no one hurts the two people I love most. You're the reason I'm here. You and Liam.

"So always remember…it'll be okay, babe. No matter what's going on, I'm here for you. Whether I'm at home or a world away. I love you and I always will.

"Your angel downrange,

"Damon"

Liam sat with Peanut on his lap.

Bill's eyes glistened, as did his parents'. He handed Grace the letter.

She silently read Damon's handwriting. His words.

"I was so wrong. All this time I thought he'd put everything else ahead of us." But Damon hadn't. For so long she'd believed his being a Ranger was the most important thing in his life, not her. She looked at Bill. "But you were right about him. You didn't even know him, but you knew."

"Damon did what he did out of love. That's how I knew." Bill cupped her face with his hand. "Because I feel the same way about you and Liam. I'm not Damon. But I love you guys. I will do anything I can to keep you safe."

It's okay now, babe.

She could almost hear Damon's voice in her head and in her heart. The heaviness inside her lifted, replaced with a peace she hadn't thought possible.

Yes, it was okay now.

Grace wasn't afraid to love a hero. She'd been terrified of losing another and having to face that deep, dark pain again.

But now she knew.

Loving was worth the risk, the hurt, the heartache. She would rather have had five days with Damon and lost him than to never have been with him. She could acknowledge her fear and forge ahead. Bill might not come home from a shift or a mission, but she couldn't let that stop her from being with and loving an incredible man. "I love you."

"I love *you*." Bill lowered his head and kissed her, a kiss full of tenderness, warmth and love. Slowly, he pulled away, then sat next to Liam again. "So here's the deal, little dude. I want to ask your mom to marry me. We can't get married right away, since we just met and I don't have a ring. But that means you'll have to stay in Hood Hamlet. Since you're the man of the house, I wanted to ask your permission. Is it okay, Liam?"

"It's fine, Daddy."

The two hugged.

Grace covered her mouth with her hands.

Bill's parents' embraced.

Liam handed Bill a present wrapped in scraps. "This is yours."

"Thanks, little dude." He peeled away the pieces of paper. "It's a ring box."

Grace gasped. "Where did you get the presents, Liam?"

"Santa," he said without any hesitation.

Santa. Great.

Bill opened the box. "Whoa."

A beautiful diamond flashed and sparkled, as did the smaller diamonds inlaid along the gold band.

"I have a feeling it'll fit you, Grace," Susannah said.

Grace had the same feeling.

Bill handed her the box. "Nice ring."

"Gorgeous." Grace turned the box over and recognized the name imprinted in gold. She couldn't breathe. "It's from a jewelry store in Columbus. Bill…"

He nodded. "So, Liam, what did want Santa to bring you this year?"

"A daddy." Liam smiled proudly. "You."

Grace's heart melted. Now she knew why Liam wouldn't tell anybody what he wanted for Christmas.

"That's awesome. You got what you wanted," Bill said. "But where did the letter and ring come from?"

Liam bounced Peanut. "I told you. Santa."

Grace joined them on the floor. "Santa gave them to you?"

"He helped me find them," Liam said.

"When?" she asked.

"Last night. I get up. You sleep."

Bill had told her about his friends coming over to make Christmas Eve more real for Liam. "I did hear something on the roof," she said.

"Santa come down the chimney," Liam said. "Angel says to go to truck. We find these."

Grace was afraid to ask. "Angel?"

Liam nodded. "Santa needed help. Angel help. I help, too."

She couldn't think straight. Letters and a diamond ring didn't magically appear. "Can you show us where you found them?"

In the garage, Liam pointed to a latched cubby in the backseat of the truck. "Ring was in here."

Oh, Damon. Grace took deep breaths so she wouldn't lose it. He would have returned from Afghanistan in time for their anniversary. Was the ring supposed to be her present? "Damon must have hidden the ring so he could give it to me when he returned home."

"What about the letter?" Bill asked.

Liam pulled a small rectangular box from under the backseat. "The letter was in here."

"I've never seen that before." She opened the lid. Letters and postcards she'd sent Damon during his last deployment were stuffed inside. A few blank envelopes and folded pieces of paper were on top—the same stationery he'd used to write her letter. "This must have fallen out of his things that were returned to me."

"Peanut hungry," Liam announced.

Susannah took his hand. "Nana will get you something to eat. And Papa will help."

The three returned to the house.

Grace waited for the door to close. "I keep trying to figure out how this could have happened."

"Maybe Liam found the items on his own," Bill suggested. "He's spent enough time in the backseat."

"That seems like the most logical explanation. When did the truck arrive?"

"Late last night. Hughes and Porter helped Thad before they went onto the roof."

"I heard them." Grace smiled, thinking about his friends pretending to be Santa. "The jingle bells were a nice touch. It sounded like Santa was coming down the chimney."

Bill's forehead wrinkled. "They didn't have jingle bells or do anything with the chimney."

"But—"

"If it wasn't them…"

Then it was someone else. Santa. And an angel.

She looked at the box of letters in her hand and the ring box in Bill's. "No way."

"What other explanation is there except for Christmas magic?"

The emotion in his voice brought tears to Grace's eyes. "You really think Santa and an angel and Christmas magic played a part in this? Not Liam?"

"Why not?" Bill tucked Grace's hair behind her ears. "This is Hood Hamlet. Anything can happen in December."

She took a deep breath. "I don't know."

"Sometimes you *don't* know. You can't always be certain. You have to take a leap of faith and just believe." He caressed her face. "Can you believe?"

"I want to."

"That's good enough for me." He handed her a jacket with the word *Rescue* printed on the sleeve. "Put this on."

"Why?"

He pressed the garage door button. "I don't want you to be cold."

Taking her hand, he led her out of the garage to the Santa statue in the front yard. "This seems like the perfect spot."

Snow fell from the sky, landing on their hair and shoulders. Grace felt as if she were standing inside a snow globe. "For what?"

"We haven't known each other long, but I have Liam's permission. And I want yours." Bill dropped down on one knee. "I love you, Grace Wilcox. Will you marry me?"

Grace wasn't sure what had happened here in the early hours of Christmas morning. She wasn't sure she wanted to know. But she couldn't mistake the joy and love overflowing from her heart. "Yes, I'll marry you."

Bill stood up and brushed his lips over hers. "Forever, Gracie."

Forget being inside a picture-perfect snow globe. Real life—real love—was so much better. She stared up at her hero, at her future. "Forever."

* * * * *

"All right. What's the plan?"

"A night off. With me. You put on your best party dress, let me take you out to dinner. You talk about yourself, not the things you're supposed to be doing. You let me take responsibility for showing you a good time. You relax. We have a nightcap in my suite, then you get a good night's sleep."

"In my own room?" Luce stamped down on the corner of her mind that was happily imagining what might happen if they were both in his room.

Ben's smile grew a little wolfish. "Well now, that's up to you."

"Really," Luce said, flatly.

"Of course." Ben looked mildly offended. "I'm not saying I won't give it my best shot. You're a beautiful woman, and I enjoy the company of beautiful women. But at the end of the night, you get the choice of my bed or the spare room. Either way you have a bed for the night."

Luce found her gaze caught on his. He thought she was beautiful? Ben Hampton actually wanted her. Sober, all grown up, not obviously crazy…and he wanted her. She could have dinner with him, flirt, kiss…more. All she had to do was say yes.

STRANDED WITH THE TYCOON

BY
SOPHIE PEMBROKE

MILLS & BOON

First published in Great Britain 2013
by Mills & Boon, an imprint of Harlequin (UK) Limited,
Eton House, 18-24 Paradise Road, Richmond, Surrey TW9 1SR

© Sophie Pembroke 2013

ISBN: 978 0 263 90156 6

23-1113

Harlequin (UK) policy is to use papers that are natural, renewable and recyclable products and made from wood grown in sustainable forests. The logging and manufacturing processes conform to the legal environmental regulations of the country of origin.

Printed and bound in Spain
by Blackprint CPI, Barcelona

Sophie Pembroke has been dreaming, reading and writing romance for years—ever since she first read *The Far Pavilions* under her desk in Chemistry class. She later stayed up all night devouring Mills & Boon® books as part of her English degree at Lancaster University, and promptly gave up any pretext of enjoying tragic novels. After all, what's the point of a book without a happy ending?

She loves to set her novels in the places where she has lived—from the wilds of the Welsh mountains to the genteel humour of an English country village, or the heat and tension of a London summer. She also has a tendency to make her characters kiss in castles.

Currently Sophie makes her home in Hertfordshire, with her scientist husband (who still shakes his head at the reading-in-Chemistry thing) and their four-year-old *Alice-in-Wonderland*-obsessed daughter. She writes her love stories in the study she begrudgingly shares with her husband, while drinking too much tea and eating home-made cakes. Or, when things are looking very bad for her heroes and heroines, white wine and dark chocolate.

Sophie keeps a blog at www.SophiePembroke.com, which should be about romance and writing but is usually about cake and castles instead.

This is Sophie Pembroke's fabulous first book for Mills & Boon!

For Holly.
I'm proud of you all the way to the moon, too.

CHAPTER ONE

LUCINDA MYLES WASN'T the sort of woman to panic, usually. But the prospect of being without a bed for the night five days before Christmas, in the midst of the coldest December the north-west of England had seen in decades, was decidedly unappealing. The city of Chester was booked solid by Christmas shoppers and by the other unfortunate academics attending the badly timed *Bringing History to the Future* conference. If the Royal Court Hotel didn't find her booking…well, she was going to need a new plan. But first she'd try dogged persistence. It had always worked for her grandfather.

'I understand that you're fully booked,' Luce said, in her most patient and forbearing voice. The one she usually saved for her brother Tom, when he was being particularly obtuse. 'But one of those room bookings should be for me. Dr Lucinda Myles.' She leant across the reception desk to try to see the girl's computer screen. 'M-Y-L-E-S.'

The blonde behind the desk angled the screen away from her. 'I'm afraid there is no booking at this hotel under that name for tonight. Or any other night, for that matter.'

Luce gritted her teeth. This was what she got for letting the conference staff take charge of her hotel booking. She really should have known better. *Take responsibility.*

Take control. Words to live by, her grandfather had always said. Shame she was the only one in the family to listen.

As if to echo the thought, her phone buzzed in her pocket. Luce sighed as she reached in to dig it out, knowing without looking that it would be Tom. 'And there are absolutely no free rooms in the hotel tonight?' she asked the blonde, figuring it was worth one more shot. 'Even the suites are booked?' She could make the university reimburse her. They wanted her here at the conference— the least they could do was give her a decent room for the night.

'Everything. Every room is booked. It's Christmas, in case you hadn't noticed. And now, if I can't be of any further assistance…' The blonde looked over Luce's shoulder.

Glancing back herself, Luce saw a growing queue of people waiting to check in. Well, they were just going to have to wait. She wasn't going to be intimidated by this fancy hotel with its marble floors, elegant golden Christmas tree, chandeliers and impatient businessmen. She'd had one hell of a day, and she was taking responsibility for making it better. 'Actually, perhaps you could check if any of the other local hotels have a free room. Since you've lost my reservation.'

'We haven't—' the blonde started, but Luce cut her off with a look. She sighed. 'I'll just check.'

While the blonde motioned to her colleague to come and assist with the check-in queue, Luce slid a finger across the touch screen of her phone to check her messages. Three texts and a voicemail. All in the last twenty minutes, while she'd been arguing with the receptionist. A light day, really.

She scrolled to the first text while the disgruntled businessman behind her checked in at the next computer. It was from Tom, of course.

*Has Mum spoken to you about Christmas Eve? Can
you do it?*

Christmas Eve? Luce frowned. That meant the voicemail was probably from her mother, changing their festive
plans for the sixth time that month.

The next text was from her sister Dolly.

*Looking forward to Xmas Eve—especially choco-
late pots!*

That didn't bode well. Christmas Day was planned and
sorted and all due for delivery from the local supermarket
on the twenty-third—apart from the turkey, which was
safely stored in her freezer. Christmas Eve, however—
that was a whole different proposition.

The final text was Tom again.

Mum says we have a go! Fantastic. See you then.

Luce sighed. Whatever Mum's new plan was, apparently it was a done deal. *'You're the responsible one, Lucinda,'* her grandfather had always said. *'The rest of them
couldn't take care of themselves for a minute out there in
the real world. You and I know that. Which is why you're
going to have to do it for them.'*

Apparently they needed looking after again. With a
Christmas Eve dinner. And chocolate puddings. Presum-
ably in addition to the three-course dinner she'd be expected to produce the following day. Perfect.

Luce clicked the phone off as the blonde came back.
The voicemail from her mother, hopefully explaining everything, could wait until Luce had a bed for the night.

'I'm sorry,' the blonde said, without a hint of apology

in her voice. 'There's some history conference in town, and with all the Christmas shoppers as well I'm afraid the local accommodation has been booked up for months.'

Of course it has, Luce wanted to say. *I'm here for the damn conference. I booked my room months ago. I've just spent all morning discussing how to bring history into the future. I deserve a room.*

But instead she clenched her jaw while she thought her way out of the problem.

'Right, then,' she said after a moment. 'I'm going to go and sit over there and try calling some places myself.' She motioned to the bar at the side of the lobby, where discreet twinkling fairy lights beckoned. This day would definitely be better with a gin and tonic. 'In the meantime, if you have any cancellations, I'd appreciate it if you'd book the room under my name.'

'Of course.' The blonde nodded, but her tone said, *You'll be lucky.*

Sighing, Luce turned away from the desk, only to find her path to a G&T barred by a broad chest in an expensive shirt. A nice chest. A wide, warm chest. The sort of chest you could bury your face in and forget about your day and let the owner of the chest solve your problems instead.

Not that she needed a man to fix her problems, of course. She was perfectly capable of doing that herself, thank you.

But it would be nice if one offered, just once.

Raising her gaze, she saw that the chest was topped by an almost unbelievably good-looking face. Dark hair brushed back from tanned skin. Golden-brown eyes that glowed above an amused mouth. A small scar marring his left eyebrow.

Hang on. That scar was familiar. She knew this man. And she should probably stop staring.

'Is there a problem with your reservation, madam?' he asked, and Luce blinked.

'Um, only that it doesn't seem to exist.' She glanced back at the reception desk to discover that the blonde, rather than assisting the next guest in the queue, was practically hanging over the counter to get in on their conversation.

'Daisy?' The man raised his scarred eyebrow at the blonde.

Luce definitely recognised that expression. But from where? A conference? A lecture? Somebody's ex? Hell, maybe even from TV? One of those reality shows about real life in a hotel? Except Luce didn't usually have time to watch such programmes. But the subconscious was a funny thing. Maybe his image had been imprinted on her brain, somehow, in eerie preparation for this moment.

'There's no reservation in her name, sir, and the hotel's fully booked tonight. I tried the usual places, of course, but everyone's booked out.'

For the first time Daisy sounded helpful and efficient. Obviously this guy was someone who mattered. Or Daisy had a huge crush on him. Or, most likely, both. After all, Luce could tell from the way he stood—feet apart, just enough to anchor him firmly to the earth—that this was a man used to the world bending around him rather than the other way round. And really, even with the scar—especially with the scar, actually—what young, healthy, straight woman wouldn't feel a certain *ping* of attraction to him?

Except Luce, of course. She had too many bigger things to worry about to waste time on attraction. Like where she was going to sleep that night. And who the hell he was.

Luce frowned. So annoying. Normally she was good at this stuff. Of course the man hadn't given any indication that he recognised *her*, so maybe she was wrong. Or just less memorable than he was.

Suddenly Luce was rather glad she couldn't put her finger on his identity. How much more embarrassing would it be to have to explain to him how he knew her while he stared at her blankly? Much better to get this whole interaction over with quickly. She'd probably figure out where she knew him from when she was on the train back to Cardiff on Thursday morning, by which time it wouldn't matter anyway.

'What about the King James Suite?' he asked.

Luce was amused to see Daisy actually blush.

'Well, I didn't think… I mean…' she stammered.

Luce, seeing her chance, jumped in. 'You thought I couldn't afford it?' she guessed. 'Firstly, you really shouldn't make such assumptions about your guests. Secondly, since you lost my reservation I'd expect that a free upgrade would be the least you could do. So I'm very interested to hear your response to the gentleman's question.'

Arms folded across her chest, just like her grandfather used to do when he was disappointed in her, Luce stared Daisy down and waited for an answer. This was it, she was sure. The moment her luck turned for the day and she got to spend the night in the best luxury the Royal Court Hotel had to offer. Never mind the gin and tonic—she was having champagne in the bathtub at this rate.

Daisy, redder and more flustered than ever, turned wide blue eyes on her boss. 'But, Mr Hampton, sir…I didn't offer her the King James Suite because *you're* staying there.'

Mr Hampton. Ben Hampton. The memory fell into place just as Daisy's words registered.

Luce winced. Apparently her day wasn't improving after all.

* * *

Ben Hampton couldn't keep from smirking when he saw his potential suite-mate roll her eyes to heaven and turn folded arms and an accusing stare on him. This was going to be fun.

Five minutes earlier he'd been about to head out for the evening when he'd seen the brunette holding up the reservations queue in the lobby. His first instinct had been to intervene, to get things moving again. Being one half of the 'sons' in the Hampton & Sons hotel chain meant that he fixed things wherever he saw them. He kept the guests happy, the staff working hard and the hotel ticking over, wherever he happened to be staying at the time. That was his job: keep things moving. Including himself. But of course staff evaluation was also important, his brother Seb would have said, and this had looked like the perfect opportunity to observe how the Royal Court's reception staff dealt with a difficult guest.

So he'd stayed back, trying not to look as if he was loitering behind the ostentatious golden Christmas tree in the lobby, and watched. He'd heard the woman give her name as Lucinda Myles and a jolt of recognition had stabbed through him. Lucinda Myles. *Luce.* They'd teased her about that, hadn't they? Such an absurd nickname for someone so uptight. Ben knew from six months of dating her university roommate that Luce Myles had been the twenty-year-old most likely to be doing extra course reading on a Friday night, while the rest of them were in the pub. And he'd been able to tell from three metres away that she was still the most tightly wound person he'd ever met.

Luce had vibrated with irritation and impatience, just as she had whenever he and the girlfriend had emerged from their bed at noon on a weekday. Ben frowned. What had her name been, anyway? The girlfriend? Molly? Mandy?

Hell, it *had* been eight years ago—even if six months was something of a relationship record for him. Was he supposed to remember the name of every girl he'd ever dated? But Luce Myles...that wholly inaccurate name had stuck with him down the years.

Casually, he'd turned his head to get a better look at her. Dark hair, clipped at the back of her head, had revealed the creamy curve of her neck down to her collarbone, shoulders, tense under her sweater. The heel of her boot had been tapping against the marble as she waited for Daisy to finish calling around for a room Ben knew wouldn't exist. She'd been knotted so tight she might have snapped at any moment, and he'd wondered why—passing acquaintance aside—he was even vaguely interested in her. Yes, he liked a woman who knew what she wanted, but usually she wanted a good time—and him. Lucinda Myles didn't look as if she'd gained any conception of what a good time was in the last decade, let alone a desire to have one.

In fact, he'd realised with a jolt, he knew exactly what she looked like. That permanent frown etched in her forehead, the frustration around her eyes—they were familiar. He'd seen them on his mother's face often enough.

But that hadn't explained his sudden interest. He'd studied her closer and eventually decided it was her clothes. Despite the 'stay away' vibes her demeanour gave out, her clothes were just begging to be touched. Straight velvet skirt in the darkest plum, a navy sweater that looked so soft it had to be cashmere. Even her sensible brown boots were suede. She certainly hadn't dressed like that at university. Ben appreciated fine fabrics, and the sight had made his fingers itch to touch them.

He'd wondered what she had on underneath.

A woman couldn't wear clothes that strokeable if she didn't have something of a sensual nature under them.

Even if she didn't know it was there yet. Maybe Lucinda Myles had an inner sensuality just begging to be let out after all these years. Ben had thought he might like to help her with that. For old times' sake.

Daisy had returned to report on the utter lack of available hotel rooms in the local area, and Luce had moved away—which simply didn't fit in with Ben's plans. So he'd stepped forward and suggested the King James Suite, which had had the added bonus of enabling him to watch Luce's face when she realised who she'd be sharing with.

Except her reaction wasn't quite what he'd been expecting.

There'd been no sign that she recognised him, for a start, which was a bit of a blow to the ego. He liked to think he was a fairly memorable guy. But then, he'd grown up in eight years. Changed just as she had. Would he have recognised her without hearing her name? Probably not. So he could forgive her that. No, the cutting part was that instead of flushing red or widening her eyes, like Daisy did, or even giving him a glimpse through her armour of tension and irritation like any other woman would have, Lucinda Myles had winced.

Winced. At the prospect of spending the night with him.

Daisy's eyes grew wider than ever and Ben decided it might be better for his reputation—and ego—if they moved this conversation elsewhere.

'Before you get entirely the wrong idea about my intentions,' he said, angling an arm behind Luce to guide her towards the bar, 'I should point out that I'm the owner of this hotel rather than an opportunistic guest. Ben Hampton, by the way.' A slow blink from Luce. Recognition? Ben pressed on anyway. 'And you should also know that the King James Suite has two very finely appointed bedrooms.'

Luce pursed her lips and eyed him speculatively before giving a sharp nod. 'Buy me a gin and tonic and you can explain exactly what you *did* mean by propositioning me in that manner while I try and find somewhere else to stay tonight.'

It wasn't entirely what he'd intended, but it would do. It would give her time to remember him, or for him to introduce himself all over again. And getting her even more tightly wound than usual would only make it more glorious when she fell apart under his touch.

CHAPTER TWO

Luce smirked at Ben Hampton's retreating back and wondered what on earth had possessed the owner of a luxury hotel like the Royal Court to offer to share his suite with a complete stranger. Unless, of course, he remembered her, too. In which case, why hadn't he just said so? She was pretty sure Ben Hampton had never suffered from the sort of crippling embarrassment that sometimes held her back even now. He certainly hadn't when he was twenty.

Ben Hampton. Of course it was. She remembered that same scarred eyebrow raised at her over the breakfast table—a subtle mocking of the fact that while he and Mandy had been out having fun she'd been in studying. Again. They'd never been friends, never had any real meaningful conversations. Not even that last night, at another of his dad's swanky hotels for Ben's twenty-first birthday. She hadn't known him and she'd never cared to. The little she'd observed of him had told her his entire personality, and from what she'd seen today he hadn't changed. He still expected the world to bend to him and women to fall at his feet, just as he always had. And she still refused to do either. They were worlds apart—maybe even more so now than they had been at university.

So why offer her his room? For old times' sake?

Not that she'd be taking him up on the offer, of course. Especially if he didn't know who she was. Still, she had no reservations about acquiring a free drink from the exchange, while she worked on finding alternative accommodation.

Pulling out her phone again, Luce saw she had another message. Great. She dialled her voicemail and prepared to decipher her mother's rambling.

'Lucinda? Are you there, darling? No? Are you sure?'

A pause while Tabitha Myles waited to see if her eldest daughter was simply pretending to be an answering machine. Listening, Luce closed her eyes and shook her head a little.

'Well, in that case, I suppose I should...maybe I should call back later? Except Tom did ask... You see, the thing is, darling, Tom's decided he should spend Christmas Day with his new girlfriend. Vanessa. Did he tell you about her? She sounds delightful. She has two children, I understand, and you know how Tom loves children... Anyway, since he won't be with us on Christmas Day we thought it might be nice to have a family dinner at the house on Christmas Eve so we can all meet Vanessa! Won't that be lovely? I think this could be a real step forward for him... after everything. And you always say the house still belongs to all of us, really. Dolly says she'll come too, as long as you're making your special chocolate puddings. I told her of course you would. And you can invite that lovely man of yours along. Been ages since we saw Dennis. Anyway, so that's that sorted. Friday evening, yes? See you then, darling. Lovely to talk to you. Bye!'

Fantastic. It was Monday afternoon and she was stuck in Chester at the conference until Thursday morning, assuming she found somewhere to stay. What the hell was she supposed to cook that was worthy of Tom's tentative first steps out of depression and into the world of love *and* went with chocolate pots for Dolly? Maybe she could amend her supermarket order if she could get online. Which just left getting the house in a state Tabitha could tolerate, explaining once again that Dennis was not her boyfriend and writing her conference report. Not to mention the completed draft she'd promised her publisher of her first book. The university did like its lecturers to publish.

'Looks like I'll be working on the train,' she muttered to herself, tugging her organiser from her bag to start a new 'To Do' list. She saved Tabitha's message and her voicemail moved swiftly onto a harried conference organiser, apologising profusely for a 'slight confusion' with the hotel booking arrangements. Luce could hear the poor girl's boss yelling in the background.

Sighing, Luce deleted the message. So, still homeless. Maybe she should call it quits and head back to Cardiff. She'd already given her lecture. And, interesting as the rest of the conference looked, it wasn't worth going without a bed for. Except her ticket was non-refundable, and the walk-up price would be astronomical. But if it meant she could just go home it might be worth it.

Her phone buzzed in her hand and Luce automatically swept a finger across the screen to open the e-mail. The cheery informality of Dennis's words set her teeth on edge from the first line.

Dr Luce! Bet you're living it up in Chester. Don't forget my summary on tomorrow's lecture, will you? D.

See? Things could be worse. Dennis could have come to Chester with her. Fortunately he was far too important and busy to spend time away from the university. That was why he sent Luce instead. Of course now she had to attend a really dull lecture on his behalf and take notes, but that was a price worth paying for his absence.

Tossing her phone onto the table, Luce scanned the bar to see where Ben had got to with her drink. She needed to formulate a plan to get through the next week, and that would definitely be easier with an icy G&T in her hand. Except it didn't look as if she'd be getting it any time soon.

At the bar, Ben Hampton had his phone clamped to his ear and was smiling at the redhead in the short skirt who'd claimed the barstool next to him. Typical. What did she expect from a man who offered to share his suite with a woman he barely knew? As if she needed further evidence that he hadn't changed since university. His sort never did. Luce remembered well enough Mandy stomping into the flat at two in the morning, more than once, wailing about how she'd caught Ben out with another woman. Remembered the one time he'd ever shown any interest in *her* at all, when Mandy hadn't been looking. Did he? she wondered. He'd been pretty drunk.

Luce narrowed her eyes as she observed him. But then he turned, leaning against the bar behind him, and raised that scarred eyebrow at Luce instead of at the redhead. A shiver ran across her shoulders and she glanced away. She really didn't have time for the sort of distractions Ben's smile promised. She had responsibilities, after all. And she knew far, far better than to get involved with men like Ben Hampton. Whatever game he was playing.

Take responsibility. Take control. She had to remember that.

Without looking up again, Luce grabbed her organiser and started planning how to get through her week.

Ben ignored his brother's voice in his ear and studied Luce instead. She was staring at her diary, where it rested on her crossed legs, and brushed an escaped strand of hair out of her eyes. Her pen was poised over the paper, but she wasn't writing anything. She looked like a woman trying to save the world one 'To Do' list at a time. His initial impression had definitely been right, even if he hadn't seen her in nearly a decade. This was a woman who needed saving from herself.

Not my responsibility, though, he reminded himself. *Not my fix this time.*

'So, what do you think?' Sebastian asked down the phone. 'Is it worth saving?'

'Definitely,' Ben answered, before realising that Seb was talking about the Royal Court Hotel, not Lucinda Myles. 'I mean, yes—I think it's worth working with.' The Royal Court was a relatively new acquisition, and Ben's job for the week was to find out how it ticked and how to make it work the Hampton & Sons way. 'You stayed here, right? Before we bought it? I mean, you must have done.'

'Dad did,' Seb said, his voice suddenly darker. 'I have his report, but…'

It was hard to ask questions about the room service and the bathroom refits when the old man was six feet under, Ben supposed. 'Right—sure. And there were concerns?'

'Perhaps.' Seb sounded exactly as their father had, whenever *he* hadn't said something that mattered. Keeping information from his youngest son because he didn't trust him to step up and do his job. To take responsibility for making things right.

Ben had hoped Seb knew him better than their father had. Apparently not.

Perhaps that was just what happened when you spent your childhood in different boarding schools. With five years between them, Ben had always been too far behind to catch up with his talented older brother. He'd always wondered what life had been like for Seb before he came along.

'Fine. I'll type up a new evaluation tonight and get it

over to you. Okay?' It wouldn't take long—especially if he could get the original report e-mailed over from head office. But work responsibilities could wait until later. First he had plans. Like finding out just how strokeable *Dr* Lucinda Myles really was under those clothes. Because *of course* she'd gone on to get her PhD. The woman was born for academia.

'That'd be great,' Seb said.

He sounded tired, and Ben could imagine him sitting behind Dad's big oak desk, rubbing a hand over his forehead. Because now it wasn't years and schools keeping them apart, it was the burden of responsibility.

Working together, especially since their father had died, had enabled Ben to get to know his brother better than ever before. They were close, he supposed, in their way. Possibly because neither of them really had anyone else.

And Seb was his brother before he was his boss. He had to remember that.

A stab of guilt at the thought made Ben ask, 'Is there anything else you need me to do?'

The pause at the other end of the line suggested that there was, but whatever it was Seb obviously didn't trust him to do it. 'Nah, don't worry about it. Enjoy your week in Chester. Take in a Roman relic or something. Or—no, you were planning on heading off to your cottage, weren't you?'

'I thought I might,' Ben said cautiously. God, after the last twelve months all he wanted was to hole up in the middle of nowhere with a good bottle of whisky, some really great music and some old movies. 'But if you need me back in the office—'

'No. You haven't had a holiday in nearly a year.' *Since before Dad died,* went unspoken. 'You deserve a break.'

Not as much as Seb did. The idea of persuading his ultra-responsible older brother to take time off was frankly laughable, but apparently Ben wasn't nearly as essential to the well-being of Hampton & Sons. Something he might as well take advantage of, he supposed. 'Well, you know where I am if you need me.'

'In bed with a hot blonde?' his brother joked, a hint of the old, relaxed Seb coming out.

Relief seeped through Ben at the sound of it. 'Brunette, hopefully.' Ben eyed Luce again. Still ignoring him. If she remembered him at all she probably felt exactly the same way about him as his father had—that he was still the same man she'd known him to be at twenty, incapable of growing up. Well, maybe he'd have a chance tonight to show her exactly what sort of man he'd grown into.

Seb's laugh lacked any real humour. 'Then I wish you luck. I'm sure you'll have her begging you for more in no time.'

'That's the plan.'

'And then you'll just have to figure out how to get rid of her when she inevitably loses her head over you.'

Quite aside from the fact that Ben found it impossible to imagine Lucinda Myles losing her head over anyone, something in Seb's words rankled.

'Hey, be fair. I'm always honest with them. They know exactly what to expect. No commitment, no strings, no future, and—'

'No more than one night together in a row,' Seb finished for him. 'I know. But they always think they'll be the one to change you.'

Ben shrugged, even though Seb couldn't see him. 'Not my responsibility. I don't do long-term.'

'Just the short-term fix.' Seb chuckled. 'Well, if that's all you want enjoy yourself. I'll see you back in London on Friday.' He hung up.

Ben put his brother's mocking out of his head. As if Seb was any better, anyway. Ben couldn't remember the last time he'd even seen him with a date.

Life was all about priorities, their father had always said. And just because Ben had never shared David Hampton's priorities when he was alive, and didn't intend to start now, that didn't make the sentiment any less valid.

His priorities weren't love and marriage. And his priority for the night certainly wasn't Seb and the business. It was Luce Myles. Grabbing two gin and tonics from the bartender, Ben was pretty sure he knew exactly how to get under her skin.

Luce's 'To Do' list was stretching to several pages by the time Ben finally returned with their drinks.

'Queue at the bar?' she asked, raising her eyebrows as he placed the glasses on the table. A girl couldn't be expected to deal with so many demands on her without a drink.

'Phone call from the office,' he countered with an apologetic smile.

She supposed that running a hotel chain did require some level of responsibility, hard though it was to imagine from Ben Hampton. On the other hand, he had described it as the 'Hampton & Sons' chain, so maybe he was just the heir apparent, running errands for Daddy, and the phone call was about him maxing out his company credit card. That would explain a lot, actually.

He folded himself into the low bucket chair, his long legs stretched out in front of him, and Luce allowed herself to be distracted from how the man made a living. A more interesting question was how did he manage to look so comfortable, so relaxed, in a chair so clearly not designed for someone of his height or size? Luce couldn't manage it, and the chair might have been made for her.

'You look like you kept yourself occupied, anyway.' He motioned at her list, and she winced.

'Busy week. Time of the year.' She started to close the cover of her organiser, but Ben's hand slipped between the pages and pushed it open again.

'Let's see what's keeping Dr Lucinda Myles so busy.'

Tugging the diary towards him, he flashed her a grin that made her middle glow a little, against her better judgement. She didn't remember him being this damn attractive. His behaviour was unacceptably intrusive, an invasion of her privacy, and her 'To Do' list was absolutely none of his business. And yet she didn't stop him. All because he had a wickedly attractive smile. Clearly she was losing her edge.

I need some time off. The thought was a familiar one, but Luce knew from past experience that nothing would come of it. Yes, some time to recharge her batteries—hell, even some time to focus on her book—would be beneficial. But when on earth would she ever find the time to make it happen?

Ben flipped through the list and gave a low whistle. 'Conference, followed by what I imagine to be a long and tedious conference report, family dinner party on Christmas Eve, Christmas Day entertaining, house repairs, cat-sitting for your neighbour, university New Year's Eve event, student evaluations, your actual day job. When were you planning on sleeping?'

'I wasn't.' Luce took a long sip of her gin and tonic. 'Especially since I still don't have a bed for the night.'

'I believe I offered you a solution to that particular problem.' Ben slammed her organiser shut, but kept his hand on it. 'In fact, after seeing your "To Do" list, I have an even better proposition.'

'So you *are* propositioning me, then?' Luce said, trying to sound accusing rather than amused. Or aroused. This was unacceptable behaviour—especially from the owner of a hotel. And she was not the sort of woman who had one-night stands in hotels just to get a bed for the night. However attractive the man. But part of her couldn't help wondering if he'd be doing this if he didn't remember her. Or, perhaps more likely, he'd never be doing this at all if he knew who she really was. *Which is it?*

Ben just smiled a lazy, seductive grin. 'Were you ever really in any doubt? Now, do you want to hear this proposition or not?'

She shouldn't. But her curious nature was what had led her into academia, into history, in the first place. She wanted to know what had happened, when and why. She couldn't help but remember all those long, dull evenings staying in to study, until Ben and Mandy stumbled into the flat, ready to tell her everything she'd missed, their eyes pitying. She needed to know what it was Ben Hampton saw in her *now* to make him waste his time trying to seduce her. 'Go on, then.'

'Take the night off.'

Luce blinked. 'That's it?'

Folding his arms behind his head, Ben smirked. 'It's elegant in its simplicity.'

'It's not possible.' Luce reached for her organiser, shaking her head. 'I need to type up my notes from today, I need to talk to my brother about this dinner, and I need to—'

'You need to slow down.' Peeling her fingers from the cover of her diary, Ben picked it up and slipped it into the pocket of his jacket.

Luce lunged across the table to try to grab it, but she was too slow. 'I need that. You can't just—'

'Trust me, it's for the best.' Luce glared at him, and

he sighed. 'Okay—tell you what. You listen to the rest of my plan, and if you honestly don't think it sounds like a good idea I'll give you your stupid planner back and you can go wander the streets of Chester looking for a hotel. All right?'

Even Luce had to admit that her options were a little limited. 'All right. What's the plan?'

'A night off. With me. You put on your best party dress, let me take you out to dinner. You talk about yourself—not the things you're supposed to be doing. You let me take responsibility for showing you a good time. You relax. We have a nightcap in my suite, and then you get a good night's sleep.'

'In my own room?' Luce stamped down on the corner of her mind that was happily imagining what might happen if they were both in *his* room.

Ben's smile grew a little wolfish. 'Well, now...that's up to you.'

'Really?' Luce said flatly.

'Of course.' Ben looked mildly offended. 'I'm not saying I won't give it my best shot. You're a beautiful woman, and I enjoy the company of beautiful women. But at the end of the night *you* get the choice of my bed or the spare room. Either way you have a bed for the night.'

Luce found her gaze caught on his. He thought she was beautiful? Ben Hampton actually wanted her? Sober, all grown-up, not obviously crazy...and he wanted her. She could have dinner with him, flirt, kiss...more. All she had to do was say yes.

She tore her gaze away.

'And tomorrow?' she asked.

Ben's smile slipped. 'Tomorrow I'm leaving town. Look, whichever way tonight goes, it's nothing sordid. Nothing to be ashamed of. We can enjoy each other's company then

go our separate ways. I'm not asking you for anything beyond tonight.'

'So romantic,' Luce muttered. She hated how unworldly
he made her feel. His matter-of-fact proposition of a one-
night stand was miles away from any date she'd been on
in the last ten years. And also the reason she couldn't give
in to it. She wanted more from a night of passion than a
kiss on the cheek at the end of it and never seeing each
other again.

'This isn't romance,' Ben said. 'It's much more fun than
that. And, either way, I bet you feel better in the morning.'

And she would. Sex aside, she'd get a stress-free evening, with no need to entertain since Ben was clearly capable of making his own fun. She could just relax and let
someone else take charge for a few hours. Could she even
do that? She wasn't sure she ever had before.

'Admit it—you're tempted.'

Ben leant across the table, that scarred eyebrow raised,
and Luce knew that she was. In more ways than one.

'By dinner,' she told him firmly. 'Nothing else.'

Ben gave her a lazy smile. 'As you like.'

It might be the worst idea she'd ever had. But at least
she'd have somewhere to sleep for the night, and the whole
week ahead would look more manageable after a relaxing
evening and a solid eight hours' rest. And maybe tomorrow morning she could tell him who she was and watch
his amused composure slip as he realised he'd tried to
seduce Loser Luce. Again. That would almost make it
worth it in itself.

I shouldn't. I have responsibilities.

But even Grandad Myles, duty and responsibility's biggest advocate, would have wanted her to take a night off
once in a while. Wouldn't he? She was stressed, overwhelmed and exhausted—and utterly useless to anybody

in such a state. A night off to regroup would enable her to better help others and get things done more efficiently. Nothing at all to do with wanting to find out what she'd been missing on all those university nights out.

Besides, hadn't she fantasised about a night in the Royal Court's best suite?

'On one condition,' she said.

Ben grinned. 'Anything.'

'I want to take advantage of your hopefully plush and expensive bathroom first.' With bubbles. And maybe champagne.

Ben's grin grew wider. 'Deal.'

'Then give me my organiser back.' She was already starting to feel a bit jittery without it. Maybe she could review her lists in the bath. Multi-tasking—that was the key to a productive life.

But Ben shook his head. 'First thing tomorrow it's all yours. Not one moment before.'

'But I need—'

'Trust me,' Ben said, taking her hand in his across the table. 'Tonight I'll be in charge of meeting all your needs.'

A red-hot flush ran across Luce's skin. Perhaps this wasn't such a good idea after all.

CHAPTER THREE

LUCE HAD NEVER seen such a magnificent bathroom.

The size of the rolltop tub almost helped her forget the sight of Ben locking her beloved crimson leather organiser in the suite's mini-safe. And the glass of champagne he'd poured her before she'd absconded to the bathroom more than made up for the way she'd blushed when he'd asked if she was sure she didn't want him to help scrub her back.

Tearing her eyes away from the bath, Luce checked the door, then turned the lock. She'd told him as clearly as she could that the only part of his offer she was interested in was dinner and the spare bed. No point giving him the wrong idea now.

Of course she wasn't entirely sure what the right idea was. Accepting an offer of a night out with a gorgeous man—whatever the terms and conditions—wasn't exactly typical Luce behaviour. She hadn't even made a pros and cons list, for a start.

But the decision was made now. She might as well make the most of it.

Turning on the taps, Luce rifled through the tiny bottles of complimentary lotions and potions, settling on something that claimed to be a 'relaxing and soothing' bath foam. Sounded perfect. After a moment's consideration she tipped the whole bottle into the running water. She was in need of all the relaxation she could get. That was the point of this whole night, wasn't it? And, since it was the only one she was likely to get for a while, she really should make the most of it.

Luce took a swig of her champagne, stripped off her clothes and climbed into the heavenly scented hot water.

Relaxation. How hard could it be?

It would be a whole lot easier, she decided after a few moments of remaining tense, if Ben Hampton wasn't waiting outside for her.

Tipping her head back against the edge of the bath, Luce tried to conjure up the image of the last time she'd seen him. After so many years of trying to forget she'd thought it would be harder to remember. But the sounds, scents, sights were all as fresh in her mind as they'd been eight years ago, at the swanky Palace Hotel, London, for Ben's twenty-first birthday party.

It had been a stupid idea to go in the first place. But Mandy had wanted someone to travel down on the train with and Ben had raised his eyebrows in surprise and said, 'Well, sure you can come. If you really want to.' And Luce *had* wanted to—just a bit. Just to see what birthdays looked like for the rich and privileged.

Much as she'd expected, it turned out. Too much champagne. Too many people laughing too loudly. Bright lights and dancing and shimmery expensive dresses. In her green cotton frock, and with her hair long and loose instead of pinned back in one of the intricate styles the other girls had seemed to favour, Luce had felt just as out of place as she'd predicted.

So she'd hidden in another room—some sort of sitting area decked out like a gentleman's library. Books never made her feel inadequate, after all. She could sit and read until Mandy was ready to head back to their tiny shared hotel room. Not a Hampton hotel, but a cheap, probably infested place three tube stops away. It had been the perfect plan—until Ben had found her.

'You've got the right idea,' he'd said, lurching into the chair next to her.

Luce, who'd already watched him down glass after glass of champagne that evening, had inched further away. 'Not enjoying your party?' she'd asked.

Ben had shrugged. 'It's a party. Hard not to enjoy a party.' His eyes had narrowed as he'd studied her. 'Although you seem to be managing it.'

Looking away, Luce had fiddled with the hem of her dress. 'It's not really my kind of party.'

'It's not really mine either,' Ben had said.

When Luce had glanced across at him he'd been staring at the door. But then his attention had jerked back to her, and a wide, not entirely believable grin had been on his face. 'It's just my dad showing off, really. There are more of his business associates here than my friends.'

'And yet you invited me?'

He'd laughed at that. 'We're friends, aren't we?'

'Not really.' They'd had nothing in common besides proximity to Mandy until that moment, right then, when Luce had felt his gaze meeting hers, connecting them—until she'd realised she was leaning forward, into him, waiting for his answer.

'We could be.'

He'd inched closer too, leaning over the arm of his chair until Luce had been able to smell the champagne on his breath.

'You're a hell of a lot of a nicer person than Mandy.'

'Mandy's my friend,' Luce had said, trying to find the energy to defend her. But all she'd been able to see was

Ben's eyes, pupils black and wide. 'Your girlfriend.' She couldn't think with him so close.

'Mandy's out there flirting with a forty-something businessman she knows will never leave his wife but might buy her some nice jewellery.'

Luce had winced. He was probably right. For a moment she'd felt her first ever pang of sympathy for Ben Hampton.

But then he'd leant in further, his hand coming up to rest against her cheek, and Luce had known she should pull away, run away, get away from Ben Hampton for good.

His lips had been soft, gentle against hers, she remembered. But only for a brief moment. One insane lapse in judgement. Before she jerked back, leaving him bent over the space where she'd been. She'd upped and run—just as she should have done the moment she'd arrived at the party and seen how much she didn't fit in.

Luce sighed and let the memory go. Much more pleasant to focus on the hot water and scented bubbles of her bath than on Ben's face as she'd turned back at the doorway. Or the humiliation she'd felt, her cheeks burning, as she'd run out, his laughter echoing in her ears, and dragged Mandy away from her businessman and back to that flea-ridden hotel.

He probably didn't remember. He'd been drunk and young and stupid. He'd certainly never have done it sober. Why else would he have laughed? The whole incident was ridiculous. Luce was a grown woman now, with bigger concerns than what Ben Hampton thought of her.

Except he was waiting outside the bathroom door, ready to take her out for dinner. And afterwards…

Luce shut her eyes and dunked her head under the water.

What the hell was she doing in there?

Ben checked his watch, then poured himself another

glass of champagne. It was coming up to three quarters of an hour since he'd heard the lock turn, and since then there had been only the occasional splash. Apparently she was taking the whole relaxing thing seriously. He should have remembered earlier how his ex-girlfriend had complained about Luce disappearing into the bathroom with her history texts and using up all the hot water on ridiculously indulgent baths. At the time he'd just found it comforting to know that the woman had some weaknesses. Now it was seriously holding up his evening.

But at least it gave him the opportunity to do some research. Unlocking the safe, he pulled out Luce's organiser again and sank into the armchair by the window to read. Really, the woman was the epitome of over-scheduled. And almost none of the things written into the tiny diary spaces in neat block capitals seemed like things she'd be doing for herself. Christmas dinners—plural—for family, attending lectures for colleagues, looking after someone else's cat… And then, on a Sunday near the end of January, the words 'BOOK DRAFT DEADLINE' in red capitals. Interesting. Definitely something to talk about over dinner.

She baffled him. That was why he wanted to know more. On the one hand, he was pretty sure he could predict her entire life story leading from university to here. On the other, however…there was something else there. Something he hadn't seen or noticed when they were younger. Something that hooked him in even if he wasn't ready to admit why. Yes, she was attractive. That on its own was nothing new. But this self-sacrificing mentality—was it a martyr complex? A bullying mother? Luce hadn't ever seemed weak, so why was she doing everything for other people?

Particularly her family, it seemed. Flicking through the pages, Ben tried to remember if he'd ever met them at university, but if he had they hadn't made much of an impression. Now he thought about it, he did remember Luce disappearing home to Cardiff every few weeks to visit them.

Obviously a sign of things to come.

Leaning back in his chair, Ben closed the organiser and tried to resist the memories pressing against his brain. But they were too strong. Another dark-haired woman, just as tired, just as self-sacrificing—until the day she broke.

'I'm sorry, Benji,' she'd said. 'Mummy has to go.'

And it didn't matter that he'd tried everything, done anything he could think of to be good enough to make her stay. He hadn't been able to fix things for her.

Maybe he could for Luce.

Laughing at himself, he sat up, shaking the memories away. Luce wasn't his mother. She wasn't tied by marriage or children. She could make her own choices far more freely. And what could he do in one night, anyway? Other than help her relax. Maybe that would be enough. Maybe all she needed was to realise that she had needs, too. And Ben was very good at assessing women's needs.

A repetitive beeping noise interrupted his thoughts, and it took him a moment to register it as a ringtone. As he looked up, his gaze caught on Luce's rich purple coat, slung across the sofa on the other side of the glass coffee table. She'd taken her suitcase and handbag into the bathroom with her—obvious paranoia in Ben's view—but he'd seen her drop her phone into her coat pocket before they left the bar.

Interesting.

He should feel guilty, he supposed, but really it was all for the woman's own good. She needed saving from herself. She needed his help.

The noise had stopped before he could retrieve the

phone from the pocket of her coat, and Ben stared at the flashing screen for a moment, wondering how one woman could have so many people needing to contact her. In addition to a missed call from her mother, her notifications screen told him straight off that she had three texts from a guy called Tom, an e-mail from a man named Dennis and another missed call from an improbably named 'Dolly'. All in the hour since they'd left the bar.

Scanning over the snippets on the screen told him all he really needed to know—every person who'd contacted her wanted something from her. Dropping the phone back into her pocket, Ben considered the evening ahead.

His plan, ill thought out to start with, had been to have a fun evening and hopefully a fun night. To show Luce a good time, then remind her who he was so they could have a laugh about it. Or *he* could, anyway. But now…he was invested.

Who *was* Lucinda Myles these days?

The last time he'd seen her must have been the night of his spectacularly disastrous twenty-first birthday party. He remembered spotting her sloping out of the hotel ballroom towards one of the drawing rooms, but after that far too much champagne had blurred the evening until the following morning and a headbangingly loud lecture from his father about appropriate behaviour and responsibility to the family reputation. Friends had helpfully filled him in on the more humorous of his antics that night, but no one had mentioned Luce.

Then the ex had broken up with him for humiliating her and 'possibly ruining her future', whatever that meant, and he'd had no reason to see Luce again. Who knew how much she'd changed in the intervening years?

Ben paused in his thoughts. She couldn't have changed

that much, given what he'd seen so far that day. In which case…

Grabbing the phone from the table next to him, he called down to Reception.

'Daisy? Can you cancel my booking at The Edge tonight?' Trendy, stainless-steel, cutting-edge fusion restaurants just weren't Luce's style, no matter who the concierge had needed to bribe to get him a table there that night. 'No, don't worry. I'll sort out an alternative myself.'

Something more Luce. More fun too, probably.

One more quick phone call ascertained that the restaurant he was thinking of still existed. Perfect. Hanging up, Ben glanced at the bathroom door and then at his watch again. He'd given Luce long enough. Time to move on to the next stage of their evening.

Pausing first to replace the diary in the safe, he gave the bathroom door a quick rap with his knuckles and then said, loud enough to be sure he could be heard through it, 'You've got five more minutes in there before I start trying to guess the pass code for your phone.'

To his surprise, the lock turned and the door opened almost instantly. Eyebrows raised, Luce stared at him and said, 'Threats aren't traditionally very relaxing, you know.'

But baths clearly were. Especially for Dr Lucinda Myles.

She'd changed out of those clothes he'd been longing to run his hands over, but since she'd replaced them with a slippery, silky purple dress he really wasn't complaining. Her hair was pinned up off her neck, with a few damp tendrils curling behind her ears and across her forehead. She smiled at him, her deep red lips curving in amusement. 'I didn't think you were the sort of man to do speechless. I like it.'

A rush of lavender hit his lungs as she swept past him,

reminding him of the château in summer, and he realised he still hadn't spoken. 'If I'd known you were using your time so well I'd have been much more patient,' he said, finding his voice at last.

Luce slipped her arms into her coat, her fingers reaching into the pocket for her phone. Time for another distraction. Ben offered her his arm and she took it, forestalling her return to the world of technology and messages from people who wanted far less fun things from her than he did. 'Now, if you're ready, won't you let me escort you to dinner?'

She still looked suspicious as she nodded, but she left the room beside him, steady on higher heels than he'd have expected her to be comfortable wearing. Ben smiled. This was going to be a good evening. He was sure of it. The hotel and the business were fine, and he had the company of a beautiful and intriguing woman for the night—one he might be able to help a little. And then he'd get to decamp to the cottage for the rest of the week, feeling good about himself.

Life was great.

There should be laws against men looking quite that good in a suit. Men she was determined to resist, anyway. If Dennis had ever looked even half as good maybe they would have managed more than a few coffees and the occasional fake date when he needed a partner for a university dinner or she needed someone for a family event.

Actually, no, they wouldn't. Quite aside from the fact that Dennis became intensely irritating after more than a couple of hours in his company, she'd never felt that... *spark*—that connection she needed to take the risk of building an actual relationship. To her surprise, Ben Hampton had a spark. Not a relationship one, of course, but maybe something more intense. Something that definitely hadn't been there the last time they met. Which was just as well, as he'd been dating her roommate at the time. But there was definitely something.

It was almost a shame she didn't have the time, energy or courage to take him up on his offer to find out exactly what.

Her phone buzzed in her pocket and her fingers itched to reach for it. She hadn't called her mother back, and she'd only worry if she didn't hear from her. Well, actually, she probably wouldn't. Tabitha saved her concern for Tom and Dolly, safe in the knowledge that Luce could take care of herself far better than the rest of them.

Still, she'd get annoyed, which was even worse, and pull a guilt trip on Luce next time they spoke.

She really should call her back. But Ben's arm held her hand trapped against his body, and she could feel the warmth of him even through his coat and suit jacket. Was that intentional? Trying to cut her off from her real life and keep her in this surreal bubble of a night he'd created?

Ben Hampton had invaded her life and her personal space since she'd bumped into him again, only a couple of hours ago, and she'd let him. Sat back and let him take charge, point out the problems in her life, rearrange all her plans for the evening. What had happened to taking responsibility and control?

Okay, she needed a new plan for the night. Something to wrest back control. At the very least she needed to know if he remembered her...

She shivered as they left the hotel lobby, the bitter night air stinging her face and her lungs. Icicle Christmas lights dangled above the cobbled streets, twinkling in the night like the real thing. Ben tugged her a little closer, and she wondered how it was he stayed so warm despite the winter chill.

'Where are we going?' she asked, belatedly realising he hadn't even told her where he was taking her. Some fancy restaurant, probably, she'd figured when pulling out the dress she'd packed for the conference gala dinner. But that wasn't the point. No one knew where she was—least of all her. It was madness. She was out in a strange city at night with a man she barely knew. A little surreptitious internet searching in the bar while he'd been fetching the drinks had told her the bare bones of his professional career since university—which mostly seemed to be doing whatever his father needed him to do—but it hadn't told her what sort of a man he was. She hadn't seen him in eight years, and she hadn't known him all that well back then. He certainly hadn't been the kind of guy the twenty-year-old Luce had willingly spent time with. This was foolishness beyond compare. Dennis would be horrified.

Of course her mother would probably be relieved. Tabitha had always been a little afraid that her daughter had inherited none of her more flighty attributes at all.

'A little French restaurant I know,' Ben said, answering the question she'd almost forgotten she'd asked. 'It's up past the Cross, on the Rows. You okay to walk in those shoes?'

'Of course.' Luce spoke the words automatically, even though the balls of her feet had started to smart as she struggled over the cobbles. *Show no weakness.* That was another of her grandad's rules to live by. If she couldn't keep the other one tonight, she might as well try to hang on to something.

'You never used to wear shoes like that.'

Luce couldn't tell if the warm feeling that settled over her shoulders at Ben's words was relief or confusion. 'You do remember me, then?' she blurted out before she could stop herself. 'I wasn't sure.'

'You think I invite strange women up to my suite all the time?'

Luce shrugged. 'University was a long time ago. I have no idea what kind of man you are now. And, actually...'

'Yeah, yeah.' Ben rolled his eyes. 'Eight years ago I'd have invited *all* women up to my room.'

'I hope you've grown up a little since then.' A hitch in Ben's step made her glance up. 'What?'

He shook his head. 'Nothing. Just depends who you ask.'

Picking up speed again, Ben led them up the very steep steps onto the medieval Rows, a second layer of shops and restaurants above the street-level ones. The historian in Luce was fascinated by the structure—the timber fronts, the overhanging storey above making a covered walkway. There was no other example in the world—the Chester Rows were unique. She should be savouring every detail.

And instead all she could think was, *He remembers me.* Well, at least she knew now. Except...just because he remembered her, that didn't mean he remembered the last time they'd seen each other.

Maybe he'd forgotten it entirely. And maybe that meant she could, too.

It was too cold for much more conversation. They made their way along the Rows, Luce tucked tightly into Ben's body for warmth, until he said, 'Here we are,' and Luce's whole body relaxed at the sight of a cosy little restaurant tucked away behind a few closed shops with sparkling Christmas window displays.

'Thank God for that,' she said, smiling up at Ben. 'I'm freezing.'

CHAPTER FOUR

SMILING UP AT HIM, complaining about the cold, Luce seemed relaxed for the first time. As if this was any usual date, not a peculiar arrangement to help an uptight woman cut loose. And she remembered him. That was a start. He wasn't sure he could have made it all through dinner without knowing.

Ben pushed open the door to La Cuillère d'Argent and let Luce walk into the warmth first. Her face brightened in the candlelit restaurant, and she glanced back at him with surprise on her face.

'I'm overdressed,' she said, taking in the rustic wooden tables and chairs. There weren't many other people eating there, but those who were wore mostly casual clothes.

'You look perfect.' He smiled at the waiter approaching. 'Table for two, please?'

Seated at a candlelit table in the window, looking out at the people hurrying past, Luce stripped off her coat and asked, 'How did you know about this place?'

'Not what you were expecting?'

She shook her head, and Ben knew what she was thinking. She'd expected somewhere impressive, somewhere fancy and expensive—somewhere that would make her feel kindly towards him when he paid, possibly impressed enough to take him to bed when they got back to the hotel.

Somewhere like The Edge. Somewhere that said, *I'm Ben Hampton and I've just inherited half of a multi-million-pound hotel chain, and I still have time to flatter and treat you. Aren't you impressed?*

But that would have defeated the object of the evening. He wanted Luce to relax, and he knew she wasn't the sort to be impressed by or enjoy over-priced, over-fiddly food. Too practical for that, with her epic 'To Do' lists and her martyr complex. She'd probably feel guilty the whole time, which wouldn't help his cause at all.

No, he needed somewhere cosy and intimate, somewhere he could actually talk to her, learn about her life since uni, find out what made her tick. This place was perfect for that. Ben blinked in the candlelight as he realised, belatedly, that he *wanted* to know her. Not just seduce her or entertain her. He wanted to know the truth of Luce Myles.

Of course seducing her was still firmly part of the plan. He just didn't mind a little small talk first.

'Have you been here before?' Luce asked, scanning the wine list. 'Do you live in Chester?'

Ben shook his head. 'Just visiting to check on the hotel. But I came here with my mother years ago. She was born in France, you see. Knew every great French restaurant in the country.' It must have been fifteen years ago or more, he realised. 'I checked while you were in the bath to make sure it was still here, actually. It really has been a while.'

'What does it mean?' Luce asked, staring at the front of the menu, where the restaurant name curled across the card. '"La Cuillère d'Argent",' she read slowly.

'The Silver Spoon,' Ben translated, tapping a finger against the picture under the words—an ornate piece of silverware not unlike the ones on the table for their use.

'I like it,' Luce announced, smiling at him over the menu.

Ben's shoulders dropped as a tension he hadn't realised he was feeling left him. That was wrong. She was the one who was supposed to be relaxing. He was always relaxed. That was who he was.

'Good,' he said, a little unnerved, and motioned a waiter over to order a carafe of white wine to start. He rather thought he might need it tonight.

They made polite conversation about the menu options, and the freshly baked bread with olive tapenade the waiter brought them, before Luce asked, 'So, if you're just visiting, where is home these days?'

Ben shrugged. Home wasn't exactly something he associated with his stark and minimalist penthouse suite. And since he hadn't been to the cottage in Wales for over a year, and the château in France for far longer, he was pretty sure they didn't count.

'I'm based out of London, but mostly I'm on the road. Wherever there's a Hampton & Sons hotel I've got a bed for the night, so I do okay.'

Across the table Luce's eyes widened with what Ben recognised as pity. 'That must be hard. Not having anywhere to call home.'

Must it? 'I'm used to it, I guess. Even growing up, I lived in the hotels.' A different one every time he came home from boarding school, after his mother left. 'I've got a penthouse suite in one of the London hotels to crash in, if I want. Fully serviced and maintained.'

'Thus neatly getting out of one of the joys of home ownership,' Luce said wryly.

Ben remembered the 'House Repairs' entry on her 'To Do' list.

'Your house takes some upkeep, then?'

'It's falling apart,' Luce said, her voice blunt, and reached for her wine. 'But it was my grandfather's house, and I grew up there. I could never sell it even if I found someone willing to take it on.'

'Still, sounds like a lot of work on top of all your other commitments.' Was this something else she was doing for her family? For the sake of others? 'Are you sure you wouldn't be happier in a cosy little flat near the university?'

He was mostly joking, so the force of her reply surprised him. *'Never.'*

'Okay.'

Dropping her eyes to the table, Luce shook her head a little before smiling up at him. 'Sorry. It's just…I worry about it a lot. But one day I'll finish fixing the place up and it'll be the perfect family home. It's just getting there that's proving trying.'

Ben shrugged. 'I guess I don't really get it. I mean, I own properties and such. I've even renovated one of them. But they're just bricks and mortar to me. If I had to sell them, or if getting rid of them gave me another opportunity— well, it wouldn't worry me.'

'You don't get attached, huh?' She gave him a lopsided smile. 'Probably a good choice if you're always moving around.'

'Exactly. Don't get tied down. It's one of my rules for life.'

'Yeah? What are the others?'

Ben couldn't tell if she was honestly interested or mocking him. 'Most importantly: enjoy life. And avoid responsibility, of course.'

'Of course,' she echoed with a smile, reaching for the bread basket. 'You never were big on that.'

There was an awkward silence while Ben imagined Luce rerunning every stupid moment he'd had at university in her head. Time to change the subject.

'So, you're in Chester for some conference thing?' he asked.

Luce nodded, swallowing the bread she was chewing. '*"Bringing History to the Future"*.' Ben smiled at the sarcasm in her voice.

'You're not a fan?'

'It's not that,' Luce replied with a shrug. 'It's just… there's so much important preservation and research to be done, and finding a way to make the importance of our history fit into a series of thirty-minute television programmes with accompanying books does tend to interfere a bit.'

'But if it's not important to the bulk of the populace…?'

'Then we lose funding and the chance to study important sites and documents. I know, I know…'

From the way she waved her hands in a dismissive manner Ben gathered this wasn't the first time she'd heard the argument. 'You have this debate a lot?'

Luce gave him a lopsided smile. 'Mostly with myself. I understand the need, but sometimes I'd rather be holed up in a secluded library somewhere, doing real research, real work, not worrying about who was going to read and dissect it without understanding the background.'

'This is your book?' Ben tore himself another piece of bread and smeared it with tapenade, but kept his gaze on her.

Luce pulled a face. 'My book is somewhere between the two. "Popular history for armchair historians," my editor calls it. Or it will be if I ever finish it.'

'What's it about?'

'An obscure Welsh princess who became the mistress of Henry I, and whose rape caused the end of the truce between the Normans and the Welsh.' The words sounded rote, as if she'd been telling people the same line for a long time without making any progress.

Ben scoured his vague memory of 'A' Level history, but they hadn't covered much Welsh history in his very English boarding schools. 'You're still based in Wales, then?' he asked.

Luce nodded. 'Cardiff. But not just for the history. It's where I grew up. Where my family lives. It's home. And when Grandad left me the house I knew it was where I was meant to stay.'

'That's nice,' Ben said absently, thinking again of the overgrown château that was his heritage from his maternal grandmother. He should probably check in on it some time soon.

The waiter brought their meals, and the conversation moved on to discussing the dishes in front of them.

'So,' he said, when they'd both agreed their food was delicious, and Luce had stolen a bite of his rabbit with mustard sauce, 'tell me more about this Welsh princess of yours.'

Her eyebrows jumped up in surprise. 'You're interested?'

'I have a cottage in Wales,' he explained. 'Down in the Brecons. It's where I'm headed tomorrow, actually. A good story might get me in the right mood for my rural retreat.'

'What do you want to know?'

Ben shrugged. 'Everything.'

The surprised look stayed, but Luce obliged all the same.

'Um…Princess Nest. She was the daughter of the King of Deheubarth, in South West Wales, and she gave Henry I a son before he married her off to his steward in Wales.'

'Nice of him,' Ben murmured.

'How things worked then. Anyway, the reason she's remembered, really, is her abduction.'

'She was kidnapped?' Letting his fork drop to his plate, Ben started paying real attention. Against the odds, this was actually interesting.

Luce nodded. 'Owain ap Cadwgan, the head of the Welsh resistance, fell in love with her. He and his men stole into Cilgerran Castle and took her.'

Ben blinked. 'What happened next?'

'A lot of things.' Luce smiled. 'A whole book's worth, in fact. Some people say she fell in love with Owain, too. But really, if you want to know the whole story, you'll have to read my book.'

'I will,' Ben promised. If she ever finished writing it, of course.

Okay, she had to give Ben Hampton this much—he was a better judge of restaurants than she'd expected. And a better conversationalist than she remembered. He'd actually sounded interested when she'd talked about Princess Nest and her book, which was more than anyone in her family had ever managed. Of course he was only doing it to get her into bed—she wasn't stupid, and he'd all but told her as much—but she had no qualms at all about turning him down at the bedroom door. She couldn't imagine for a moment that someone with the charm and self-confidence of Ben Hampton would have any trouble shaking off that kind of rejection.

She, on the other hand, had absolutely no desire to be the one being ushered out of the bedroom before breakfast the next morning, when he'd got what he wanted and lost interest in her.

The waiter cleared away their dessert plates and deposited the coffees they'd ordered in front of them, along

with two oversized liqueur glasses with a small amount
of thick amber liquid pooled at the base.

'Calvados,' Ben explained, lifting his glass to his lips.
'Apple brandy. It's a traditional Normandy *digestif*.'

Luce followed suit. The brandy taste she remembered
from occasional late nights with her grandfather during
university holidays was deepened by the hint of fruit. 'It's
good.'

Ben shrugged. 'I like it.'

While she was drinking it he paid the bill. She realised
too late to insist on paying her half. 'Let me give you
something for my—'

'Absolutely not.'

Ben clamped a hand down over hers as she reached for
her purse, and she felt the thrill of a shiver running up her
wrist to her shoulder. It must be the brandy, she decided,
affecting her judgement. Because, however attractive Ben
Hampton was, and however intense his focus on her and
her conversation made her feel, she was not going to sleep
with him tonight.

She couldn't help but wonder, though, how all that con-
centration on the moment would feel if he was focusing it
on her body. Her pleasure.

Luce shook her head. Too much Calvados. Some fresh
air would sort that out.

Ben slipped her coat over her shoulders, and that same
frisson ran through her as he stood close behind her. Luce
wondered whether her room in the suite had a lock on its
door. For keeping him out or her in, she wasn't entirely
sure.

The cold night air bit into the exposed skin of her face
and hands. Luce glanced at her watch: nearly midnight.
She needed to get some sleep if she was going to make
that lecture for Dennis in the morning. She huddled into

her coat and felt Ben's arm settle on her shoulders, holding her close against him again.

'So, feeling any more relaxed?' he asked.

'Lots,' Luce answered honestly. 'But that might just be the alcohol.'

'True.'

They walked a few more steps, and Luce almost thought he might drop the subject.

Then he asked, 'So, what do you think might relax you a little more?'

Truly great sex, Luce thought, but didn't say. The sort that made you forget your own name, just for a little while. The sort that let you sleep so deeply you woke refreshed and energised, however much of the night you'd spent exploring each other's bodies.

Not that she'd ever actually *had* sex like that herself, of course. But Dolly was adamant that it existed.

'Um…handing in my book draft on time?' she said finally, when she realised he was still waiting for an answer.

'And how do you plan to do that when your "To Do" list is full of stuff you need to do for other people?'

It was a question she'd asked herself often enough, but hearing it in Ben's relaxed, carefree voice made her bristle. 'What do you care? If you're so against helping others, why do you care if I get my book in or not?'

Ben shrugged. 'Well, I've listened to Nest's life story this evening. I'm invested now. I told you—I want to read the damn thing when you finish it.'

'Oh.' Luce tried to hide her astonishment.

'Besides, I didn't say I was against helping others. I'm here in Chester because I'm doing a favour for my brother.'

Apparently he wasn't going to stop surprising her any time soon.

'What favour?'

'The person who was supposed to be checking out the hotel this week got sick, so I offered to swing by on my way to a week off.'

Ben smiled down at her, and Luce felt it in her cold bones.

'So, you see, it's not helping out others I object to.'

'Then what is it?' Luce asked, remembering that she was supposed to be annoyed.

'I object to you giving up your whole life to serve others. I think you need to put your own wants and needs first for a while.'

It sounded so reasonable when he said it. So tempting. But then Luce remembered the pages of 'To Do' lists filling her stolen organiser. 'And how, exactly, do you suggest I do that?'

'Well, actually,' Ben said, grinning, 'I do have one idea.'

They were nearly back at the hotel now. Luce stopped walking and raised her eyebrows. 'Are you really trying to tell me that sleeping with you would solve all my problems?'

Ben chuckled. 'No. But it would be a good start.'

Luce closed her eyes and laughed. 'You are incorrigible.'

'Come on,' he said, tugging her forward again. 'Let's get inside.'

CHAPTER FIVE

THE SUITE WAS almost too hot after the bite of the December night air. Ben stripped off his coat and jacket, rolling up his shirtsleeves as he made his way across to the bar area. 'What can I get you? More brandy?'

'Um…peppermint tea?' Luce asked.

He couldn't help but smile at her. 'Is that to help you resist my charms?' he asked.

'To help me get up for this lecture in the morning.'

Luce sprawled into the chair he'd been sitting in earlier, and Ben admired the way her slim calves stretched out in front of her. She'd kicked her shoes off the moment they'd got into the room, and she pointed her toes as she flexed her feet.

There was absolutely no reason at all for that to be sexy. And yet…

Flicking on the kettle, he said, 'I wanted to talk to you about that, actually.' If she wasn't going to let him help her relax the way he knew best, maybe he could at least draw her attention to some of the unnecessary things that were stressing her out.

Luce raised her eyebrows at him and waited for him to continue.

'What is it, exactly, that you'll get out of attending this lecture for a colleague?'

'It's a favour,' Luce said. 'I'm not expecting to get anything out of it.'

'So this guy won't do the same for you at a later date? It's not somehow tangentially related to your own research and might prove helpful one day? The university won't look fondly on your actions and bear it in mind in the future when it comes to promotions and such?' He was watching carefully, so he saw her squirm a little in her seat. Had she never considered how little she got back from all she gave out?

'Well, no. Not really.' She shifted again, looking down at her hands. 'Dennis doesn't like leaving the university much, and I can't imagine he'll let on to anyone at the university that I went for him in the first place. Plus the topic's pretty dull.'

The kettle boiled and Ben poured hot water onto a tea bag in one of the fine china mugs. Then he poured himself a large brandy while it brewed. 'In that case, I can only assume that this man is important to you in some way. Are you dating?'

'No!'

The answer was so quick and so vehement that Ben suspected he wasn't the first person to suspect it. But maybe it wouldn't bother her so much if it wasn't him asking. He could hope, anyway.

'Then why are you doing it?'

'Because he asked,' Luce said, sounding miserable.

'And you can't say no?'

Her glare was scathing. 'I said no to you, didn't I?'

Ben took her the tea before he replied. 'You told me you wouldn't stay here tonight, and now you are.'

'I told you I wouldn't sleep with you. I'm holding firm on that one.'

He chuckled, and saw her frown grow deeper. Had she

always been this much fun to tease? How had he not noticed? 'We'll see. Anyway, the point is you do all these things for other people and you get nothing back. You need to think about what you want for yourself.'

Luce sighed into her cup of tea. 'I know.'

She sounded defeated, which wasn't quite what Ben had been going for. She hadn't stopped fighting him since they met in the lobby. He kind of liked that about her.

'But there's just never any time. If I don't take care of things for Tom, or Dolly, or Mum, it'll just cause a bigger mess further along the line that I'll have to clear up.'

'Tom and Dolly—your brother and sister?' He didn't remember her even talking about her family at university. Not that they'd ever really had any long, meaningful talks about their lives, of course. But he was starting to wish they had. Maybe then Luce would make more sense to him.

Luce nodded. 'They…they're not very good at getting by on their own. Neither is Mum. It was different when Grandad was still alive. But now…'

'They all rely on you.' Ben slouched down in his chair, stretching his foot out to nudge against hers. 'Sounds to me like you need someone you can rely on for a change.'

Her head jerked up in surprise. 'You cannot possibly be suggesting that person is you.'

'Good God, no!' Ben shuddered at the very thought. 'Good for one night only. I have a rule.'

'Of course you do. Every girl's dream.'

Ben gave her a wry smile. 'You'd be surprised.' There were always enough women looking for exactly that.

'So, what are you suggesting?' Luce asked.

The hint of desperation in her voice, the pleading in her eyes, told him she was really hoping he had an answer. She was in so deep she didn't even know how to get out.

'Stay here tonight with me, like we planned. And tomorrow, first thing, head back to Cardiff. Screw your colleague and his lecture. Forget about your family for a couple of days. You're supposed to be in Chester until Thursday, right? So no one will know you're home. You can knuckle down, sort out your book, and then spend Christmas relaxing instead of stressing out about all the work you should be doing.'

Luce's gaze darted away. 'I'm not sure I even remember how to relax.'

Ben smiled. 'Spend the night with me and I'll remind you.'

Oh, it was so, so tempting. Not just the sex—although that was bad enough. But the thought of three whole days with nothing to do except work on her book. No one asking her for anything.

Luce bit her lip. 'What about the lecture? Or my conference report? Or the Christmas Eve dinner?'

'Screw them,' Ben said, raising his glass to her. 'Decide, right here and now, that *you* are more important than what other people want from you. Decide that your book is what matters most to you at this moment in time and focus on that for the week. Make your family help you for a change. Get some priorities for once.'

He was right. The world might stop turning on its axis because of it, but he, Ben Hampton, was actually right. Maybe he'd been wrong every time he'd called her boring or obsessed at university—or maybe he hadn't been. But now he was right. She needed priorities. And maybe, if nothing else, three days alone would help her figure out what they were.

'Maybe I can get my ticket refunded. Or changed to tomorrow,' she mused. The conference organisers had bought the original ticket, but after the fiasco with her hotel room she didn't feel inclined to trust them to re-arrange her travel home. She'd head down to the station in the morning—see what they could do.

'I'll buy you a ticket,' Ben said carelessly. 'First-class. You can work on the train.'

Luce raised her eyebrows at him. 'What? As payment for services rendered? I'm not sleeping with you, remember?'

'As an apology.' Sitting up straighter, Ben fixed his gaze onto her own, and she found it impossible to look away. 'From Hampton & Sons. For losing your booking. I don't pay for sex.'

He looked more than insulted. He looked hurt. Luce's gaze darted away. 'Sorry. I didn't mean...'

'Yes, you did.' Ben sighed. 'Look. You're pretty much out of options here, Luce. I'm leaving tomorrow, and I have no doubt that this suite will be booked up for the rest of the week. You can try and find somewhere else in the city with a cancellation, or you can go home. And once you're there it's your choice whether you let anyone else know you're back.'

'Why are you doing this?' Luce asked. 'Trying to help me, I mean?' Could he possibly be so determined to get her to sleep with him that he'd try to fix her whole life to achieve it? Surely even Ben Hampton couldn't be that single-minded.

More to the point, how the hell was she meant to keep on resisting him if he was?

But Ben just shrugged. 'Because I can. Because fixing things is what I do for a living. Because it's so blatantly obvious what you need.' His words were casual, thrown away without thinking. But there was a tightness around his eyes that suggested something more.

Did he remember that night in the library? Was that what he was trying to make up for by helping her?

And, really, did it really matter? It was eight years ago. But she might never see the man again after tomorrow, and she knew the curiosity alone would drive her insane. 'Do you remember the night of your twenty-first birthday?'

Ben didn't even blink at the change of subject. 'Barely. Mostly I remember the hangover the next day. That kind of misery stays with you.'

He didn't remember. And if he didn't remember, it was as if it had never happened. She could forget it, too. Let the past go.

'I do know that I got dumped because of my actions that night.' Ben raised an eyebrow at her. 'Care to fill in the missing memories?'

Luce smiled. 'Maybe one day.' Except there wouldn't be another day, would there? Tomorrow she'd take the train home and forget all about Ben Hampton.

She tried to remind herself that this was a good thing.

Ben drained the last of his brandy and got to his feet. 'Well, I guess I'd better let you sleep on your decision. Unless…' He gave her a hopeful look.

'I am not sleeping with you.' Whatever her rebellious body was hoping. She could feel a tightness growing in her belly just thinking about it.

He laughed, far more cheerful than she'd expected him to be about being turned down. 'In that case, if you'll excuse me, I have a long drive ahead of me tomorrow.'

Bending down, he brushed a kiss against her cheek. His lips were softer than she'd imagined. Not that she'd been thinking of them.

'Goodnight, Luce.'

She watched him place his glass on the counter and

saunter into the bedroom, closing the door firmly behind him. And yet she was still staring at the door.

Her fingers brushed her cheek, as if she could trace the kiss his lips had left.

Damn him. Somehow she knew that all she'd dream about that night was what might have happened if she'd said yes.

Ben was not naturally an early riser, but his father had been, and Seb had inherited the trait, so he'd had to learn to function well before seven-thirty. And, given the motivation of breakfast with Luce before he packed her off to her new and improved existence in Cardiff, he was awake, showered and dressed before the sun was fully up the next morning. Which wasn't as impressive in December as it would have been in July, but Ben still felt a little pleased with himself as he knocked on Luce's door.

At least he was until she answered it moments later, already dressed in some sort of knitted jumper dress and those incredibly enticing boots.

He'd spent a lot of the previous evening thinking about those boots. And what Luce might be wearing under that dress. It hadn't been his most restful night's sleep ever, but his mind had at least been happily occupied.

'You're up at last, then,' Luce said, eyebrows raised.

'Were you always so smug in the mornings?' he asked as Luce wheeled her already packed suitcase into the living area. He had Seb for smugness. He really didn't need any more *smug* in his life. At least not unless he was getting to feel it for once.

'Probably.' Luce flashed him a superior smile. 'But you were mostly sleeping in while I was up working. You might not have noticed.'

Taking her suitcase and resting it against the wall by

the door, Ben decided it was time to change the subject. 'So, have you decided what you're doing today?'

Luce bit her lip. 'Heading back to Cardiff, if that offer of a train ticket still stands?'

Ben nodded. 'Of course. And when you get there?'

'I finish my book. In secret.'

A sense of relief washed over him. 'Good.' He'd done it. He might not have been able to bring his mother back from the brink before she jumped ship, but he'd fixed this. He'd fixed that little bit of Luce's life that he could influence and now he could move on, forget all about her.

That, right there, was one good day's work.

'I've ordered us breakfast,' he said, just as a knock on the door indicated its arrival.

'If nothing else, the Hampton & Sons hotel chain has certainly fed me well during my stay,' Luce said, taking a seat at the table in the dining area. 'I should write to the management.'

'I'll pass on a message.' Ben let in the room service staff member and took his own seat as platters of food were laid on the table. Eggs, bacon, toast, pastries—and plenty of hot coffee. Should keep him going on his drive through Wales, and it would make sure Luce had one more good meal before she lost herself in research and writing for the rest of the week.

'Shall I open the curtains, sir?' the room service guy asked, and Ben nodded.

Helping himself to eggs as Luce poured the coffee, Ben couldn't help but think how domestic this was. Far more couply than he'd ever managed, even with women he'd actually slept with. It was a good job she was leaving today, or she'd be straightening his tie and calling him 'honey' in no time. She was that sort.

'I'll call the station when we've eaten,' he said as light

flooded into the room from the opened curtains. 'See what times your trains are.'

But Luce wasn't listening to him. Instead she stared out of the window, coffee cup halfway to her mouth. Ben followed her gaze.

Outside, rooftops and roads were coated in a thick layer of snow, gleaming white and icy. Heavy flakes fell lazily from the sky, adding to the perfect Christmas scene.

'Huh!' Ben said, watching it fall. 'When did *that* happen?'

'I should never have gone out for dinner,' Luce muttered to herself as she waited on hold for the station. If she hadn't gone out for dinner with Ben Hampton she'd have had to try to find somewhere else to stay. When that had inevitably failed she'd have had no option but to get a train home. She'd be warm and cosy in Cardiff, watching the snow fall as she worked on her book.

Except, if she was honest with herself, she knew she wouldn't be. She'd have called her mother as soon as she got back to sort out the Christmas Eve dinner, and then she'd have been caught up in the responsibility net again. She'd be at her family's beck and call, sorting out their problems and organising their Christmas season. The book wouldn't have got a look-in.

Of course she would still have had a roof over her head, which was more than she'd have right now if the trains weren't running.

The hotel room door slammed open and shut and Ben walked back in, his hair damp with snowflakes. 'It's really not stopping out there,' he said, shrugging out of his coat. 'I spoke to Reception—apparently all trains are subject to significant delays, and a lot simply aren't running.'

Luce pressed the 'end call' button and dropped her

phone onto the sofa before perching on the arm herself. 'Fantastic.'

'You're thinking this is all my fault somehow, aren't you?'

'Yes.' What the hell did she do now?

Ben pulled up a chair and sat opposite her. 'Okay, well, let's see what we can do to fix this.'

Luce rolled her eyes. 'I know you pride yourself on being able to solve problems in hotels, but I think the British railway network might be beyond even your capabilities.'

Ben ignored her. 'Daisy on Reception says this room's booked out for tonight, and the guest has just called to confirm they'll still be coming, despite the snow. So that's out. We might possibly be able to find you another room if we get some cancellations, but there's no guarantee. Or...'

'Or?' Luce sat up a little straighter. Another option was exactly what she needed right now. Unless, of course, this was another Ben Hampton plan to seduce her.

'I'm driving south today anyway. Headed to my cottage down in the Brecons. Apparently it's not so bad further south just yet, and I'm confident my four-by-four can handle it.' He shrugged. 'Wouldn't be too far out of my way to take you on down to Cardiff. I can always stop for the night in one of our hotels there if the snow worsens.'

Blinking at him, Luce considered. It would mean hours in a car with Ben, on bad roads, but somehow she felt he was a surer bet than the trains. And not even he would try to seduce her in a snowdrift, right? 'You'd do that?'

'I still owe you for the room mix-up, remember? And this is cheaper than a first-class train ticket, anyway.'

He made it sound like nothing, but Luce knew better. He was fixing her life again. But if it got her home and her book finished maybe she should just let him. Accept help for once.

Grandad hadn't had a saying to cover that one, but Luce thought there might be potential in it all the same.

'Okay, then,' she said, grabbing her phone and standing up. 'Let's go.'

CHAPTER SIX

SOMEWHERE AROUND WELSHPOOL Ben finally admitted to himself that this might not have been the best idea he'd ever had.

The integral sat nav in the car had wanted him to cross over the border and drive south through England, before nipping back into Wales just before Cardiff. But Ben had done the drive south through Wales to the Brecons and the cottage enough times to feel confident in his route, and he didn't need advice for the uninitiated. Besides, the travel news had reported a pile-up on the A49 that would make things incredibly tedious, so really a drive through the hills had been the only option.

Right now, though, he'd take a three-hour traffic jam over these roads.

Daisy on the front desk had assured him that the snow was worst in the north. What she hadn't mentioned was that it was heading south. Every mile of their journey had been undertaken with snow clouds hovering above, keeping pace, and dumping more of the white stuff in their path as they drove.

Ben's arms ached from gripping the steering wheel tightly enough to yank the car back under control as the road twisted and slipped under them. His eyes felt gritty from staring into the falling snow, trying to see the path ahead. And Luce was not helping at all.

To start with she'd just looked tense. Then her hands had balled up against her thighs. Then she'd grabbed onto the seat, knuckles white. Ben had stopped looking over at her as the road grew more treacherous, but he'd bet money that she had a look of terror on her face now.

'Are you sure this is the best way to go?' Luce asked, her voice a little faint.

'Yes.' At least at this point it was pretty much the only option.

'Do you think…? Is the snow getting heavier?'

'No.' Except it was. Any idiot could see that. But the last thing Ben needed was Luce freaking out on him in the middle of a snowstorm.

'Are you just saying that to make me feel better?'

That sounded more like the Luce he'd had dinner with last night. Sharp and insightful.

'Yes.'

'Thought so.' She took a breath and released her death grip on the seat. 'Okay. What do you need me to do?'

'Keep quiet and don't freak out.' Ben ground the words out. Distraction was dangerous.

'Okay. I can do that.'

He wasn't sure if she was reassuring herself or him, but she did seem to relax a little. At least until they hit the Brecon Beacons National Park.

As the car climbed the hills the skies darkened even further, looking more like night than afternoon. The falling flakes doubled in size, until his windscreen wipers couldn't keep up, and the slow progress he'd been making dropped to a crawl. The road ahead had disappeared into a mist of white and the hills were blending into the sky.

They were never going to make it to Cardiff tonight.

'Okay. New plan.' Running through the road systems in his head, Ben prodded a couple of buttons on the sat nav and decided that maybe, just this once, he'd take its advice. Anything that got him off these roads, out of this car and somewhere warm. Preferably with a large drink.

'What? Where are we going?' Luce peered at the sat nav, which was insistently telling him to turn right. 'We need to get to Cardiff!'

'We're never going to make Cardiff in this.' Ben swung the car slowly to the right and hoped he'd hit an actual road. 'We need to get somewhere safe until this passes.'

'Like where?' Luce asked, her tone rising in incredulity.

'My cottage,' Ben reminded her. 'It's a damn sight closer than Cardiff, and a lot safer than these roads.'

There was silence from the passenger seat. When Ben finally risked a glance over, Luce was staring at him. 'What?'

'You planned this,' she said, her words firm and full of conviction. 'This was the plan all along.'

'Getting stuck in a snowstorm? I know I'm a powerful man, Luce, but the weather's up there with the rail network on the list of things I can't control.'

'That's why we came this way. You *knew* the snow would be bad, so you planned to kidnap me and take me to your cottage. You're still mad I wouldn't sleep with you last night.'

Was the woman actually insane?

'Trust me—sleeping with you is the last thing on my mind right now. I'm more concerned with us—oh, I don't know—not dying.'

'I should have taken the train.' The words were muffled as Luce buried her mouth into the long fluffy scarf wrapped around her neck.

'Next time I'll let you,' Ben promised, relief seeping

through him as he made out enough letters on the next road sign to reassure him they were nearly at the village nearest his cottage. Two more turns and they'd be there. Once they got onto the last rocky upward track. 'Hold on,' he warned her. Then he took a breath and turned the wheel.

Luce had never liked rollercoasters. Or fairground rides. Or ferries, actually. And the journey through the hills with Ben had felt far too much like all three for her liking. Rising and falling, rocking, swaying in the wind... She could feel breakfast threatening to rise up in her throat as they bumped over the rocky track Ben had just violently swerved up.

All she wanted was to be at home. Warm, safe and merrily lost in the Middle Ages. Was that so much to ask?

But instead she was...*where*, exactly? Somewhere in the Brecon Beacons, she supposed. Risking her life on an unsafe track to get to Ben's love-nest in the hills. Somewhere to wait out the storm and focus very hard on reasons not to indulge in a one-night stand with Ben.

Suddenly Cardiff felt a very long way away.

The car jerked to a halt and Luce rubbed at her collarbone where the seatbelt dug in.

'We're here.' Ben threw open the door and jumped out into the snow, as if any amount of cold were better than being stuck in the car with her.

He was still mad about her suspicions, then. And, yes, okay—rationally she knew he probably hadn't intended this to happen and couldn't actually control the snow.

But it was still all a little too convenient and willpower-testing for her liking.

Unfastening her seatbelt, Luce followed, stepping gingerly into the soft piles of snow and wishing she'd packed more practical boots. Peering through the snow, she followed Ben's tracks up what she presumed must be a path under all the white and saw, at last, Ben's cottage.

Luce wasn't sure what she'd expected, exactly. Maybe a collection of holiday chalets attached to a hotel. Or an ostentatious, look-how-rich-I-am manor house sort of thing that could only be called a cottage ironically. Whatever it was, it wasn't this. An actual, honest-to-God stone cottage in the hills.

It was perfect.

'Come on,' Ben said, and she realised the front door was open. 'If you freeze to death you'll never forgive me.'

'True,' Luce said, and hurried in after him.

With the door closed fast behind them, the wild winds and swirling snow seemed suddenly miles away. It wasn't hot in the cottage, by any means, but it was warm at least. Ben turned his attention immediately to the stone fireplace that dominated the lounge, stacking sticks and paper with practised ease.

Luce stared around her, taking in the unexpected surroundings. It certainly wasn't the sort of space she'd imagined Ben feeling comfortable in. Yes, it had a modern open-plan layout, but there were none of the bright white surfaces and stainless-steel accessories she'd expected, even after seeing the rustic outlook of the place. Instead the large main room was decorated in earthy colours—warming, welcoming reds and browns and greens. The battered leather sofas had tawny throw blankets and cushions on them—perfect for curling up in front of the fire. And the sheepskin rug before the fireplace made even the grey stone floor more warming.

Not Ben. Not at all.

'When did you buy this place?' she asked, stripping off her coat and scarf and hanging them over the back of a kitchen chair before removing her boots.

'A couple of years ago. I wanted somewhere separate. Somewhere that was mine.'

Luce thought she could understand that. Of course she encouraged her family to treat her house as theirs, but technically it belonged to her. That mattered.

'Did you get someone in to decorate?' Because this was the perfect rustic-cottage look. The sort of thing that either happened naturally or cost thousands via an interior designer. She didn't see Ben as the naturally rustic type.

'I did it,' Ben said, without looking up from the tiny flame he was coaxing.

Luce tried to hide her surprise. 'Well, it's gorgeous,' she said after a moment. Because it was—even more so, somehow, now she knew it was his own work. It wasn't beautiful, or tasteful, or on trend. It was warm and cosy and she loved it.

As the fire caught Ben flashed her a smile—the first she'd seen since they left Chester.

'So glad you approve.'

In that moment the cottage itself ceased to be the most attractive thing in the vicinity. Luce swallowed, looked away and said, 'Um…so, how long do you think we'll be stuck here?'

Standing up, Ben straightened, brushing his hands off on his jeans. 'Until the snow stops, at least. Don't think we'll be going anywhere until tomorrow.'

Tomorrow. Which meant spending another night in close proximity to Ben Hampton. Another night of not throwing caution to the wind and saying, *Seduce me*. Just to find out, after eight years of wondering, what it would be like.

The look he gave her suggested that he'd read her mind—but imperfectly. 'Don't fret. There's a spare room. It even has a key to lock it from the inside, if you're still worried that this is some great master plan to get into your knickers.'

Heat flushed in Luce's cheeks. She should probably apologise for that at some point. But since he was the one who'd point-blank propositioned her the night before maybe sorry could wait. Besides, just as the night before, she was more concerned that she'd need the lock to keep herself in, rather than him out.

Not thinking about it.

'What do we do until then?' she asked.

Ben shrugged. 'Up to you. Work, if you like. Personally, I'm going to make myself an Irish coffee and warm up by the fire. Then, once this snow slows down, I'm going to walk down into the village and see if the Eight Bells is serving dinner. I'd invite you to join me, but I'd hate for you to get the wrong idea about my intentions.'

'I do still need to eat,' Luce pointed out. 'And besides, Hampton & Sons have once again failed to make good on their promise—I was supposed to be in Cardiff by now. The way I figure it, you owe me another dinner.'

Ben raised an eyebrow. 'Really? Seems to me that you relying on me for a bed for the night—without, I might add, any of the activities that usually make such a thing worthwhile—is becoming a bit of a habit. So, is that dinner *instead* of a night's free accommodation in a charmingly rustic cottage?'

Luce considered. 'Maybe we could go halves on dinner?'

'Good plan.' Ben moved into the kitchen area and pulled a bag of coffee from the cupboard. 'So, do you want the grand tour?'

Luce spun round to smile at him and nodded. 'Yes, please.'

'Right, then.' Waving an arm expansively around the

living, dining and kitchen space, he said, 'This is the main room. Bathroom's over there. That's my room. That's yours.' He pointed at the relevant doors in turn. 'Back door leads out to the mountain. Front door leads to the car and a lot of snow. That's about it. Now, how Irish do you want your coffee?'

She should take advantage of the afternoon to work, really. But her laptop was still in the car, and she was cold and tired and stuck with Ben Hampton for another night. She deserved a warming drink and a sit by the fire, didn't she?

Luce perched on a kitchen stool and watched him fill the coffee maker. 'Make sure it's at least got a decent accent.'

Ben grinned at her. 'Will do.'

Ben had been more concerned with getting in and getting warm than studying Luce's expression when they arrived at the cottage. But now, watching her sink into the sofa, coffee in hand and feet stretched out towards the fire, he smiled to see her looking so at home there.

It wasn't an impressive cottage. He knew that. None of the homes in a ten-mile radius had more than three bedrooms; anything bigger would have been ostentatious. Ben wanted to fit in here. So when he'd bought the tumbledown stone building he hadn't extended it, just rebuilt it as it would have been. And it wasn't the most expensive of his properties—not by a long stretch. But it was his favourite. Not least because it was the only one that was really *his*. Bought with his own money, chosen by himself, decorated by himself. The penthouse in London, impressive as it was, belonged to the company and had been decorated by their interior designer. And the château... That still had his grandmother's favourite rose print wallpaper all over it. He really needed to get out there and start sorting that place out.

But not now. This was his week off. His week of relaxation in his favourite place. Albeit with an unexpected, suspicious and snappish guest, and the prospect of a round trip to Cardiff in the snow tomorrow.

Sipping his own coffee, Ben let the warmth of the cottage flood his bones, relax his muscles, the way it always did when he came home.

Home. Luce had asked him where it was and he'd said he didn't have one. He hadn't explained that he didn't want one. He'd had a home once, only to lose it when his father's obsession with work drove his mother away.

He didn't need a home that could be taken from him. He just needed a bolthole to hide out and recharge. Could be anywhere. Right now it just happened to be here, that was all.

I need to spend more time here.

Once he'd deposited Luce home he'd come back and look at his work schedule for the next twelve months. Figure out where there might be a break long enough to get back to Wales again. Maybe even over to France.

Luce drained her coffee and said, 'So, this pub you mentioned?'

'The Eight Bells. Best pint and best pies this side of the border.' They'd missed lunch in the snow. She was probably as starving as he was.

'Sounds promising,' Luce said, but she didn't sound convinced.

Ben decided to put her out of her misery. 'And, for you townies, there's a pretty decent wine list, too.'

'Oh, thank God.' Her face brightened.

Ben chuckled. 'Less than a day with me and you're already desperate for a drink? What? The coffee not Irish enough for you?'

'It's lovely,' Luce said. 'But after this day I'm ready for a hearty meal and a large glass of wine.'

Ben enjoyed one more moment of warmth by the fire, then got to his feet. 'In that case, I guess we'd better prepare to face the elements again. You ready?'

Luce grinned and took his hand to let him pull her up. 'As I'll ever be.'

CHAPTER SEVEN

AFTER A SNOWY, freezing and downright treacherous walk into the village, Luce stamped the snow off her boots, unwound her scarf and let Ben go and find menus and drinks while she settled into a chair at the rustic wood table by an inglenook fireplace. The Eight Bells was certainly a lot nicer than she'd expected in a local village pub, but then, she supposed they were in the heart of tourist Wales around here. Made sense to cater to the townies.

Not that there were many of them around tonight. Only a handful of tables were occupied, and those were by locals discussing the weather and when the roads would be cleared.

She shouldn't have been surprised that Ben would find a cottage near fine dining and local shops that delivered organic produce, she supposed. That was just who he was. How had she forgotten that?

It was the cottage, she decided. It was so homely. Somewhere she could imagine actually living herself. Nothing like the fancy hotel he'd been living in when she and Mandy had visited from university. Not even anything like the suite at the Royal Court in Chester. And yet it was his. Maybe there were nuances to Ben Hampton she was missing after all.

'Check out the pie list.' Ben dropped a couple of menus

on the table, then placed a glass of white wine in front of her. Wrapping her fingers round the stem, she took a long sip. Ben was right; this place had really good wine.

'You recommend the pies, then?' she asked, scanning the menu.

'I recommend everything on the menu.' He wasn't even looking at it, she realised.

'You come here often?'

'As often as I can.' He sipped his pint. 'The owner's an old friend of mine.'

That was one constant. Ben had always had a lot of friends around. When Mandy had started dating him Luce had assumed that his hangers-on were after his money, or the parties he could get them into. But over time it had become clear that they genuinely enjoyed his company. Ben was one of those people with a talent for making people like him.

Not a talent Luce had ever claimed to possess.

'I'll try the chicken pie, then,' she said, closing the menu. Ben nodded, and went to place their order. Watching him go, Luce studied the width of his shoulders, the confidence of his stride. Apart from a little extra muscle and size, how much had he really changed in the last eight years? Was he still the same boy who had kissed her in the hotel library?

Would he try again?

He was back before she had anything approaching an answer to that question.

'So,' he said, settling himself into his chair with practised ease, 'Old Joe over there tells me the snow should be over for now, but we might get another load tomorrow night. Hopefully the roads will be clear enough tomorrow to make a break for Cardiff before it hits. A few of the locals plan to take the tractors out in the morning and clear them.'

'That's good.' Getting home tomorrow would still give her a day and a half to work, at the least.

'Until then I'm afraid you're stuck with me. So, in the meantime, I believe this is the part where we make small talk. What topic do you want? Politics? Religion?'

'Tell me what you've been doing since university.' He looked surprised, so she added, 'I bored you about Nest last night. Now it's your turn.'

She needed to know where he'd been, what he'd done, so she could understand who he was now. For some reason it seemed vitally important that she make sense of him before they headed back to the cottage and their separate beds. Luce very carefully ignored the small part of her brain that murmured, *And if I understand him, if I know him, I'll know if it's safe to ask him to kiss me tonight.*

But Ben just shrugged and said, 'Pretty much as expected. Graduated and went to work for the family business...'

'It seems to be doing well enough.'

His smile was a trifle smug. 'Doubled the profits in my first five years. On track to triple them in the next two.'

That Ben was familiar. The one who thought money was the most important thing in the world. 'Your father must be very proud,' she said, thinking of the stern grey-haired man she'd met that one fateful day she'd spent in Ben's world. She didn't mean it to sound so dry, so sarcastic, but it came out that way regardless.

'He died about a year ago.' Ben's eyes were on his glass rather than her as he spoke, and a sharp spike of sympathy pierced Luce's chest.

'I'm so sorry.' She knew how that felt. That hole—the

space where a person should be. Trying to find a way to live without someone who'd defined you all your life.

But Ben rolled his shoulders back and gave her a strange half-smile. 'I wouldn't be. To be honest, I've barely noticed the difference. Just means that now it's my brother Seb checking up on my methods instead.'

There he was. The boy who'd had so little regard for the things that mattered—family, friends, responsibility, doing the right thing—had grown up exactly as she'd expected. Into a man who still had no respect for the things that mattered to her. A man she couldn't consider sleeping with even if she was sure it would be magnificent. *And* a sure way to find that relaxation he promised.

Except there was something in his eyes. Something else. 'You must miss him, though?'

'He wasn't really the sort of father you missed.'

She wanted to ask more, to try to understand how his father's death could have had so little impact on him. But before she could find the right question the waitress brought their food and Ben had switched the conversation to pies and homemade chips.

In fact, Luce realised as she tucked into her truly delicious meal, he seemed almost too keen to keep the conversation light and inconsequential. As he started another story about a hotel somewhere in Scotland that had served compulsory haggis to its guests for breakfast every Sunday Luce smiled politely, nodded in the right places and tried to think of a way to get him to open up. He was hiding something, she was sure, and her incurable curiosity was determined to find out what it was before she had to return to Cardiff.

'Let's have another drink before we head home,' she suggested, when he paused in regaling her with his tales.

Home. Oh, God, she'd just called the cottage 'home'. If

ever anything was guaranteed to send a man running in the opposite direction, laying claim to his house as your own before you'd even really been on a proper date was probably it. But Ben hadn't flinched or reacted. Maybe he hadn't noticed. Maybe Luce really could be that lucky.

'Sure. But I warn you now: I'm not carrying you back in that snow.'

'I think I can manage.'

Ben studied her carefully, as if he suspected an ulterior motive, but at least he didn't seem terrified at her presumption. Luce tried not to shift under his gaze and pretended very hard that she'd said nothing of consequence at all.

'Okay, then.' Ben got to his feet. 'You have a look at the pudding menu while I get the drinks.'

Now, *that* was a mission Luce could get stuck into. Then all she had to do was figure out a way to get Ben to open up to her.

Ben rested his weight against the bar, waiting for their drinks, and watched Luce from the corner of his eye. Not that she'd notice. She seemed completely absorbed by the dessert menu, and he wondered if she'd go for the chocolate mousse or the sticky toffee pudding. She didn't seem like a fruit salad girl. It was one of the things he liked about her.

That was a surprise in itself. The Lucinda he'd known so many years ago hadn't been someone you liked. She hadn't let anyone close enough to find out any of her likable qualities. Locked up in her room studying, running off to the library or covering the tiny kitchen table in the flat with papers and textbooks. That was how he remembered her. The way she'd always run off to her room when he and Mandy had arrived home. Apart from a few hastily eaten dinners together, when Mandy insisted on them 'getting to know each other', that was all he'd known of her. He'd never been able to understand how someone as outgoing and fun-loving as Mandy could even be friends with her. Hadn't believed her when she'd said that Luce could be fun sometimes.

He could see it now, though. She was the sort of woman who grew into herself. Her confidence and self-possession had let her beauty, humour and personality shine out at last. And she'd grown into her body, too. Had she grown into her sexuality in the same way?

It bothered him how much he wanted to find out.

And now the weather had given him the perfect chance to do just that. It might not have been a plan in the way Luce had accused him, but it certainly was an opportunity to take advantage of.

One night in a secluded cottage was even more perfect than one night in a luxury hotel. As long as it was just one night and the snow didn't strand them there any longer. Two nights in a row and women started to get ideas, Ben had found. Which was why he'd committed to his one-night rule.

And Luce was up to something; that much was clear. Given another glass of wine, he was pretty sure he could figure out what, and how it might affect his seduction plans.

The barmaid handed over their drinks and Ben took them with a wide, friendly smile before heading back to Luce. He had hopes for what was going on here, and if he was right the evening could be set for a much better ending than he'd dared to assume the night before.

'So, what are you fancying?' Ben put the drinks down on the table and tried not to smirk when Luce looked up, eyes wide and face flustered.

'Um…' Her gaze flicked back down to the menu. 'The sticky toffee pudding?'

'Good choice.' Dropping into his chair, Ben reached his arms out across the back and felt his muscles stretch. 'Tracy says she'll be over to take our order in a moment.'

'Great.' Placing the menu back on the table, Luce folded her hands over it.

Ben braced himself for whatever line of questioning was coming next.

'So, what do you do when you're not working?'

To his horror, Ben actually had to think about an answer. When had he become so obsessed with work? That was Seb and Dad. Not him.

'Oh, you know. The usual. Fine dining. Trips abroad.' That sounded obnoxious. She already thought he was obnoxious. He really shouldn't make it any worse. 'I have a château in France—well, my grandmother did. She left it to me. I'm renovating it.' Or he should be. He *would* be. As soon as he found the time.

Luce raised her eyebrows and Ben cast his gaze over to the bar to see where the hell Tracy the barmaid had got to.

'You're interested in property development? First the cottage, now the château?'

'Yes,' Ben lied. It had nothing to do with making money. He'd done up the cottage so he had somewhere to escape to. And he wanted to do the château because…well, he couldn't just leave it there to crumble, now, could he?

'So what's next?' Luce asked, then glanced up and said, 'Oh, the sticky toffee pudding for me, please.'

It took Ben a moment to catch up, to realise that Tracy was standing patiently behind him with her notebook. 'Same for me, please.' He gave her a smile and watched her walk back to the bar. Maybe Luce would get cross enough at him paying attention to another woman that she'd stop asking questions he didn't want to answer.

No such luck.

'So?' she repeated. 'What comes after the château?'

'No idea,' Ben said with a shrug. 'You know me—I'm a take-one-day-at-a-time kind of guy.'

Except he wasn't any more. Not really. He couldn't be—not when Seb was relying on him so much these days. He knew exactly what would be next. More visits to more hotels. More reports on what was working and what wasn't. Long, long meetings with Seb and his team about where the company was going. More spot inspections on long-standing members of the Hampton & Sons chain. More firing old managers and putting in their own people. More budget meetings where the accountants told them they should get the hotels to improve drastically without giving them any money to do it.

Business was business, after all.

'Still?' Luce asked. 'I suppose I shouldn't be surprised. People don't really change at heart, do they?'

Ben looked at her, sipping her wine across the table, her gaze too knowing, and for once he wanted to tell someone the truth. That sometimes he was sick of all the rules he'd set for himself. That sometimes he did want to stop. To stay in one place for a while.

Downing the rest of his pint, he said, 'I need another drink,' and headed to the bar before the urge became too strong.

CHAPTER EIGHT

BEN RETURNED WITH another pint for himself and another glass of wine for Luce. She hadn't drunk more than half of the glass she already had, but she accepted it gracefully anyway. She had a feeling that he wasn't so much trying to get her drunk to take advantage of her, more to distract her.

Clearly he'd never experienced the Myles curiosity in full flow before.

'So, you left university, joined the family business, and you're still there?' She tipped her head sideways to look at him. 'So either you really have changed a little bit, or there's something about your job you truly love. Because the Ben Hampton I knew couldn't stick at anything for more than six months.' Which had, incidentally, been the exact length of his relationship with Mandy before the kiss in the library. Not that she'd counted.

Ben's hand was already on his pint. 'It's a job. It pays me very, very well and I don't have to sit in an office all day.'

Now, *that* sounded like the Ben she'd known. But it still felt wrong, somehow. And Luce had drunk enough wine to tell him so. 'That doesn't sound like it makes you happy.'

'Are jobs supposed to make you happy?' Ben asked, eyebrow raised.

'Mine does,' Luce said, in an immediate unconsidered response.

'Really?'

'Of course.' At least as long as she didn't think too much about the particulars. A lecturing position at the university and the opportunity to do her own research into areas of history that fascinated her. That was all she'd ever wanted.

It was just that day-to-day, dealing with the academic system, the obscure rules and regulations of academia, funding, and other colleagues…well, it could be a little… frustrating.

'So, which part do you love the most?' Ben asked. 'Attending dull lectures your colleagues can't be bothered to go to? Grading unoriginal essays? Applying for funding all the time just to actually do your job?'

Which was just a bit too close to her own thoughts for Luce's comfort. 'I'm not saying there aren't downsides, or days that aren't particularly joyous. But at the heart of it I love discovering the past. I love finding out about the lives of women long dead and how they influenced the world around them. That's what matters to me.'

Ben's gaze was curious now. How had this got turned around? Wasn't *she* supposed to be questioning *him*?

'In that case,' he asked, 'why aren't you spending all your time on your book? Looking at a linked lecture tour or even a TV programme? Why are you wasting time writing reports for your lazy colleague?'

'This is just how it works,' Luce said, reaching for her glass as an excuse not to look at him. 'It can't be all fun, all the time. There has to be responsibility, too.'

'And that's why I'm still working for the family business,' Ben said. 'Told you I could be responsible sometimes. Ah, look—pudding.'

Tracy put their bowls on the table with a curious glance between them. How many women had he brought here? Luce wondered. Was she the latest in a long line? Did she not fit the usual stereotype? Was that why everyone kept looking at her tonight?

She couldn't think about that now. What did it matter, anyway? Tomorrow she'd be back in Cardiff. She'd probably never think of Ben Hampton again.

Liar.

'Okay, then,' she said, reaching for her spoon. 'What would you be doing if you weren't working for the illustrious Hampton & Sons?'

Ben's spoon paused halfway to his mouth. 'Honestly? I have no idea.' He looked as if the concept had never even occurred to him. As if he'd never thought about what he'd actually *like* to do. He'd just fallen into his job and kept going.

Which was so entirely out of keeping with what Luce had thought she knew about his character that she forgot about pudding entirely.

'Well, what do you love doing?' she asked. 'Renovating properties?'

'I suppose.' He put his spoon back in his bowl and looked at her. 'Look, you seem to have the wrong impression here. I am very good at my job, and it serves the purpose I want it to serve—namely paying me more than enough to enjoy my life. Doing my job well keeps my brother and the investors happy. And I get to live my life my way. I never wanted my job to be my life, so this arrangement suits me pretty much perfectly.'

Explanation over, he dug back into his sticky toffee pudding and ignored Luce completely.

Which was fine by her. No need for him to see the utter confusion she was sure was painted across her face.

She just couldn't get a handle on this man. Every time she thought she understood something—that he'd changed, that he hadn't—he pulled the rug out again. Just when she was sure that he was a man stuck in a job he hated, searching for something to fulfil him, he turned round and told her that was the last thing he wanted.

She just didn't understand.

'You're looking baffled,' Ben said.

Luce glanced up to see him smiling in amusement. 'Just…trying to understand.'

His mouth took a sympathetic downturn, but his eyes were still laughing. 'I know. It's always hard for over-achievers to understand that work isn't everything.'

'That's not… There are plenty of things in my life besides work.'

'Oh, of course. Like running around after your family and friends, making their lives run smoothly.'

'Aren't you doing the same for your brother?'

Ben shook his head. 'Not at all. My job is my job, and I am compensated very handsomely for it, thank you.'

'There isn't a price you can put on love.'

'No,' Ben said, his voice suddenly, shockingly hard. 'There isn't. But what you do for them? That isn't love. That's pandering.'

Luce's emotions swung back again. No, he hadn't changed. Not at all. He still thought that he and his thoughts, his wants, his opinions, were the only things in the world that mattered. Couldn't begin to imagine that he might be wrong. That it might be different for other people.

'No—listen to me.'

Ben reached out and grabbed her hand with his own as he spoke, and Luce looked up into unexpectedly serious eyes.

'What do you want more than anything in the world?'

His skin against hers. His attention firmly placed on her. Those were the only reasons she felt a jolt of lust through her body at his question. The only reason her mind answered, *You.*

Luce pulled her hand away. *Note to self: I do not want to sleep with this man. It would be disastrous.*

'I want my family to be happy. Settled.' Because, she admitted, to herself if not out loud, if they were—if they didn't need her so damn much—maybe she could go out and find what made *her* happy.

'Because that would set you free?' Ben said.

Luce's gaze shot to his in surprise.

'Because if they were happy you wouldn't have to worry about them. But, Luce, they're never going to be happy and settled without you as long as you're still there bailing them out at every turn. You'll give and give until there's nothing of you left. And then you'll crack. My mother—' He stopped, looked away. 'I've seen it before. You can't give up your own life for your family.'

Luce swallowed. 'You have no idea what you're talking about.'

'I think I do.' The words were bitter.

But he didn't. And Luce couldn't tell him. How could she explain a grandfather who'd worked hard all his life for the little he had to a man who'd been born with everything? How could she explain the importance of doing the best job she could, giving it everything she had so she could be proud of herself at the end of the day? His job meant nothing to Ben, was just a means to an end. It was all about the money. So how could she explain the passion she felt when she uncovered a hidden bit of women's history? When she brought untold stories to light?

'You don't. My grandfather's last words to me… He made me promise to take care of my family. I'm the only one, you see. My mother's a wonderful woman, but she's lost in her own world most of the time. And my brother and sister inherited that. They don't see the real world. None of them do. That's why they need me.'

'They're not your responsibility.'

Ben's voice was gentle, but the words still stung.

'And maybe it's time for a change. For them to learn to look after themselves.'

Luce shook her head. 'I told you. They are what they are. They're not going to change now.'

'Not if you don't give them the chance.'

That wasn't fair. 'People don't change. Not really.'

'Not even you?' Ben asked, eyebrow raised.

Luce laughed. 'Especially not me. I'm exactly the same Lucinda Myles you remember from university, right?'

Ben's gaze trailed slowly across her face, down her body, and Luce felt her blood warm.

'Not exactly the same.'

'That's not the point. My family are my responsibility, whatever you think.' Because they were all she had, too. And wasn't that a sad thing, at twenty-eight, to have nothing else but a family that needed you? Luce drained the last of her wine. 'I think it's time to go home,' she said, and Ben nodded.

They were halfway to the cottage before she realised she'd called it 'home' again.

They walked back to the cottage in silence. The snow had stopped, at last, but the paths were still slippery underfoot. The air stung Ben's lungs as they climbed the path, making it too painful to talk even if he'd had any idea of what to say.

Why was she so entrenched in solving things for her family? Because she'd promised her grandfather? That didn't seem enough. There had to be something else, but he was damned if he could figure out what. When would she learn? You couldn't fix everything for anyone. So you did what you could and you moved on. You couldn't let other people pull you down.

Had she been like this at university? He couldn't remember. She must have gone home a lot, though, since he and Mandy had often taken advantage of the flat being empty at weekends. A sliver of self-loathing jarred into him. Of course *that* was what he remembered. Why hadn't he paid more attention to Luce then?

Or perhaps the better question was, why was he paying so much attention to her now?

Finally they reached the cottage and Ben dug in his pockets for the keys. Luce waited silently at his side for the door to open. Inside, the under-floor heating was doing its job admirably, which was just as well as the fire had all but burnt out. They both stripped off their outer layers, and Ben took the coats and hung them by the back door. When he turned round Luce still stood where he'd left her, looking at him, her eyes huge and sad.

'Do you really believe that your family aren't your responsibility?'

She looked distraught at the idea that anyone could believe such a thing. *She should have spent some time with my old man.*

He wanted to say the right thing. Words that would make her smile again, as she had over dinner. But he wasn't going to lie to her.

'I think that your family need to learn to manage without you for a while. You can't mortgage your own life, your own happiness, for theirs.'

Luce just shook her head. 'We really haven't changed at all, have we?'

Despite her assertions that people didn't change, she sounded so forlorn at the idea that Ben moved closer, his body determined to comfort her even if his mind knew it was a bad idea. His hands settled at her waist as she spoke again.

'We're exactly the same people we were at university.'

'No.' Even to his own ears his voice sounded harsh. 'We're not.'

Luce looked up at him. She was so close that he could see the uncertainty in her eyes.

'Aren't we? I may not wear jeans and baggy jumpers every day, but I'd still rather be working than in the pub. Tonight notwithstanding,' she added, a small smile on her lips.

'You came to the pub, though. That's new.'

'Maybe. And what about you? Back then…'

'I spent every night in the pub and didn't care about work,' Ben finished for her. 'I promise you that tonight is not representative of my adult life.'

'Back then,' Luce repeated, 'you cared about yourself first. Your own happiness was most important, and you didn't want the responsibility of anyone else's on your shoulders.'

A memory struck him—something long forgotten and hidden. A book-lined room and a dark-haired girl in the moonlight, a plain dress draped over her body, fear and confusion in her eyes as he moved closer. Had that really been him? No wonder Mandy had ditched him. He hadn't cared about Luce's happiness then, had he? Or the responsibility he had to his girlfriend. *Hell.* Did Luce remember? She must. That was why she'd asked. No wonder she needed to know if he'd changed.

'I care enough about you to try and help you finish your book. Reclaim your life.' He was grasping at straws, he knew. Trying to find something to show her he *had* changed.

Luce tipped her head to the side. 'Do you? Or are you just trying to get me into bed?'

'I can't do both?' Ben joked, but Luce's face was serious. He sighed. 'Trust me, I wouldn't do all of this just for sex.' He pulled away, but her hand brushed his arm, a silent request to stay close, and despite the desperate urge to leave this conversation behind and retreat to his room with a bottle of whisky, Ben found he couldn't move.

'I have to know. Do you really not remember your twenty-first? Are you sure you're not trying to make up for that night?'

Ben shook his head automatically. It hadn't even occurred to him that he should.

'Or finish what you started?'

'I didn't even remember until just now. I…I knew I hadn't been kind to you back then. Maybe that was why I took you to dinner last night. Gave you somewhere to stay. This is something entirely different.'

Her teeth sank into her lower lip as she stepped forward, closer than before, so close that he could feel her breath through the cotton of his shirt. She looked up, her eyes bright, and Ben felt his breath catch in his chest.

'Then the only thing I can think is that you wanted me here so you could hear me beg you to seduce me.'

God, yes. Heat flooded through his body at her words, fierce and unchecked. Her lashes fluttered shut over her eyes and Ben knew this was his chance. This was the closest she'd let herself get to asking for what she wanted. This was the moment he should sweep her up in his arms and off to bed, like Owain kidnapping Nest.

And he couldn't.

He couldn't be what she remembered—alcohol on his breath as he pushed a kiss on her, whether she wanted it or not. He was a different man now, and she needed to know that. People really did change.

Stepping back caused him physical pain. His muscles were aching to stay with her, to pull her against his chest and hold her close.

'Not like this,' he said, his voice hoarse.

And then he walked away.

CHAPTER NINE

LUCE WOKE UP on Wednesday morning determined not to spend one more sleepless night on Ben Hampton.

She was through. From nights spent waiting for him and Mandy to kick everyone else out of the flat and go to bed at university, to the long, long night after she ran away from him in the hotel library, to that night in Chester, to last night, spent wondering and wondering. It was enough.

It didn't matter if he'd changed his mind about seducing her. In fact it was a good thing that he hadn't. Because the very last thing Luce needed at the moment was someone else needing her to take care of their lives. She had a book to write, after all, and Ben Hampton's life was a mess—even if he was too busy trying to fix hers to notice it.

Actually, she told herself, staring up at the uneven ceiling of the cottage, it was probably all for the best. She'd made a decision eight years ago not to get involved with this man. A decision she'd renewed and confirmed in Chester, and again yesterday when he brought her to the cottage. She might have nearly broken that resolution because of too much wine and conversation, or because of a brief, misguided hope that people really could change, but that wasn't enough. She should thank Ben, really, for *not* taking advantage of her vulnerable position and letting her stick to her beliefs.

Not that she was going to, of course.

Shifting under the sheet, Luce turned over with a sigh. The problem was that she wanted him. She might not be the most obviously sexual person in the world—but she was an academic, not a nun. Although they might as well be the same thing at the moment. Too much time working, researching, writing, lecturing… It didn't leave a lot of time for romance. Or even just a fun encounter with a gorgeous guy.

But Luce wasn't supposed to want that, was she? It wasn't the way she was made. Wasn't in her history. No, she was supposed to study, to learn, to improve herself. Sex didn't improve anything in her admittedly limited experience. Hell, even Nest, in her restricted, disapproving time, had managed to have more sex with considerably more guys than Luce had.

Her head flopped back against the pillow and she finally admitted the truth to herself. She'd wanted Ben Hampton last night. And, more than that, she'd wanted him to make the first move—to take her—so that she could rationalise away her desire this morning. She'd wanted to be able to say it was a weak moment, that it was the wine and the romantic snowbound cottage. She'd wanted to be able to move on and forget it without admitting that sex with him was something she really wanted.

Craved. Needed.

Well, she was just going to have to get used to going without. Because there was no way she could ask him for it now. Humiliation really wasn't her colour, and she wouldn't risk him turning her down again.

Damn it.

With a deep breath, Luce sat up. 'Time to move on,' she said softly.

Her room—the spare room—had a desk, a king-sized

bed and an *en suite* bathroom. If you had to be stranded in the middle of nowhere, Luce figured this was the sort of place you wanted to be stuck. It wasn't a particularly feminine room, but then, Luce wouldn't have expected it to be. Ben had decorated it, after all. The huge bed was draped in a wine-red quilt, soft and cosy, with cushions and pillows piled up at the head. Beside the bed stood a chenille-covered armchair, perfect for curling up with a book. And under the window was the desk—sturdy, probably antique, and exactly what she needed. Slipping out of bed, Luce ran a hand across its scarred wooden surface and for the first time could imagine herself finishing her book. Telling Nest's story to the world, finally, the way she wanted it to be known.

Might as well make the best of a bad situation. She was stuck there at least until Ben woke up. She'd retrieved her laptop from the car before their trip to the pub, so she could at least get some work done.

Luce listened for movement outside her door and, hearing nothing, risked slipping out long enough to make a pot of tea and some toast and sneak it back into her room. Then, wrapped up in her pyjamas, socks and an old jumper she'd found in one of the drawers, she settled down at her desk.

Ben Hampton didn't matter any more. All that did matter was telling Nest's story the right way.

There was no sign of Luce when Ben emerged from his room the next morning. Which was probably for the best. His surge of nobility, admittedly spurred on by a determination to prove that he *had* changed in the last eight years, might not have lasted in the face of Luce in pyjamas. Or a nightdress. Or maybe nothing at all...

After a night of contemplating the possibilities, and

imagining what might have happened if he'd just kissed her properly and carried her off to bed, those images were firmly burned onto his brain. God only knew what it was going to take to get them out again. And knowing she was just metres away, probably still in bed, really wasn't helping.

Ben eyed the closed bedroom door, grabbed his keys and headed out. Fresh air and distance was what he needed. And he could check out the state of the roads while he was at it.

Ben took the drive into the village slowly. The snow showed no sign of melting, but the roads were clearer than he'd expected—obviously some of the local farm vehicles had already been out. Ben parked up outside the Eight Bells and decided he deserved a warming cup of something, and maybe some of Tracy's homemade cake, before he hit the village store for supplies and a weather forecast.

Johnny, the landlord, raised his eyebrows from behind the pumps at the sight of him. 'Didn't expect to see you out of bed so early.'

'It's gone ten,' Ben pointed out, leaning against the bar.

'Exactly.' Johnny reached behind him to flick the coffee machine on. 'Tracy said it looked like you and your new friend were planning to hit the sheets for the rest of the week when you left here last night.'

'Well, Tracy was wrong,' Ben said, trying not to think about how close to right she might have been. 'Besides, Luce is an old friend—not a new one. We were at university together.' No need to get into the details.

'Hmm.' The corners of Johnny's mouth dipped down for a moment, as if to say, *Okay, then. If you say so,* as he handed over a cup of coffee.

'What?'

'Just… You do realise she's the first person—male or female—you've ever brought to my pub?'

'So?'

'Is she the first person you've taken up to your cottage at all?'

An uncomfortable feeling crept up Ben's back. 'Yeah. We were driving to Cardiff when the snow got heavy, so we stopped off here.'

'That explains it, then, I guess. We just figured she must be someone important.' He didn't sound pleased at the explanation. 'So. Old friend?'

'Yeah, you know. Nice to catch up and stuff.' Ben picked up his coffee, and motioned to one of the tables by the window. 'Anyway, I'd better drink up and get back to her. Lousy host, really.'

'I can imagine,' Johnny said.

But the frown line between his eyebrows told Ben he was still a little disappointed by the set-up.

Why? he wondered as he made his way over to the table. Was it so inconceivable that he'd bring a friend to visit? Just because he hadn't done it in the last few years? Why *hadn't* he, actually? He supposed it hadn't occurred to him. The women he spent time with all preferred a night at one of the hotels, the swankier the better, and since Hampton & Sons didn't have anything under five stars except their newest acquisitions—in this case, the Royal Court, which had a measly four—it was easier just to check into the nearest one. And if he was meeting friends it was the local pub or the curry house. No need for them to trek all the way to the middle of nowhere in Wales. Besides, the cottage was *his* place. It was where he went when he needed to escape from the real world. There'd never been much point in bringing the real world with him.

Luce wasn't the real world. This brief sojourn in the

snow had nothing to do with reality. Once he'd taken her back to Cardiff the brief time bubble would be over and he'd forget all about her for another eight years, while he got on with his life and she refused to. Easy.

His phone rang as soon as he sat down. 'Hampton.'

'Other Hampton.'

Seb's dry voice sounded out of place as Ben sat staring across at the Welsh mountains. Seb was urban and urbane. He was the city, and the company, and the polished wood of his office.

He'd definitely never invited Seb up to the cottage. Maybe he should.

'What can I do for you today, oh, fearless leader?'

'Stop calling me that, for a start.'

On the other end of the line Ben heard his brother shuffling papers before he continued.

'I just got through reading your report from Chester.'

'And?'

A pause. Never good.

Then Seb said, 'When are you back in London?'

'Tomorrow night was the plan. Might make it Friday—snow dependent.'

'Can you stop by and see me on Friday? I know it's Christmas Eve, and you're supposed to be off the rest of the week…'

'I can,' Ben said. 'But if there's a problem with my report I'd rather you just tell me now.'

Another pause.

'It's not a problem, exactly.'

Seb didn't sound annoyed, or let down, which Ben was pretty sure their father would have done. That was something.

'Just an idea I want to talk through with you.'

Now, *that* was new. For the last six months Seb had

been making the decisions and Ben had been making them happen. That was how they operated, and it worked well. But if Seb was willing to let him in, loosen his grip on the reins… *Maybe he won't turn into Dad after all.*

'Okay. So, how's London coping without me?'

'Never mind London,' Seb said. 'Tell me about this brunette from Chester. Did you actually take her to your cottage? The forbidden inner sanctum?'

It felt wrong to hear Luce described that way, and Ben regretted ever mentioning her to Seb. He clamped down on the surge of anger filling his chest, reminding himself that Seb was only talking about her the way Ben himself had, last time they'd spoken.

'It's not… She's an old friend,' Ben said, repeating the line he'd used with Johnny and wondering why it felt like such a lie. Because they'd never really *been* friends, he supposed. 'I was driving her back to Cardiff and we detoured to the cottage because of the snow.'

'Wow. You *did* actually take her to your fabled cottage? I was kidding about that part. She must be pretty important.'

'More that I didn't want to die in a snowy crash,' Ben assured him. 'Her train was cancelled, I was headed this way anyway, so I drove her. That's all.'

'Hmm.'

Ben didn't think Seb needed to sound quite so disbelieving. 'Yeah, well, I should get back to my host duties,' he said, draining his coffee. 'I'll see you on Friday.'

It didn't matter what Seb thought about Luce, he reminded himself as he stood and put on his coat. Because after today she'd be out of his life again.

Which was a good thing. Right?

Except if he wasn't going to see her again… The thought of not having her, just once, burned at his heart.

He needed to touch her, to feel her—hell, even just to hold her. The memory of her swaying into his arms the night before wasn't fading. How could he *not* experience more than that?

But after turning her down the night before…? Ben wasn't stupid. She wasn't going to ask again. He'd head back to the cottage, they'd pack up the car and drive to Cardiff, and that would be it. He'd blown the only chance he'd get with Luce Myles.

But as he left the Eight Bells a leaflet in the rack for tourists caught his eye, and Ben realised that maybe there was one more thing he could give Luce before they parted ways. Something for her to remember these strange, snowy few days by.

Pocketing the leaflet, he headed over to the village shop, his mood suddenly a whole lot lighter.

It hadn't been Luce's most productive morning ever.

She'd started well—up with the lark and at the desk with her computer cursor blinking at her. Outside, the snow looked as if it might be starting to clear, which gave her hope that they might make it to Cardiff today. She'd heard the front door slam after she'd been working a couple of hours, and reasoned that Ben had probably gone to check on the conditions. She'd have to wait until he got back to face him. Heat had flooded to her cheeks at the very thought. Really no hurry on that one. Then they'd be on their way and it would all be over. She'd be home again.

In the meantime, the book wouldn't write itself.

The first couple of pages of the section dealing with Nest's life at Cilgerran Castle, before her abduction, had come in an inspired burst, leaving her feeling buoyant and excited. And then…nothing.

After another half an hour of staring at the screen and

adjusting punctuation, Luce had given up and indulged in a long soak in the bath instead. Hot water and bubbles were almost guaranteed to help inspiration strike, surely?

Except when she settled back down at the desk, fully dressed in a long knitted skirt and wine-red sweater, she still had nothing.

'Going well?'

Luce spun round to see Ben leaning against the door-frame, arms folded over his chest and his eyebrow raised. He betrayed no sign of his rejection the night before—which was a small point in his favour, Luce supposed.

'I think I'm getting some really useful stuff,' she lied, and hoped he hadn't heard the bath water draining out.

Ben held up a bakery bag. 'Well, brunch will help. I brought ham and cheese croissants.'

Luce's stomach rumbled at the very mention.

As they sat down together at the small kitchen table Luce asked, 'What are the roads like? Can we make Cardiff today?'

Ben nodded, already chewing. 'More snow due tonight, but we should be able to beat it.'

She should be relieved. Thrilled that she was heading home. So what was with the strange, sad part of her that was already missing the cottage before they'd even left?

And not just the cottage. The company.

Luce stared down at her plate. Definitely time to go.

'I should go and get packed up, then,' she said, even though the only things she'd really unpacked were her laptop and notes.

'Actually…'

Ben paused and she looked up at him. Was he going to ask her to stay? No. That was ridiculous.

'There's somewhere I'd like to take you. Before you go. It's not exactly on our way, but I think it'll be worth it.'

Luce frowned. 'How out of our way? Where is it?'

'It's a surprise.' Ben's smile was slow and teasing. 'But I promise you you'll like it.'

The problem with that, Luce reflected, was that what she liked and wanted wasn't always good for her. But if this was her last ever day with Ben, how could she turn down the chance to spend a few more hours with him?

'Finish your croissant first,' he said, and she obeyed.

Twenty minutes later they were all packed up. Pulling on her thick coat and boots, Luce followed Ben out to the car, her eyes drawn to the way his upper body filled out his coat. He really had grown into his size over the last eight years. How was she supposed to forget how good it had felt to be held against that chest the night before when he was just *there*, looking gorgeous?

Of course after today he wouldn't be.

Sighing, she got into the car, fastening her seatbelt without looking at him again. Instead, she looked back at the cottage as they drove away, and wondered if there was any chance she'd ever see it again.

'You okay?' Ben asked as they reached the main road out of the village.

'Fine.' She flashed him a quick smile, then glanced away. So much pretty countryside to look at, all white and sparkling. Why should she look at him anyway? 'Are you really not going to tell me where we're going?'

'I told you. It's a surprise.'

Luce didn't know the area well enough to be able to guess where they were headed, and by the time they hit the bigger roads she was too absorbed in her own thoughts and the snow-capped hills and frosted trees around her to pay attention to road signs. What would this countryside have looked like in Nest's time? Would she have ridden through these hills? How had it felt when she'd had to leave this landscape behind and move to England?

What would Ben do if she kissed him?

Luce closed her eyes. *No.* Back to what mattered. Nest. Her book. Not her sex drive.

Although Nest had obviously had enough of one, given the number of men she'd been connected to and the number of children she'd borne.

Not the point. Okay. Enough about Nest the woman. Focus on the book itself. The structure. Should she break Chapter Seven into two parts? Should she ask Ben in for dinner when they got to Cardiff? Or more…

Oh, God, this was hopeless.

'We're here,' Ben said, his voice amused, and Luce realised belatedly that the car had stopped moving.

Fumbling with the handle, Luce threw the door open and stepped out into the snow. She smoothed down her skirt with one hand, aware that Ben was walking around the car towards her.

'Figured out where we are yet?' he asked.

He was standing too close for her to think straight. She could feel the warmth of his breath on her neck, a wonderful contrast to the wintry chill.

She stepped away quickly and looked up. 'Oh!'

The twin round towers of Cilgerran Castle loomed overhead, grey and dark against the sky, snow capping them, and Luce's breath caught in her throat. She'd have known where she was in an instant, even without the information board at the edge of the car park. This place mattered. This was history made real, right before her. 'This is it. This is—'

'Cilgerran Castle. Where they say Nest was abducted from.'

Ben moved behind her and she could feel his warmth through her coat.

'Good idea?'

She nodded, her head jerking up and down hard to show him just what a fantastic idea she thought it was. This was what she needed. To get close to Nest physically as well as intellectually. She needed to stand where she had stood, needed to feel the stone walls around her. Needed to understand how Nest had felt so many years ago.

Why hadn't she come here before? Oh, she had, she supposed, back when she was studying for her Masters and Nest had been just a passing interest in half a module of her course. But never since. After all, she'd done it already. Why waste the day getting there and back to Cardiff again when there was so much else she needed to do?

But she'd never felt then what she felt now. The feeling that all of history was coming together in one place, just to help her understand.

'I hadn't realised it was so close,' she murmured, and felt Ben shrug behind her. He was so close, too.

'A couple of hours. You were daydreaming on the way here.'

Had it really been that long? They could have got to Cardiff and back already. 'I was thinking about Nest.' Mostly.

'I saw a leaflet for it in the Eight Bells rack earlier. Thought it looked like your sort of thing. And when I remembered how you told me Nest had lived here, was taken from here, I had to bring you.'

Luce spun round, finding herself nose to chest with him. How had she forgotten he was so close? His hand settled on her waist to steady her when she stumbled on the uneven ground and heat radiated through Luce's body. Raising her gaze to meet his, she said, 'Thank you.'

'You're welcome.'

The words were simple, but the emotions they evoked were anything but. His lips were just inches away. If she went up on tiptoes she could kiss him so easily. It would be a thank-you kiss, nothing more, but she'd get to feel his mouth against hers. And, oh, how she wanted to…

She bit down on her own lip to try to curb the temptation. But Ben's fingers still pressed against her waist. Then he glanced away, hands dropping from her body, and she saw his Adam's apple bob as he swallowed.

'Shall we go in?' he asked.

Luce stepped back and nodded again. Nest—that was why she was here. And then she was leaving. She really had to try to remember that.

CHAPTER TEN

BEN WATCHED LUCE'S rear move enticingly under that touchable flowing skirt as she gripped the handrail of the bridge over the moat, struggling to keep her footing on the icy wood as she made her way into the castle. It had seemed like such a good, obvious idea to bring her when he'd seen the leaflet. Killing two birds with one big hunk of tumbledown rock. Lots of Brownie points for him for thinking of it, meaning she'd be thinking kindly of him again as they drove to Cardiff. Maybe even enough to say yes if he asked her to dinner again. He could spend the night in Cardiff, head straight to London in the morning. Because this wasn't over yet. It couldn't be.

Memories of his twenty-first birthday flashed through his mind again. He'd wanted to seduce this woman eight years ago, before he'd even really known her. And now that feeling was a thousand times stronger.

He was pretty sure she'd go along with it this time, if he did. Last night's awkward resolution notwithstanding, he'd seen the signs. The way her body swayed into his whenever he got close, the way her eyes widened when her gaze caught his. And the way her teeth had pressed down into her lip, displaying just how plump and kissable it was. Her resistance was definitely crumbling.

He had to stop thinking about this. He had to wait. Otherwise he'd be seducing her up against a very cold stone castle keep.

Inside the castle walls Ben found a bench near an information board, brushed off the snow as best he could and sat down to watch the show. Cilgerran was a nice enough castle, he supposed, but not exactly his main area of interest. That, right now, would be Luce.

The castle had free entry until the end of March, but no one else was taking advantage of it. Clearly the weather had scared them off, but they were missing out, Ben thought. Luce flitted from wall to wall, from snow-covered step to window, from arch to arrow-hole, the breeze keeping her skirt plastered against her curves under her short jacket, her colour high and eyes bright. From time to time she'd call out to him, telling him about what she was looking at, what had happened here. The wind whisked away every other word, but it didn't matter. Ben didn't care about the castle. He was too entranced by her.

She was beautiful.

It wasn't as if he hadn't noticed before, of course. But it had always been a pale, reserved beauty. The sort you could look at but not touch. Hell, she'd practically had 'Keep Out' signs plastered all over her. But here…here she was radiant. She was real. And how he wanted to touch her.

He couldn't have said how long it was before she jumped down from the low remains of an interior wall, sending a puff of snow flying up. Time seemed to pass differently when he was absorbed in watching her.

Her cheeks were pink and flushed as she flung herself onto the patch of bench he'd cleared beside him. 'This place is fantastic,' she said, sounding slightly out of breath from hopping around the castle walls.

'I'm glad you like it.' The urge to lean back against the bench, stretch an arm around her shoulders and pull her into him was almost overpowering. In an attempt to resist, Ben leant forward instead, resting his forearms along his thighs. 'It must have been pretty impressive back in the day.'

'It's impressive now.'

Luce's voice held a tone of reverence, and he knew she saw something here that he never could—something beyond his world. It didn't matter. He was content to enjoy it through her, to see her eyes light up at the history she saw here. He'd bring her back every week if he could. Just to see that sparkle, that life in her face.

Except maybe it would wear off over time. Maybe they'd have to tour all the castles in Wales. And the rest of Britain. And overseas. *I wonder how she feels about French châteaux?*

Or maybe he'd take her back to Cardiff and never see her again, as planned.

That thought made the winter air colder, the clouds overhead more threatening. Ben squinted up at the sky. The reports said no more snow until that night, but those skies just screamed bad weather. They should get going or they might not make it to Cardiff. Again.

But he didn't want to leave. Not yet. He wanted a little more time with this Luce first. Excited, vibrant, castle Luce. Was that so much to ask?

'So, where do you think Nest was taken from?' Ben got to his feet as he spoke, reaching a hand out to pull Luce up again.

She rolled her eyes as she stood. 'The castle would have looked completely different then. Most of what you see today was probably built in the thirteenth century—a hundred years or more after Owain took Nest.'

'Okay, so tell me what it would have looked like then.'

'Earth and timber building, probably. We can't really

be sure.' Luce gazed around her again and Ben realised he was staring at her the same way she looked at the castle. He didn't stop.

Luce carried on talking, almost as if to herself. 'It doesn't matter that it looks different now. The landscape's the same. The feeling. She was here, and now I am. And I feel... It's ridiculous.' She dropped her head.

'Go on,' Ben said, trying to resist the desperate temptation to move closer to her.

Luce reached out to place a hand against the stone of the castle wall, palm flat, as if she were connecting herself to the site. 'I feel like I can understand her better here. Make more sense of her life and what happened to her. There's so few facts that we can be sure about. But here they come together better.'

'So it's helped?'

She looked up, her eyes wide and shining, and smiled at him. Ben felt the moment he lost himself as a dull ache in his chest.

'It's helped a lot,' she said. 'Thank you.'

It was too late, now, he realised. He'd been hers since the moment he saw her again in Chester. Maybe longer. Maybe since that night in the library. It didn't matter. None of it mattered any more. He just had to have her.

Stepping forward, he raised his hands to her cold face, his body moving into her space as she fell back to rest against the castle wall.

'We should get going.'

Sharp white teeth bit down on her lip again after she spoke, and Ben almost groaned at the sight.

'I know.' But he didn't move away.

'Kiss me,' she said, anyway, and he lowered his mouth to hers, the wind whipping round them, cold and icy and utterly unimportant in the moment.

Her lips were soft and sweet under his as he teased them open, drinking in the taste and the feel of her. Luce's arms wrapped around his waist, her hands firm against his back, pulling him in deeper, closer, even as he pressed his body against hers, the softness of her curves driving him wild.

As the first cold drops hit the back of his neck, Ben pulled his mouth away, his hands tugging her body into the warmth and safety of his arms. Luce rubbed her cheek against his coat and he kissed the top of her head.

'We need to get out of here,' he said, and she moved away, leaving him cold and bereft.

She blinked up at him and snowflakes landed on her lashes. 'It's snowing again.'

'And it's going to get heavier. But, more importantly, I need to get you somewhere more private than a ruined public castle.' He took a breath. 'So—Cardiff or the cottage?'

Luce's lips quirked up in a naughty smile, and the expression was so utterly unexpected that Ben bit back a laugh.

'Whichever is closer,' she said, and he grabbed her hand as they ran for the exit.

Finally, Ben thought, as the car doors slammed behind them and he set a course back to the cottage. Finally something was looking up.

The journey back to the cottage seemed to take twice as long as the trip to the castle had done, and that was only due in part to the increasingly heavy snowfall. It seemed worse even than the drive from Chester had been. Cardiff would have to wait another day, apparently, but somehow the thought bothered her far less now. She couldn't have left without having this, having *him*, just once.

Ben drove steadily through the worsening weather, taking bends and dips in his stride. Luce kept her hands clenched against her knees, more to stop herself touching him than from fear of the drive.

'You okay?' he asked finally, just as the sky went from grey to black and Luce made out a sign welcoming them to the Brecon Beacons National Park through the falling snow.

'I'm fine,' she said.

'Really?'

No. I want you to pull over so I can ravish you in the back seat. Luce felt her eyes widen at the very thought. Not a very Dr Lucinda Myles type desire at all.

'You're not over-thinking this?'

She looked up at Ben as he spoke. His eyes were still firmly on the road, his arms braced tight to the wheel. He looked as if every muscle in his body was taut. Was that because of the weather? Or because he was resisting a similar urge to hers?

Luce gave herself one moment to believe it was the latter, then realised she still hadn't answered his question. With a soft laugh she said, 'Honestly, Ben, I'm barely thinking at all right now.'

She was watching, so she saw him blow out a long breath, saw his shoulders sink, his body start to relax. Had he really been that worried about her?

'I'm not going to fall apart because you kissed me, you know,' she said, forehead furrowed with the effort of trying to figure out what he was thinking.

His mouth slipped into a half-smile. 'Yeah, but I might if I don't get to do it again soon.'

The heat that pooled in her belly seemed hotter, more desperate at his words than it had been even in the castle. Back there she'd told herself it was the location, the romanticism of the castle and its history. But here, when he should be focused on the road, he was still thinking about kissing her.

'Are we nearly there yet?' She could hear the wanting in her own voice, and Ben obviously did, too. He glanced over at her, just for a moment, surprise on his face.

'Nearly,' he answered, his voice low and full of promise.

Luce was almost certain that the rest of the journey took considerably less time than it should have done. But he had to slow down again as they reached the twisting path up to the cottage itself, and Luce gripped the edge of her seat as the car slipped and slid over the still falling snow. *Not going to be fun trying to get back through this to Cardiff, even tomorrow.*

The thought was too depressing to dwell on. Instead, Luce focused on thinking about what might happen when they got inside the cottage and bit her lip.

'Okay, this is as close as we're getting,' Ben said eventually, wrestling the car onto the side of the road and pulling on the handbrake. They hadn't even made it to the parking spot they'd managed the day before. This snowstorm was making yesterday's look like a mere sprinkling. 'Think you can walk from here?'

Luce nodded because, honestly, she could do anything if it meant Ben was going to kiss her again soon.

He trudged round to the other side of the car, helping her out into the snow, and pulled her arm through his so he held her tight against the side of his body. Together, heads down against the snow flurries, they made their slow way up the last of the hill to the cottage, with Ben yanking her upright whenever her boots slipped.

And then, just when Luce had started to fear they were never going to make it, the cottage appeared through the snow, and warmth burst through her despite the weather.

Ben fumbled the door open and in moments had slammed

it shut behind them and pressed her up against it, his hands cold as they found their way under her coat and jumper to bare skin. His lips were hot, though, warm and demanding, and Luce let her head fall back against the wood and surrendered herself to his kiss.

Then he wrenched himself away again and Luce's body ached with the loss.

'This is what you want?' he asked.

Luce nodded furiously. 'Of course—'

'For *you*,' he interrupted. His eyes were dark with want, but his face was serious. 'Not because someone else wants you to, or because it's what you should do, or even because you're trying to be something you weren't in university. Because you want it.'

'Yes.'

'And you know…you know what this is?'

At last Luce realised what he really wanted, and even though she'd promised herself she wouldn't give it to him, the need that burned through her body meant she couldn't stop the words even if she wanted to.

'I want you, Ben. Me. I want your hands and your mouth and your body on me. Just for tonight. Just one night.'

His hands tightened around her waist as she spoke and Luce swallowed at the heat in his eyes. Then she said the words she knew he was waiting for.

'Seduce me.'

That was all Ben needed to hear. With a growl of satisfaction he captured her lips again, even as his hands pushed her coat from her shoulders.

'You're wearing far too many clothes,' he murmured, working his kisses down her throat.

She bent her neck enticingly, to give him better access, and he allowed himself a moment to admire the pale skin there, and the line of her throat to her shoulders. How had he never noticed how beautiful she was when they were younger? Maybe she was more confident now, better dressed, more aware of her own attraction. But her beauty had always lain in the essence of her, the bones and the lines, and he just hadn't been looking carefully enough.

Except for that one night, drunk and stupid. Then he'd seen it.

'It was cold in the castle,' Luce said, and Ben had to concentrate to remember what they'd even been talking about. He was past words already.

God, how had she bewitched him so completely, so quickly? Taken charge of his senses so that all that mattered was getting her in his bed as quickly as possible? Hell, he didn't even care about the bed. He was on the verge of taking her right here against the door.

He needed to regain some control. He needed to be able to walk away from this tomorrow. The wild, blood-boiling feeling that had taken over had stripped away what he knew of himself. He needed this to be back on his terms.

With more effort than he would have liked, he pulled her away from the door. 'Bedroom,' he said, sentences still beyond him.

Luce glanced around as though she'd forgotten entirely where she was, hadn't even noticed the splintered door at her back. At least he wasn't the only one losing control.

She followed him without argument as he tugged her towards his bedroom and kicked the door shut behind them. He'd worried that she might be spooked when they were finally there, that once it became too real she'd change her mind. But instead she melted into his arms as he stripped off her clothes, her fingers already dragging his jumper up over his head.

Skin to skin, touch to touch, Ben laid her back on the

bed, covering her with his own body. She was so smooth under his hands, and every touch made her arch and moan and mew, responsive in a way he could never have imagined. And he responded in turn, his fingers and his mouth reaching deeper, more demanding, until finally, *finally*, he slid home into her and felt her moan against his shoulder.

'Okay?' He kissed her ear as they stilled for a moment, letting her adjust.

'More than,' she whispered back, and then Ben couldn't help but move and move, until she was falling apart under him, and his whole world narrowed to the feel of her, to a pinpoint of sensation that made his body tense until it might break...

Afterwards, once enough of his brain had returned to his body, Ben rolled onto his side, pulling Luce with him so she was tucked safe in his arms. Her breathing was the only sound, deep and even, as if she were trying to bring her body back under her own control. It was too late, though. He'd already seen the wildness at the centre of her, the free parts she kept locked up tight. The hidden side of her that wanted, wanted—wanted so much.

He couldn't let her lock that up again.

CHAPTER ELEVEN

THE ROOM LAY under a strange hush, as if nothing existed beyond the bed in which they lay. Luce supposed it was the snow, blanketing the world outside and deadening the sounds. But maybe it was the sex as well. After all, such a moment deserved a reverential silence, surely?

Because it wasn't just sex. Luce felt a stab in her chest at the realisation, and she must have flinched, because Ben's arm tightened around her, pulling her closer into that magnificent chest. She felt his mouth brush against her hair, soothing, comforting. As if he was trying not to startle her.

'Freaking out?' he asked, his voice a murmur. But the grip on her body told her he wasn't letting go even if she was.

'A little,' she admitted, and cursed herself even as she spoke. The last thing she needed Ben to know was that sex had reduced her to a gibbering wreck.

Except it wasn't the sex. The sex had been phenomenal, taking her everywhere she'd needed to go and then some. Her whole body was thanking her for the sex in its own languid, melted way. No, the sex was just fine.

It was the feelings that went along with it that caused the problems.

She wasn't deluded enough to think that Ben would break his one-night rule for her. But, lying in his arms, it was hard to imagine how she would tear herself away the next morning.

But she had to. Because Ben wasn't a man looking for responsibility, family, a wife. And she knew herself. She wasn't Nest, for all that she'd been taken from Cilgerran Castle and bedded tonight. She had a family she had to take care of, and Ben would never be able to bear to have anything take affections away from him. If she were to fall in love, to find someone to make a life with, it had to be someone who supported her, helped her, understood that she had other responsibilities.

Ben Hampton was not that man. Ben was so far from being that man it was almost funny. Or hugely depressing.

The best she could hope for with Ben was an occasional night together when he happened to be in town and it suited him—and even then never more than one night in a row. And that wasn't enough for her. He wanted her to think about her own needs? Well, she needed more than that from a relationship.

'What can I do to help you relax?' he asked, his voice soft and seductive.

Luce felt her body reacting even though every muscle in it was already exhausted.

'I'm never going to be able to sleep if you keep thinking so loud. Normally a woman is more relaxed after I finish my work.' He sounded faintly put out at that.

Luce bit her lip. She had to leave tomorrow morning. She knew that. But that didn't mean she couldn't make the most of her one night.

Shifting in his arms so she was facing him, Luce let him pull her flush against him, her breasts brushing against the hairs on his chest, his right leg pressing between her thighs.

'Maybe you haven't finished work for the night, then,' she said, and watched his eyes darken as he smiled.

Yes, if she only got one night with Ben Hampton, Luce was going to make sure every moment counted.

According to the clock on the bedside table, it was late morning when Ben awoke, but the room remained dim and close. *Guess it hasn't stopped snowing, then.* He supposed he could get up and look, see what they were dealing with. But the bed was so warm, and when he shifted Luce snuggled closer into his arms.

Yeah, he wasn't going anywhere in a hurry.

And neither, he realised, was she. Not if the snow was as heavy as it had looked before they'd retired to the bedroom for the night. If he hadn't been able to get the car all the way up to the cottage yesterday afternoon, they'd be lucky even to get back to it this morning. No point even trying.

Not, of course, that logic meant she wouldn't need some convincing of that fact. Ben smiled. Given how responsive she'd been to his 'convincing' the night before, he didn't see it being a particularly arduous task.

'Are you awake?' Luce asked, her voice fuzzy with sleep.

'Yeah,' he murmured, and she turned over in his arms to face him.

'Has it stopped snowing?'

She was blinking up at him, her hair falling into her eyes, her face pink and sleepy, and Ben thought she looked more beautiful than he'd ever seen her.

'Don't know.'

Wriggling out of his embrace, she wrapped the extra blanket from the bottom of the bed around her and padded to the window, ducking under the curtain to look out.

Then she swore. Ben didn't think he'd ever heard her do that before. He hadn't even been sure she knew such words.

Flinging the curtains open, she turned to him with an

accusing glare. 'Look at it! It's piled up halfway to the window! We're never going to get back to Cardiff in this!'

Shuffling into a seated position, lounging against the headboard, Ben shrugged. 'So we spend another day here. Is that so bad?'

'Yes!' Luce ran a hand through her tangled hair and almost lost her grip on the blanket. 'It's Christmas Eve *tomorrow*, Ben. I have to get home. Never mind the book. I've got to get things ready for my family. I haven't even *thought* about dinner for tomorrow.' She yanked the blanket up again, covering all but a hint of her cleavage. 'This is all your fault.'

'I thought we'd established that I can't control the weather?' Ben said mildly.

'Maybe not. But you said it wouldn't snow again until last night. And you didn't tell me it would be heavy enough to drift!'

Ben winced. That much was, in fact, true. He'd known how bad the snow would be and still brought her back here, instead of taking her home. 'I gave you a choice: the cottage or Cardiff. You chose here.'

'Because I didn't have all the information! You *trapped* me here.'

She looked so anguished Ben almost felt sorry for her. Except that she was trying to blame him for her decisions and accusing him of imaginary plots. Again. As if he hadn't done all he could to help her for the last three days. As if what they'd shared was nothing more than an attempt to get her into bed. Well, if that was what she thought— fine. Let her believe him to be exactly the sort of man she'd always thought. She'd never believe he'd changed, anyway. So why should he change? What had he been thinking to believe for even a moment that this could be more than a one-night stand? They were as different now as they'd ever been.

'Trapped you here?' Ben raised his eyebrows in deliberate disbelief. 'Why would I do that? You know my one-night rule. Trust me—I'm as ready to get back to civilisation as you are.'

He wished he could take back the words the moment he'd spoken them. Not least because he knew he'd put an end to any chance of spending another day—and night—in bed with Luce. But mostly because of the way her face froze, eyes wide, mouth slightly open, fingers wrapped in the blanket as she held it tight to her chest.

The moment lasted too long—a cold chill between them as the silence of the snow pressed in. Then Luce broke. She took a step back, towards the door, and shook her head just a little. 'Of course. If we're stuck here I need to work. Tell me when it clears enough for us to leave.'

She didn't even slam the door behind her. Instead she closed it carefully, letting the latch click quietly into place. And Ben fell back down onto the bed and wished he'd never heard of Cilgerran Castle.

Luce fumbled her way into her clothes with chilly fingers, trying to convince herself that it was only the cold making her shake. But the anger still bubbling up in her chest told her different.

She was furious. With Ben, naturally, for being exactly what she'd always known he was. And she was even more angry with herself.

Dropping to sit on the bed as she yanked on thick socks over her woolly tights, Luce tried to calm down. She'd never get any work done like this.

How could she have been so stupid? She knew beyond a doubt exactly what sort of a man Ben was. Hell, he'd told her himself! His ridiculous one-night rule was a prime example. As if only spending one night together could make falling in love less likely.

Not that she was in love with Ben Hampton. Not even *she* was that idiotic.

She'd brought this on herself. *Take responsibility. Take control.* Well, she'd take the responsibility, anyway. Control seemed to be entirely out of her hands.

This was her punishment for taking what she wanted for a change—for forgetting about her obligations, about her family. Would the snow clear for them to get through? The thought of spending another night in the cottage, even in her own room, made her shiver. And what if she didn't make it home for Christmas Eve and Tom's dinner? Or, worse, Christmas Day itself?

If giving in to her foolish desire to sleep with Ben Hampton ruined Christmas for her family they'd never forgive her. Hell, she'd never forgive herself.

In a flurry of movement Luce crossed the room and settled into the chair, flipping open her laptop and tapping her fingers against the wood of the desk as she waited for it to bring up her manuscript. Work. That was what she needed. Something to distract her and give her purpose. Except…

How am I supposed to concentrate on ancient history when my own past and present is naked in the next room?

No, she needed to focus. Nest. What happened after Owain took her from Cilgerran? Henry I intervened. So, how to frame it? Consider how one woman, a Welsh princess, caused uproar in the English court? Or tell the more personal story of her ex-lover coming to the rescue of her reputation?

Her lips tightened. God only knew what her grandfather would make of *her* reputation right now if he were still alive.

Nest had it easy. One quick kidnapping and she was set.

With a sigh, Luce turned her attention to the document in front of her and pushed all thoughts of Ben, the night before and what the hell happened next out of her head. The only thing she could fix right now was her book.

Ben was still cursing himself for an idiot two hours later when, as he waited for the kettle to boil for an apologetic cup of peppermint tea, the lights went out. Cursing, he flipped a few switches on and off, then stalked off towards the fuse box. Chances were it was a power cut, given the snow, but his luck had to turn some time. Maybe it was a tripped switch.

It wasn't. And by the time he returned to the kitchen Luce stood in front of the fire, arms crossed over her chest, glaring at him. 'What the hell's happened *now*?'

'Power cut,' Ben said. 'At least best I can tell. Might be a line down somewhere.'

'So what do we do?' Luce asked, a snap in her voice. 'Don't you have an emergency generator or something?'

At least she was talking to him. He supposed he should be grateful for that. 'No generator. Now we build up the fire, keep warm and survive on whatever in the fridge doesn't need cooking.' Maybe he had some marshmallows they could toast somewhere at the back of a cupboard.

Luce glared out of the window and he followed her gaze to where the snow was still fluttering to the ground. 'I'm thinking very fondly of the Eight Bells right now.'

'We'd never get down the path,' Ben said.

'Just as long as it clears enough for us to get to Cardiff. I'm not staying another day here with you.' Luce's tone was firm, as if daring the weather to disagree with her again. But, given the way the snow had started to drift, driving anywhere in the next few days would be a really stupid idea.

Of course getting snowed in at his cottage, during a power cut, with a furious Lucinda Myles was also kind of idiotic. Apparently there was something about her that made him lose his mind.

'Are you hungry?' he asked, checking his watch in the firelight. He wasn't sure what meal they were on, but it had been a while since either of them had eaten.

'That depends on what's in your fridge.' Luce eyed him with suspicion, as if he might be about to add poisoning to his list of crimes.

'I picked up some bits from the village shop yesterday. There should be enough to tide us over.' Just about. He'd only planned on having to feed himself, after all.

'Fine. But the power had better come back on before my laptop battery runs out.' Turning on her heel, Luce stalked back towards her room. 'Call me when the food's ready.'

Ben sighed and watched her go. Apparently any sort of reconciliation was still a way off.

There wasn't much to prepare. Ben arranged cheeses and bread on plates, adding some cold meats he'd picked up, then carried them over to the low table in front of the fire. Then, as an afterthought, he grabbed a bottle of red wine and two glasses. Wine always made things more of a feast.

'Grub's up,' he called, and moments later Luce appeared. She'd added another jumper on top of her outfit from earlier. With the electric under-floor heating out of commission the cottage was becoming very chilly, very quickly. 'Sorry it's not much.'

Luce took the glass of wine he'd poured for her and sat at the end of the sofa nearest the fire. 'Better than nothing.

At least it's warm in here.' Her words were short, terse. And she still wasn't looking at him.

With a deep breath, Ben sat down beside her, reaching for his own wine. 'That's not all I'm sorry for.'

Slowly she turned to look at him, without speaking. It wasn't much, but Ben took it as a sign she was at least willing to listen. 'I'm sorry about what I said. About...'

'Your one-night rule?'

'Yeah.'

'Fine.'

She'd turned her attention back to her plate again, picking at the bread. Ben watched her, waiting for something more, but it wasn't forthcoming.

'Not feeling inclined to apologise for accusing me of trapping you in this cottage purely to seduce you?'

'Not really.' She reached for her wine glass. 'Apart from anything else, you *did* seduce me.'

She had a point there. And somehow Ben knew that saying, *You asked me to* wasn't going to make anything any better.

'How does it even work, anyway?' she asked, after a long moment's silence in the flickering firelight. 'Your stupid rule? What? You just live your life going from one-night stand to one-night stand?'

'No.' Ben rubbed a hand across his forehead. *Now* she wanted to talk about this? There was a reason he usually had this talk before he hit the sheets. 'Of course not.'

'Then what?' Putting down her plate, Luce turned her body to face his, all attention on him. 'Come on. I want to know.'

For a moment she thought he wasn't going to answer. But, Luce rationalised, as a victim of his stupid rule, at the very least she deserved to understand it.

Finally Ben spoke. 'I date women. Same as anyone. I just make a point not to spend more than one night with them at a time.'

'Because twenty-four hours is too much like commitment?' Luce said, rolling her eyes. Men. What were they so damn scared of?

Ben sighed. 'Because if one night becomes two nights then it's all too easy for it to be three nights. A week. A month. More. And suddenly she's expecting a ring and a life. Something I can't give her.'

'You've tried, then?' Luce folded her legs up under her, twisting so her feet were closer to the hearth. With just the flickering fire to light the room it felt smaller, cosier. As if the world were only just big enough to encircle the two of them and their shadows.

'I don't have to. I've seen it before.' The way he said it, Luce knew that whatever he'd witnessed it had been up close and far too personal.

Frowning, she made an educated guess. 'Your parents?'

'Yeah.' Ben topped up their wine glasses, even though neither of them had drunk very much. 'Dad…his life was the business. Everything came second to Hampton & Sons. Even the sons.'

How must that have felt? Knowing he was less important than a building? Luce couldn't imagine. Her family might expect a lot from her, but at least she always knew they needed her.

'And your mum?' she asked.

Ben blew out a long breath. 'Mum would follow him around from business opportunity to networking dinner, smiling when he wanted her to smile, wearing what he wanted her to wear. She gave up her whole life to satisfy him, until finally she realised she'd given up herself.'

'She left?'

'When I was eight.' Ben stared into the fire. 'She just… she couldn't do it any more. We didn't see her much after that. And then she died two years later.'

Luce swallowed, her heart heavy in her chest. 'I'm sorry. I never knew.' She could almost imagine him, ten years old, perfectly turned out in a suit at his mother's graveside. His heart must have broken. Was that when he'd given up on family?

Ben shrugged. 'No reason you should. Anyway, that's why. My life—it's all about fixing things and moving on. Just like Dad. And I won't subject a wife or a child to that.'

'So you just don't let anyone get close enough to want it?' Couldn't he see how bleak that existence was?

'Seems easiest.' He drained his wine and poured himself another glass. 'So, what about you? What is it that makes *you* believe that bricks and mortar are important? I mean, I'm all for lucrative property opportunities. But your house is more than that to you, isn't it?'

'It's home,' Luce agreed. 'It always will be.'

'So tell me. What makes it home?'

Luce glanced over and saw that Ben's eyes were closed, as if by not being able to see her he was distancing himself from the question he was asking. But if he wanted to understand what made a house a home, she wasn't going to deny him.

'It was my grandfather's house, originally. I told you that, right?' She trailed her finger around the stem of her glass, trying to find the words to explain what the house meant to her. 'He bought it after he moved to Cardiff with Grandma and made a little money, back in the fifties. It's not in a great area, but it's still more than I could afford to buy today. And it's close to the university.'

'He left it to you?'

Luce nodded. 'When he died, yeah. We grew up there,

you see. My father left when Dolly was a baby, and my Mum…that's when she retreated to her own bubble. Grandad moved us in, helped bring us up. Grandma had been dead for years, and the house was too big for just him, he always said.'

'You were his favourite, though,' Ben said. 'If he left you the house instead of your mum or your brother and sister.'

The unfairness of that act caught in Luce's chest every time she thought about it. 'It wasn't that, exactly. He relied on me to take care of them. The house needs a lot of work, and I don't think he thought they'd manage it. They all know it's still their home, too.'

'So you even give them your house?' Ben's eyes opened wide to stare at her. 'You really do give up everything for them, don't you?'

The cosy warmth of the fire started to cool and Luce pulled away a little. 'I don't expect you to understand,' she said, leaning back against the arm of the sofa.

Ben shrugged. 'Like I told you, home for me was hotels, after Mum left and Dad gave up the house. I used to think maybe I'd missed out, when I was a kid away at boarding school. But I like moving on—finding new things, new places.'

'But you bought this cottage,' Luce pointed out. 'You did it up, made it a home. You brought me here.'

She regretted the words as soon as they were spoken. She knew she shouldn't read more into that than a whim, an emergency pit stop in the snow. But it was so hard not to.

When she looked up his face was closed, his eyes staring over her head. 'The cottage is an investment. I'll probably sell it soon.'

The thought of Ben giving up his escape, the closest

thing he'd had to a home in years, without even realising what it meant, was too depressing to contemplate.

Looking away into the fire, she said, 'Doesn't look like the power's going to come back on tonight.'

'Yeah, I doubt it.' Ben gave her a look she couldn't quite read, then added, 'We'll have to see how the roads look in the morning.'

No. No way. Maybe she understood him a little better now, but that didn't mean she could stay here any longer and not go crazy. 'I'm sure they'll be fine.' Getting to her feet, she added, 'And a good night's sleep will do us both some good before the drive. I'll see you in the morning.'

She didn't look back, didn't check his expression, didn't wait for him to wish her goodnight. Even so, she barely made it to the door before the sound of his voice stopped her in her tracks.

'What if I said you were worth breaking my rule for?' he asked, so low she almost thought she must have misheard.

She turned back to face him, her heart thumping against her ribcage. 'But I'm not. I'm just the same Lucinda Myles you made fun of at university.'

Ben shook his head. 'You're so much more than I ever saw.'

Luce gave him a half-smile. 'So are you.'

And then, before she could change her mind, she shut the bedroom door behind her and climbed, fully clothed, into the freezing bed.

CHAPTER TWELVE

BEN HAD PASSED a fitful night on the sofa, his dreams filled with dark hair and brick walls. But at least he'd been warm, he reasoned. Luce must have been half frozen in her lonely bed, if the way she'd appeared in front of the freshly banked fire before the sun had risen was any indication.

'Happy Christmas Eve,' she murmured as she held her hands out to the flames. Her suitcase leant beside the front door, just as it had in Chester, waiting to leave.

He sat up, blankets falling to his waist, and motioned at the case. 'You're still hoping to make it back to Cardiff today, then?'

'I have to.'

'To cook dinner for your family,' he said, a little disbelievingly.

'To spend Christmas with them,' she corrected. 'Don't you want to get back to London to spend it with your brother?'

'I think Seb wants me there for a business meeting rather than to sing carols round the piano.' Come to think of it, what *did* Seb want him there for? He'd been so preoccupied with Luce he'd barely given the strange conversation with his brother another thought.

'Fine. Maybe you don't care about family, or home, or Christmas. But I need to get back. Will you drive me?'

She looked down at him, eyes wide and dark, her hair curling around her face, and Ben knew he couldn't say no to her.

'If the roads are clear.' It wasn't a promise, but it felt like one all the same.

Luce nodded. 'I'll pack up the car.'

The roads weren't clear, not by anyone's definition. But the snow had stopped, and by lunchtime the tractors were out clearing some of the local thoroughfares. Once Ben had spent another hour digging his four-by-four out of the snow that had built up around it, and reversed onto the track, the journey looked manageable.

Still, it wasn't until they got out of the Brecon Beacons National Park and onto larger roads that Ben finally felt his shoulders start to relax as he settled into the drive. He'd driven through worse weather, especially up in the hills in France, by the château, but that didn't mean it was his preferred time to travel. Didn't mean he wasn't still annoyed with Luce for making him.

That's why. That's the only reason. Nothing to do with her leaving me.

Something he wasn't going to think about until this drive was over.

As they entered Cardiff Luce gave quiet, monotone directions to her house and Ben could feel his time with her slipping away. Being wasted. But what was the point? Her family would always be more important than him. And he would never be able to give her enough to make her stay. Neither one of them was going to change now, if they hadn't already. Why put himself through that?

Eventually he pulled up outside a row of townhouses, most of them converted into flats. Luce had the car door open almost before he'd switched the engine off, so he got out and went to open the boot for her.

'Want me to carry this in for you?' He hefted her suitcase out of the car and rested it on the pavement, his fingers still on the handle.

Luce shook her head. 'I can manage.'

And wasn't that her all over? 'Fine,' he said, relinquishing his hold.

She paused, biting down on her lip again, and Ben tried to ignore the heat that flooded through him at the sight.

'Thank you,' she said, finally. 'For this week.'

'I know it wasn't what you planned. But I hope you found the time away...useful.'

'I did, actually.' She sounded surprised.

'Good.'

What else was there left to say?

Awkward silence stretched between them until Luce motioned towards her front door and said, 'I'd better go and get ready.'

'The dinner party.' Ben nodded, his neck feeling stiff. 'Of course.'

'I know it doesn't seem like—'

'It's your life,' he interrupted, too tired to have the argument again. 'Do whatever you want, Luce.'

As he got back into the car he could have sworn he heard her say, 'That's the problem.' But by the time he turned round she'd already gone inside.

He thought about going straight back to the cottage, but he knew the memory of her would linger there. He'd call his usual cleaning lady, get her to clear the place out so that all reminders would be gone by his next visit.

He could check into a hotel, he supposed, if any had a spare room on Christmas Eve. But suddenly he wanted to see his brother. He wanted to know what Seb had planned next for the business. Something about this time with Luce had left him unsettled, unsure. And he needed something to throw himself into.

Decision made, he climbed back into the car and headed east, watching the snow that had disrupted his life thin and finally disappear as he sped along the M4.

He drove straight to Seb's office, figuring—correctly—that even late on Christmas Eve his brother would still be hard at work.

'You look terrible,' Seb said, as Ben sprawled in the visitor's chair on the opposite side of their dad's antique desk.

The usual unease and uncertainty rose up in Ben, just as it always had when Dad had been in residence behind the desk, but he clamped down on it, folded his ankle up on one knee and leant back, arms spread along the arms of the chair. Disrespectful and uncaring. Because Seb didn't need good posture to know he had his respect, and his dad wasn't there to care any more.

Neither is Luce.

'Hell of a drive in,' Ben said. 'Hills are practically snow-bound.'

Seb's eyebrows pulled down into a frown. 'This could have waited, you know. Until the weather cleared, at least.'

Ben shrugged. 'Needed to get back anyway.'

With a knowing look, Seb settled back in his chair. 'Ah. Time to let the latest girlfriend know she was only temporary, right? I'm just amazed you managed more than one night. Time to retire your rule at last?'

'No,' Ben said, shortly. 'The rule stays. And it's Christmas Eve. She had some family thing she had to get back for.'

Ben stared out of the window, trying to ignore the sense of wrongness that filled him when Seb talked about Luce as one of his girlfriends. Why did it feel so different?

Hadn't it followed the exact same pattern it always did? A bit of fun, discovering they were entirely different people, and then going their separate ways. Except this time they'd known just how different they were before they even went out to dinner. They'd wanted each other anyway.

Seb hadn't said anything, Ben realised. When he drew his attention back to his brother he found Seb watching him, a contemplative look in his eye.

'What?' Ben asked, shifting to sit properly on the chair.

'Nothing. Just…she was different? This girl?'

'Luce,' Ben said, automatically. 'And I don't know what you mean.'

'You said she was an old friend,' Seb clarified, and a sense of relief came over Ben.

'Yeah. We knew each other in university. So what?'

'Nothing,' Seb said again.

Ben didn't believe him. Time to change the subject. 'So—come on. I've driven through snowstorms and London traffic to get here. What did you want to meet with me about?'

Seb blinked, tapping a pen against his desk as if trying to remember. Finally he said, 'I've got a new job for you. If you're interested.'

'A "your mission, should you choose to accept it" type thing?' He hoped so. Preferably something far away, completely absorbing and with no reminders of Luce. That sounded pretty much perfect.

'Sort of.' Seb sighed. 'Look. I'm trying to find the right way to say this.'

'Sounds ominous.'

'I don't want you thinking you're not good at your job.'

'I am excellent at my job,' Ben said. 'And since when do you worry about my ego?'

'Since when do you take women to your cottage?' Seb countered.

'Just say it. Whatever it is.'

'Okay. So… Although you are passably good at your job—'

'Excellent at, I think I said.'

'You don't love it.'

Ben looked at his brother in surprise. 'It's a job, Seb. I don't have to love it. I just have to do it.'

'Maybe not. But I think you could love it.'

Things started to fall into place for Ben. 'I know what this is. You're worried that I'm still angry Dad left control of the business to you. I told you—I don't want it. Too much responsibility for me. I like the travel. I like the money. I like making things happen. I don't want to be stuck behind that desk for the rest of my life.'

'Like you think I will be?' Seb looked at him. 'You think I'm going to turn into Dad.'

'Not if you choose not to.' Ben shrugged. 'Besides, it's different. You haven't got a wife and kids like Dad did.'

'Maybe I'd like to have those things, though. One day.'

'Really?' Ben shook his head. 'Nah—can't see it. You'll sit there and manage the business, I'll go out and about and make things happen, and neither of us will drag any kids from boarding school to hotel for their entire childhood. It's all good.'

'And that would be enough for you?'

'Yeah. Of course it would. What are you thinking? That I need a private jet to make my life complete?'

'Honestly? I think you need a home. I think you need someone to come home to. I know everything with Mum screwed up that ideal for you, and maybe it was easier for me, being away at boarding school already. But it wasn't your problem to fix. You can't fix problems, only situa-

SOPHIE PEMBROKE   133

tions. And, Ben, it's time to move on. Time to grow up at last.'

But Seb hadn't seen it. Hadn't seen their mother falling apart day by day. He'd already been away, engrossed in school and friends and sport. He'd already moved on before Mum had.

Ben had been the only one there to try to make things right for her. And he hadn't been able to.

'I think you're crazy.' Pushing against the arms of the chair, Ben stood up. 'And if that's all you wanted to talk to me about—'

'I haven't finished.' When Ben remained standing, Seb sighed. 'Just sit down, Ben. I promise to stay on topic. Business only. Your shambles of a private life is your own.'

'Yeah, like yours is any better,' Ben grumbled. But he sat.

'I'm working on it,' Seb said with a lopsided smile.

'Really? Am I missing something here? Did something happen while I was away?'

'Business only, right?' Seb grabbed a folder from the corner of his desk and handed it across to Ben.

Opening the file, Ben felt his heart lurch against his ribcage at the sight of the reception desk at the Royal Court Hotel, Chester. *So much for a distraction from Luce.* Slamming the folder shut, he said, 'Been there. Done that. What's next?'

'I want you to go back.'

'Why? It's fine. It's running well. I've made my recommendations for streamlining some processes, making things more effective. Other than that…' He shrugged.

'I want to try something new.'

Against his better judgement, curiosity welled up in Ben. Something new. Something different. That was something they'd never been able to do while their father was alive. He'd had an unalterable system. Buy the hotel, make it look and run like all the others in the chain, move on to the next project. Every time.

'New how, exactly?'

Seb gave him a slow smile. 'Knew that would catch your attention. Trust me, you're going to like this plan.'

Ben wasn't so sure about that. But he was willing to give his brother the benefit of the doubt. 'Okay. I'm listening.'

Luce barely had time to toss her suitcase in her room before her phone rang. Glancing at the display, she saw it was her mother and let it go to voicemail. *Sorry, Mum, but if you want dinner tonight you'll have to wait for me to call you back.*

Okay, it was almost five in the afternoon. Two hours until her guests arrived. Long enough to cook something fantastic if she had any food in the house—which, having missed her supermarket delivery, she didn't. Long enough to clean and tidy the house if she didn't have to do anything else—which she did. And long enough to make herself look presentable if she could bring herself to care what she looked like—which she couldn't.

Collapsing into her favourite armchair, Luce pulled out her organiser and started her list. The most important thing about the evening was that it go well for Tom. After his break-up with Hattie, and the misery and depression that had followed, he'd not introduced them to a new girlfriend in two years. This was big. This was a turning point. Luce needed to make it as successful as she could. And pray that the turkey she'd yanked out of the freezer the moment she walked in defrosted in time for tomorrow.

Obviously at this stage a gourmet feast was out of the question. Instead Luce raided the corner shop for whatever was left at this point in the Christmas panic buying—

mostly mismatched canapés and mince pies. Halfway to the till she remembered to grab vegetables for the next day. She'd just have to hope she had enough of everything else in to make do.

The house itself wasn't in too bad shape—after flinging everything that didn't belong in the lounge, dining room or kitchen into the bedroom, Luce figured it would serve. Candles and cloth napkins on the table, lamps instead of overhead lights, and they were set to go.

Of course by that point it was seven, and she was still wearing the skirt and jumper she'd travelled home from Brecon in. A shower was out of the question, she supposed, but she'd hoped to at least change and put some make-up on. The ringing doorbell suggested she was out of luck.

'Are you running late?' Dolly asked, looking her up and down as she answered the door.

'However did you guess?' Luce ushered her sister in. 'I just got back a couple of hours ago. You're lucky I'm here at all.'

'Tom's lucky, you mean. I had plans for tonight, you know. This new girl of his had better be worth the effort. Does this mean you didn't have time to make the chocolate pots?'

Luce glared, and Dolly held up her hands in self-defence. 'Okay, okay. Next time. You go and get changed and I'll get us something to drink. Is there wine in the fridge?'

'As always,' Luce called back as she went to try to excavate something from her wardrobe that didn't need dry cleaning.

In the end the best option she had turned out to be the purple dress she'd worn to dinner with Ben in Chester. Luce tugged it on, trying not to notice the way his scent still clung to the fabric. Shoving her feet into low heels and pulling a cardigan over it made it feel a little less dressy—

more suitable for a family occasion. *And it matches the culinary sophistication level better. Or maybe I should put on jeans...*

By the time she'd run a brush through her hair and thrown on the minimum amount of make-up her mother would let her get away with, the doorbell had rung twice and Luce could hear voices in the lounge, along with clinking glasses. 'Showtime,' she whispered to herself, and tried not to wish she was still at the cottage.

Five hours later, as Dolly watched her load the dishwasher while eating the leftovers she was supposed to be putting in the fridge, Luce had to admit it had been worth coming back for. Even with her mum's pointed comments about the food.

'Did you think she seemed nice?' Dolly asked.

Since the others had already left, Luce didn't bother hiding the surprise in her voice. 'I did.'

Dolly laughed. 'I know. I wasn't sure whether to expect another monster, or what. But, no, she's nice. A little bossy, maybe. It'll be weird not having Tom here for Christmas Day, though.'

'It will. But he seemed happy.' That was by far the most important part. Tom hadn't been remotely happy for a very long time.

'He did.'

Dolly paused, and Luce looked up at her, forehead creasing.

'You don't.'

'I'm fine,' Luce lied.

Dolly boosted herself up onto the kitchen counter. 'What happened this week?'

'I went away. To a conference. And ended up taking a bit of a detour home, what with all the snow.'

'And were you alone?' Dolly pressed, eyebrows raised.

'Not entirely.' The memory of Ben kissing her against the castle wall invaded her mind and she bit her lip and tried to concentrate on her little sister, in the here and now.

'I knew it! Who did you go with? Oh, no—it wasn't Dennis, was it? That would explain why you're so miserable.'

'It was *not* Dennis,' Luce said, with feeling. 'Wait—I thought you liked Dennis?'

Dolly rolled her eyes. 'Mum liked Dennis. And only because she thought he was what you wanted. Boring, staid and uneventful. But if you weren't with Dennis…'

'My train got cancelled and an old university friend offered me a lift home. We got stuck in the snow and holed up at a cottage in the hills for a couple of days.' She shrugged. 'That's all.'

But Dolly wasn't content to leave it at that. The same curiosity that drove Luce to discover the past had made her sister incurably nosy about the present. 'And was this friend male or female?'

'Does it matter?'

'Yes!' Dolly bounced down from the counter, her eyes bright and intense. 'If you're finally getting a life I want to know all about it. Hell, I want to throw a party in celebration.'

'It's not… There's nothing to celebrate.' Because she was probably never going to see Ben again.

Dolly's mouth turned down at the corners, her eyes full of sympathy. 'Do you want to—? Ooh, I bet that's him!' she interrupted herself as Luce's phone rang.

'I doubt it— *Oh.*' Ben's name flashed across the screen. Of course he'd have programmed his number in on one of the many occasions when he'd stolen her phone. No respect for personal boundaries, that man.

Dolly had already swept up her coat and bag and was halfway out through the door. 'I'll be along tomorrow for my Christmas dinner,' she said with a wave.

Luce stared at the phone again. And then she pressed 'answer'.

CHAPTER THIRTEEN

IT WENT AGAINST all his usual rules about women and relationships, but Ben needed to talk to someone. And for some reason the only person he wanted to talk to was Luce.

He sprawled across his bed, waiting for her to answer, wondering if she would just ignore it. It was late, after all. Gone midnight. She might be asleep. Or maybe her dinner party was still going on. Maybe Dennis of the annoying e-mails was there. Maybe—

'Hello?'

Maybe she would answer after all.

'Hey. Merry Christmas. You okay?'

'Happy Christmas to you, too.' There was a rustle of fabric on the other end of the phone. Was she in bed? 'I'm okay. Tired.'

'How did dinner go?' That was what you did, wasn't it? When you wanted someone to stay in your life even if just as a friend? You asked about stupid things you didn't care about.

'You can't tell me that you're suddenly interested in my family gatherings after all the time you've spent maligning them this week.'

Luce's voice was amused, but Ben could hear a sharper edge under it. He'd hurt her, even though he'd tried so hard not to.

'No, not really.' Ben sighed. 'I just don't understand why it was so much more important to you than...everything else.'

'Because you never asked,' Luce responded promptly.

She had a point. Unfortunately, he'd found, she usually did. 'Okay, then, I'm asking. What was so important about this dinner?'

'Hang on,' she said.

Ben heard the click of her phone being put down somewhere. There was more rustling, then she picked up the phone again.

'Were you just getting undressed?' Ben asked, the image waking up his exhausted body instantly.

Luce gave a low laugh. 'It's gone midnight and I am more than ready to be out of this dress. Besides, if we're going to have this conversation I want to be comfortable while we're doing it.'

'What conversation?' The word made Ben nervous. He usually tried to avoid being in any situation with a woman that required him to have a serious conversation.

'The one about my family and why you're so offended by my taking care of them. And don't think I didn't notice that we managed to *not* have this conversation at any point where we couldn't just hang up on each other.'

'Well, we were a little preoccupied at certain points.'

'Ben?'

'Yeah?'

'We are not having phone sex.'

Damn. 'I know that. So—go on. Tell me about this dinner.'

Luce sighed. 'It wasn't just a dinner. It was for my brother Tom. He's had a rough time of it the last few years. Longer, really. But when his marriage broke down a couple of years ago he totally fell apart. And because he was in such a state my mother was beside herself, too. It was just when Dolly was applying to drama schools and, well…'

'You got stuck trying to hold everyone together?'

'Yeah. Anyway, this was the first time since then that Tom's met someone he's wanted to introduce us to. First time he's seemed interested in anything, let alone anyone, since Hattie left him.'

'And you didn't want to risk it not happening?'

'I just… It was a big deal for my family. And he'll be with her tomorrow. This was our only chance to be all together.'

'I get that.' Ben thought about Luce, alone in that big house, trying to make her family happy so that she could finally relax enough to find some happiness herself. 'I guess I just don't get why they're all *your* responsibility.'

'Who else would look after them?'

It was a throwaway comment, Ben knew. Self-deprecating, accepting the inevitable. But could he hear a real question under it? Was she ready to cast off some responsibility?

'Maybe it's time they learned to look after themselves.'

'Maybe.' She didn't sound entirely convinced, but it was a start. 'Did you make your meeting with your brother in the end?'

'I did.' It was the reason he'd called, actually. 'He has some new ideas for the business. A new role he wants me to take on.'

'Sounds interesting.'

'It is.'

'You don't sound sure.'

'It's a lot to take on.'

'A big responsibility.' To her credit, she didn't mock him for that. 'Tell me about it.'

How to explain? 'Well, you have to understand when my dad ran the business it was all about turnover. He bought up a hotel, made it a functional and decent place for businessmen, then moved on to the next one. Over time they became higher and higher end, with more amenities and luxurious surroundings, but the basis was the same. It was somewhere to work.'

'And that's where you grew up?' Luce said, surprising him with the sympathy in her voice. 'That must have been—'

'It was fine,' Ben interrupted. 'I got to travel the country before I was ten and the world before I was twenty. Not many kids had that chance.'

'No, but most kids had a home instead of a hotel.'

She sounded as if she wanted to ask more questions, and Ben really wasn't in the mood to be psychoanalysed, so he moved on quickly.

'Anyway, Seb wants to change the model. He wants us to look at adding more boutique hotels to our chain. Maybe even some family-friendly ones.'

'That sounds great. He wants *you* to run this?'

She sounded surprised, but Ben was too tired to be offended. 'Starting with the Royal Court in Chester.' Ben closed his eyes, remembering Seb saying, *'Just because you're good at doing what Dad did, it doesn't mean it's what you have to do. It doesn't always have to be about the quick fix and moving on. I think you'll enjoy the challenge of long-term development more.'*

Was he right? Ben supposed he'd find out soon enough.

'So you're heading back to Chester?' Luce asked.

'Not yet. Got to visit some of our hotels on the continent first. But I should be able to get there in a few weeks.'

'So you'll be away a while?'

'About a month.' Normally the idea of getting away, of waking up in a different city every few days, would be appealing. Especially after an interlude with a woman who was getting too close for comfort. But today…it seemed too long.

There was a lengthy pause, and Ben cast around for something else to say to keep her on the phone. It had been so much easier when they were in the cottage, shut away from the rest of the world. Where he'd had her all to himself without having to share her.

'Should I…?' He took a deep breath and started again. 'Can I call you when I get back?'

Luce's voice was soft as she replied, 'Yes, please.'

Luce was surprised, in a way, at how easily she slipped back into her old life. Her pre-Ben life. There was no reason to be, she supposed. After all, she'd lived without Ben in her life for a lot longer than when he'd been there. But still, those few days at the cottage had been transformative, somehow. She wasn't the same person she'd been before she went. Even if it wasn't obvious in her everyday life.

'What are these files?' Dolly asked, poking at a stack of folders on the dining room table a few weeks later, when she came over to indulge in Luce's tea—and her biscuit tin.

Luce glanced over. 'Just some stuff Dennis wants me to sort through for him.'

Dolly raised her eyebrows. 'And this is more important than your own work because…?'

'It isn't.' Luce swept the files into a box on the nearby dining chair. 'That's why I haven't done them yet.' Besides, Dennis was still sulking about her missing the lecture in Chester. Given the way she'd snapped at him when he whined, he probably wouldn't be asking her to do anything else for him any time soon.

'Good.' Dolly settled herself onto one of the other chairs, tipping it back to rest against the wall behind her. 'You've changed, you know. In a good way,' she added hurriedly. 'But you definitely seem different since you went away last month.'

Luce stopped tidying. 'Do I?'

'Yeah.' Dolly slanted her head to the side and looked her up and down for long enough to make Luce blush. 'Maybe more self-assured, I guess. Which is good.'

'More self-aware, I think.' Luce bit her lip as she considered her sister.

She needed to tell someone her news, and Ben was still away. She'd thought about calling a few times, always late at night when she was tucked up in bed, but she couldn't tell him this over the phone. It wasn't fair. But Dolly... She seemed more of an ally than she ever had before lately. She'd always been the baby, the one who needed the most looking after, but recently she'd been more of a friend than an obligation. Someone who cared about Luce rather than just needing things from her. She could tell Dolly.

'What's going on?' Dolly let her chair tip onto four legs again, leaning forward to rest her wrists on her knees. 'Come on—tell me. It's obviously something big. You're actually blushing.'

Luce's face grew immediately hotter in response. 'Okay. But you can't tell Mum. Or Tom. Or anybody just yet.'

Dolly's eyes widened. 'Now I'm *really* intrigued.'

Gripping the edge of the table, Luce summoned her courage and said it out loud for the first time. 'I'm pregnant.'

For a long moment Dolly just stared at her in silence. Then she clapped her hand over her mouth, not quite muffling the squeak that came out.

Luce sank into a chair. 'I know. I know. It's absurd.'

'It's wonderful!' Jumping up, Dolly wrapped her arms around her, and Luce relaxed into the hug. 'I'm going to be an aunt!'

'You are,' Luce said firmly. She'd considered the other options—of course she had. But this was her baby—hers and Ben's—and it might be her only chance. She was financially capable of looking after it, she had her family around her...

'God, how the hell are you going to baby-proof this place?' Dolly asked, looking around.

...and she lived in a death trap.

'That's on my list of things to figure out,' Luce said. 'To be honest, given the length of the list, it might take me a while to get around to it.'

Dolly perched on the table beside her, looking down through her long dark hair. 'Okay, I'm not asking the obvious question, because I figure you'll tell me when it's right. But just promise me it's not Dennis's.'

Luce laughed. 'Trust me. The father is about as far from Dennis as you can imagine.'

'In that case, I really want to meet him,' Dolly said. 'I take it it's the old university friend, then? The one you got snowed in with?'

Luce nodded. 'That's him.'

'Funny...I didn't even know you were still in touch with any of your friends from then.'

'You mean, you didn't know I had any in the first place.' She hadn't, really. Mandy had been her housemate, but had only been friendly when it suited her.

'That, too.'

'We weren't...close then.' Understatement of the year.

Dolly nudged her with her shoulder. 'You obviously are now. Have you told him?'

God, how had things changed so that Dolly was the one asking sensible questions? Luce had imagined this conversation the other way round all through Dolly's teenage years. 'Not yet. He's away on business. I don't want to tell him over the phone.'

'Fair enough. How do you think he'll react?'

Luce thought of Ben recounting his life rules over dinner in Chester, his explanation of the one-night rule, and said, 'Badly.'

Really, who wouldn't? Yes, he'd asked if he could call her when he got back from his business trip, but that wasn't the same as having a lifetime tie to another person and the responsibility of a baby thrust upon him. Of course he was going to react badly. It was what he did next, once he'd calmed down, that mattered. How would he try to fix her life this time? Because if his answer was to throw money at the problem, rather than time or love, she was done with Ben Hampton.

'Then he's an idiot. Clearly having you in his life would be the best thing to ever happen to him.'

Luce looked up, astonished. 'Thank you.'

'And, anyway, it doesn't matter what he says. Auntie Dolly will be here to make things brilliant every step of the way.'

To her surprise, Luce found that made her feel a whole lot better.

Ben stared up at the building of the Royal Court Hotel, the February wind whipping down the cobbled streets and through his coat. How the hell was he going to look at this place objectively, think about changing anything, without thinking about Luce? Hell, she was all he'd thought of for over a month. In every Hampton & Sons hotel he'd visited there'd been something to remind him of her. A bedspread or a cushion in the same soft fabric she loved. A gin and tonic at the bar. Shining dark hair glimpsed across a room. She was haunting him, and he couldn't even figure out why. Was it because he'd left her as broken as he'd found her? Maybe more so? Or was it as simple as a bruised ego? He'd offered to break his rules for her and she'd turned him down.

He'd considered finding someone else—someone to prove the validity of his one-night rule—but none of the women he'd met seemed to appeal. Nothing did. Not the New Year's Eve party he'd found himself at in New York, nor the cutting-edge restaurant in Sydney. And as the jobs dragged on and delays crept in all he wanted was to be back in his cottage. With Luce.

He'd even thought about calling, asking her to join him, but he couldn't bear to hear her say that she couldn't leave her family, her job, whatever else it was that mattered more than he did.

The woman might think she wanted to settle down, find true love, but until she cut those ties—or at least slackened them a little—no man stood a chance.

Besides, it wasn't as if *he* was looking to settle down anyway. His job—his life—still involved travelling the world, getting out there, and what woman would put up with that long-term?

She could come with me. Write on the road... Except she wouldn't. And so he wouldn't ask. Even if the thought of waking up next to Luce Myles every morning was incredibly tempting.

Shivering, Ben pushed open the door at last, and memories made him grit his teeth at the sight of the lobby. The desk where he'd first seen her. The bar where he'd stolen her diary. And, upstairs, the suite where she'd taken that long, long bath. God, knowing what he knew now, he wished he'd just walked in on her then. All that time wasted...hours and hours when he could have had her in his arms and hadn't.

And even more of them ahead.

'Mr Hampton!'

The blonde behind the reception desk beamed at him and Ben tried desperately to remember her name.

'It's so wonderful to have you back so soon.'

Which meant that the entire hotel staff were panicking about why he needed a repeat visit, and wondering if it was a sign that their jobs were in danger. *Great*. 'It's lovely to be back…'

'Daisy.'

'Daisy. Right.' Ben rubbed a hand over his aching forehead. 'Sorry—long flight.'

A look of carefully schooled concern settled onto her face. 'Why don't we get you checked in, then, sir? I've put aside the King James Suite for you again, if that's okay?'

'Wonderful,' Ben said, taking the key. Not a chance in hell of getting any sleep there without Luce beside him. *Great*.

Even the walk to the lift was full of memories. Ben distracted himself by watching the other guests instead, trying to observe them in a professional manner, figure out their wants and needs and how the hotel could meet them.

The businessmen by the bar were easy; Ben's father had known exactly what they needed. A comfortable room, with a desk or table to work at, all-night concierge and room service, meeting rooms and wireless internet access, a business centre with photocopiers and fax machines, and admin assistants they could hire by the hour. A well-stocked bar and well-served restaurant. All done. The Royal Court had them covered. Of course so did every other business hotel in every city.

But what about the couple canoodling by the pot plant? What did they want?

Well, if they were anything like him and Luce…privacy, a sturdy bed, champagne in the mini-bar, a big, deep bath. Maybe a romantic restaurant for dinner, breakfast from room service. Nothing unusual. And, honestly, the couple by the plant were so wrapped up in each other that it didn't look as if it mattered where they were, as long as they had each other.

Which just left him wondering why he and Luce had never managed that. Which was depressing. Time to move on.

But the family waiting by the lift, with two huge suitcases and a small boy with an oversized rucksack… They didn't look happy.

The father was in a suit, tie knotted tightly, jacket still on, briefcase in hand. This wasn't a man who'd left work and gone straight on holiday with his family. This was a man who was still working. And, from the frown creasing his wife's forehead, she wasn't too happy about it. The boy just looked miserable.

Ben knew that look. That was the *another day, another hotel* look. The *will I get to see my dad between meetings?* look. The *did I bring enough books to read?* look. That boy knew his family weekend was going to be spent watching his parents arguing, then his mother putting on a brave face while his father disappeared to yet more meetings.

Ben had been that boy. And Ben knew what would happen when the mother couldn't take any more.

He couldn't change another family's future—couldn't explain to every father dragging his wife and kids to business hotel after business hotel instead of actually taking a holiday what could happen and how it felt. But maybe he could make it a little more fun for the families wait-

ing for their husbands, wives, mothers or fathers to finish
their meetings.

Pulling his mobile from his pocket, he called his brother.
'Seb? That new style of hotel you wanted? I've got an idea.'

CHAPTER FOURTEEN

IT HAD BEEN eight weeks. He'd said he'd be away for a month, and now it was nearly two. Luce dropped her bag by the front door and collapsed onto the sofa, preparing herself for another evening of not hearing from Ben.

Damn him.

She should have known better than to believe him when he said he'd call. Hadn't he made it perfectly clear what they were? One night only. He wasn't going to call again.

But eventually she'd have to call him. He deserved to know.

Her head ached, her body was exhausted, and constant low-level nausea left her weak and miserable—and, damn it, she wanted to tell him! Wanted the secret off her shoulders. Wanted to share it with someone else.

Dolly knew, of course, and had been more wonderful than Luce had imagined possible. Her little sister had grown up unexpectedly, and Luce loved seeing this new, responsible side to her. Having her onside made things bearable. But soon she would have to tell other people—her boss, her mother, Tom. God, she'd even have to tell Dennis eventually. But Ben had to know first.

She'd have to call him. If he wasn't back soon she'd have to tell him over the phone. Except then she wouldn't be able to see his face, his reaction, the truth about how he felt.

She'd imagined it a dozen different ways. Sometimes, if she was feeling excessively romantic, he fell down on one knee and proposed instantly. Most of the time he looked shocked, stunned and slightly horrified. That was okay. She expected that. But sometimes, after that, her imagination had him take her in his arms and tell her they'd figure it out together. And sometimes it had him walk out without looking back.

She'd cope, whatever his reaction—she knew that. She just needed to know what it was. If he wanted to be involved in his child's life or not. Then she could start making plans. Until then…this horrible limbo persisted.

Time to move the action back into her own hands. *Take responsibility. Take control.* 'If he doesn't call tonight I'll phone him.'

'You've been saying that for weeks,' Dolly said from the door.

Sad, but true. 'Yeah, but now I'm desperate. I'll do it.'

Dolly sighed, shut the front door behind her and came to sit on the sofa, lifting Luce's feet to rest them on her lap.

'Has it occurred to you that you might be better off without him? I mean, he's basically disappeared off the face of the earth for two months now, Luce.'

'I know. And it has.' Luce sighed. 'Chances are he'll run like the wind when I tell him anyway. But he needs to know. And *I* need to know.'

'This is all because you can't write your "To Do" list before you tell him, isn't it?'

Luce chuckled. 'Partly.'

Dolly tilted her head to look at her. 'Are you in love with him?'

Rolling her eyes, Luce gave her sister a shove to the shoulder. 'You've asked the same question every day for two months now. What on earth makes you think my answer might have changed? No, I'm not in love with him. But he's the father of my child, and the responsible thing is to let him know that and have a conversation about whether he wants to be involved. That's all.'

Dolly's smile was sad. 'I think you're getting less convincing every time you say that. Come on—I'll make us some tea.'

The worst thing was Dolly was right. As ridiculous as Luce knew it was to have fallen in love with someone based on three days in a cottage in the middle of nowhere, she was starting to be very afraid that was what had happened.

She missed him. More than she'd thought she possibly could. When he'd called that first night she'd hoped that maybe they'd speak again while he was away. Then, when he hadn't called, she'd been grateful for a while—after she took the pregnancy test and realised she had to tell him in person. She hadn't been sure she could keep it from him if they spoke.

But now? Now she just ached to see him. She fell asleep wishing she had his arms around her and woke up missing his morning kisses and the way, the one morning they'd woken up together, the first thing he'd done was pull her closer, kissing her neck. She missed the way he told her she had to stop working sometimes, to relax and have fun.

And she really wished he was around to help her figure out what to do about Tom.

Dolly brought the tea tray back to the coffee table: thick slices of ginger cake on a plate next to the teapot, milk jug and cups. 'I picked this up from the deli down the road. They said the ginger should be good for nausea.'

'Smells wonderful.' Luce picked up her plate and took a slice. Still warm.

Once she'd poured the tea Dolly settled into the armchair on the other side of the armchair. 'Okay. Now that you're fed and watered we need to talk.'

'Look, Doll, I'm going to tell him. But—'

Dolly put up a hand to stop her. 'Not about that, for once. We need to talk about Tom.'

Luce sank back against the cushions and ate some more cake. 'I know we do. I just—'

'Don't want to. I understand.' Dolly took a deep breath. 'I think you need to tell him about the pregnancy.'

'How on earth would *that* help?'

'He's talking to Mum about how he and Vanessa should have the house. Since she's got kids already and they need the space.'

Luce blinked. 'But it's *my* house. Grandad left it to me. And besides, they've been together—what?—three months? And they're already talking about shacking up in *my* home with *her* kids?' Luce could hear her voice getting higher and squeakier as she talked, but she couldn't seem to stop herself.

'Okay, you need to calm down. Think of the baby.'

Luce rolled her eyes, but settled back obediently against the cushions. 'As if I think about anything else.' Except the baby's father.

'Look, I don't know if he's just testing the waters, or what. But Mum's so happy to see him settled with someone that I think she'll go for anything that keeps him that way.'

'But it's my house,' Luce repeated, calmer this time.

'I know. But you've always given in to them before. To me, too.'

'You make it sound like I'm a doormat.'

'It's not that. It's just that you're always working so damn hard to make sure we're all happy and okay.'

'And that's a bad thing?'

'Not in itself, no. But Mum and Tom…they expect it now. They can't imagine it any other way.'

Everything Ben had ever said about giving in to her family, about giving up her life for them, came back in a rush. He was right. He'd been right all along. This was her life, and she needed to live it for herself. And she'd have someone else even more important to live it for when the baby came. She'd have her own little family to be responsible for. She couldn't let her mother and brother run her life any more.

'You honestly think they expect me to give up the house?'

Dolly shrugged. 'Mum and Tom both treat this place like it's theirs anyway, when it's convenient.'

'Not when the roof almost caved in or the stairs needed replacing.' Funny how they'd been nowhere to be seen when she'd needed money or time to help fix the place up.

'Exactly.'

'Exactly…what?'

'They have no idea what they'd be taking on. But Tom's so used to you doing whatever he needs I don't think it's crossed his mind that you won't just happily move out into some little flat somewhere while he moves his instant family in here.'

'That's crazy!'

'Luce…' Dolly put her cup and saucer back on the tray, and leant forwards. 'You've never said no to him before. No one has—except Hattie, and look what happened then.'

'So you're saying I should give him my house to avoid his mental breakdown?'

'Hell, no!' Dolly shook her head violently, her long dark hair flying across her face. 'I'm saying it's time you *did* say no. Unless you want to get the hell out of this crumbling museum before the baby comes. In which case, make him buy it from you.'

Luce looked around her at the antique furniture, the threadbare rugs and the splintering floorboards. Yes, the place was falling apart. But it was her home—would be her baby's home. It was all she had left of her grandfather. He'd left it to *her*, not to Tom or Dolly or their mother, and he'd done that for a reason.

No way in hell she was parting with it.

'No. It's my home. I'm staying.'

'Fine. Then we need to make that clear to Tom. And then we need to go and buy some yellow paint for the nursery.'

Dolly clapped her hands together with excitement. Luce wasn't sure whether it was the painting or the standing up to Tom that was filling her with glee. It didn't matter.

'There's something else I need to do first,' she said. 'I need to tell Ben.'

Ben was wrestling with the hotel key card when his phone rang. As the door fell open he dropped his suitcase and put the phone to his ear.

'How did it go?' Seb asked.

Ben kicked the door shut behind him. 'It went well, I think.' Meetings with investors were usually Seb's domain, but he'd insisted Ben take this one. It was his baby, after all.

'Good. Full debrief when I get there tomorrow? I got Sandra to book us a meeting room.'

'Sure. Just need to get some sleep first.'

Seb laughed. 'Welcome to the world of real work, brother.'

The cell was cut off as Seb hung up, and Ben tossed the phone onto the coffee table. There was truth in Seb's words. This was *real* work—trying to expand and transform a hotel chain that had been stuck in one mindset for too long. It was work Ben would never have been allowed to do while their father was alive—work he hadn't even known he wanted to do until Seb had suggested it to him.

But now? He was good at this. Better than he'd used to be. Because he cared about making these hotels right for their guests. Not just the businessmen or the couples. He wanted a chain of boutique hotels that felt like a home away from home for the families that stayed in them. That made the kids feel safe and happy—not scared of another sterile white room with a too-big bed. Not a free-for-all family hotel with everything in red plastic either, though. This was a hotel for grown-ups, too. It just didn't exclude or alienate children.

He had a plan, and he had convinced the backers, but he had a hell of a lot of work ahead of him.

But first he needed to sleep.

The phone rang again before he could make it to the bedroom. He intended to ignore it until he saw the name flashing across the screen.

Luce.

Snatching the phone up, he said, 'Hey, I was going to ring you. I just got back into the country and I'm in Cardiff for a few days.' He didn't mention that he'd scheduled this particular leg of the trip in the hope of getting to see her.

'That's lucky,' she said, her voice warm and familiar. 'I really need to talk to you.'

'Okay. Want to do it over the phone? Or meet me for lunch tomorrow?'

'Um…neither. Look, could I come over? Where are you staying?'

Ben felt ready to drop. His eyes itched with grit and his very bones ached with tiredness. But the thought of Luce in his arms again… 'Of course. I'd love to see you.'

There was a sigh of relief at the other end and Ben felt the first pang of concern at the sound. What did she want to talk about, anyway? He *had* hoped whatever it was was an excuse—just a reason to see him. He'd have to wait and see, he thought as he rattled off the hotel's details for Luce. She'd be here soon enough, and he really needed to shower first.

He barely made it. The knock on the door came as he towelled off his hair. Pulling a tee shirt over his head, he padded barefoot to the door in the comfiest jeans he'd packed and hoped Luce wouldn't be too disappointed if he wasn't up to hours of bedtime fun tonight.

When he opened the door he stopped worrying about that and started worrying about her instead. Her hair was scraped back from her face and he could clearly see the redness around her eyes, the puffiness of her skin.

'Are you okay? You look dreadful.' He ushered her in, keeping an arm around her shoulders as he guided her to the sofa.

Luce gave a watery chuckle. 'Just what every girl likes to hear.'

'Sorry. But…what's happened?'

'God—everything.' She sighed. 'Um…my brother Tom.'

'The one you rushed back to cook a dinner for?' Ben tried to keep the censure from his voice. He wasn't sure he was entirely successful, though.

'Yeah, that was… I shouldn't have. I know that now.'

Ben blinked at the unexpected victory. Except if she'd changed her mind *that* thoroughly… 'What did he do?'

'He wants my house.'

'What?'

Luce rubbed at her eyes. 'He and his new partner want to move in together, with her two kids, and Tom thinks it's only fair that *they* get the family house, since there's more of them.'

'That's crazy. It's your home.'

'That's what I'm going to tell him. And...'

She trailed off, and Ben felt fear clutch at his insides. What else had her brother done? 'Go on. Tell me.'

Luce looked up at him, holding his gaze with her own. Her eyes still looked tired and watery, but they were clear as she said, 'I need to tell him I'm pregnant. But I couldn't do that until I'd told you. That's why I wanted to see you tonight.'

'You need to tell him... Wait—what?' The world seemed to have gone fuzzy. Luce's voice was buzzing in his ear, making it impossible to make out the words. 'But... What?'

'I'm pregnant.' The words cut through the haze of confusion, clear as a bell, but still Ben couldn't make sense of them.

'Pregnant?' he repeated numbly.

'Yeah. I know we used protection, but that first time...'

'I was too desperate for you.' Stumbling to his feet, Ben moved to lean against the back of the sofa, hands braced against the edge, staring down at the cream leather. 'God, this is just...'

'I know it's not what either of us planned,' Luce said from behind him.

She sounded brave, calm—but then, she'd had more time to figure all this out, hadn't she? How long had she known? Long enough to make a twenty-five-point plan for dealing with it, he was sure. Whereas here he was, half-asleep and dead on his feet, trying to get his mind around the idea that in seven months he would be a *father*.

God, how could he be? When he'd just promised Seb he'd take on the whole new business? He couldn't drag Luce and a baby from hotel to hotel with him, like his father had. He'd lose them in a heartbeat. And Luce would never trail around after him while he worked anyway. She had her own career, and her own family tying her to Cardiff. He wasn't foolish enough to think she'd give those up for a man she barely knew and had spent just a few days with, even if she was mad at her brother right now.

So what did that leave?

Luce touched him on the shoulder and he flinched in surprise, spinning round to see her watching him with wide eyes. 'Look, I know this is a surprise—'

'Surprise?' Ben shook his head. 'It's a shock. A disaster.'

Her face hardened at that, and he wanted to take it back, but it was the truth, after all. What was he going to *do*?

'Okay. Fine. I just wanted you to know so you could decide what involvement you want in your child's life. Obviously the answer to that is clear. So I'll just—'

'Wait. No. I just… I need a little time here, Luce.'

She nodded. 'That's understandable. Why don't I meet you for lunch, later in the week, and we can talk? Come up with a plan?'

'No! I don't want you to go. And I don't want to come up with a plan! This is our whole lives being turned upside down. A "To Do" list isn't going to fix that.'

'It's a start.'

'It's an end. It's giving up on any other options.'

Her face turned stony. 'Options?'

Ben stared at her, his eyes widening when he realised what she thought he meant. 'Not that. No, never that. I just… I don't know how we could make this work right now. The business… There's a lot going on right now, and Seb needs me to do it…'

Luce took a step back, her mouth twisted in a cruel smile. 'So now your work matters to you? Right.'

'There's a new project,' Ben started, but it sounded weak even to his own ears.

How could he explain to her again, in a way she'd understand, that he couldn't be the man his father had been? He couldn't lose her and his child that way, have them hating him for never being there. But he still had too much to do. He couldn't give up his dreams for a life in an office, nine to five, never going anywhere or seeing anything. Where would they even live? A never-ending series of hotel rooms would be terrible for a child, despite the new project, and by all accounts her house was falling apart. They didn't even have a home—how could they be a family?

'I just need some time, Luce.'

She shook her head. 'No. You've made your priorities very clear, thanks. I can do this on my own. I have my family to help me.'

'Would that be the same family that's trying to take your home away from you? And how the hell are you going to look after a baby in that place anyway?'

'What? You think we'd be better off here?'

She glanced around her and Ben knew she was taking in the sharp corners and sterile white and metal furnishings. Nothing like the cottage at all.

'I think you'd be better off with me.'

'Living out of hotel rooms? Never settling down? Isn't that what you said you'd *never* do to a child?' The words stung as she bit them out. 'Or will it be you, gone for months on end, sleeping with every woman who smiles at you in a hotel bar? No, thanks. A family takes more than a one-night rule, Ben.'

He swallowed back an angry denial, not least because he knew everything she said was true. His father hadn't been able to do it, and Seb wasn't even trying, for all his talk. Ben wasn't content to be one of those once-a-month visiting dads. So maybe Luce was right. Maybe there was no place for him at all.

'I can help. Financially.'

She threw him a scathing look. 'I don't want it,' she said.

Ben heard, *I don't want you.*

'Money isn't going to give you a quick fix this time.'

Why was he even surprised? he wondered as Luce walked out, slamming the door behind her. He'd never expected his father to love him more than his work, or his mother to love him more than her freedom. He certainly couldn't expect Luce to love him more than her child.

Their child.

'Hell,' he whispered, and went to pour himself a very large whisky from the mini-bar.

CHAPTER FIFTEEN

LUCE REFUSED TO CRY.

She stayed resolutely dry-eyed while flagging down a taxi. She remained calm as they drove through the dark Cardiff streets and as she paid the driver. She didn't even give in while she fumbled with the keys to get into her house.

But at the sight of Dolly, asleep on her sofa with a blanket over her knees, having obviously failed in waiting up for her to get home, Luce fell apart and sobbed.

Dolly awoke with a start, jerking upright and tossing back the blanket even as she stumbled to her feet. 'What happened?' she asked, her voice bleary.

Luce shook her head and pulled Dolly down to sit on the sofa with her. 'I can't… Just…don't ask, please.'

'Idiot,' Dolly whispered. 'Tell me he wasn't more of an idiot than Tom?'

'It's a toss-up.'

'Useless. All of them. We should run away to some women's commune and raise her there.'

'It might be a boy.'

'Doesn't matter. We'll dress him in skirts.' Dolly shook her head. 'Except then Tom would just steal the house while we were gone, and that's no good. So we'll stay here.'

'We?' Luce blinked up at her sister

Dolly took a deep breath. 'I thought I could move in and help you. If you want me. And not at all in a house-stealing sibling way. Because you already have one of those. I know I haven't always been much help in the past, but I think it might be time for me to grow up and take care of myself.'

Luce tilted her head to look at her sister. 'You *have* grown up. I don't know what changed.'

Dolly shook her head. 'Doesn't matter. The only thing that does is that I want to be here to help you with the baby. To look after you for a change.'

'That would be wonderful.' Relief started to seep into her chest. She didn't have to do this alone. Even if Ben wasn't there she still had Dolly.

'And besides, I thought the rent money might help you with doing this place up a bit. Making it safe for the baby.'

Luce stared at her. 'You don't have to pay rent. You're still my baby sister.'

'And I'm a grown-up now, remember? I can pay my own way.' Dolly smiled a lopsided smile. 'Maybe we can help look after each other. Because it seems to me that there's going to be someone soon who needs your love and care a lot more than me or Tom or Mum.'

'Especially if I'm the only parent it's got.' Luce slumped back against the arm of the sofa.

'Idiot,' Dolly muttered again. 'But it doesn't matter. You'll be the best mum any child could hope for. And I'll be the coolest auntie.'

'Of course.'

There was a pause, then Dolly asked, 'What did he say?'

'He's got a lot of work on at the moment. He offered me money.' That was a reasonable summary, Luce felt.

'How dare he!' Dolly's voice grew ever more vehement.

'The thing is, he's not a bad man. He…he looked shell-shocked at the whole thing. Trapped. Like he couldn't see a way out.'

Dolly shook her head. 'Doesn't matter. He should have manned up and supported you.'

'Yeah, I know.' Luce twisted her hands in the blanket. He should have. Of course he should. And she couldn't quite believe that he hadn't.

'But...?'

Luce looked up at her sister. 'The thing is, I think I might be a little bit in love with him.'

Dolly laughed and pulled her into a hug, her arms warm and comforting around her. 'Oh, Luce. Of course you are. I've known that for weeks.'

'Then how come I only just figured it out?'

'Because you were too busy trying to come up with a sensible plan for all this. Except love isn't sensible, and it can't be planned.'

'Is that why you fall in love so often? Because you're not sensible and can't be planned either?'

'Exactly.'

How had her baby sister grown up so smart? Luce laid her head against Dolly's shoulder and stared out into the darkened room. She knew where every stick of furniture was, exactly where each painting hung on the wall. They'd been there her whole life, after all. 'What do I do now, Doll?'

'You just take each day as it comes. It gets easier, I promise. And I'll help you.'

Luce nodded. Time to try life without a 'To Do' list for a while.

Ben woke feeling jet-lagged and hung-over, and cursed his alarm clock before he'd even opened his eyes. A headache pounded behind his temples, beating a rhythm that sounded like a door slamming over and over again. Still, he had work to do. And since, after last night, work was all he had, he supposed he'd better make the most of it.

Dragging himself out of bed, into the shower and then into a suit took twice as long as normal. He skipped breakfast, his stomach rebelling at the idea. How much had he drunk after Luce had left? The mini-bar looked suspiciously empty.

Seb was waiting for him in the meeting room and raised his eyebrows at the sight of him. 'Jet-lag?' he asked, pouring Ben a coffee.

Ben dropped into an empty chair and pulled the saucer closer. 'Amongst other things.'

'Thought you'd be immune to that by now.'

'Twelve time zones in eight weeks is hard on anyone's body.' Which was true. It just wasn't why Ben felt so awful.

Seb tilted his head, looking sympathetic. 'You need some time off?'

Ben shook his head. 'I need to work.'

'Why?' Seb's brow furrowed. 'What's going on, Ben? You've been different lately. First your trip away with your "university friend" then a sudden desire to revamp our hotels for the family market. Anything you need to tell me?'

'She's pregnant,' Ben said, his voice flat.

Seb's eyebrows shot up. 'Really? Well, that explains a lot. When did you find out?'

'Last night.'

'Oh. So the hotel thing was…?'

'Coincidental. I hadn't seen her since we came back from the cottage. She stopped by last night and told me. I…reacted badly.'

'You were exhausted last night, Ben. I'm sure if you call her, talk to her…'

'No. She's right. It's better that I'm not a part of the baby's life.'

'She said that?' Seb shook his head. 'That can't possibly be true.'

Ben shrugged. 'What could I give a child? I have no idea how to be a father, my job means travelling pretty much all of the time, and I won't force a kid to come along with me like Dad did. This is something I can't fix. She told me as much.'

'You mean you won't try.' Seb's tone was flat. Disappointed.

Ben glared up at him. 'You don't think I would if I could?'

'I think you're scared. I think you've got so used to swooping in and solving a crisis before retiring victorious you've forgotten that some things take more than that. Some things are worth more than that. More than just throwing money at a problem, or hiring and firing people.'

'That's my *job*,' Ben snapped.

'Yeah, and this is your life. Your future. It deserves more than a quick fix. Your child deserves more.' Seb stared until Ben flinched. 'You need to decide right now that you're in this for the long haul.'

The long haul. For ever.

With Luce.

After the last couple of months of being miserable without her, how could he give that up without a fight?

Ben swallowed. 'Okay. Say I'm in. What the hell do I do? She still thinks I'm the same person I was at university, with no sense of responsibility. She thinks I've never grown up.'

'Then maybe it's time to prove her wrong,' Seb suggested.

Ben blinked at his brother. 'What do you mean?'

Seb got to his feet, coming round to lean against the front of the conference table, next to Ben's chair. Ben appreciated the gesture. It made it easier to remember that Seb was his brother, not just his boss, and definitely not their father all over again. Brothers. That was good.

'You're not that kid any more. I remember you at university. You're miles away from that now. You work hard, you value your friends, you want to make a home—'

'Where did you get that one from?' Ben asked with a laugh. 'I live in hotel rooms.'

'Maybe. But I've heard you talk about your cottage. About your plans for the château. What are they, if not homes?'

An image of Luce, leaning against the kitchen counter in the cottage while he cooked, flashed into his mind. Then one of her curled up on the sofa with a book and a blanket. Working at the desk. Sprawled across his bed, smiling at him, waiting for him to join her.

The buildings weren't home. Whatever he did to them, however he filled them, they couldn't be—not on their own.

They needed Luce there. *Luce* was home. Luce and their child.

'Oh, God,' he said, collapsing back in his chair. 'I'm in love with her.'

'Well, I thought that was obvious,' Seb said. 'Now, what do you want to do about it?'

'What *can* I do? She thinks I'm an idiot, and I still can't imagine how I could have a family right now.'

Seb picked up the phone. 'Business Services? Could you get us some more coffee in here, please? And we're going to need the room a little longer than anticipated. We need to have an important planning meeting. Right now.'

'Do you want me to send in some pastries, too?' came the muffled reply.

'Definitely,' Seb said, looking at Ben. 'Now, come on. Let's find a way to make this work.'

'I can help with that, you know,' Luce called up the stairs, behind the struggling Dolly and her suitcase. 'I'm pregnant. Not an invalid.'

'You're trying to save me again,' Dolly yelled back.

'No, I'm not. I'm…' But Dolly had already reached the top of the stairs and disappeared into her new bedroom. Since she wasn't allowed to help with any of the fetching and carrying, Luce decided to go and make tea instead. At least that was useful.

As she entered the kitchen her phone rang, as if it had known she was coming. Luce stared at it, sitting on the counter, with Ben's name scrolling across the screen. Just the sight of those three letters made her heart clench. She'd need to talk to him eventually, she knew. Give him another chance for some sort of involvement—with the baby, not her. She was all set without him, thank you. She had her own not-a-plan and she was sticking to it. Just her, Dolly and the baby.

Ben had been right about one thing—even if he was wrong about almost everything else. She needed priorities and she needed to stick to them. And for the foreseeable future her priority was her child, and staying healthy and stress-free so she could look after them.

Neither Ben nor her brother were conducive to that.

The phone stopped ringing and Luce went to put the kettle on. She'd talk to him soon. Just not yet.

'Anyone home?'

Luce's shoulders tensed at the sound of Tom's voice. She hadn't heard his key in the lock, but maybe Dolly had left the door open while she was dragging in her assorted bags and boxes.

'In the kitchen,' she called back, and schooled her face, ready for the showdown.

'Oh, good. I'd murder a cup of tea,' said Tabitha.

Luce bit her lip. She hadn't expected Mum, too. Oh, well, maybe it was best to get it all over with in one go, anyway.

'I'll make a pot,' Luce said. Maybe she could busy herself with the teacups and cake until Dolly came down. Moral support was always appreciated.

'I think that's the last of it,' Dolly said as she entered the kitchen. 'And just in time, too. Hi, Mum. Tom.'

Luce placed the tea tray on the kitchen table. 'Help yourselves,' she said, and settled into the chair at the head of the table.

'Now, Lucinda,' Tabitha said, taking a tiny sliver of cake. 'We wanted to talk to you about Tom's idea. He says you dismissed it rather out of hand, but I don't think you can have listened to all the details. He's put a lot of thought into this, you know.'

'He wants to live in my house with his new girlfriend and her children,' Luce summarised.

'Well, yes. But we thought that you could have Tom's flat in exchange! Wouldn't that be nice? This house is far too big with just you rattling around in it, anyway.'

'Tom's flat is rented,' Luce pointed out. Best to address all the problems with Tabitha's statement in turn, she decided.

'Well, yes, but the rent's very affordable for you on your salary. And, after all, you've been able to live here rent-free for the last few years. Isn't it time Tom had the same opportunity?'

Luce blinked and looked over at Dolly, who appeared

equally baffled by their mother's attempt at reasonable argument.

'She's lived here rent-free because it's *her* house,' Dolly said.

'Only because Grandad left it to her,' Tom put in. 'But it's always been the family house, hasn't it? Luce always says it belongs to all of us, really.'

'Except for the part where it's *her* house. Grandad left you other stuff. And me.'

Dolly's voice grew louder. Her grasp on staying restrained and reasonable wasn't going to last long, Luce suspected.

'Not a house, though,' Tom said, his tone perfectly reasonable.

Luce frowned. 'Is that what this is really about? You're jealous because Grandad left me more valuable property than you?'

Tom straightened his back and stared at her. 'It's not about jealousy. It's about fairness. I need the house more than you, that's all. We're a family. We share.'

The really scary part, Luce thought, was that he truly believed this was a reasonable demand. She'd spent her entire life giving and giving to these people, and now they couldn't imagine that there might be something she wasn't willing to hand over to them.

But Dolly had grown up, grown out of that dependence. She'd changed when Luce had never really believed it was possible.

And that meant Tom could, too.

'Do you know why he left it to me?' Luce asked, mildly. Tom shook his head.

'He left me a note in the will explaining. He said, *"You're going to spend the rest of your life looking after the lot of them, because God knows they can't do it them-*

selves. Think of this as your salary." And I think I've more than earned it over the last few years.'

Tom stared at her, his eyes wide and disbelieving, and Luce squashed down a pang of guilt. She needed to do this. For all their sakes.

'Sounds fair to me,' Dolly said gleefully. 'And that's another reason I have no problem paying you rent.'

'Rent?' Tabitha said, faintly.

'Yep. I'm moving in with Luce. Figure that the rent I pay can help her fix up this place. Trust me, Tom, you wouldn't want the house if you'd seen the damp in the attic.'

Tom finally found his voice. 'But I told Vanessa we could—'

'Well, you shouldn't have,' Luce interjected. 'This is my place, Tom. And while you, and Mum—and Vanessa, if she sticks around—are always welcome here, this is *my* house, *my* home. And I'm afraid all of you are going to have to get better at looking after yourselves. I'm going to have bigger concerns for the next decade or two.'

'Like what?' Tom asked.

'Like my own family. I'm pregnant.'

'You're…? Well… That's lovely, darling, I'm sure.' Tabitha's brows were furrowed, as if she were missing some vital part of the conversation.

Luce wondered if hearing what Grandad had really thought of her had sent Tabitha even further into her own world, reliving past events with new eyes. She was sure her mother would catch up later and demand answers and information. But for now Luce was glad of the respite.

Tom, however, had no such reserve.

'Pregnant! You can't be. Who's the father? Or is this some desperate attempt to find love from a child instead of actually falling in love? Some "must start a family by the age of thirty" plan?'

Anger bubbled in Luce's stomach, acid and biting. She'd known Tom wouldn't take the change in the status quo well, but to hear such words from her own brother—the brother she'd tried so hard to look after and protect—it made her heart ache. And told her it was past time to cut him off. Fighting to keep her voice even she said, 'That's none of your business. Now, get out of my house.'

'I thought we were always welcome here?' Tom said, sneering.

'Not when you talk to her like that, you're not,' Dolly said, grabbing his arm. 'Come on—time to go. Mum, I think you might be better off at home this afternoon, too. We'll see you soon.'

Luce collapsed back in her chair as she heard Dolly bundle their relatives out of the house. Reaching for a piece of ginger cake, she said, 'I can't believe I just kicked them out.'

'I can't believe it took you this long,' Dolly said cheerfully as she sat down and helped herself to her own slice. 'Buck up, sis. You know they'll be back. Tom will calm down and beg for forgiveness, then pretend he never said that stuff. But they need to stand on their own four feet for a while. You did the right thing. And besides, you still have me!'

'Yes, I do,' Luce said. 'And everyone needs an adoring sister to run them a bubble bath from time to time…'

Dolly rolled her eyes. '*Another* bath? Really? Okay. But only because you're pregnant. This stuff stops once the baby's here.'

'That's okay. You can bath the baby then, instead.'

Dolly laughed as she headed off to the bathroom, and Luce thought that maybe, just maybe, things would be okay after all. Not great, perhaps. They couldn't be—not without Ben. But she'd be okay. And that was enough for now.

*　*　*

Just one more try. Ben stared at the phone in his hand for
a minute before taking a deep breath and pressing 'call'.
Just because she'd ignored his last four phone calls, that
didn't mean she'd definitely ignore this one, did it?

Still, as the phone rang and rang, Ben started to have
his doubts.

'Hello?'

'Luce?' The voice didn't sound quite right, but international phone lines did that sometimes.

'No, it's Dolly.' The sister. *Great.* 'You must be the "old
university friend".'

'Ben Hampton. Is Luce there?'

'She's in the bath. In there all the time now she's pregnant.'

'She was bad enough before.' Ben took a breath, and
took a chance. 'Look, I know she's avoiding my calls. I
was...'

'An idiot?'

'Last time we spoke. Yes. But I was jet-lagged and
exhausted—and stupid, mostly. I've had a chance to let
the news sink in, and I'm ready to make it up to her.'
Ready to make her the centre of his world if she'd let him.

'Convince me,' Dolly said, her voice firm.

Ben blinked at the phone. 'What?'

'Convince me you're worthy of my sister. Make me
want to help you.'

Dolly spoke slowly, as if she thought he was an idiot.
Which, actually, she probably did.

'I don't know how.'

'Then try. Or you're on your own.'

Ben stared out across the gardens of the château and
thought. He needed this. Needed Dolly's help if he was
ever going to get Luce out here and convince her that they

could be a real family. But convince her he was worthy of Luce? Impossible.

'I'm not,' he said, finally. 'I'm not worthy of her. Nobody could be.'

'Right answer,' Dolly said. 'Now, tell me your plans and I'll see what I can do. Because, I'm telling you, she's absolutely miserable without you.'

Ben smiled for the first time in a week and told Dolly his plan.

CHAPTER SIXTEEN

'AT LEAST TELL me where I'm going,' Luce said as Dolly threw more clothes into her suitcase. 'And how long I'll be gone. I need to call work…' Which would be fun. Dennis was still speechless over the pregnancy thing.

'Already done,' Dolly said. 'I told them you'd be back next week. If you decide not to… Well, call them once you're there.'

'Where, exactly?' Luce asked, frustrated. 'And if I'm there longer than a few days that skirt won't fit me any more. Three months and I'm already starting to show.'

'You're glowing,' Dolly said. Then she stopped and looked at her. 'Well, sort of. Right now you just look stressed.'

'I can't imagine why.'

Dolly slammed the lid of the suitcase shut and fastened it, leaning hard on it with her elbow to keep it closed. 'Look, just trust me on this one. It's for the best, and everything's going to work out fine. You need a break. You need looking after. And, most importantly, you need to not be in the house while they're fixing the attic. God only knows what they're going to find up there, and all that dust would be bad for the baby. Even the builder's told you to get out for a few days.'

'I could have just booked into a hotel round the corner for the weekend,' Luce pointed out.

'Except I know you.' Dolly gave her a look. 'You'd be back here every five minutes, wanting to check on things. No. This is my first chance to be the grown-up and in-charge sister, and I'm taking it. I have booked you a long weekend and you are going. End of story. I'll take care of everything here, so you don't need to worry at all.'

Luce opened her mouth to speak, and then closed it again. Telling Dolly she couldn't go, that she'd worry too much, was tantamount to telling her she didn't trust her to look after things. How could she do that when Dolly was trying so hard?

'And, look,' Dolly said, pointing to the carry-on bag next to the suitcase. 'I'm letting you take your research notes and your laptop, aren't I? I know how close you are to finishing the revisions on your book. So it can be a working holiday. Perfect.'

Luce bit her lip at the memory of her last accidental, snowy working holiday. 'Thanks, Doll. I just…'

'You just need to relax. Come on—let's get you to the airport.'

In the end Luce decided it was easier just to cave in to Dolly's boundless enthusiasm and go. A weekend away did sound wonderful, and it was nice to have someone else take care of the planning for a change.

Or so she thought until her plane landed in Nice and there was no one there to meet her.

This was why she took care of things herself. As hard as Dolly was trying, organisation and responsibility still didn't come naturally to her. And now Luce was stuck in an airport with no idea where she was supposed to be going.

Fishing her phone out of her bag, she called Dolly. 'I

thought you said there'd be a car here to meet me? With, you know, a driver? To take me to the hotel?'

'He's not *there*?' Dolly's incredulous voice screeched down the line. 'Hang on. I'll call you back.'

Luce took her bags and sat down on a nearby bench to wait. The Arrivals lounge began to empty out a bit, waiting for the next influx of passengers from the following flight, and she glanced around her, trying to see if she'd missed a sign with her name on it or something. Dolly had been so sure it was all arranged…

The doors in front of her opened with a bang, and Luce looked up to see Ben Hampton—paint on his face, jeans, shirt and in his hair—running towards her just as her phone rang.

'Dolly.'

'He's on his way,' Dolly said quickly. 'There was a mix-up—'

'He's already here.'

'Oh.' Dolly paused. 'Are you cross?'

'Possibly. I'll let you know later.'

'Okay.'

Luce hung up. 'You and Dolly came up with a plan. You and Dolly. Together.' The two people least likely to work together or to come up with a coherent, responsible plan.

Wincing, Ben said, 'Yeah. Guess it's no surprise it didn't quite work. I thought you weren't due in for another hour.'

'And you still dressed for the occasion?'

Ben glanced down at his paint-splattered clothes. 'I lost track of time. Come on—let me take your bags.'

'Where are we going?' Luce asked as she followed him out to where his car was parked at a wildly illegal angle on the kerb. 'Another hotel?'

Ben shook his head. 'We're going home.'

* * *

She looked incredible. Three months pregnant, straight off an aeroplane, annoyed with him—and she was still, by far, the most beautiful thing he'd ever seen.

'Where is home, exactly?' Luce asked as they pulled out of the airport.

'I told you about my grandmother's château?'

'That's where we're going? So—what? You're moving to France?'

Ben sighed. 'If you just wait—just a little bit—I promise I can do grand apologies and romantic gestures in style once we get there. And maybe once I've changed clothes.'

'It's not your clothes I'm worried about you changing. And I'm not interested in romantic gestures.'

She had her arms crossed over her chest, her creamy breasts pushing against the silk of her top. Were they bigger? *Not the time, Hampton.*

'Just the apology, then?'

Luce nodded. 'And I'd rather have that sooner than later.'

Ben smiled despite himself. 'No patience at all, have you?'

'Oh, I don't know. I think I've waited quite long enough.'

She had a point. 'I made a plan and everything, you know. There was a list.'

'Dolly's been telling me for weeks that plans need to be flexible. That's why we're painting the nursery yellow.'

'You and Dolly?'

'She's moved in. She's paying rent so we can fix up the house and make it baby-safe. And it means I won't have to be alone when the baby comes.'

Ben clenched his jaw. She wouldn't be alone. She shouldn't ever have thought she had to be alone. *Never mind the plan.*

'I'm sorry, Luce. For reacting the way I did.' Ben glanced across at her. She stared out of the window, intently focusing on something in the distance, or maybe on nothing at all. Either way, she wasn't looking at him, which was all Ben cared about. 'I was an idiot. I know that. Seb told me, and Dolly told me.'

'She wrote a song about how much of an idiot you are, you know.'

Ben laughed. He was starting to actually like Dolly, against the odds.

'The thing is, I knew I was wrong. I knew losing you, and our baby, would be the worst decision I ever made. I just couldn't see any way out of it.'

Now Luce looked at him, eyebrows raised, and Ben looked away and concentrated on the road again, just to avoid the anger in her gaze.

'You couldn't just say, *We'll figure it out together*?'

Ben winced. 'Apparently not. I was jet-lagged, tired, not thinking straight. But mostly I just didn't want to turn into my father.'

'You can't let your parents' marriage define your life.'

'I know. But Seb wanted me to take on this new work, travelling all the time, and I couldn't drag you and a kid around with me—hell, you'd never let me. And even if you did you'd hate it so much you'd leave me eventually. But I couldn't see myself staying in one place either. And I don't want to be one of those dads who's never around and then shows up for a couple of days in a whirlwind before disappearing again.'

'So you made all these decisions for me and our child without talking to me about it?'

Luce's words were cold and hard, and Ben turned off the *autoroute* with relief. Nearly home. If he could just get her to the château…

'I'm trying to make up for it now,' he said. 'Just give me the chance.'

Luce shook her head. 'I'm not sure that you can, Ben.'

The pain in her voice made his heart clench. 'Let me try.'

They drove the rest of the way in silence, and by the time Ben pulled up in front of the château the sky was growing dark. Grabbing her bag from the boot, he opened the door to help her out, and watched her as she stared up at the building.

'It's beautiful,' she said.

'It's nothing compared to you.' She turned to him in surprise, and he shrugged, moving away towards the front door.

'You know flattery isn't going to win this one for you?'

'It's not flattery if it's true,' Ben called back. And besides, he'd try every trick he could think of if it meant getting Luce to stay.

Inside, the château was cool and dark. The spring evening had turned chilly, and Luce wrapped her cardigan tighter around her as Ben flicked on the lights. Lamps around the walls flared into life, lighting the wide entrance hall and sweeping staircase.

'You want the tour?' Ben asked, and Luce nodded.

She followed him through the first door on the left.

'Drawing room,' Ben said, waiting while Luce looked around.

Everything looked dusty, unloved. Sheets lay over the chairs and sofas and the candlesticks and brassware were tarnished. There was none of the careful design of his hotel rooms, or even the cosy decoration of his cottage. This was somebody else's home—not Ben's. Not yet, anyway.

'When did you get here?' she asked as he led her back into the hall and through the next door.

'A week ago,' Ben said. He flipped on the light switch, revealing case after case of dusty leather books. 'Library, obviously.'

'You flew straight here the day after I told you?'

'I had work to do.'

Of course. For someone who said he didn't want to turn into his father, Ben seemed to be doing his damnedest to become exactly the same sort of workaholic.

He led her across the hallway to show her a front sitting room and a formal dining room. More antique furniture, more dustsheets. More floral wallpaper and heavy curtains.

'This place doesn't seem very *you*,' she commented.

'It isn't yet. Lot of work to do.'

'Is that why you came straight here as soon as you got back from your work trip? Or is there a hotel nearby you're looking at acquiring?'

'Always with the questions…' Ben took her arm, tucking her hand into the crook of his arm just as he had that night in Chester. 'Come see the kitchen, then I'll explain everything.'

The kitchen stretched across the back of the house, with huge full-length windows leading out to the garden. The units were old and battered, but Luce could see what a fabulous space it could be, redone properly. The whole house had huge potential. Small for a château, she supposed, but plenty big enough for any modern family.

Not that she would be moving to France, of course. Ben hadn't even suggested it. In fact she had no idea at all what he wanted from her.

'It's a lovely kitchen,' she said, rounding on him. 'Now, talk.'

Ben smiled, and the love in his eyes as he looked at her shocked her. He looked…open. Free.

'I spoke to Seb,' he started. 'The morning after I saw you. Told him what an idiot I'd been. Told him I couldn't see how I could fix it—having you and a family—with my job. But without the job I couldn't support you, and being stuck in an office five days a week would drive me crazy.'

'I know that. I'd never ask you to do that.' Luce pulled away from him. 'I told you—you don't have to be involved if you don't want to be. But why you dragged me out here to tell me this again—'

'I didn't,' Ben said, grabbing her hands. 'Just listen—please. Actually, come upstairs with me.'

'Only if you talk as we go,' Luce said, hating the burning tears she could feel forming in her eyes. Damn hormones. They confused everything. She just wanted answers. No need to get upset.

'Okay,' Ben said with a laugh. 'You've been very patient with me.'

Holding her hand, he walked them back into the hallway and up the staircase.

'Seb asked me what I really wanted,' he said. 'And I realised it was the same question I'd kept asking you. You hadn't been able to answer it. But suddenly I could. The only thing in the world I wanted that morning, and every morning since, was you in my life. You and our child. No one-night rules. No running away. Just you. Always. However you'll have me.'

Luce looked up in surprise and the stair carpet slipped under her foot. Ben wrapped a strong arm around her waist and she grabbed at his shoulders as she found her balance and tried to get her heartbeat back under control.

Ben smiled at her, carrying on as if nothing had happened. 'So Seb ordered coffee, and we worked out a plan to make it all work. A long-term, lasting plan. You'd have been so proud of us.'

'I already am,' Luce murmured. He'd made the right choice. It had taken him a couple of days, maybe, but he'd chosen to stay, to fight. Chosen responsibility and grown-up life over running away like a teenager. 'So, what was the plan?'

'We tackled work first, because I was so worried about making the same mistakes Dad did. I offered to quit, but Seb had a better plan. I'm going to keep developing our new hotel line—family-friendly, boutique business hotels—but I'm going to get help to do it. You can come with me, whenever you want, and we'll structure it so I'm not away more than two weeks in every month.'

Luce blinked. 'So—wait. You want to be with me—with us—when you're in the country?'

Ben grinned and pulled her up the rest of the stairs. 'I love you, Luce. I want to be with you all the time. Did I miss that part out?'

'Yes.'

'Well, I do. I want to be a real family with you. And I know now what a real family needs.'

'What's that?'

'A home. Or, in our case, several.' He threw open a door off the landing and Luce looked in to see sunny yellow walls and boxes of nursery furniture piled in the centre of the room. 'I'd hoped to get at least the crib put together before you arrived. Painting took longer than I remembered.'

Luce bit her lip. 'You want us to live here?' That would mean leaving Dolly—and Tom and Mum. Leaving Cardiff. Leaving her job. Giving up everything she loved. Would he really ask her to do that?

'Sometimes.' Ben wrapped his arms around her waist and pulled her against him. 'I figure we'll fix up your Cardiff house and live there most of the time. I mean, I don't imagine you're going to want to suddenly give up your home and your work or anything, but we can spend summers here at the château.'

Hope flared up inside her. Maybe he did understand after all. 'And any time we need a weekend to get away from it all we can go to the cottage?'

'Exactly.'

Ben smiled down at her and Luce tried to remember if she'd ever seen him looking so happy. She didn't think so. Not even after making love.

It all sounded perfect. More than she'd ever hoped or dreamed for. To be with him, just their little family, all the time. Except... 'I told you Dolly moved in, right?'

'I don't care. As long as I get to be with you. Besides, we might need a babysitter.'

Luce laughed. 'Very true.'

'So you'll do it?' Ben asked. 'You'll take the chance that I've changed? Grown up?'

Luce smiled up at him. 'I love you, you idiot. Of course I will.'

Ben lowered his lips to hers and kissed her softly. 'That's okay, then.'

'Well, seeing the château did make a bit of a difference. And I like the idea of homes in two countries...'

Ben shook his head. 'That's what I realised. These buildings aren't home. *You* are. You and our baby. That's home to me.'

Luce's shoulders relaxed as she tucked her head against his chest. That was what she'd needed to hear.

Things weren't just going to be okay any more, she knew. Their life together would be magnificent.

* * * * *

A sneaky peek at next month...

Cherish™

ROMANCE TO MELT THE HEART EVERY TIME

My wish list for next month's titles...

In stores from 15th November 2013:

❏ Snowflakes and Silver Linings – Cara Colter

& Snowed in with the Billionaire – Caroline Anderson

❏ A Cold Creek Noel & A Cold Creek Christmas Surprise – RaeAnne Thayne

In stores from 6th December 2013:

❏ Second Chance with Her Soldier – Barbara Hannay

& The Maverick's Christmas Baby – Victoria Pade

❏ Christmas at the Castle – Marion Lennox

& Holiday Royale – Christine Rimmer

Available at WHSmith, Tesco, Asda, Eason, Amazon and Apple

Just can't wait?

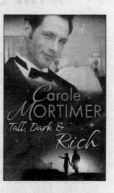

Wrap up warm this winter with Sarah Morgan…

Sleigh Bells in the Snow

Kayla Green loves business and hates Christmas.

So when Jackson O'Neil invites her to Snow Crystal Resort to discuss their business proposal… the last thing she's expecting is to stay for Christmas dinner. As the snowflakes continue to fall, will the woman who doesn't believe in the magic of Christmas finally fall under its spell…?

4th October

www.millsandboon.co.uk/sarahmorgan

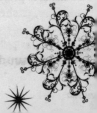

1013/MB435

Come home this Christmas to Fiona Harper

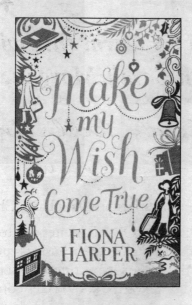

From the author of *Kiss Me Under the Mistletoe* comes a Christmas tale of family and fun. Two sisters are ready to swap their Christmases—the busy super-mum, Juliet, getting the chance to escape it all on an exotic Christmas getaway, whilst her glamorous work-obsessed sister, Gemma, is plunged headfirst into the family Christmas she always thought she'd hate.

www.millsandboon.co.uk

Meet The Sullivans...

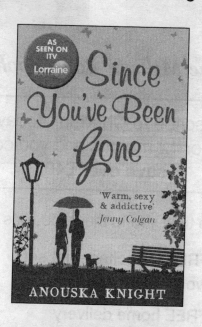

Join the Mills & Boon Book Club

Subscribe to **Cherish**™ today for 3, 6 or 12 months and you could **save over £40!**

We'll also treat you to these fabulous extras:

- 🌹 **FREE L'Occitane gift set worth £10**

- 🌹 **FREE home delivery**

- 🌹 **Rewards scheme, exclusive offers…and much more!**

Subscribe now and save over £40
www.millsandboon.co.uk/subscribeme